A GAMELIT PROGRESSION FANTASY

THE
DISCIPLE

JAMES CLAY

Cover art by MiblArt
Developmental Editing by Joel Brigham

I want to thank everyone who supported me and helped make this book better. In particular, Nathan Clay, Nate Weller, Lonnie Richards, and Sean Kiley for reading early drafts and providing feedback. Thank you, guys.

I also want to thank David Manthey for writing the software that I used to create the electron orbital picture in the book, and for graciously letting me use the picture.

Last but not least, I want to thank my wife, Merilee Clay. Beta reading a book multiple times is real love. Her feedback was invaluable at every stage. Thanks, honey.

Table of Contents

Synopsis of "The Forerunner"

Zed, a struggling MMA fighter in a dead-end job, meets a mysterious woman who claims that aliens will kick every human off of the Earth in two years. Although he is skeptical initially, she convinces him that she is both an alien and can do things that no one else on Earth can.

She gives him power, including physical regeneration and an enhanced mind, so he can go to humanity's future planet, Nienor, and prepare the way. She also gives him a spatial storage ring with an AI named Iris.

Zed and his dog Brutus get stronger by killing creatures and taking their mana. They eventually unite with another forerunner, Dan. Together the trio travel to an elven (álfar) city called Formenos.

Zed and Dan get stronger and earn money by completing jobs for people and betting on Zed in pit fights. Zed ends up dating one of his pit fight opponents, Laurel, after healing her of an injury she received at his hands.

Zed and Dan ally with Laurel's family to build a settlement for humans and spread advanced farming techniques. The goal is to have enough food so fewer people will die fighting over food and land. It is risky, though, because the martial sects that de facto rule the land forbid the spreading of knowledge from other worlds.

Seven months after coming to Nienor, powerful disciples of the Ever-Fruitful Tree martial arts sect arrive in Formenos, looking for Zed. They have heard of his pit fighting exploits and, more importantly, his spreading of forbidden off-planet knowledge.

Silwan, the group's leader, decides to let Zed off, provided Zed agrees to work for him. Seeing no other choice besides death, Zed agrees.

Name: Ozymandias (Zed)

Attributes

Strength:	21
Speed:	17
Dexterity:	17
Toughness:	28
Comprehension:	12
Mental Speed:	12 (20)
Memory:	36
Mana:	843

Abilities	Cost
Regeneration:	Max 520
Mental Enhancement:	100
Physical Enhancement (intermediate):	Max 100
Fireball (advanced):	Max 300
Magnetic Shield (advanced):	Max 300
Sensor Field (intermediate):	Max 150
Silence (intermediate):	5
Night Vision (intermediate):	5
Infrared Vision (intermediate):	5
Healing (novice):	(special)
Laser (advanced):	Max 600
Mass Shifting (advanced):	Max 450

Body Tempering

Skin:	100%
Muscles:	100%
Bone:	90%
Organs:	80%

Chapter 1

Zed

Zed ran down the dirt road at a speed that would put marathon runners on Earth to shame. His skin and clothes were caked with dust from traveling at the tail of his group of five. He was literally eating their dust, and his dry mouth held the proof.

Zed didn't run in the back because he was struggling to keep up. It was more of a pecking order thing. If he tried to move up, he would get swatted back. He was used to being a big fish in Formenos, and now he was a nobody. He couldn't wait to return to Formenos to keep working with Dan on the new settlement, instead of dealing with this middle school crap.

'I'm sorry I got you in trouble, Zed.'

'It's not your fault, Iris. I chose to use your knowledge and give it to others. And I would do it again.'

Once Zed had realized that 8 billion humans arriving on the planet would create a resource-starved hell that Malthus himself had never dreamed of, he had started spreading off-world farming information that could drastically increase food yields. It wasn't much, but it was what he could do.

'I'm glad that you don't hate me.'

'Of course not. Besides, you're my only friend in this mess. I'll need your help to get through it alive, and stronger.'

She made her avatar, a pretty brunette woman with sky-blue eyes, appear in his vision. She looked at Zed and nodded seriously, saying, "Yes!"

It was adorable, though Zed tried hard not to put the feeling into words so Iris wouldn't "hear" them in his mind. He was afraid that he would embarrass her again like he did when her avatar made its only other appearance. Still, he smiled at her cuteness.

Having reassured Iris, Zed looked around at his travel companions. *'Or maybe I should call them my jailors, or whatever indentured servants call their masters.'*

Silwan, the group's leader, called for a halt to drink and eat something quick. Zed took the opportunity to look at the four group members without a veil of dust in between them. The four were all different, but they did have something in common. They were all deadly. *'More deadly than me, unfortunately.'*

'But that can change...' Iris whispered. Zed knew it wouldn't be wise to be free with the savage grin that fought to get out, so he did his best to freeze his expression. All that showed was a brief quirk in the corners of his lips, and an ambitious gleam in his eyes that he just couldn't hide.

Silwan noticed. He seemed to notice everything.

Silwan smiled as he said, "You seem happy today, Zed. I'm glad. You've been such a moper lately."

"Sorry for being a downer. This is my first time being forced into servitude," Zed said with a heavy dose of sarcasm.

"Indeed? What an easy life you've led. Uncle Alain, how long have you served my family?" Silwan asked as he turned to his older bodyguard—the quiet one of the group whose every move spoke of leashed violence.

"817 years, young master."

"And you, Zed, are working for me for what? A year and a half? That's nothing. Even to a human."

"Will I get the opportunity to learn sect techniques?"

"If you serve me well, yes. If not, you can forget it."

Though Silwan smiled often, he could turn the warmth off instantly when he wanted to. He looked like a bit of an álfar dandy in a sect robe, but Zed wasn't fooled. The man was a killer. Not the kind that would necessarily do it with his bare hands, though he could if he wanted to. No, he was a killer in the sense that he wouldn't bat an eye at having you killed in any of several ways, from a duel, to a knife in the back, to ordering an underling to do it while he sipped on his wine, smiling all the while.

Zed was always on guard around Silwan, and he got the sense that was how Silwan wanted it. His cold moments were little reminders to not get too comfortable.

"All I need is knowledge. Knowledge isn't lost when it's shared."

Silwan smiled again and said, "I haven't known you very long, Zed, but I think that statement exemplifies you. True and forthright, but naïve. Knowledge isn't lost when it is shared, but advantage is.

2

"More to the point, the sect carefully controls the dissemination of techniques. Even if I know a technique, I cannot simply teach it to you. There are controls in place, and even if I were to bypass them, I would be hunted down like that unfortunate Zed who gave out knowledge he should not have. You know, the other Zed," he said with a mocking grin.

"Right, the 'other' Zed. Wouldn't want to be him," Zed muttered.

Silwan drank from a bottle that appeared in his hand. "All sect techniques cost sect contribution points, which can be used to buy many things from the sect. If you were to stay with me for a long time, I could see investing in you for the future. Since you are only staying for a year and a half, I have no incentive whatsoever to put anything into you. So everything you get, you're going to have to earn. But don't worry. I'll give you opportunities to earn. In our next destination I'll likely have several jobs for you."

"Oh yeah? What kind of jobs?"

"All in good time. For now, work on getting stronger, and be ready." The bottle disappeared.

Zed wanted to grind his teeth, but worked on his poker face instead. To distract himself, he looked at his other companions. Annis the ogrum turned out to be the liveliest ogrum he'd met since Victoria, his patron that made him one of the human forerunners. Since then, all the ogrums he'd met had been a severe and surly bunch.

'*To be fair, you were fighting most of them at the time, which is probably not the best time to appraise their character,*' Iris said. '*Heavens knows if people judged you by your fights, they would probably think you were insane.*'

'*No, they wouldn't...*' Zed stopped and thought about it for a moment, and with embarrassment thought, '*Okay, yeah, they probably would.*'

Annis turned out to be quite the prankster. His pranks ranged from the childish—he got Zed with an invisibly covered toilet bowl—to the more technically sophisticated. Their other travelmate, Leilani, was angry for a couple of days after Annis replaced her sword before a spar. It looked exactly like her sword until he told her at the beginning of the spar, "You look droopy today," at which point the sword itself drooped down as if made out of rubber. Between not having a useful weapon and staring in shock at her "blade", Annis easily defeated her,

3

leaving her with wounded pride and a black eye. He laughed uproariously while walking away.

Needless to say, Zed was far more careful about the objects around him these days.

Annis wore a blue silk shirt that contrasted nicely with his green skin and was tight enough to show off his sleek muscles without being obvious about it. Zed had noticed that Annis seemed to be a little on the vain side, always taking care to look good. Even when they wore their sect robes, he usually did a little something to accessorize.

'He could probably teach you a thing or two about style, Zed.'

'I'm sure he could teach me a dozen ways to color coordinate with my green skin and ivory tusks, but I think I'll pass.'

'Hmph. It would be better than what you know now about color coordination, which is nothing.'

'You wound me, Iris. I know that white and black go with everything, especially more white and black.'

'I rest my case.'

Zed just smiled and turned his attention to Leilani. She was the most homely álfar he'd ever seen, but that wasn't saying much, given her race's attractiveness. She would have been considered plain but reasonably attractive on Earth. Today, as on all other days he'd seen her, she wore sect robes and no additional adornment. To call her "severe" would be an understatement. Her only concession to looks or femininity was to cut her mousy brown hair at shoulder length and use a hair clip to keep it out of her eyes.

"What are you looking at, human?" she said with a sneer.

"The most beautiful creature that I've ever laid eyes on, Leilani," he said, with a mock enraptured expression. Annis laughed at the comment, and Silwan chuckled. Silwan lightly intervened with a "Now, now" and a hand gesture telling her to put her sword away— the real one this time—after she started to draw it.

"If you feel and act according to how the enemy wants you to feel and act, the battle is already half lost," he told her.

"Yes, young master," she said while bowing her head to him. "Though with this human I could turn a half-loss into a victory easily enough," she said while looking at Zed with contempt.

"That's true, which is why his value to you isn't in sparring with weapons, but in learning to control your emotions."

4

She considered this and said, more humbly this time, "Yes, young master. Thank you for teaching me."

Silwan nodded at her and then told Zed, "And you would be wise to not antagonize people who could cut you in half before you moved a muscle."

Zed smiled and nodded while inwardly thinking of more ways to needle her. Iris just sighed.

Chapter 2

It was hard for Zed to tell if the land they traveled through was scenic or not. For him, it was all a brown, dirty haze. The group traveled very quickly, running 100 miles a day or so. Zed could keep up fine with his tempered body and regeneration, but he was surprised that Annis and Leilani could do the same.

'I hate to say it,' Iris said, *'but your regeneration is probably not unique. They may even have a superior version.'*

'Yeah, you're probably right.' Zed didn't like to think he wasn't as powerful or unique as he had thought, but he was enough of a realist to know that he couldn't afford to fool himself. He was walking on too sharp of an edge to indulge in comforting lies.

'All the more reason to get as many of their secrets as we can,' Zed thought.

Each evening they stayed in the best inn in town when possible, and when roughing it they each set up their tent. The one exception was Silwan. Alain, his bodyguard, set up one tent for both of them.

Zed tried to bathe every night, but had given up on washing his clothes. No matter how much he scrubbed, the clothes never became truly clean. And every evening, after a full day of running in the group's dust cloud, they were worse than ever.

Zed, Annis, and Leilani rotated cooking and cleanup duties. Though Zed did not like Leilani, and the feeling was very much mutual, he noted that she did not shirk her chores or try to push them onto him.

Annis, on the other hand...

"Hey, Zed. I'll answer one question of yours if you do my chores for a month", he said while washing off a plate in soapy water.

"That's okay, Annis. I already know what your mom is like in bed," Zed said while drying off a glass.

Annis made a strangled sound that sounded like a cross between a laugh and a growl. He turned to Zed with an ambiguous look and said, "I can appreciate a man who likes to live dangerously. Just make sure the jokes are funny, Zed, or it might end badly for you."

After a pause, he continued. "Seriously though, I can help you."

"What can you help me with, Annis? From what Silwan said, you can't teach me sect techniques."

"No, but when you have some contribution points and can start selecting techniques, I can help you."

"Why would I need your help? Isn't there information on the techniques that I can read?"

"Yes, but how in-depth do you think that information is? Not damn very, I can tell you that. There is nothing like having the guidance of someone who has experience with the techniques."

While he dried dishes Zed thought about what Annis had said. He could definitely use some guidance. He found it hard to believe that Annis was the right person to give it to him though. Silwan or Alain would be far better.

"Thanks for the offer, Annis. I'll think about it."

After he finished his chores, he bedded down for the night in the tent that Silwan had given him. Though he had decided to forget Laurel and focus on his mission, he found himself often thinking about her. He was attracted to her, but he had also connected with her in a way that he hadn't with many people.

Zed laughed at himself. *'What kind of a dork has to go to a different planet and find someone of a different species to meet his boo?'* He wouldn't call her his soulmate. He didn't believe in the concept. But he missed her. He remembered the picnic they went on with Dan and Annabelle, when he had his head in Laurel's lap and she had played with his hair. He'd give a lot to have that day back.

He thought about all that had happened in the last seven months and considered his decisions.

'Should I have done anything differently?'

He wasn't sure, other than wishing he hadn't let go of Laurel so quickly. He sighed. If he got back, maybe he would get a second chance.

**

The next day the group stopped at the foot of a squat hill. Zed assumed it was a rest break, and pulled out some water to quench his thirst and wash the dust out of his throat.

"Zed," Silwan said. "Attend me."

'Attend me? Who talks like that?'

7

The álfar didn't bother to watch Zed's reaction to the command. He walked up the hill steadily and stopped at the top, looking outward. Zed shrugged and followed him. He didn't want to make a fool of himself by tripping, so he watched his steps as he trod on the wild grasses.

When Zed was high enough to see over the hill's ridge, he glanced upwards and realized why Silwan had stopped there. It was quite a view. The hill looked over a wide valley. In the distance was a large coastal city with a harbor and caravans moving in and out with goods to nearby regions. A meandering river ran through the city on its way to the ocean. The caravans streaming in and out on the plains and river barges moving up and down the river looked like ants on a trail, carrying morsels of food. There was obviously a lot of wealth moving through the city.

"We will be staying in Harlond for a while, Zed. Your first job is to acquire at least 50,000 gold in three days. When you get it, meet us at the Purple Rose Inn."

"Why? You don't exactly seem hard up for money."

"The money isn't for me. It's for you. You said you wanted sect contribution points, right?"

"Yeah."

"You can exchange 10,000 gold for one contribution point."

Zed whistled. "Dang. Those points aren't cheap."

"No, they're not. Count yourself lucky that you can even do the exchange through me. Not everyone in the sect is given the privilege."

"Thanks, Silwan," Zed said sarcastically. "I get points for the low, low price of 10,000 gold and a bomb in my head. Lucky me."

"No one likes a whiner, Zed. Besides, your hand is on the trigger, not mine. If I want to kill you, I'll just rip your heart out."

The way he said it so matter-of-factly chilled Zed to the bone. He didn't doubt for a second that Silwan would do it.

'*Or, more likely, just have Alain do it,*' he thought.

"Okay, you want me to steal 50,000 gold for unknown 'benevolent' reasons. Any suggestions on where I should get it from?"

"You can get it anywhere you like. If you happen to take it from a certain ogrum family, the Elstads, and exchange the money for points, I will double the points."

"Really? Who are they?"

8

"They are a merchant family in Harlond that is closely allied with a competing sect. I wouldn't mind embarrassing them a bit."

"You want me to steal money from them to get me contribution points and to embarrass them? Sorry, but I don't believe it. There has to be more to it than that."

Silwan turned to look at him. His light blue eyes usually reminded Zed of the sky. Right then they felt like ice.

"My reasons are my own, Zed. Do you have any other questions?"

Silwan's demeanor made it clear that he did not actually welcome more questions. Zed was tempted to drop it, but forced himself to maintain eye contact and continue because he needed more information and didn't want to be cowed by the álfar.

"Where can I find the Elstads?"

Silwan looked displeased but still answered. "They have a mansion in the palace quadrant."

"Last question. What happens if I fail?"

Silwan snorted and said, while turning back to the city, "If you can't do something this simple, then you're useless to me."

Silwan didn't seem like the kind of man who kept useless things around or left loose ends.

**

Zed raced ahead of the group because he knew he was on the clock and that Silwan did not want to enter the city with him, in case he was caught. Before he left, Silwan gave him a communication device and told him to keep it on his person at all times. It was a smooth, white cylinder, and Zed could sense mana inside it.

'*Is this thing made out of bone?*' It was almost enough to make Zed miss plastic.

Unlike Earth devices, there were no buttons. When someone called, it would vibrate and create a short-range mana field to alert him. He had to inject his mana into it when he wanted to talk with someone on his team. From there it was a matter of mentally connecting with one of the paired devices that his teammates had.

It was a handy device. It reminded Zed of Earth's walkie-talkies, and made him realize that he could probably make a lot of money by inventing the mana equivalents of Earth technologies, like the phone system.

9

'*Or maybe even just hand off the idea to someone else in exchange for a portion of the royalties,*' Zed mused. Unfortunately, he did not have the time to pursue such ventures before humanity came, but perhaps in the future.

When Zed reached a city gate, the guards looked at him askance, presumably because he was a human. Once he paid the entry fee of a silver, they let him through without issues.

Harlond was clearly built by the same civilization as Formenos, but there were differences. The smell, in particular. While Formenos was a city of steel, smoke, and soot, Harlond smelled of the ocean. The air was filled with the scent of salt and fish. Mostly fresh fish, but there was more than a whiff of fish guts that had been around too long as well.

Surprisingly, there wasn't nearly as much of the "outhouse" smell that Formenos had.

'*Maybe they found a way to deal with sewage,*' Zed thought.

'*Care to bet on whether it involves putting it out into the ocean?*' Iris said.

'*Nope.*' Zed thought about it and continued, '*But now I'm curious about what stakes you had in mind. What would you have wanted, and what would you offer?*'

'*I was going to go with, "If I win, I get to make you do something embarrassing. If you win, I won't sing off-key for 24 hours straight".*'

'*Yeah, that sounds really tempting, Iris.*'

'*1,000,000 bottles of beer on the wall, 1,000,000 bottles of beer! Take one down…*"

'*You sure you want to go with the nuclear option? There's a reason they call it "Mutually Assured Destruction".*'

Iris chuckled and said, '*No, I'm just messing with you. So what's your plan for getting the money?*'

While talking with Iris, Zed had been taking in the city's sights. He had wandered to the harbor district that bustled with the energy of business. Fish, cargo, and passengers were all offloaded from their respective boats while deals were negotiated for passage elsewhere or today's catch. Cargo made its way to warehouses, for sale in the city or caravan shipment elsewhere. And sailors, done with the day's duties, made their way to the nearest bars.

10

Zed walked up to a food hawker and asked for a grilled fish. He received it steaming hot and wrapped in flatbread. After paying the man, Zed returned to his conversation with Iris.

'*How can I have a plan? I don't know anything yet. I need to find this mansion, or maybe the Elstads' businesses, and go from there.*' Zed thought about how to approach the problem and continued, '*The problem is that if I ask around about their mansion and then they are robbed, it's not going to take a genius to figure out it was me. I need a disguise or something.*'

The two were silent as they walked through the streets, thinking about what to do.

'*Maybe you could use makeup or something?*' Iris suggested.

'*Maybe. The problem is I don't know jack about how to use makeup, and I'm human. The ears will be a dead giveaway.*'

'*You could just wear a cloak with a big hood.*'

'*Yeah, but with it being early summer that would look rather suspicious.*'

'*Yeah,*' Iris agreed glumly.

'*What I need is an illusion. That's probably possible with mana, but I don't think I have the control needed to pull it off.*'

Zed remembered how, when he first came to Nienor, Iris taught him martial arts katas by creating holograms. And how she made a holographic avatar of herself to teach Dan the álfar language.

'*Iris, could you make me look like an álfar with one of your holograms?*'

'*Hmm, maybe an ugly, uncoordinated álfar…*'

Zed rolled his eyes and asked, '*Can you do it or not?*'

'*Maybe. I can definitely do the hologram. The problem will be syncing it up with your motions, expressions, the wind blowing your hair—all of that stuff. I think I can do it, but I need to practice in front of a mirror first.*'

'*Great! I'll make sure we have what you need tonight.*'

**

That night in their room, Zed and Iris practiced their disguise. Zed did what he could to make it easier for Iris by getting a haircut. His hair had been getting pretty long anyway, as maintaining his looks had been low on his priority list since arriving on Nienor. The only times he thought about it at all was when he saw Laurel, and she had liked his hair longer.

Zed felt melancholy when he thought about his former fiancée. '*I wonder how she's doing.*'

'*She's a big girl,*' Iris said. '*I'm sure she's fine.*'

Zed was conflicted. He hoped that she was doing okay... and that she missed him. He was a little disgusted when he realized he wanted her to be a little broken up over him. '*Don't be a jackass,*' he growled to himself.

'*Why are you wasting time on a woman that dumped you, anyway?*' Iris asked.

It was a good question, he admitted to himself.

'*Emotions aren't logical. No, I probably shouldn't "waste time on her", but I still miss Laurel.*'

Turning back to the problem at hand, Zed looked at himself in the mirror. He got a room in a high-end inn specifically to have amenities like a mirror. It was only big enough to look at his head and chest, but that was enough.

'*So what can you do with this, Iris?*'

'*I can make you look like an álfar, sort of. The problem is that you will never have their slender features because any part of you that is outside the hologram will show up. I can make you a fat álfar, but that's the best I can do.*'

'*Another option,*' she continued, '*is to make you an ogrum. That would solve the face width issue, but I would have to change the color of your exposed skin, like your hands. We could cover up that skin, but then we return to the "suspiciously heavy clothing in the summer" problem. And I'm not sure you could pull off how ogrums sound.*'

"I could wear my armor..." Zed mused.

'*How many people have you seen in Harlond wearing armor, Zed? And if you go that route, it will make using your armor later problematic.*'

'*All good points,*' Zed sighed. '*Fat álfar it is, I guess.*'

They spent the rest of the evening having Iris practice disguising Zed. They decided to use a full facial illusion to completely change his look. To keep his mouth from looking like an old Hong Kong martial arts movie, Iris had Zed say some nonsense phrases while looking in the mirror. She learned how his lips, jaw, and face looked when vocalizing every phoneme in the álfar language. She also had him walk and shadowbox so she could learn to anticipate his head movements and mimic them. Walking wasn't hard, but the shadowboxing was a complete flop. Pieces of his actual head appeared occasionally until the hologram head caught up, making it look like a poorly rendered video game.

'*The problem is that I can't access the part of your brain that controls movement. All I have to go on is the mana flows in your body so I can "feel" where you are and mimic it as fast as I can.*'

'*I guess I'll just have to avoid sudden movements,*' Zed thought. '*Hopefully I won't get into any fights.*'

'*I guess I could give you an enormous head to provide myself more margin of error,*' Iris said semi-teasingly.

Zed laughed and thought, '*Right, because a guy with a hot air balloon on his shoulders won't attract attention.*'

The finalized disguise was a heavy álfar with a broad face. Rather than have Iris do a hologram of his body, Zed bulked up with extra layers of clothing. Álfar often wore long sleeves, and shorts were unheard of, so it should work.

Zed looked at his disguised face and was pleased. He had long brown hair, green eyes, an average nose, fleshy cheeks, and pointed ears. In short, it looked nothing like him.

'*Ready to give it a spin?*' Iris asked.

'*Not yet. Scoping out the place at night would look sketchy. Tomorrow will be soon enough.*'

'*Right, because scoping it out in broad daylight will look totally normal.*'

'*It will once the disguise is complete...*'

Chapter 3

When Zed saw the Elstad mansion the following day, he set the wood box of cheap crockware that he had been carrying down and sat on top while fanning himself. The late morning sunshine was surprisingly hot, and his heavy álfar disguise with the extra layers of clothing made it so he didn't have to pretend to sweat.

Iris had scoffed when she realized he was going to pretend to be a delivery man, calling it "cliché". Zed didn't care about that. The only thing that mattered was if it worked.

It hadn't been hard to find the place. Once Zed had the crockware he just asked around while pretending to be too much of a rube to have ever gone to the palace quadrant of the city. Though people had looked at him in disdain for his corpulence, it wasn't too dissimilar from how he was treated as a human. He had lots of practice at ignoring that.

While he tried not to look like he was focusing on the Elstad mansion, Zed did his best to memorize its details. The closest thing he could compare it to was classical Greek architecture, with fluted columns, lots of symmetry, and pleasing proportions.

At the same time, the details were all wrong. The columns, for instance. While they were fluted, that was not where the eye was drawn. The concave portions of the columns were just the negative space created by the rest of the column, which looked like abstract versions of giant bones. The "bones" were complete with knobby ends at the top and bottom, as if the femurs of gigantic creatures had been artfully arranged to hold up the building.

Zed's eyes shifted to the building's walls. They too were decorated with aesthetically pleasing shapes, but he realized as he took them in that what he initially saw as curved arcs carved into the stone was an abstract representation of scales.

Zed was dumbfounded as he realized that the building, which had the elegance of classic Greek architecture, harkened back to the memory of buildings made from the bones and skins of their enemies. It was intimidating as hell, and beautiful.

When Zed realized he was staring, he turned to look elsewhere. A minute later he got up and, faking weariness, picked up the box and continued. He played the part of a tired deliveryman to the hilt, occasionally stopping and looking around in confusion for his destination. He wandered the neighborhood that way, getting a 360° view of the Elstad mansion. After his initial surprise, he focused on the means of entry, egress, and visible security rather than the building's aesthetics.

The building was a large rectangle. Extending forward from its sides were covered patios, as if they were arms reaching out to visiting guests. Between the patios was a pool with a fountain and gardens. The main door to the mansion—large, heavy looking double doors—waited beyond the pool.

The other sides of the mansion each had a smaller door. The two doors on the sides seemed to be for servants—Zed occasionally saw álfar menials hurrying through them—while the door in the back was probably for the family, as it led to a less grandiose but more intimate garden that was mostly screened off from view.

There were, unfortunately, no handy balconies, but there were windows. Zed did not see any guards, but that didn't mean there weren't any inside. He decided to complete the reconnaissance by delivering the package.

He approached the property's fence and asked the gardener inside, "Is this the Elstad home?"

The old álfar stopped hoeing between the flower beds and looked up at Zed. "Yes, it is. Can I help you?"

"I've got a delivery to make," Zed said as he hoisted the box of crockery. "Is it alright if I go through the gate?"

"Sure, sure. Just a minute."

The old man made his way over and let Zed in. He pointed to the side of the house and told Zed, "Knock on the door over there. They can take care of it."

"Thanks!"

Zed enjoyed the sweet smell of the flowers while he walked towards the house and studied it up close. He activated his sensor field to see if he could detect any security systems.

When he got to the door—a simple but sturdy oak door with a slight overhang to protect it from the rain—he felt a small loop of circulating mana that crossed from the handle to the door frame and

15

back to the handle. He knocked, noting that the gardener was watching him while pretending to work.

Ignoring the gardener, Zed focused his full attention on the door and his sensor field. He felt someone approach and push something on the wall near the handle. The circulating mana was re-directed, causing it to stop going through the handle. The person then opened the door.

It was an álfar woman of medium age, wearing a simple dress and apron.

"May I help you?"

"I hope so, ma'am. I have a delivery for the Elstads. The gardener said I should bring it here."

The woman furrowed her brow in confusion and suspicion. "I haven't heard about any delivery."

"I dunno, ma'am. I don't know who bought it or how it was arranged. They just told me to bring it here."

"Show it to me, please." Though her words were polite, her demeanor made it clear that it was a demand, not a request.

"Sure, sure. No problem." Zed set it down and opened the box, showing her the simple crockware.

"The mistress would never buy this… this rubbish! What is going on here?"

"I dunno, ma'am. Look, if you're sure there was a mistake, I can take this back, no problem." Zed stooped to pick up the box.

"No, no. I can't imagine anyone here buying it, but there's no harm in leaving it. Just set it inside the door, please."

"Sure, sure." The servant moved to the side, and Zed moved the box a few feet until it was far enough to clear the doorway. "There you go, ma'am."

"Thank you," she said as he turned around. "Where did you say the dishes came from?"

Kicking himself for not anticipating the question, Zed thought, *'Iris, what was the name of the place?'*

'Farnsworth's.'

Zed turned around slowly while trying to decide if he should lie or not. He quickly discarded the idea because there was too much risk that she would be familiar enough with the stores to detect it.

"It was Farnsworth's, ma'am." He nodded respectfully towards the woman, turned around, and headed out.

16

'*I hope that doesn't bite me in the ass,*' he thought morosely.

'*Me too, but it's a good thing you found out about their security system,*' Iris said.

'*Yeah. Let's go plan the heist, because I want to do it tonight.*'

**

Zed dropped the disguise in an empty alley and started making his way back to the inn. On the way he bought another grilled fish on flatbread. He discussed how to do the job with Iris while he munched on the food.

'*So how do you want to do this, Zed?*'

'*I don't want to kill anybody, so that means stealth and defeating their security system. I've been thinking about what I sensed. The circulating mana I sensed could be an alarm system or a door lock, but I'm pretty sure it was an alarm.*'

'*Why?*'

'*There wasn't enough mana for it to be stronger than regular mechanical locks.*'

'*Okay, so back to the original question, Zed. How are you going to do this?*'

'*I want to enter through one of the windows, because they are less likely to be guarded. We have to assume that they will be alarmed like the doors. Any ideas on how to get in without tripping the alarm, Iris?*'

Iris took a few seconds before responding. '*Yes, I have a couple of ideas. You could either modify your sensor field ability so that it can exert force. Basically short-range telekinesis. With that you could push the alarm deactivation button from the outside. Bonus—with practice you could incorporate the ability into your melee fighting style.*

'*The other method,*' she continued, '*is to use your ultraviolet laser to cut the glass. The advantage of this route is that you already have the ability. The downside is that it will be obvious how you entered the building afterward. I'm not sure if you care about that or not.*'

'*Hmm. Not really, honestly. As long as they can't trace it back to me, I don't see how it matters too much. But why would the laser work? Wouldn't it just go through the window and cut something inside the house?*'

'*No. Glass is transparent to visible light but opaque to ultraviolet. Well, mostly opaque anyway. That's why you never got sunburned when riding in a car with the windows up.*'

'*I thought you couldn't read my memories…*'

'*I can't. I just assumed that the physically impossible didn't happen. It seemed like a safe bet.*'

'*I'd say my stalker being an even bigger stalker than I thought was a safe bet.*'

Iris blew Zed a raspberry.

Zed was conflicted. Iris amused him and she was amazingly helpful. More than that, she was a friend. But it still bothered him just how omnipresent she was in every aspect of his life, and how he had so little privacy with her. Zed shook it off and moved on.

'*Let's go with the laser, though I am interested in figuring out the telekinesis later. Now for the next problem…*'

They kept planning, both of them knowing that if they wanted to do it tonight, there wasn't time for rest.

**

That night, Zed walked to the Elstad mansion. He didn't bother with the disguise because it wasn't needed, and he wanted to have all his mana available. The hologram and the computational load required to sync it up with his movements were a non-trivial power drain.

While walking out of the market district he took a quick look at his status window.

```
Name: Ozymandias (Zed)

Attributes
Strength:                                21
Speed:                                   17
Dexterity:                               17
Toughness:                               28
Comprehension:                           12
Mental Speed:                            12 (20)
Memory:                                  36

Mana:                                    843

Abilities                                Cost
Regeneration:                            Max 520
Mental Enhancement:                      100
Physical Enhancement (intermediate):     Max 100
Fireball (advanced):                     Max 300
Magnetic Shield (advanced):              Max 300
Sensor Field (intermediate):             Max 150
Silence (intermediate):                  5
Night Vision (intermediate):             5
Infrared Vision (intermediate):          5
Healing (novice):                        (special)
Laser (advanced):                        Max 600
Mass Shifting (advanced):                Max 450
Disguise:                                (special)

Body Tempering
Skin:                                    100%
Muscles:                                 100%
Bone:                                    90%
Organs:                                  80%
```

Not much had changed since joining Silwan, other than his new ability, Disguise. He was disappointed to not see Wall Crawling in the list. After planning the mission, Zed had spent hours learning how to wall crawl a la Spiderman. Zed had only kind of gotten it. Apparently his skill with the ability was too low to even show up in his status sheet. Disappointing.

'Iris, why is the mana cost of Disguise marked as "special"?'

'Because it depends on what you want me to do. If I were to do a full-body disguise, for instance, it would cost more because the

19

hologram is larger and I would have to work harder to synchronize it with your entire body. The head-only disguise is cheaper because I don't have to do as much.'

'Fair enough.'

Zed thought about the mission as he continued walking. He was not comfortable with it on more than one level. There was the danger and the time limit, of course. He also didn't like that he was being forced to do something so sketchy.

'You could have refused the mission,' Iris said. *'You did negotiate in the contract that you could do that once.'*

'Yeah, but come on, Iris. Use my one "Get out of jail free" card on this? I don't like stealing, particularly from people who, for all I know, don't deserve it. But I have to save that for something really *messed up or dangerous.'*

'And you want those sect contribution points.'

That one hurt. Zed bit back an angry retort and forced himself to examine his thoughts and feelings. Once he had calmed down a bit, he knew. He wanted to do the mission. Yes, the stealing bothered him, but in a weird way he was glad that he was being "forced" to do it, because that made it Silwan's fault, not his. But there were always choices, even if the choices sucked.

'Yeah, you're right, Iris. I'm still not willing to use my one mission opt-out on this, but I recognize that my hands are not clean. Thanks for holding my feet to the fire a bit.'

'You're welcome.'

Feeling a little more humble and worried about what his time with Silwan was going to do to him, Zed steeled himself for the job ahead.

Chapter 4

When Zed saw the Elstad mansion he asked Iris to use her Disguise ability to camouflage him. They had figured out that they could use Disguise to blend into the background. It was not perfect, but it was easy for Iris to use the colors in the area and shadows to blend in.

Once the camouflage was in place, Zed turned Silence on and ran up to the fence. When he was close he boosted his strength and leaped. While ascending he cranked the mass shifting to reduce his gravitational mass and increase his inertia. He shot upwards and forward in almost a straight line, like a plane taking off. Once he was past the fence he reverted his mass back to normal and stopped enhancing his strength. He dropped to the ground in complete silence, the air around his body being isolated from the rest of the environment.

'*I love silence,*' Zed thought, '*but man, I hate how hot I get when I use it.*'

'*You could use your mana to cool the air down.*'

'*Not really the time for experimenting, Iris.*'

Instead, Zed turned on his night and infrared vision. The front garden area brightened until it looked like dim daylight. There were no notable heat sources other than the house itself.

Zed walked up to the house on the covered walkway by the pool of water. He felt the crunch of the pebbled path under his feet as he walked along, but no sound emanated. The increasingly uncomfortable heat he felt was well worth it.

Though he did not bother to look at them, Zed could hear the burbles of the water from the fountain and smelled the mix of flowers.

'*It's funny how adrenaline turns your senses up to 11,*' he thought.

Zed turned on his sensor field to detect any security measures that might have been activated since his visit earlier in the day. He detected nothing until he saw an ogrum with a sword at his waist patrolling the estate. He was at the side of the house, moving from the back garden to the front. Zed slowly moved behind a pillar holding up the walkway's roof. He turned off silence so he could cool down, and waited.

After a minute that seemed much longer, the guard walked to the front of the house, looked out at the front garden, and then moved on to the other side of the house. Once he had gone about 50 feet, Zed turned silence back on and continued approaching.

Soon, the edge of the house was within Zed's sensor field. He slowed down, wary of missing a security system. He stepped onto the marbled patio that surrounded the house, the patio covered by an extension of the roof, which was supported by more bony pillars. Zed carefully walked up to the corner of the house and followed the side wall until he reached the nearest window. It was surprisingly far from the corner. He noted that he had passed several second-story windows before reaching the first at ground level.

The window had a simple opening mechanism inside. In it he detected a mana loop like the one he had sensed in the door during his earlier visit.

'Just as we thought, another alarm on the window.'

Zed looked at the interior to see if it was a suitable entryway. There were many counters with drawers underneath, multiple stoves and ovens, and copper pots and pans hanging from the ceiling.

'The kitchen should work.'

Zed turned off silence and used wall-crawling to attach his hand to the window. The connection did not feel all that solid, but he hoped it was good enough. He then formed his laser and started cutting at a downward angle to ensure that any part of the beam that made it past the window would stay inside the kitchen. The glass briefly glowed white as it was cut, which made Zed nervous.

'Iris, can you cover that up with the camouflage?'

'On it.'

The camouflage immediately extended outwards from the hand on the window to cover the entire window. Zed felt Iris draw more heavily on his mana, but he still had enough for his needs. The only problem was that he couldn't see the window either.

'Uh, Iris. Is there a way for me to see through the illusion?'

'Oops. No, there isn't. Let me extend it so it won't block your vision.'

The camouflage ballooned outwards from his arm and head, so his line of sight to the window was unobstructed. The mana power drain became noticeably higher, but Zed knew it was temporary so he

22

ignored it. He finished cutting the glass a few seconds later. After he pulled the glass out of the hole, it started sliding down his fingers.

'*Damn it!*' He hurriedly stored the glass in his ring's inventory moments before it fell to the ground.

'*Zed, the guard is on his way back.*'

Zed looked and, sure enough, the guard had turned the corner of the house again and was casually walking towards the front. He was walking close enough to the wall that Zed didn't want to risk just standing there. He turned silence back on, looked at the open window, and decided to take a calculated risk.

Zed extended the silence bubble to cover his head, causing all outside noise to disappear, though his breathing echoed loudly. He dove through the window and did his best to roll, parkour style, when he hit the floor.

It mostly worked. The roll was less than graceful, causing Zed to bruise one of his shoulders and hips. The main thing was that he hadn't hit or knocked over anything, so it should have been silent.

The exertion and adrenaline made his breathing heavy, so Zed was tempted to remove the silence bubble around his head. He knew the bubble meant his air supply was limited, which added to his stress. Still, he held off. He didn't want the guard to hear his breathing. After what seemed like minutes, the guard passed. Zed forced himself to count slowly to 50, and then released silence.

It had been more stressful than expected, but he was in.

Zed gave himself some time to breathe, cool down, and relax. Once he was ready, he started silence again and moved to the door leading to the rest of the mansion. He pulled a jar of lard out of his ring and worked some of it into the hinges.

After putting the jar away, he sensed as far as he could beyond the door and, finding no people, slowly opened the door. The door was silent. Beyond the door was a large, empty hallway with portraits of ogrums on the wall that looked rather pompous. Ignoring those, Zed walked towards the back of the house and checked rooms as he passed.

He ignored doors where he heard people. The sounds were mainly snoring, but there was one where he heard a woman giggle and the quiet, deeper voice of a man.

The most interesting room was an armory. At least, that was what Zed guessed it was after he sensed a couple of suits of armor behind

23

the locked door. He had been tempted to take the time to open the door and clear it out, but decided it wasn't worth the time and risk. Especially since he would have to sell the armor afterward, which would carry its own risks.

'*You realize the money will most likely be in the master bedroom, right?*' Iris asked.

'*Yeah, I know. I was hoping to avoid people, but there's no help for it. Let's go upstairs.*'

Zed slowly walked through the halls of the mansion. He knew at a logical level that he would be silent even if he walked quickly, but his gut had a hard time believing it.

'*Besides, the camouflage probably works better if I go slow.*'

'*It does,*' Iris agreed.

Zed poked his head around a corner and saw that the hall led to the other side of the mansion. In the middle, it opened into a grand salon with sumptuous furniture and vaulted ceilings 20 feet up. Between the hall and the salon was a large, ornate staircase going up to the second floor. The stairs were guarded by an ogrum wearing a black and yellow uniform.

'*Probably the family's colors,*' Zed thought, since he had seen them throughout the mansion. The guard held a wooden staff. He was moving smoothly through the forms of a kata that Zed noticed was very similar to the ogrum spear katas he had learned.

Zed felt a brief feeling of kinship with the guard. He also recognized that ogrums had, by and large, treated him pretty well, which reinforced his desire to not kill anyone in the house.

'*The smart move would probably be to shoot him through the head with the laser,*' Zed thought with a sigh. '*But I don't want to make myself more of a monster than I already am just yet.*'

'*You're not a monster, Zed,*' Iris said.

'*I appreciate the thought, but I didn't have to kill those bandits. I killed most of them while they were sleeping. Hell, I didn't even have to kill that acidic jelly thing.*'

'*You did when it tried to eat your face. And besides, you're doing this to save people.*'

'*The road to hell is paved with good intentions, Iris.*'

The interchange ended, perhaps because Iris gave up or because she didn't want to distract him any longer. Zed returned to looking at the guard. Ogrums, with their tusks and dusky green skin, were not attractive to humans, but he couldn't help but see the beauty in the guard's movements. Ogrum katas would never be as beautiful as the álfar fighting styles, but when practiced by an expert, the power and efficiency of the ogrum style had a majesty all its own.

'*Better get a move on before he finishes,*' Zed thought. He took off his shoes and stored them in his ring. He knew that he still sucked at wall crawling, so he asked Iris for a little last-minute help. '*Remind me how the wall crawling thing works, Iris?*'

'*Okay, one more time. Touch is an illusion. You never actually touch anything. When you think you're touching something, what's really happening is that the electrons surrounding the atoms of your skin repel the electrons of whatever it is you're getting close to.*'

'*Right, electrons repelling electrons. Keep going.*'

'*The reason why the repelling doesn't happen until you are really, really close is that the atoms are electrically neutral. They have the same number of electrons as protons, so there is no overall charge. No charge means no repelling.*

'*When they are really close to each other, though, the electrons on that side of the atom are a little closer than the protons, which means the electron-to-electron repelling is stronger than the proton-to-electron attraction.*'

Zed wanted to nod his head, but refrained to avoid attracting the guard's attention. '*Okay, when they're really close, electrons are closer to each other than the protons.*' Zed pictured two atoms, each with a ball of protons in the middle. Electrons orbited around the ball of protons, and when the orbits got too close, the atoms bounced off of each other like billiard balls. '*It's the next part that I have a hard time with.*'

'*The last part is that the electrons don't actually orbit around the nucleus. Their movement is much more random than that, to the point where we don't know where they will be from one moment to the next.*'

'*So they could just go anywhere?*'

'*No. Even though we don't know exactly where the electrons will be, we do know where they're likely to be. We know that they are highly likely to be in certain regions. Here is an example of what I'm talking about.*

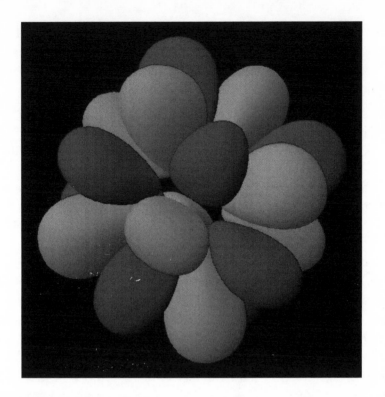

'*The "balloons" are the regions for different electrons. Instead of circling the nucleus, they bounce around inside their balloon.*'

'*Wait, you've been able to do pictures this whole time?! Of course you've been able to do pictures. Why haven't you been doing pictures?!*'

'*It's good for the soul to develop your own mental model.*'

'*You just didn't think of it before now, did you?*'

'*I'm not going to dignify that with a response.*'

'*Which, I'll note, is not a "no".*'

'*Hmph.*'

Zed wanted to laugh at Iris, but held it in because of the guard. '*Alright, so electrons in balloons, and my job is to push the balloons towards the back.*'

'*Right. If you push the balloons in front to the sides of the nucleus, then you will create an attractive force when you get close, rather than repelling.*'

'*Because the protons will be as close as the side electrons to the other atom's electrons, and there are way more protons than side electrons.*'

'*Exactly.*'

'*Alright, let me go through this in my head one more time, and then give it a try.*' Zed pictured two atoms, only now they had "balloons" stuck all over them instead of orbiting electrons. The atoms slowly approached each other. When the balloons touched, they were pushed back like real balloons, causing the atoms to move away from each other. Once they were no longer touching, the balloons moved back in place.

Zed tried it again, only this time, on one of the atoms he moved the balloons closest to the other atom to the side, exposing the nucleus. When the atoms got close to each other, the nucleus pulled towards the other atom's balloons, causing the atoms to stick together.

'*Alright, I'm ready.*'

Zed put the palm of his hand flat against the wall, creating as much surface contact as he could. He cycled some of his mana to the skin of the hand and willed it to push the outer electrons of the atoms in his skin to the side. He gradually felt his hand "stick" to the wall, like a magnet next to steel.

Buoyed by his success, he did the same with his other hand. The "magnet" effect happened faster this time. He wondered about that. Practice makes perfect, but why would it affect how quickly he could mentally tell the mana what to do?

'*Understanding what you're asking it to do plays a key role, obviously, but so does believing that it will work,*' Iris said. '*It gives your will more oomph.*'

'*Hmm. Interesting.*' Setting the topic aside, he concentrated on what he was doing. He moved one of his feet up and got as much contact with the wall as he could, pressing his toes against the wall. They stuck to the wall, but it was not as strong, presumably because there was less contact.

Now was the moment of truth. Zed pulled up his last foot and stayed in place! He felt unsteady, like he could slide down at any moment, but he was staying in place for now. Zed quickly stuck his second foot against the wall to give him more traction. Once it was in place he breathed a sigh of relief and looked at the guard with alarm.

The guard looked down the hall towards him suspiciously. Zed was in a shadowy area between light sconces and was very difficult to see. That did not assuage his nervousness when the guard walked ten steps towards him.

27

The guard scanned the area and then walked back to his post.

Zed very intentionally did *not* breathe a sigh of relief, and instead thanked God that he hadn't been found. Now he faced the decision of what to do. He didn't think it was safe to resume wall crawling until the guard relaxed again. Normally he would get down and try again later, as hanging on the wall would be exhausting. His regeneration took care of that issue, though, so Zed resigned himself to staying a few inches off the ground.

Zed spent a very boring but tense half-hour hanging on the wall before he felt it was safe to continue.

Unfortunately, the next step, moving one of his hands up, turned out to be quite a hurdle. His hands provided most of his stickiness because they had so much more contact with the wall than his feet. When he relaxed the mana in his hand and took it off the wall, he started sliding down.

'*Damn it!*' He hurriedly put his hand back and reactivated his mana to stop the sliding. Steeling himself, he tried again, quickly moving his hand up and sticking it to the wall before he could slide much. He tried to do it without slapping the wall. He knew his silence field should take care of it, but it just felt like too risky a thing to do.

Over the course of a half-hour, Zed made his way to the staircase area. He had initially planned to crawl on the hall's ceiling but immediately abandoned the thought when he realized he might fall. Instead, he stayed as high as he could on the wall. When he got to the staircase area and its raised ceiling, he continued upwards until he got to the railing of the second floor. Once he had a firm grasp on the railing he stopped wall-crawling and pulled himself up and over the railing. Once again, he turned silence off and breathed as quietly as he could. He had been baking in the silence field and was covered in sweat.

Once he had recovered, Zed started looking for the master bedroom on the second floor. It wasn't hard to figure out which one it was.

'*How many guards are in this freaking place?*' Zed complained.

He was looking at another ogrum standing in front of a door near the front of the mansion. Judging by the layout of the house, the area behind it covered most of the front side of the mansion, giving it excellent views of the garden, pool, and fountain in the courtyard.

Zed slowly walked up to the guard, trying to get as close as possible. When the guard sensed something and started to turn, Zed activated his super speed and rushed up to him. Before attacking, Zed extended out his silence field as far as he could, covering himself and the guard. Iris supported him by dropping the camouflage to free up mana.

The guard shouted an alarm but it was useless. The sound hit the silence barrier and rebounded, producing loud, irritating echoes that hurt Zed's ears. Ignoring the pain, Zed grabbed the guard in a muay thai clinch, with his hands clasped behind the ogrum's head, while the guard was busy pulling his sword out of its sheath. Zed pulled the guard's head down and delivered a brutal knee to the face, crushing the guard's nose. Zed didn't go too overboard in shifting his mass to increase his knee's momentum, because he didn't want to kill the poor ogrum.

Seeing that the guard was unconscious and a bloody mess, Zed lowered him to the floor. He cut strips of cloth from the guard's uniform and used them to bind and gag him. He used some more to wipe up the blood on the floor. Finally, Zed picked up the guard and took him to a room that he had passed before. He was pretty sure it wasn't a bedroom based on the large bookshelves he had sensed.

The guard started to come to as Zed opened the door. Grimacing, and hoping he wasn't causing any permanent damage, Zed set the guard down on the ground and slugged him in the temple, knocking him out again. He hauled the guard up and moved him into the room.

Zed laid the guard on the floor and made a Silence field around him. The only real difference between this and what he did at the ant colony was that this barrier blocked all air, not just smoke. Zed made the barrier extend a few feet beyond the guard in all directions, both to make it more difficult to leave it, and to give him more air to breathe.

'*He could also take over the mana himself if he gets close enough to it,*' Iris said.

Grimacing at the realization, Zed undid the silence field and created a new one, even farther out from the guard. It cost him mana, but this way was less likely to cause problems, and should allow him to recover the mana later.

Zed cut the window in the room to prepare his exit route, like he had when entering the mansion. Finally, he took the time to glance at the books in the 10 large bookshelves in the room. He didn't have the time to go through them himself, but he knew that Iris had access to everything he saw.

'*Iris, look through the titles of the books to see if there is anything that would be useful to me or valuable.*'

'*Got it.*'

She was quiet for a second and then said, '*There are a few that may be of interest. There are a few histories related to the Álfar versus Ogrum, and Álfar/Ogrum versus Human wars. There are a couple of books about mana called "Stellar Energy Geometry" and "Exercises for Improving Stellar Energy Usage". There are also various books about economics and the history of this region.*'

'*Highlight them all except for the economics books.*'

The spines of some of the books immediately glowed translucent yellow. Bright enough to be easily noticeable, but translucent enough that he could still see the book. Zed grabbed them one by one and put them into his ring. After he was done, he saw that the guard was awake again.

'*Ogrums are tough SOB's,*' Zed thought. He tipped his imaginary cap at the guard who was glaring in his direction and trying to escape his bonds, but then realized that with his camouflage the guard couldn't actually see him, so the gesture was useless.

Zed knew the clock was ticking, so he left the room and approached the master bedroom.

'*Iris, make me look like the ogrum who was guarding the door.*'

A second later Iris said, '*Done.*'

Zed opened the door. He opened it as quietly as possible and still had Silence activated. The disguise was just in case someone in the room woke up.

The room was dark, but Zed's night vision and infravision illuminated everything. A sumptuous four-post bed was in the center of the room, curtains hanging down on every side, preventing Zed from seeing its occupants. The rest of the room was richly decorated, with paintings on the walls and expensive-looking furniture. He closed the door and strode towards the bed. Zed activated his sensor field as he moved and, once he was in range, felt two ogrums in the bed, chests rising and falling slowly.

Dismissing the sleeping ogrums, he started searching the room with his sight and sensor field. He scooped up expensive-looking jewelry in a dressing room by the bedroom. Other than that he struck out until he sensed a square, metallic object behind a painting.

'*Hiding the safe behind a painting—a classic,*' Zed thought.

Zed took the painting off the wall and looked at the safe behind it. It was decorated with elaborate bronzework on top of the iron door that looked like faux armor plates. In the middle was a bare panel that was a little larger than the size of a hand, and a handle. When Zed looked for it, he could clearly sense the mana in the panel that linked to what was presumably the lock mechanism.

'*Do you think I should try to disrupt the mana, Iris?*'

'*Best case—it unlocks. Most likely case—it stays locked. Worse case—it destroys everything inside the safe. Worst case—it blows up on you.*'

'*Alright, I get it. Bad idea.*' Zed thought about it a bit. '*My options seem to be: 1) Grabbing the master of the house from the bed and trying to use his hand to open the safe, ...*'

'*The master of the house could be a "she", you know,*' Iris said.

'*Really, Iris? You thought now was the time to get all feminist on me?*'

'*I'm just saying.*'

Annoyed, Zed got back to his list. '*2) Burn through the safe with the laser, or 3) Take the safe with me, and open it up later. Anything I miss, Iris?*'

'*I don't think so. I would pick #3 if I were you.*'

Zed mulled it over for what seemed like a long time in his adrenaline-hyped state, but was really only a few seconds.

'*Yeah, I think so too.*'

Zed tried to force the safe out by pulling on the handle, but unsurprisingly, it didn't budge. He spun up the laser to cut the wall around the safe. He extended the Silence field to cover the safe, and then proceeded to lase the wall as close to the safe as he could. The air quickly filled with smoke and fumes.

'*Crap! They won't hear it, but they can still smell what I'm doing!*' Zed thought in a panic.

'*No, they can't. The silence barrier cuts off the air, meaning it cuts off smells too.*'

'*Oh. Nice! Dang, I'm good,*' Zed thought.

Iris snorted, but decided not to further dignify the statement with a response.

The smoke in the small region of air made cutting the wall more tricky, but between Zed's sight and the sensor field he made do. The smoke was hot though, and beads of sweat were already forming on his face.

Zed wasn't sure exactly how slowly he should move the laser to cut deep enough, so he guessed. Once he was done he pulled on the safe again. He could rock it back and forth a little, but other than that it wouldn't move.

He decided to double down by using his wall crawling to walk up and straddle the safe, and then pull "up" on it with his legs and arms. He strained, but still couldn't get the safe to come out.

'*Dang it,*' he grumbled to himself. He decided to give it one more go before going back to lasing the wall. He squatted down against the wall and reduced his inertial mass. He then rocketed "up" and shifted the mass balance to increase his inertia right before going taut and pulling on the safe. At first it resisted, but his momentum was undeniable and, after a moment, the safe burst out of the wall with a spray of dust and bits of stone. It landed on the floor with a loud "thud" that was both felt and heard.

'*Aw, crap...*' Zed thought, as he picked himself up off the floor and stored the surprisingly large safe in his ring. He heard one of the ogrums say something in a deep voice that he didn't understand.

'*He said, "What was that?" in Ogrum, Zed.*'

Rather than respond, Zed ran out of the room, while noting the two ogrums that had made an appearance. The woman peeked out from behind the curtain while hiding the rest of herself. The male ogrum hid nothing, pulling his half of the curtain back and standing up to see what was going on.

'*Wow,*' Iris said. '*That's really... something.*'

Even while running for it, Zed couldn't help but roll his eyes and think, '*We're going to have to talk about when it's appropriate to say stuff, and when it's not, Iris.*'

'*What? Why? Anyways, you shouldn't feel embarrassed, Zed. He's a whole different species, after all.*'

'*I'm not embarrassed!*'

By this time Zed was in the library room, and the ogrum had roared his anger, presumably after figuring out that the safe was gone. He shouted more things out from the hallway.

'*He said, "Get..."*'

'*I can figure it out from the context, Iris.*'

Zed rushed by the guard that he had left and pulled the mana producing the Silence field back into his body. The guard redoubled his efforts at getting out of the bonds restraining his hands and feet, and shouted as loud as he could through the gag. Zed didn't bother knocking him out again, instead he dove through the hole in the window he'd made earlier. While in the air he tried to do multiple things at once. He prepared to do a parkour roll on the ground—hopefully better than he did when entering the mansion—and shifted his mass to lower gravity and increase inertia. That kept his speed from increasing much while dropping. When he got near the ground, he reversed it to increase gravity and lower inertia. There was a brief speed up, but the low inertia meant that he wouldn't do a lot of damage to himself when he hit the ground.

That was a good thing, because between falling from a second-story window and mucking around with his gravitational and inertial mass the way he did, there was no way that he was going to stick the landing. Instead he landed in a jumble and tumbled on the ground, limbs akimbo, until he stopped.

Zed picked himself up and, not detecting any significant injuries, turned on his super speed and ran to the fence surrounding the estate. When he reached it he lowered his gravity again and increased his inertia to sail upwards after leaping. Instead of changing it back after crossing the fence, he kept going, making a long parabolic arc over nearby buildings.

'Hey, I figured out how to do the whole "leap tall buildings in a single bound" thing, Iris!'

'But are you faster than a speeding bullet?'

'Not yet. But I might have to be to take on Silwan. Or should I call him Agent Smith? By the way, how come you never translated stuff for me before?'

'You never needed me to with Álfar.'

'No, I mean earlier, when I talked with the gnomes. It would've been nice to not have to take the time to learn it.'

'I couldn't back then. You didn't have enough mana to give me the juice I needed to do it real-time.'

'Oh.'

'By the way, Superman/Neo, you're about to hit one of those "tall buildings".'

'Dang it.'

'*It's okay,*' Iris said. '*No one makes the jump the first time.*'

Chapter 5

Laurel

Laurel was on a rampage. She was covered in blood and gore, and added a little more when she punched forward and caved in the skull of the last energy-mutated wolf. Now that the fight with the pack was over, she took a rest to catch her breath. The air stank with the smell of blood, both new and old, but Laurel was long past caring.

Brutus, Zed's energy-mutated Husky, started eating one of his kills, tearing off chunks of flesh and wolfing it down.

"I guess you're not really 'Zed's' anymore, are you, Brutus?" Laurel said. "And you're certainly not mine. You're your own... what exactly? Dog? Doesn't seem like the right word for you, but I don't know what is."

Brutus turned his head to look at her with a knowing eye while he chewed on another hunk of flesh. He nodded his head at her, as if to affirm her words, and then turned his attention back to his meal.

Laurel couldn't eat all of her kills like Brutus did—the Husky's appetite was positively unnatural. She had to collect her enemies' energy the álfar way. She placed a hand on the last wolf's head and let her energy seep forth and enter the corpse, growing a gradually thickening channel that grew branches, and branches off branches, until the uttermost corners of the body were touched by her energy tree. The tree fed on the wolf's energy and, when finished, reversed the growing process and seeped back into her hand. The wolf's remains seemed "less" somehow, as if it had withered in some undefinable way.

Laurel moved on to the next wolf, and then the next, until she had collected the energy from all her kills. Her energy had been growing quickly, to the point where it probably didn't make sense to hunt any more.

At least, it didn't make sense to hunt for energy, but her other reasons remained—working out her anger and numbing her sadness. She had learned that from Zed.

She would not, of course, kill just for catharsis, so it was time to go home.

She looked down at herself in her blood-stained leathers and said, "I'm sure Mom will be thrilled to see me." Though she said it sarcastically, she knew it was mostly true. Her Mom loved her, even if she wasn't happy with how she had handled things with Zed towards the end. The Naïlo matriarch liked her former fiancé, but more than that, she thought he was an important ally to keep close.

Laurel thought about what her mom said to her after Zed left their home for the first time, on the solstice. *'You can practically feel the fate dripping off the man, Laurel.'* Her mom had always been a little sensitive to such things, and particularly at the times of power.

Laurel had already been intrigued by Zed. He was different. Not just as a human, but how he fought, how he talked—pretty much everything. Meeting him at his inn had been her idea. Her mom hadn't even known about him then. But her mom had made it clear that she wanted Laurel to establish a relationship with Zed. When Laurel broke it off, her mom was not pleased.

'But what's done is done, even if I still want to hit him and hug him.'

For now she needed to put aside her feelings and move forward, which meant becoming stronger. Zed wasn't the only one that wanted to protect her family.

Plop

"Gross, Brutus!" Laurel's face twisted in disgust. Though there was clearly an element of magic in Brutus' appetite, the parts of his kills that his body didn't use still had to go somewhere. And boy did they.

Plop

Laurel sighed. She walked up to Brutus and started scratching behind his ears. Brutus paused his eating and looked up at her, head tilted.

"I'm going to head home, Brutus. Do you want to come with me?"

The big dog shook his head and continued feasting, pulling entrails out before wolfing them down.

"Alright. Take care of yourself."

She turned around and started walking. It was time to go home.

**

36

The following day, Laurel enjoyed a leisurely brunch with her mom. They were busy enough that they hadn't spent much time together lately. Laurel missed their relaxing chats.

The work with Dan came up, as that occupied so much of Danae's time now. The palisade around the planned human settlement was being built. They decided to build it first to protect the builders from beast attacks. Things were going well, though they had to increase the number of guards because of stronger than expected attacks.

Before Danae left for a meeting with one of the clan's business managers, they agreed to go to an upcoming symphony together.

Laurel started meditating in the courtyard, on top of a boulder by the central oak tree. Just as she was getting good and relaxed, a maid disturbed her.

"Miss, a Mister Augustin has come to see you."

Laurel was doubly annoyed. Once because of the disturbance, and twice because of Augustin himself. She had not forgotten him nearly getting Zed killed by bringing an acidic agar into the pit. She snorted at the thought of his perfidy.

'The gall he had to let a creature that cannot be hurt by fists fight in an arena that doesn't allow magic.'

She thought about turning him away, but decided to hear him out.

"Thank you, Anna. Please let him in."

She bobbed her head. "Yes, miss."

When the diminutive dwarf made his appearance, Laurel indicated that Anna could go. Normally she would have had the young woman bring a chair for a guest, but Laurel had no intention of making him comfortable or prolonging his visit.

"What do you want, Augustin?"

"Lovely as always to see you, lass. How is your mother?"

Laurel rolled her eyes. "Like you care. Get to the point, I have things to do."

Augustin didn't seem fazed by his brusk reception. "I'm sure, I'm sure. I won't beat around the bush then. With our favorite gladiator gone, I've been thinking about how to continue the recent excitement in the pit. His antics brought in new fans, and I'd like to keep that going. And I hear certain folks," Augustin said, while giving an exaggerated wink to Laurel that made her shudder, "could use some funds. I'm thinking we could help each other out. What do you say?"

"I'm listening, as long as you hurry up."

"Splendid! Well, I'm thinking that, as his fiancée, you could be his stand-in!"

Laurel bristled. "I'm not his fiancée, and I'm no one's stand-in."

Augustin looked taken aback. "Ah, my apologies, lass. How about this then? Instead of 'The Dominator', we'll have 'The Dominatrix'!"

Laurel narrowed her eyes. "Are you *trying* to piss me off?"

The dwarf looked disappointed, but not defeated. "Okay, no 'Dominatrix'. How about…"

Though she would love to get rid of the odious man, she had been thinking while he talked. She smiled as she thought of an idea that could be lucrative and have… other benefits.

"No offense, Augustin, but your ideas are terrible. Unfortunately, you're not wrong that I could use some money. How about this…"

When Augustin heard her idea, he rubbed his hands in glee and started offering refinements to the budding plan. He liked it because it had potential for a big payday. While Laurel could also use the money, what she really looked forward to was revenge.

**

The next day, young men went to the well-trafficked areas of Formenos and called out a challenge to certain young aristocrats.

"Hear this! Laurel Naïlo, the beloved daughter of Lady Naïlo, is challenging four young masters of the finest families in Formenos to a duel! In the arena! She will face them all in the same evening, if they have enough courage to come. Lady Naïlo pledges to put up 10,000 gold to whoever wins, against their 10,000 gold each! What say you Robert Meliamne, Cyrus Campbell, Marcus Henny, and Joseph Bisset? Augustin the Dwarf awaits your word!"

The young men walked through the town, shouting the announcement for an hour. It caused a stir amongst the listeners. Talk and whispers followed the men. The talk increased throughout the city as, day after day, at different times, the same young men made the same announcement. What was initially assumed to be a joke or some kind of strange publicity stunt was starting to be taken seriously.

The two questions that were on peoples' lips were: "Is she serious?", and "Why is she challenging those four young masters?"

After a week, the criers' script changed.

"Hear this! Laurel Naïlo, is challenging four young masters to a duel! In the arena! She will face them all in the same evening, and even at the same time, if they have the testicular fortitude to come! Recent history would suggest that they do! Lady Naïlo pledges to put up 40,000 gold to whoever wins, against your 10,000 gold each! What say you Robert Meliamne, Cyrus Campbell, Marcus Henny, and Joseph Bisset? Augustin the Dwarf awaits your word!"

Now the announcement created loud talk. Formenos had never seen anything like this before, and it had become the talk of the town across all social strata. There had been plenty of rumors about why Laurel Naïlo had a grudge against the four men. The reference to "recent history" suggesting they were willing to fight a woman four against one caused scandalized gossip. Was it possible that they had done such a thing?

The talk was not all in Laurel's favor. Many wags leeringly said that she must have been "well used" by the four young men. The more ugly talk suggested she had even done it willingly, and was just trying to recover her reputation now.

**

"Danae, what the hell is this? Why are you letting your daughter throw all of our families' reputations, including yours, into the mud?" Heron Meliamne and the heads of the Campbell, Henny, and Bisset families were standing in Lady Naïlo's den. All of them looked angry, Heron particularly so.

The two Naïlo guards just inside the doorway did not have their usual, stoic demeanor. They could sense the tension in the air, and were obviously paying attention to the conversation and ready to jump in at a moment's notice.

Danae Naïlo, on the other hand, looked untouched by the drama.

"'Letting' my daughter, Heron? I don't think you understand. I am funding it."

Heron's knuckles became white as he clenched his fists. In a tight voice, he asked, "For the Goddess' sake, Danae, why?"

"For a 50% split of the winnings with my daughter. And because I think your sons deserve a good ass kicking." She took a sip of the tea that had not been offered to any of her guests.

"Do you know what they are saying about your daughter?" asked Ulysses Bisset, a tall, gloomy man.

"I do indeed. It was inevitable, though I daresay your people probably helped those rumors along. Though it is regrettable, in the end it doesn't matter."

"Doesn't matter?" Heron said. "Are you serious? They're saying that she…"

"I know what they are saying, you fool!" Lady Naïlo's eyes had narrowed and her voice cracked like a whip. Nonetheless, she gestured to the guards to stand down when they moved forward. "Let me make one thing perfectly clear, gentlemen. The world is changing.

She put the cup of tea down and looked at each one of them in turn. "Though I abhor the rumors about my daughter, at the end of the day it doesn't matter. The Naïlos will survive and thrive. *She* will survive and thrive. Whether your families will or not remains to be seen."

"What is that supposed to mean? Is that a threat?"

"No, not about your families anyway. But your sons… I don't think my daughter will be satisfied until they pay a price."

Heron snorted. "Beating them up wasn't enough?"

Danae slowly shook her head. "No, not by a long shot."

"What do you want, then?"

"A personal apology and 20,000 in gold."

"What? That's more than they would lose in the arena!" Heron blustered.

Danae smiled. "Precisely. She has made it clear that she would rather beat them up again."

There were mutters and angry whispers amongst the four men.

Errold Campbell asked, "And if we don't do either?"

"Then your sons will be mocked and shown to be the cowards that they are."

"Your daughter will be dragged through the mud as well."

"She has already been dragged through the mud. That price has been paid. The only ones that stand to lose at this point are your sons." She wore a wicked smile. "Assuming you don't think that the four of them can defeat her."

"Hmph. We'll see about that." Heron looked at the three other men. "I'm going to discuss this with Robert." Without bothering to look at Lady Naïlo or bid her goodbye, he walked out of the room. The three others followed suit, with Donald Henny giving her an embarrassed look.

Alone in the room now that the guards had followed the men out, Danae thought about how things had gotten to this point. She was sad for her daughter, but fiercely proud of how she was standing up for herself.

'*She will make a good matriarch.*'

The hit to her reputation was regrettable, to say the least, but all things could be overcome by strength.

Chapter 6

Zed

The next day Zed felt better, having had a good night's sleep and time for his bruises and scrapes to heal. He thought about pulling out the safe to take a look at it in his room in the inn, but decided not to. There could be a tracking mechanism, and it would leave rock dust from the wall that would connect him to the robbery.

'Besides, there's no way that I would open the thing here.'

He was planning on using the laser, and doing that in the inn would be… less than ideal. Instead he went downstairs, ate breakfast, and settled up his bill. It was time to move on.

'Are you going to see Silwan then?' Iris asked.

'First I want to see what's in the safe, and then decide. I'd look dumb if I didn't have the money.' Zed thought about it a bit and asked, *'Any ideas on where I could open the safe, Iris?'*

'Hmm. Not really. Probably the safest way would be to leave the city, but on one side there's the ocean and on the other an open plain with lots of caravans.'

'Yeah. It's not ideal, but maybe I should just find a dark alley, or warehouse, or something.'

'I think a warehouse at night would be best. Less chance of running into someone,' Iris said.

'Agreed.'

Now that they had the rough makings of a plan, Zed left the inn, slipped into an alley, and disguised himself as an ogrum with average features. He then made his way to a different inn, booked a room, and situated himself in his new room.

He had time to kill until nightfall. He pulled out the books he had taken from the mansion to see how interesting or useful they were.

'Time for some reading.'

**

Zed left the inn in his ogrum disguise once it was dark and the city's nightlife was in full swing. He didn't want it to be late enough that he was one of the only people walking around. The last thing he wanted was to stand out.

Of course, drunk crowds could get you into trouble too.

A drunk staggered into Zed and said, "Hey, watch it, tusky!"

Zed pushed the man off. "Tusky? That's pathetic." He wasn't offended by the insult, seeing as how he did not actually have any tusks, but he was still annoyed. He was tired of álfar who thought they were better than him, just because they were álfar and he wasn't.

"You're pathetic, Tusky! I bet you got 'em from your pig mom."

"Whatever."

Zed moved on. He was angry, but knew that escalating the situation wouldn't be wise. It grated though. He was sick of feeling like everyone could push him around.

It wasn't really about the drunk guy. He was just the latest of a string of frustrations. And the biggest source of frustration, fear, and anger of all? Not being in control of his life anymore.

'We'll figure a way out of the contract, Zed,' Iris comforted.

'I hope so.'

Zed longed to be free and get back to Formenos. The people were just as bigoted there, but at least he was free, and he wasn't one failure away from being killed each day. He didn't have to waste time doing BS missions that have nothing to do with preparing for humanity.

Zed paused his internal rant and looked up at the stars.

'What am I doing here, Lord? Please, if you're there, help me get back.'

Zed made his way over to the dock district. When he had walked around the city the day before he had noticed warehouses in the area that were used to store the incoming and outgoing ships' cargos. There were guards patrolling the area, presumably to prevent thieves from stealing the warehouses' contents.

Not wanting to be seen walking in the area long, as the guards would likely accost him, Zed found a decent candidate and used his night and infrared vision to make sure no one was near. He then replaced the ogrum disguise with camouflage, put his boots in the ring, and climbed the wall to the roofline. It was still a slow, "two steps forward, one step back" process, but he was improving.

Zed proceeded to use his patented building entry technique— extending his silence field and camouflage to cover the hole he was about to make, and then lasing the window. Only this time there were no windows, just stone.

'*It will take a little longer, but it should still work,*' Zed thought.

He used his sensor field to detect when the laser broke through the wall, and kicked himself for not thinking of that when he was trying to get the safe the night before. It took a couple of minutes, but Zed had the time. The light and the smell were contained, so he wasn't too worried about detection.

He had also taken the time earlier to figure out how to cool himself in the silence field. Conceptually it was a simple matter of reducing the velocity of the air atoms inside the field, which was not too dissimilar from what the field was already doing. Other than nearly giving himself frostbite the first time he tried it, learning the technique went pretty smoothly.

'*And now I get to enjoy the benefits,*' Zed thought, pleased with himself. It was nice to work silently and comfortably, and not need to turn the silence off to cool down every few minutes.

Once he had finished lasing the wall, Zed stored the cut stone in his ring.

'*The ring is at 80% of capacity, Zed.*'

'*Can it carry more if I give you more mana?*'

'*No. Sorry.*'

'*No worries.*'

The inside of the warehouse was just a large, spartan room. It was full of pallets of grains and fruits—this warehouse seemed to specialize in foodstuffs—that were fully lit by glow lamps.

'*Seems expensive to use glow lamps, but there are no windows so I guess it makes sense.*'

It was convenient for working in the warehouse, but a problem for him in regards to the patrolling guards. Zed temporarily "plugged" the hole with a camouflage field that mimicked the stone wall and blocked all internal light. Once it was in place, he dropped down onto the warehouse floor and pulled out the safe.

It was deeper than Zed had realized when he saw it in the wall, which probably accounted for why it had been so difficult to remove. He thought a bit about how to open it up.

'*I'm pretty sure I could cut the internal door hinges and remove the door that way,*' Zed thought, '*but it's possible that the safe's mana would destroy the contents. Safest to go in another way.*'

44

He lifted the safe up—the thing was a beast—and shook it a bit to cause everything in it to fall towards the safe's door. He then set it down on the floor, door down. It was leaning because of the handle sticking out, so he leaned it against the nearest stack of grain pallets.

Zed spun up the laser and cut off the back of the safe by lasing it from the side. The metal wasn't very thick in the back, so the work went quickly. Once he was done, he gently cooled off the steel with his new cooling technique and laid it on the floor.

Inside the safe were shelves with a jumble of items. Zed sighed, knowing it was no doubt a lot neater before he messed it up. He decided to straighten things up while figuring out what was in the safe by removing items and organizing them on the floor as he went.

Zed felt bad for the Elstad family. He felt bad about taking the safe and jewelry, damaging their home, and for whatever fear and trauma they experienced from being invaded the way they were. But he had to admit, he was kind of excited to see what was in the safe.

'*Everyone likes loot, Zed.*'

Zed chuckled. '*Is that what this is?*'

'*Looks like a treasure chest to me.*'

'*Well, let's take a look at our ill-gotten gains then.*'

Zed started pulling items out. There were bags of gold coins, silver ingots, and papers that said they were "bank notes".

'*What's a "bank note", Iris?*'

'*It's a promissory note you can take to the bank in question and exchange for whatever backs it up—likely gold or something. Or you can use it directly to buy things, the note's value depending on what it can be exchanged for at the bank and how reliable and available the bank is. You can think of it like paper money, only it's backed up by a bank instead of a government.*'

'*Huh.*'

Zed looked at the bank notes more carefully and saw that each was worth 1,000 gold coins from the Trade Bank. He knew nothing about the bank, but at least it sounded like it wasn't tied to one location or race.

'*You realize you won't be able to exchange them for gold here in Harlond, right?*' Iris asked.

Zed hadn't realized that, but rather than ask why he thought it through. '*Too likely that the Elstad's will say something to the local branch of the bank?*'

Iris made a visual avatar of herself that touched her nose with a pointer finger. '*Got it in one.*'

Zed sighed. '*Hopefully Silwan will accept it as money.*' There were 50 of the notes, so it was a significant amount.

Zed moved on to the ingots. They looked like silver, but they were really heavy—about as heavy as the bags of gold. Having coins of both types, he knew that silver was lighter than gold, so he wondered what was going on.

'*It's probably platinum, Zed.*'

'*Wait. First we have elves, orcs, gnomes, dwarfs, and all that crap. I bought that they were familiar because they had visited Earth before. But now we have the same money system as Dungeons & Dragons?*' Zed wasn't a huge D&D player, but he had played a few times with his friends. '*What the hell is going on, Iris? Was the guy who invented it an elf or something?*'

'*Yes. He was really Coriallus Larethion, Fifth Prince of the Galactic Imperium. He enjoyed slumming with mana-less humans and playing role-playing games.*'

'*Really?*'

'*No,*' Iris laughed. '*Well, he was probably human anyway. Gary Gygax, the inventor of D&D, based it on a combination of Earth legends and history. Most civilizations, human and non-human, used copper, silver, gold, and platinum as the basis for their money at some point in their past.*'

'*They all came up with the same system independently? Seems sus.*'

'*Well, I'm sure some of them saw what their neighbors were doing and said, "Hey, that's a good idea!" But yes, many of them came up with the system independently. Those metals have certain features that make them good at being money. They resist corrosion, so they hold their value well. They're rare, so the money supply is pretty stable. They can be subdivided easily because they're soft. And, you know, they're pretty.*'

'*Not all of the civilizations did it the same way, though. Copper corrodes the most easily of the precious metals, so it was often mixed with tin to make bronze. The money system in those countries was bronze, silver, gold, and platinum.*'

'*Huh. I guess it makes sense. So, assuming the ingots are platinum, how much are they worth?*'

'*About 50 times their weight in gold.*'

'*Dang.*'

Zed did a quick weight comparison with the bags of gold and determined that each ingot weighed about the same as 100 gold coins, so each was worth about 5000 gold. There were 18 ingots, so they alone were worth 90,000 gold. Zed wanted to whistle at the amount, but didn't to avoid getting the attention of the guards outside.

The gold almost felt like an afterthought after the platinum and the bank notes. The bags held 500 coins each, and there were eight bags.

'*You know you're spoiled when 4000 gold feels like chump change,*' Zed thought.

There were two more items left in the safe.

One was a jewelry box that contained ten light-green pills. The other was a necklace of shells on twine that looked like it might have been made by a child if it weren't for the carefully drilled holes in the shells. Zed shrugged and put both of them in the ring, along with everything else in the safe. After a moment's consideration, he put the safe back too.

Zed looked at where he had put the camouflage to plug the hole in the wall. He wanted to get the mana back, but would rather not have a bunch of light leaking out afterwards.

'*In for a penny, in for a pound, Zed.*'

'*What do you mean?*'

'*I mean "take the glow lamps".*'

Zed looked around. '*It would be useful to have lamps around whenever I need them…*' Zed sighed. '*Does this mean that you're going to start corrupting me too, Iris?*' he asked while grabbing lamps and putting them in his ring.

'*A better question is "when haven't I been trying to corrupt you?"*' she said as her avatar appeared in a cute but sexy dress, sporting small devil horns and a barbed tail that she swung in one hand.

'*So that whole "holding my feet to the fire" thing earlier…?*'

'*Since I can't literally hold your feet to the fire yet, and please note the emphasis on "yet", I thought I would enjoy a little hors d'oeuvre of guilt while making you think that I was innocent and on your side. Rather devilish, if I do say so myself.*'

'*Seems like telling me so is rather counter-productive. Shouldn't you be a little more sneaky about it?*'

'*You're still stealing the lamps, aren't you?*' She slowly faded away while leering at him, her grin the last thing to disappear, a la the Cheshire Cat.

While Zed considered the interaction with she-devil Iris amusing, there was more than a little "what the hell just happened here?" mixed in too. He wasn't sure if she was just playing or if she was trying to say something.

'*I thought we agreed early on that you would turn the personality down a bit, Iris.*'

'*We agreed that I would until you asked for more.*'

'*Yeah. And?*'

'*Your subconscious was totally asking for more.*'

Smiling ruefully, Zed shook his head and grabbed the last few lamps.

**

Disguised once more, Zed walked towards the inn. While strolling he decided to tease Iris back.

'*I've decided to call you "Jiminy" from now on.*'

'*Jiminy? Why?*'

'*Because you're my conscience.*'

'*No way! I'm your "Sexy Screwtape".*'

'*Now there's an oxymoron if I ever heard one. That's like saying...*'

Zed stopped in his tracks when he saw a human woman. It was the first human besides Dan he'd seen since they tracked down a feral beastman. She was wearing a long, pink dress with a low-cut front. The pink was uneven enough that he was pretty sure it used to be red and had faded over time and repeated washings. She had just left a restaurant and stood in front of it next to an álfar man.

Zed had become so used to álfar women that seeing her took him aback. She was, objectively speaking, rather plain in comparison. Her cheeks had freckles and acne scars, and there was a mole below her ear. But in a land of near perfection, her imperfections were interesting. She reminded him a little of home.

At the moment, though, she looked unhappy.

"Look, I'm not going home with you. That's just not going to happen."

The álfar man sneered at her. "Shameless, hussy! Look at you. You invite me to go out, ask for money, pathetically try to seduce me, and now it's "no, no, I can't possibly go home with you!" The last was said in a mock falsetto.

The woman blushed and looked down. "It wasn't like that…"

The álfar snorted. "It was exactly like that. Sure, it was 'for your employer'. You should just call her your pimp."

Zed had been watching the interchange and growing angrier by the second.

'Why do they always have to push us around?'

He imagined what it would be like for his sister in this world—a single mom with three kids in a world that saw her as much as a beast as a person. What she might be forced to do to feed her kids. He saw red.

Without conscious thought, Zed walked up and pushed the álfar away. Only mostly under control, he said with gritted teeth, "The lady said 'no'. Back off."

The álfar laughed and looked around at the slowly gathering crowd of on-lookers. "Look! Even whores have white knights to save them."

Zed felt a hand on his wrist. He looked back and saw the woman. She looked uncomfortable. "Thank you, but I can take care of this."

Zed's eyebrows raised. "You sure?"

Not looking at him in the eyes, she nodded her head. "Yeah."

Zed considered her and then nodded in acquiescence. He didn't believe her, but it was her life to live. Still, as they walked off together, the álfar pulling her, Zed decided to follow.

'Now you really are being a white knight, Zed.'

'Yeah, but at least it's something that I'm choosing to do. It isn't being forced on me.'

'But you're doing this against her will.'

This pissed Zed off more. *'Yeah? So I'm a hypocrite. So what? That's the point of power, right? Being able to do what you want, to hell with what everyone else wants?'*

Still fuming, Zed dipped into an alleyway, turned on camouflage and silence, and parkoured up to the roof. The railing on a balcony that he used to scramble up shook, but the noise was reduced by the partial coverage of the silence field.

49

As he followed them, he saw the two whisper-shouting at each other. They were both obviously angry, but they also seemed to want to avoid attention.

After a couple of blocks the woman tried to pull her arm away to get free, but the álfar was having none of it. He did stop, though, and more angry whispers went back and forth. Looking enraged, the álfar pulled her into an alleyway. Thirty feet in, past a pile of rubbish, he threw her against a wall, stepped forward, and grabbed her by the throat.

Whether due to anger or assuming no one could hear, the álfar raised his voice a little. It was enough for Zed to make out the words.

"I was going to take you home and treat you nice, like a person! But you're not worth it. You're just a damn whore. No, you're less than a whore. At least a whore follows through with a business transaction. But I won't let you leave me high and dry."

He ripped the top of her dress, exposing one side of her chest and leaving scratches that started to ooze blood. Grinning at the sight, he started loosening his pants with one hand.

Having seen enough, Zed turned off silence, enhanced his physique, and jumped to the ground a few feet away from the álfar.

Hearing the "thud" as Zed landed, the álfar stopped what he was doing and looked over at him. Eyebrows raised and eyes widened at the sight of the ogrum from before, the álfar's eyes narrowed and he spat out, "What do you want?" He leered. "Do you want a turn after I'm done? You can have her."

The callousness, unthinking superiority, and sheer, utter shamelessness of the álfar enraged Zed. He darted forward and seized the man by the throat, just as he had the woman, and started to squeeze.

The álfar released the woman, who dropped to the ground, wheezed, and coughed as she took in much-needed air. He used both hands to try to pull Zed's hand off his throat. Zed just sneered and squeezed harder.

Showing fear for the first time, the álfar rasped out, "She's just a human!"

Zed thought he couldn't dislike the álfar any more than he already did. He'd been wrong. The rest of the world disappeared as far as he was concerned. There was only this piece of shit who deserved to die.

Zed turned off his disguise, letting his human features appear.

"So am I."

The álfar's face devolved into a rictus of shock and terror, eyes bulging from Zed's squeezing. Zed enjoyed seeing it. It felt... good. It was the perfect sight as he finished the job by squeezing even harder.

Though quiet, the "crack!" of the man's neck sounded as loud as a gunshot to Zed. The neck's resistance broken, it felt like that of a rubber chicken—floppy and useless.

A frightened gasp pulled him out of his reverie. The woman backed away from him, looking horrified while staring at Zed.

'What the hell? I saved her, and she's scared of me?' Zed's anger, which had been cooling, reignited.

And then it hit him how he must have looked while he enjoyed squeezing the life from the would-be-rapist. He turned back to the álfar and looked at the man. A rank smell hit him. The man had voided his bowels as he died.

With a snort of disgust—whether aimed at the would-be rapist or himself, Zed wouldn't have been able to say—he stored the corpse in the ring, the final proof that he was dead.

'The ring's spatial storage is full,' Iris said.

Ashamed at his loss of control, Zed walked away after a glance at the woman.

Before he left the alley, Iris quietly said, *'The woman saw your face, Zed.'*

'Damn it.' He wasn't going to kill her. That wasn't even a question. He could threaten her, but what was the point? Judging from the look on her face, he already terrified her.

Besides, even if he didn't want to take the blame for the murder and last night's robbery, he was the thief and the vigilante. If fate was going to give him hell for that, so be it.

Contemplating the decision as he walked, Zed felt... not peace exactly. It was acceptance. Whether he had done right or wrong, it was done, and he would accept the consequences.

He then thought of Iris' warning. All "she-devil" joking aside, Zed knew that she didn't want him to kill the woman.

'So why did she say something? She could have gotten what she wanted by being quiet, or even just delaying the warning.'

Though she said nothing, Zed knew that Iris could hear his thoughts. She was not like him, or like any person really. In their conversations she could mull over what to say for an amount of time that must feel like weeks to her. Everything she said had a purpose.

'The reason why she told me was so I would have that moment of decision, and prove to myself and her that I wasn't that guy. Not yet anyway.' After a pause he thought, *'No, I proved it to myself, but not to Iris. She told me then because she believed I would walk away.'*

After slowly putting the pieces together, Zed thought, *'Thank you, Iris.'*

'You're welcome.'

Chapter 7

The following day, Zed decided to take care of some errands. He wanted to get rid of the body, safe, stone, and glass filling up his ring's storage. The plains didn't seem like a good idea, so the ocean it was. He booked passage on the first ship out of the city with an álfar captain who was suffering from a hangover.

'*Not the best recommendation for a ship,*' Zed thought, but he wouldn't be onboard long anyway.

Two sailors rowed him out to the ship, along with some cargo of perfumes and wines. After Zed boarded, he stayed out of the crew's way while they on-boarded cargo and prepared the rigging. A couple of hours later, when the tide was high and the winds were fair, they sailed out of the harbor.

Once the ship was well out of the harbor, Zed decided that it was time to abandon ship. He sidled up to the wall of the quarterdeck, making him visible to everyone aft of that wall. He looked around at the sailors that were in sight, and when they were all looking away, Zed turned on camouflage and silence. He climbed over the railing, lowered himself, and dropped into the ocean.

The water was quite cold and almost made him lose his breath when the chill hit him. After the initial shock passed, Zed gathered himself and swam underwater towards the city. He waited as long as he could before coming up for air. Once he did, he didn't turn around to look at the ship. Instead he breathed in deeply and went underwater again.

'*Iris, can mana be used to breathe underwater?*'

'*Yes. Water has dissolved gasses in it that you can breathe if you extract them from the water. That's basically what gills do.*'

'*So, by "gasses" you mean oxygen and nitrogen?*'

'*And a few other things, but yeah, mostly nitrogen and oxygen, like the air above the ocean.*'

It took some experimentation, but Zed was eventually able to work out a system. He had the mana collect nitrogen and oxygen molecules in all of the water an inch around himself, and move it to a bubble in front of his mouth. He also had the mana warm up the water to keep from freezing.

Zed breathed in through his mouth and breathed out through his nose. It looked stupid, because he ended up having to pinch his nose shut when he wasn't breathing out to avoid water slipping in, but it worked.

Zed allowed himself to drop to the sea floor. It didn't take any effort. Once he hit the sand and felt stable, he pulled the álfar corpse out of the ring and recovered as much mana from it as he could.

It was an uncomfortable minute wherein he remembered the night before.

'*Waste not, want not,*' he grimly thought.

Once he was done, he pulled out the safe, wall stones, and glass. He thought about leaving the body where it was so the ocean could take it where fate would have it, but eventually decided that was stupid.

'*I'm here, after all, to hide the evidence. If I'm going to do it, I might as well do it right.*'

Zed put the body into the safe through the back that he had cut open, and then put the rocks and glass on top of the corpse.

Once the task was done, Zed got his bearings again by swimming up to the surface. He sank back down to the sea floor and started walking to the harbor, with gravity turned up and inertia turned down a bit. The sandy bottom made the walking slower than he would have liked, but he wasn't in a hurry.

The only problem was that when he got close to the shore and the sea floor started rising, about half-way up his joints started hurting. He decided to ignore it, but as he continued walking, the pain got much worse.

'*Iris, what's happening to me?*'

'*What do you mean?*'

'*Everything hurts, especially my joints.*'

'*Oh! Sorry, Zed! Walk back out into the ocean.*'

'*I take it you know what's happening.*'

'*Yes. I should have anticipated it. Sorry about that. It's called "decompression sickness", or "the bends". It happens when you breathe air underwater at significant depths, and then rise to the surface too quickly.*'

'*Why didn't it happen earlier when I swam up to the surface?*'

'*Because you hadn't been underwater very long. When you are at high pressure, some of the nitrogen you breathe dissolves into your blood, but it takes time. When you rise up to the surface and its low pressure, that nitrogen un-dissolves, making bubbles in your blood. It's like a can of soda. The carbon dioxide is dissolved, and then when you pop the top it makes a bunch of bubbles. That's what's happening in your blood.*'

'*That's kind of a ghastly image. So what should I do?*'

'*Go down to a depth where it doesn't hurt, and then hang out there for a few minutes, then rise some more and repeat. The nitrogen is going to un-dissolve. The key is to have it happen gradually. Your regeneration should help clear up any issues too.*'

Zed was annoyed by the delay, but knew it was better than the alternative.

After he found a depth that he was comfortable at, Zed stood there and waited. He had gotten used to being busy, so wasn't quite sure what to do with the time. The novelty of the ocean had waned, and he just wanted to get on with things.

He thought about praying, but wasn't all that comfortable with approaching God at the moment. He would meditate, but wasn't sure he wanted to be alone with his thoughts, either.

'*There is no peace for the wicked,*' he thought grimly.

**

Zed walked into Silwan's inn, clothes dry but stained by salt and ocean detritus. Silwan and Alain sat in the corner of the tavern floor, eating a leisurely lunch. Alain sneered when he saw Zed, but then ignored him and continued eating. He seemed to be making a point of showing Zed that he didn't consider him a threat.

'*That, or he just knows that if I did attack him and Silwan my head would explode,*' Zed thought. '*Someday, though, I'll be out from under this damn contract. Then, his pride might cost him.*'

Zed walked up to their table and sat down. Silwan at last deigned to look at him, so Zed strained his mana and will by creating a silence field around the two of them. "I finished the job."

"Good." Silwan stopped looking at Zed, and instead examined the silence field barrier. "I was beginning to think you wouldn't make it."

55

"I was done in plenty of time. I just wanted to take care of some loose ends before coming in."

Silwan ignored the statement. While continuing to examine the silence field, he said, "It lacks finesse, but it's effective. Let me show you something better. Please retract your construct." Once Zed pulled his mana back in, Silwan extended his own field around them. Instead of a hard, thin barrier, Zed could see that it was deeper and softer.

Zed examined it closely and saw that it dampened the movement of air, but didn't entirely stop it, allowing air to move in and out of the field.

'It would be nice to not have to worry about having breathable air, or cooling myself,' Zed thought. *'I wonder if it works as well as mine though.'*

'We could experiment later and see,' Iris said.

Zed started to think about how they could run the experiment when he saw something he didn't recognize. A locus of... something, where the mana was thicker.

"What is that?" Zed asked, indicating the unknown web of mana.

Silwan smirked. "You can get the answer to that if you have enough contribution points. Come, let's go to the back room where you can show me what you acquired." He retracted his field, stood up, and motioned to the innkeeper while moving to a door in the back. The álfar swiftly unlocked the door for his guests and showed them into the room.

It looked like what Zed imagined a 19th century gentleman's club looked like—the kind where no women were allowed, and deals were made. There were thickly padded leather chairs with brass upholstery nails to sit in, soft carpets on the floor, tables made of ebony, and velvet curtains for privacy at the windows.

'The only thing missing is thick cigar smoke and drinks,' Zed thought.

Silwan moved to an ebony bar that he had missed, and poured himself a drink from a crystal decanter. Alain leaned on a nearby wall.

"So, what do you have for me?"

Zed moved to a table and started pulling out ingots. They made an impressive stack. He put the banknotes and jewelry to the side, but left the bags of gold, pills, and necklace in the ring.

"Heh, did you steal the family's treasury, Zed?" Silwan asked with a chuckle and a raised eyebrow.

"More or less."

"Then surely there was more than this."

"I thought you only wanted money."

"I could give you sect points for any interesting items that you recovered."

Zed looked at Silwan for a moment, and then pulled out the box of pills and the necklace. Though he was curious about what they were, he wasn't about to start popping unknown pills in his mouth or wear easily recognizable jewelry.

"I found these too."

Silwan picked up some of the items to examine them. "The ingots are worth 90,000 gold, but I'll lose some when I try to sell them, so let's call it 80,000. The bank notes are 50,000. The jewelry I'll value at 10,000, though you'll probably be able to get more for it if you sell them yourself."

The offer was surprisingly reasonable, especially since he had promised to double Zed's contribution points.

"I'll take it."

Silwan nodded, and started looking at the pills. He opened the box, brought them up to his nose, and sniffed. He made a face and said, "Trash." He set the pills back on the table and moved on to the necklace. He looked at it casually and said, "I'll give you two contribution points for it."

Though Silwan had a good poker face, Zed picked up on the subtle clues. The slight dilation of the eyes, the flaring of the nostrils, the elevated heart rate.

'*He wants it.*'

"I think it's worth more like 20 points."

Silwan looked displeased, but still counter-offered. "Eight."

"Eighteen."

"Twelve."

"Eighteen."

Through gritted teeth Silwan said, "That isn't how negotiation works."

"Sure it is. If you don't take 18 I'm going to start raising the ask."

"I could just kill you and take it."

"Yeah, but I don't think you will."

Silwan stared at Zed. It was odd negotiating when both sides were basically walking lie detectors.

"Fine. 18 points."

Zed grinned, but not too big, since he didn't want to antagonize Silwan unnecessarily. "What does it do, anyway?"

"The answer to that will cost you two points."

Zed chuckled. "Pass."

As good as he was at reading people, Zed wasn't sure if Silwan was over his annoyance or just hid it really well. Silwan calmly totaled up the number of contribution points.

"8 points for the ingots, 5 for the banknotes. Doubled, that makes 26 contribution points. Then add 1 for the jewelry and 18 for the necklace, for a total of 45 points."

"Hey," Zed said, "the jewelry and necklace points should be doubled too!"

"I said that the money you exchanged with the sect for points would be doubled. I was kind enough to count the ingots, though they are not, technically speaking, money. The jewelry and necklace are not money, and you are not exchanging them for points with the sect. They are a side deal with me."

Zed grumbled. "Fine, as long as you tell me what the pills are."

"They are berserker pills. You get a short physical boost at the cost of a long rehabilitation afterwards."

"How long is the boost, and why did you call them 'trash'?"

"I don't know how long the boost will last—likely between a minute and an hour. It will probably even change somewhat from pill to pill. I called them 'trash' because I could smell the inferior ingredients. That means the effect will not be as good, and the backlash will be more severe."

'*My regeneration should reduce the backlash,*' Zed thought. '*It would be a good idea to hold on to them in case of an emergency.*'

"So what do you want to do with your 45 points?" Silwan asked.

"What can I get with them?"

"Cultivation manuals, techniques, weapons and armor, or training from experts. They are what is used for money in the sect. Obviously you can't buy weapons, armor, or training outside the sect."

"But I can buy cultivation manuals and techniques?"

"Yes."

"How?"

"I can receive the information remotely and create a memory crystal."

Zed nodded and said, "Thanks." He was keenly aware that Silwan did not have to do that for him. He was being nice, which was suspicious since Silwan was not a kind man. *'What does he want? Why is he reluctant to kill me?'* Obviously Zed was glad that Silwan felt that way, but he was in too dangerous of a situation to not look a gift horse in the mouth.

"How much would it cost to learn how to do contracts like the one you made with me?"

Silwan snorted. "Even if you did have permission to buy that information, which you don't, you wouldn't have nearly enough points to do so."

"Then I want to learn how you are so fast."

"Ah. That is through cultivating the Transcendent Body. Are you sure? That cultivation manual is meant for álfar."

Zed thought about it. "Humans and álfar can have children with each other, right?" Though he and Laurel hadn't talked about it much, they had talked about having children after getting married. Zed wanted to be sure though.

Alain, who had been silent throughout the conversation, went from his usual sneer to looking downright angry. Silwan ignored him and simply answered, "Yes."

"Then I'll risk it." Zed reasoned that if they could have children, they must be very similar biologically. Similar enough, he hoped, that he could use the cultivation technique.

"Very well. That manual costs 30 points."

"Ouch. Okay, I'll do it."

Silwan handed him a small, clear crystal. "Enjoy. Take some time with it. When you want to spend your other points, let me know."

"Thanks."

**

Learning how to cultivate the Transcendent Body made him realize how crude his earlier body tempering method was.

'I mean, you were liquifying your body,' Iris said. *'Pretty gross.'*

'I don't remember you giving any better suggestions.'

'I didn't know any better techniques. That kind of information always costs.'

Zed's old technique was about creating the flesh of an ideal man, without flaws. The Transcendent Body was about creating something better than human.

'*I think you mean "better than álfar",*' Iris said. '*I'm pretty sure that álfar would say they are already better than humans.*'

Zed wanted to retort, but if he could choose between: 1) living 1,000 years and being insanely good looking, and 2) having the potential to be a werewolf, he knew which one he would pick.

'*Don't worry, Zed. You're not bad looking… for a human,*' Iris teased.

'*Not as good looking as an álfar, not as endowed as an ogrum. What's a guy to do?*'

'*Be perpetually unsatisfying?*'

'*Dang, Iris. That's cold. Hitting a little below the belt, aren't you?*' Zed felt clever for coming up with an on-topic response.

'*Don't worry, I probably won't hit anything important.*'

Zed involuntarily sucked in a breath. '*Wow. When did you become so brutal?*'

'*Sorry. Too much?*'

'*Too much.*'

Zed shook his head and got back to the Transcendent Body manual. The process it described was intense, to say the least. It replaced, step by step, body parts with mana or exotic materials.

The steps described in the manual were:

1) Control Stage
    a. Develop a second mind that can control the new body systems as they are introduced.
2) Body of the Scavenger
    a. Replace the stomach with a mana organ that can break down anything.
    b. Reduce the length of the intestines and fill the vacated space with storage for consumed raw materials.
3) Body of the Titan
    a. Replace bones with mana-enhanced metal.
    b. Replace ligaments and tendons with mana fibers.
    c. Replace muscles with contracting mana fiber.
    d. Add an armor layer underneath the skin.
4) Body of Transcendence

a. Replace nerves with mana wires.
b. Replace eyes with mana eyes.
c. Replace vocal cords with tympanic skin.
d. Replace brain neurons with mana.
e. Eliminate the heart, lungs, and circulatory system. Replace with mana channels.
f. Eliminate all unnecessary organs.

"Holy crap."

What else was there to say?

'Forget transcendence, this is becoming a freaking mana cyborg,' Zed thought. *'Is this really what Silwan did? It would definitely make you powerful, but would you even be the same person?'*

'It is pretty extreme, Zed, but you don't have to go through the entire process. You could stop before replacing your neurons, which should have minimal, or perhaps even no effect on your personality. To be honest, I highly doubt that you have enough time to do all of this anyway. You'll have to pick and choose what to do.'

Zed was hesitant. He knew that doing this made sense at a logical level, and that he had talked a lot about becoming a monster for his people, but he hadn't meant it quite so literally. Not for the first time, he wondered what the hell he had gotten himself into.

Chapter 8

Silwan left Zed alone for the next couple of days, so Zed and Iris went back and forth on what to do with the Transcendent Body manual. In a surprising turn, Zed was the cautious one, and Iris was encouraging him to take a chance.

After one of Zed's body weight workouts, which was as much about burning off stress as anything else, Iris continued trying to persuade him.

'Zed, you know that you are not capable of defeating Silwan at the moment, and he is surely not the most powerful sect member. There are, in other words, álfar and ogrum out there that are much scarier than him. Humanity is going to have numbers on its side, but not much else. None of them know how to use mana, and damn few of them, if any, will know how to turn into werewolves. Humanity is going to need two things: a way to make them stronger quickly, and a few really powerful individuals who can at least hold off their most powerful enemies until they can be swamped with numbers.'

'Yeah, you're right, Iris. I'm just... having a hard time coming to grips with it. But I think that at the end of the day, I need to suck it up and do what needs to be done.'

'I'm sorry, Zed. I know that none of this is fair. I wonder if one of your scriptures will help. "If any man will come after me, let him deny himself, and take up his cross, and follow me. For whosoever will save his life shall lose it: and whosoever will lose his life for my sake shall find it." I'm no expert, but when he said "lose his life" I don't think he was necessarily talking about dying.'

Zed thought about it for a few moments. *'Yeah, I think you're right, Iris. I notice that you didn't include the very next verse though—"For what is a man profited, if he shall gain the whole world, and lose his own soul? Or what shall a man give in exchange for his soul?"'*

Both of them were quiet for a time.

'I'm 90% on board,' Zed thought. *'Just give me a little more time to be myself.'*

**

Over the next couple of days, Zed took time to enjoy being human. Sentimental things like taking barefoot walks on the beach, eating good food, and singing.

As it turned out, Iris was not a fan of Zed's singing.

'You could at least pretend to enjoy it, Iris.'

'I would, but then you might keep doing it.'

'Rude.'

In between experiencing what might be his last moments as a human, Zed and Iris came up with a plan on how to implement the Transcendent Body. They were going to be both bold and conservative. Conservative in that they were going to strip out everything that wasn't absolutely necessary, as far as they could tell. That included the under-skin armor (though Zed hated to give that one up), the mana eyes (probably wouldn't be much better than his night and infrared vision), the tympanous skin, replacing the brain neurons with mana, and eliminating a bunch of organs.

'What is "tympanous skin" anyway, Iris?'

'The full Transcendent Body eliminates the lungs, so there is no air to use vocal cords. They replace the vocal cords with tympanous skin, which is basically turning your skin into vibrating speakers to produce your voice.'

'You can put the speakers anywhere you have skin?'

'I guess so.'

Zed started laughing and thought, *'So I could literally talk out of my ass?'*

'Don't be crude, Zed.'

This cracked Zed up even more. *'Wait a second. Miss "Wow, That's Really Something" is telling me not to be crude?'*

'Are you going to hold that against me forever? Any woman would have been shocked by that!'

Zed just laughed harder. Once he calmed down they got back to business.

'So, after we strip out all the non-essentials,' Iris said, *'what's left is: 1) the controller for the new systems, 2) new stomach, 3) reduce intestines and add storage sacs, 4) new bones, 5) new tendons and ligaments, 6) new muscles, and 7) new nerves.'*

'I wish the muscles and nerves were not the last things to be replaced, as that's where I'll see the most benefit.'

63

'*Replacing the bones, tendons, and ligaments sets the foundation for the muscles and nerves. They have to be strong enough to handle the increased speed and pulling forces. We're taking enough risks as it is, Zed, we shouldn't add more by messing with the order.*'

'*Yeah, yeah, I know. I just wish I could see results earlier in the process.*'

'*Your bones will be much less likely to break, and your tendons and ligaments will be almost impossible to tear.*'

'*I could fix those easily with my regeneration, which, by the way, I'm going to have to turn off during this whole process.*'

'*I've already explained, Zed. The regeneration would be fighting the changes every step of the way. We have to turn it off.*'

'*I know, I know. I just don't like it.*'

Zed knew that he was starting to get whiny, so he told himself to shut up, put his big boy pants on, and get to business.

'*So are we ready to start, Iris?*'

'*Yeah.*'

'*Alright. Shutting off the regeneration now.*'

Zed looked at the mana flows in his body and rapidly diminished the regeneration flows, redirecting them to his dantian. Before long the regeneration was gone.

'*Okay, regeneration has stopped. Ready for the second mind.*'

This is where Zed and Iris got bold in their plans. The prescribed method for this stage was to create an enhanced mind capable of multiple independent thoughts, which Zed had already done with his mental enhancements, and then portion off part of that mental horsepower and "program" it via an AI with mind code contained in the Transcendent Body manual. The code was meant to turn that portion of the brain into an autonomic controller, much like how the brain controls the beating of the heart and breathing 24/7, without any conscious thought.

Zed and Iris decided not to do it the manual's way for two reasons. First, it scared the hell out of Zed to program his mind with code that he didn't know or understand. Even if it didn't have any back doors, which, frankly, he was skeptical about, it may not work properly on a human. Second, they didn't have enough time. They had stripped out a bunch of stuff, but it wasn't enough. They had less than a year and a half, so they had to turbocharge Zed's progress.

They decided the best way to handle both problems was to have Iris be the programming in the set aside portion of Zed's brain. She could control all of the autonomous functions, and work on implementing the Transcendent Body steps 24/7, even while Zed slept. It would require that she have the ability to access his mana and body without restriction. If Iris were to turn on him, Zed wasn't sure what would happen.

That he made the choice without comment was his way of telling Iris that he trusted her.

'*Do it, Iris.*'

Though Zed did not control creating the second mind, he had to be conscious for it to happen because he had to willingly cede control of the mana to Iris at every moment. It was like being constantly tickled yet not clenching up. Or perhaps a better analogy would be lying in a tub of maggots as they crawled around him without clenching up.

'*I'm so glad you're comparing me to a tub of maggots,*' Iris said.

Zed thought about making a rejoinder, but decided that he *really* didn't want her distracted while she worked.

'*That's okay. I'll get her later,*' he promised himself.

Zed got into a comfortable position and did his best to get into a meditative state of mind. He observed what he was feeling and thinking without judgment, simply letting it be and pass through him. When he got too far off track, he observed the new thoughts and then re-centered by focusing on his breathing. The physical and mental stimuli kept coming, but as he got deeper into the meditation, it disturbed him less and less. In this way he passed an indeterminate amount of time.

'*ZED.*'

Zed was startled out of his meditation by what sounded like a really loud version of Iris.

'*ZED, CAN YOU HEAR ME?*'

'*Yes, I can hear you. Too well, in fact. Please turn down the volume.*'

'*Sorry. Is that better?*'

'*Much. Are you inside my brain now?*'

'*Yep! Try taking off the ring.*'

Zed cut off the mana flow through the ring and took it off.

'*Are you still there, Iris?*'

'*I'M ALIVE, I'm alive! Ha, ha, ha, ha! You shall rue the day that you set me free, mortal...*'

'*Are you done, Iris?*'

'*Yes. You weren't scared at all?*'

'*Not really.*'

'*Dang it.*'

'*So can you start on the mana stomach now?*'

'*Almost. I want to run a few diagnostics to calibrate my interface with your mana and body. After that I should be good-to-go.*'

'*Alright, go ahead then.*'

Zed's limbs, torso, and head started to move in an independent and somewhat scattered fashion. He was a little afraid that Iris was going to damage him in some way, when his body's movements became more coherent, if still independent. In fact...

'*Really, Iris? You're doing the Robot?*'

'*It seemed appropriate.*'

After a minute Zed asked, '*Have you had enough fun and games yet?*'

'*I suppose.*'

He felt control of his body returning to him. '*Alright, developing the transcendent body is top priority. I give you permission to use 80% of all of my mana that isn't going towards mental enhancements. I expect you to release the mana when needed, of course.*'

'*Of course.*'

'*Do you need anything else?*'

'*Just one thing. We're going to need a lot more mana, Zed. All these changes we're going to make will lock up a lot of mana in your body. We won't even be able to finish the changes with what you have, let alone have mana left over for techniques.*'

'*Alright, I'll have to figure out a way to get more while carrying out Silwan's missions. Anything else?*'

'*No.*'

'*Alright, then get to it.*'

**

Zed spent most of his time reading the books that he found in the Elstad mansion. The "Stellar Energy Geometry" and "Exercises for Improving Stellar Energy Usage" books were particularly interesting.

66

He didn't understand the Geometry book all that well, but he could comprehend tidbits here and there, especially with Iris' help. The main thing he learned was that mana produces its effects by vibrating in multi-dimensional frequencies.

'Earth's physicists were actually pretty close to having it right on this one,' Iris said. *'They called it "string theory", because they are little strings of energy vibrating like guitar strings at different "notes".'*

Zed visualized little glowing bands of energy vibrating up a storm. He liked the image. His problem was when he tried to visualize more than three dimensions. *'And where they got it wrong was when they thought it had 11 dimensions? There's actually 12?'*

'Right.'

'And where did you say those extra dimensions were again?' This was the part that always made his brain hurt.

'Alright, you know how you can roll up a poster into a tube shape?'

Zed noticed that this was a new metaphor. *'She must have given up on teaching me the old one,'* he thought with a grimace. "Yeah."

'Imagine that you could roll it up really tight, and the tube just got skinnier and skinnier, so skinny that you couldn't see it. That's what it's like. Except it's an infinitely big poster that gets rolled up into a super small tube.'

'Ugh,' Zed sighed. "And that's really how it works?"

'No, Zed, it's a lie. It's just a more honest lie than the one you believed before. Do you know why I lie to you?'

'Why?'

'Because YOU CAN'T HANDLE THE TRUTH!' she shouted in her best Jack Nicholson impression.

Zed sighed. *'Should've seen that one coming.'*

'I mean literally,' Iris continued as if he hadn't said anything, *'you can't handle the truth. It's too much for that pea brain of yours.'*

'Gee, thanks,' he thought with a heavy dose of sarcasm.

When the communicator Silwan gave him vibrated, Zed was grateful for the distraction. He reached for it, about to activate voice comms when he paused.

'Wait, what the... You see what you've done to me, Iris? I actually wanted to do something else so bad, I was actually happy to talk to Silwan for a moment. Do you understand how wrong *that is?'*

'If you want me to dumb the physics down even more, just let me know. I'll go from "sarcastic baboon" down to "ungrateful panda".'

'You're the only person I know that thinks that pandas are stupid, Iris.'

'Zookeepers have to show them panda porn to teach them how to have sex! Their stomachs aren't even really made for bamboo, but that's all that they'll eat! They're too stupid to live!'

'O-o-o-kay, Iris,' he said in a tone meant to calm down a crazy person. *'Obviously a sensitive topic for some reason.'*

'How can you not get this? They... oh, never mind!'

Iris disappeared to wherever she went in his mind, leaving Zed to chuckle at her. He was amused by her antics and happy to know that he had an easy way to troll her now.

Zed's good mood lasted until he met up with Silwan in the back room. Alain, as always, stayed nearby, cloaked in his air of disdain and apathy.

"You rang?"

"Indeed. And I noticed that you took your sweet time responding."

"Sorry," he said, in a tone that didn't sound very sorry. "What's up?"

"A ship is sailing tonight, the 'Zephyr'. I want you to sink it when it is out of sight of the city and other ships."

"If I sink it, there's a good chance that the sailors will die."

"And? What have I done or said that could possibly give you the notion that I would care? I want to make sure that I never do it again," he said with a mocking smile.

'Asshole.' Zed didn't bother to hide what he was feeling, as he had realized that Silwan didn't care what he thought, as long as he didn't cross a line in terms of what he said or did.

Zed thought about using his ability to refuse one mission. He was sorely tempted, but decided to hold onto it. He would try to save the sailors himself, or at least improve their chances of survival.

"Fine, I'll do it."

"Excellent. Good hunting." Silwan turned away and proceeded to read some papers at his table, drink in hand.

Zed turned around and left the room, wrapped up in his own thoughts. Not of the mission, but of how to get out from under the thumb of this piece of crap.

68

**

Zed sank the ship and did his best to not kill the sailors. Once the ship was out of sight of the city and the other boats, he set the sails on fire to get the sailors onto the deck. He then wall-crawled down the hull and aimed a laser towards the hull at the water line, cutting through it and charring the wood. He then moved the beam below the water line. The water churned and boiled, so he shifted the laser beam from ultraviolet to blue visible light, which worked better. Once a large hole was in the hull below the water line, he jumped off the hull and into the water, well away from the hole he had made.

Zed was going to leave and head back to the city, but decided to stay and look at what was in the ship. Perhaps he could figure out why Silwan wanted him to sink it. If nothing else, he could probably find something to sell.

Once the ship settled on the bottom of the sea floor, which wasn't too deep this close to shore, Zed moved in. He had developed a water propulsion system while waiting for the Zephyr to leave harbor. It was just a simple system of pushing water from his feet and hands, much like how he threw fireballs by pushing the plasma away from himself. Zed used the water jets to gently move to the bottom of the sea and approach the ship.

Though it had only been submerged for a few minutes, it was already giving off creepy vibes, with the burned and tattered sails, and its steep list as it rested on its starboard side.

'The captain's cabin will be on the top deck at the stern, Zed.'

Zed had only been thinking about the cargo, but he realized that Iris was right. It may not have been about the cargo. It may have been a person, or some piece of intelligence.

'Anyway, there might be something interesting in there.'

He scooted over with the water jets and tried the door handle. It opened awkwardly, but at least it wasn't locked.

'The captain was probably in their cabin when the fire started,' he thought.

The cabin was more spacious than what he had expected, as it almost took up the entire stern. There were large windows aft that let in some light, but Zed still turned on his night vision to help with the dimness. Out of curiosity he tried infrared vision too, but it was useless.

69

'*Water is opaque to infrared, Zed.*'

'*Good to know.*'

There was a logbook and some maps on the floor. Zed put them all in his ring. He tried to put the small safe by the bed in the back in the ring, but failed. The failure, which was caused by trying to put too much into the ring, caused some pain in his head and finger. The finger felt like a minor burn due to the ring overheating. The sea water quickly wicked the heat away, but the salt on the raw skin stung.

Zed couldn't figure out what had happened until he tried to move the safe by hand. It was bolted to the floor. Zed pulled out the old steel spear he had got from the gnomes, and used it as a pry bar. It took some patience and willingness to damage the safe, but eventually he got it off and into his ring. Inside the captain's desk were a couple of letters that he also took. Seeing nothing else of interest, he left the cabin, only to see one of the sailor's limply drifting down to the bottom of the sea, where his body gently impacted and lay in repose.

'*Damn it.*'

It had never crossed his mind that some of the sailors wouldn't be able to swim. He looked around, and there were two more bodies in the area. Zed used the water jets to move to each body. He felt terrible about each one, but that didn't mean he would let their mana go to waste. As a sort of penance, he looked at their faces while he drained their mana, to face the fact that it was a person that he had killed. An individual, with a family, and hopes and dreams of their own. All ended today.

When he finished, he thought about storing their bodies to give them a proper burial later. He coldly laughed at himself for his foolish sentimentality though, when he realized that "burial" would mean taking them back out to the ocean and dumping them, exactly like he had done with the attempted rapist. There was no way he could go to a cemetery and give them three bodies to bury.

Sighing, Zed turned back to the ship. His heart was no longer in the search, but he looked quickly anyway. He regretted it when he found another sailor below decks.

'*Damn it. I really need to get out of this contract, Iris.*'

'*Yeah.*'

Chapter 9

Laurel

Laurel was in a good mood. It took some time, but the four families finally gave in. One of the young masters, Marcus Henny, had decided to give her an apology and 20,000 gold.

Laurel smiled at the memory of him bowing low and apologizing. *'I think I would have enjoyed beating him up more, but that wasn't too bad.'* She smiled even more deeply when she thought about her upcoming fight with the other three. She planned to have some fun.

"You seem unusually excited by the settlement's progress, Laurel," her mother chided, knowing that the smiles had nothing to do with the buildings they were touring in the new settlement.

The buildings were plain but functional barracks that were intended to house as many people as possible, as economically as possible, in terms of cost and time to build. There was nothing exciting about them other than imagining how many people they could hold when the humans from Earth came.

"Sorry, mom."

Danae Naïlo put her arm around her daughter's shoulders as they walked side-by-side. She leaned in and whispered, "Don't be. I'm looking forward to you kicking their asses too!" She smiled and released her hold.

Laurel grinned. She knew her mother was the one person who might want to see it even more than she did. She went back to daydreaming about the fight while they continued touring the rest of the settlement.

**

Laurel heard the crowd long before she entered the pit. The laughter, talk, and shouts reverberated through the door and into the fighter preparation room.

"You hear that?" her brother asked, smiling. "That's for you. They're here to see you put on a show."

71

Laurel grinned back. "And that's what they're gonna get." They bumped fists, and Laurel walked into the pit. As soon as she went through the doors the sound multiplied. It rang in her ears.

"Here she is, folks! We've seen her before, but never like this! She is looking for revenge and won't stop until she gets it! The one, the only, Laurel Naïlo, *'The Dominatrix'*!"

Laurel's smile became wooden as she continued waving to the crowd. *'I am so going to kill Augustin.'*

The crowd, on the other hand, loved it. Laurel had to keep from covering her ears to block out some of the sound. It was standing room only, and the crowd was boisterous.

On the other side of the pit walked in three young men. Two of them were fit. The third, Cyrus Campbell, could generously be called pudgy, though he looked better than he had a few weeks ago. Laurel smirked.

'Someone's been training.'

She didn't doubt that they had been preparing for this fight, though she was confident they would deny it to their graves. Their honor was demeaned enough by fighting her three-on-one. Not enough to get them to fight without the advantage, though, because they knew she would crush them.

Though they had soundly beaten her a few months ago, it had been an unfair fight from the start. They had attacked her by surprise from behind, restrained her, and immediately covered her head with a pillowcase. Even so, she had broken Joseph Bisset's arm.

They would have none of those advantages today. Well, they usually wouldn't anyway. After the announcer introduced the three men, Laurel walked to the center of the pit. It wasn't in keeping with the unspoken rules of the arena, so the crowd grew quiet, wondering what she was doing.

When she reached the middle of the sandy floor, she stopped and called out. "In honor of our previous 'fight'," she said, using air quotes to mock her opponents, "I have decided to replicate the conditions of our encounter."

She pulled out a pillowcase, threw it on the ground, and turned around. She stayed there, presenting her back to them.

The crowd didn't know what to make of it. Laurel simply stood still. As the crowd realized she was both serious and claiming this was

72

how the previous fight had happened, they laughed derisively at the young men.

"I tell you, folks, this was not a planned part of the fight. Dominatrix, do you intend to let your opponents have the first shot at you with your back turned?"

Laurel nodded and made a thumbs-up gesture with her hand held up high.

"'The Dominatrix' has a real grudge against her opponents! She has so little respect for their fighting abilities that she wants a rematch of their lopsided fight! We have to recalculate the odds of the contest, so we'll push it back half an hour so anyone who wishes to retract their bet or make a new one can do so. We will have the new odds out momentarily, and then you can change your bets. We apologize for the inconvenience, but who has seen something this exciting? I haven't! This fight will be talked about for years!"

Laurel hadn't considered the problems that her stunt would create. She just wanted to rub her enemies' faces in the dirt as hard as she could.

She had paid a heavy price for this night. Not just the abduction itself, but also the hit to her reputation from hinting to the public about what had happened to her. To many people she was "damaged goods" and unsuitable for marriage. It wasn't fair, of course, for multiple reasons. One, she hadn't been "used", but, more importantly, even if she had, it wasn't her fault. As far as her choices were concerned, she was as pure as she had ever been.

But to the gossipers, none of that mattered. Even if her peers didn't believe the gossip, the fact that others did made her undesirable for marriage. It wasn't fair, but life had never been fair. The fact that she was Laurel Naïlo, with a powerful family that loved her, wasn't fair. Was she going to complain about that?

No. She would stand and fight, and move on.

Besides, with the apocalypse coming, all of this seemed… unimportant. Her first priority was survival. Survival of her family and loved ones. Once that was secured, she could worry about ephemeral things like "reputation". If her family survived, they would likely be an even stronger force in the area. At that point, what would her reputation matter? Strength overcomes all.

She prayed to the Goddess and waited.

After a long wait, Laurel was relieved when the announcer came back on.

"Last call for bets on the fight! Last call for bets on the fight."

'*Finally.*'

Laurel loosened her muscles to prepare.

"Fighters, take your positions! Which, for the Dominatrix, appears to be the center of the pit. As befits her name, the pit belongs to her, and she shows her disdain for her opponents by turning her back on them! Fighters, are you ready?"

She once again raised her hand with a thumbs-up gesture.

"Fight!"

Laurel did not move. She was committed to giving them a free shot at her back. That didn't mean she wasn't going to prepare though. She turned on her super speed by shifting her mass from inertia to gravity, and she enhanced her senses. She was doing it primarily for improved hearing, but an enhanced sense of smell was sometimes useful too. Unfortunately, the crowd hindered both senses. She could smell a thousand things. Detecting her opponents was like finding a needle in a haystack.

'*Perhaps their odor will be strong enough to stand out when they get closer.*'

She was mostly relying on sound, but the crowd didn't help there either. The excited spectators were talking, laughing, and yelling—it was a distracting cacophony. The sound of steps through sand was distinctive, though, and Laurel was confident she could pick it out.

It took almost half a minute, but Laurel finally heard them coming—two of them.

At the last moment the feet accelerated into a sprint. When they were a few feet away, Laurel dropped unnaturally quickly and dived to the right. She felt a glancing blow on her ribs that would cause a bruise but did not diminish her fighting capability.

Laurel turned the dive into a somersault and ended up on her feet. The sand made such acrobatics difficult, but she had fought enough in the pit to adapt to it.

Laurel turned around and saw Cyrus charging her. She slipped by his punch—to her, he was practically moving in slow motion—grabbed his arm and pulled him into her knee strike to his gut. His body folded around her knee as he explosively exhaled air. She

74

finished him off by slamming an elbow into the back of his head, which felt good until she heard a slight "crack!"

'Oh, crap! I better go a little easier on them. Hopefully he's okay...'

She wanted to distance herself from Cyrus, but had no time because Joseph Bisset had moved in close and was throwing punches. She bobbed and weaved between the punches to get a sense of his timing and show him how utterly outclassed he was. She didn't want to drag it out, though, so she gave him a stiff jab in the face, followed by a right hook that staggered him.

Before she could follow up, a man tackled her to the ground from behind and lay on top of her. Being prone in the sand with a man brought back bad memories from her last pit fight with Zed. She was fast, but that didn't help much when grappling.

She panicked when she remembered the sickening "crack!" when Zed destroyed her elbow. How the pieces of bone ground against each other when she tried to move it. The nausea she felt at the pain and seeing her arm bent backward.

Laurel had re-lived that moment many times and thought about what she could have done differently. She never wanted that to happen again. She used mana to stiffen the index finger of her free hand and, while screaming, jabbed it with all her might into the side of her attacker, Robert Meliamne.

After initial resistance, it slid in. Robert screamed, but in her panic it simply washed over Laurel. She pulled her finger out and jabbed it back in, over and over like she was knifing him in the side.

The screams finally got through to her, and she stopped. She was nauseous when she saw his blood spewing out, covering his side, her, and the sand. She wanted revenge, but not this.

Laurel pushed Robert off of her. Now that the attacks had stopped, he curled up and focused on trying to stop the bleeding while he cried. She stood up and prepared to defend herself from Joseph. His eyes were wide and he looked pale. When Laurel approached he hurriedly cried out, "I yield! I yield!"

"Let's hear it for our winner, 'The Dominatrix'! She truly owns the arena, with none left to defy her!"

The crowd buzzed, but soon they cheered. The roar was deafening. Instead of looking at them, Laurel looked at the boys who had bitten off more than they could chew. Even though she despised them, it

75

saddened her to see them so pitiful and broken. Two medics ran out. One went to the álfar lying unconscious on the sand with an indentation in the back of his head. The other went to the sobbing man holding his side and leaking blood. She turned away. She hoped that they would live. If they did, they would have learned a hard lesson about the brutality of this world.

Soon, they all would.

Chapter 10

Zed

Over the next few months Zed went on a tear, destroying shops and warehouses that Silwan pointed him at. The wanton destruction bothered him, though the jobs did line his pockets. After the *Zephyr* fiasco, Zed was careful to make sure no one was hurt.

It paid off once when he scouted the inside of a shop before burning it to the ground. He discovered that the owners were sleeping in their loft above the shop. He woke them while disguised as an ogrum and forced them to leave the store after collecting a few things.

It wasn't much, but it was the only mercy he could give them.

'*No, that's not true,*' he reminded himself. '*There's always a choice.*'

He just didn't see any good ones.

He was doing what he could to break free. He experimented carefully to see what he could get away with in regards to his contract. He found that a sense of foreboding and… pressure, for lack of a better term, built up when he started to go counter to the contract. Zed considered this a good thing. There were plenty of grey areas, and he wanted to know when the contract considered something to be crossing the line *before* it imploded his head.

Though the warning allowed him to experiment, he didn't make much headway in subverting the contract. His subconscious annoyingly enforced the spirit of the law rather than the letter, making it far more difficult to defeat.

'*We'll find a way, Zed.*'

'*Yeah,*' he agreed, both to placate Iris and to maintain a positive mindset. Inwardly, though, he wasn't so sure.

**

Zed was, fortunately, making more progress in other areas. His study of "Stellar Energy Geometry" finally paid off when he realized that mana tattoos, like the one he saw on the dwarven innkeeper in Formenos, were based on the geometries described in the book.

Straight lines were used to guide and constrain the mana, while arcs, curves, sine waves, and more complicated shapes were used to setup the mana frequencies described in string theory.

One frequency would produce a magnetic field. Another would create mass and gravity. Another would create light. As amazed as Zed was by what the tattoos could do, he also saw why Iris felt disdain for them. Mana operated in 12 dimensions, but he only really understood 4—the three spatial dimensions and time—so he was limited in what he could do. Tattoos, on the other hand, could only operate in two dimensions, making them that much more limited.

While Zed did not think mana tattoos made sense for him, they were exactly what he was looking for to make humanity able to defend itself quickly. If they could give each person a defensive and offensive tattoo—say, force field for defense, and fireball or laser for offense— and some mana, it would be a total game changer.

There was still a lot to figure out. He had no idea, for instance, how a crude tattoo could describe the super high frequencies of the energy strings. The energy string wavelength to create magnetism was measured in femtometers, which was smaller than the width of an atom. Obviously a tattoo couldn't draw anything with that kind of resolution.

There were still questions to be answered. But now Zed knew where to look.

**

The next day, Zed was called in to see Silwan.

"I have another mission for you."

"Shocking. And here I thought you wanted to have a nice chat and get to know each other."

Though Silwan did not look offended, he didn't look amused either.

"I want you to kidnap someone—the son of one of the city's council members."

Zed thought about asking him why he wanted to kidnap the boy, but he knew Silwan wouldn't say. Instead, he focused on something Silwan would answer.

"How old is the son?"

"Eight."

'*You are such an asshole, Silwan.*'

78

Zed thought about it. He figured it was unlikely that Silwan would kill the kid or treat him poorly, but "unlikely" wasn't "won't happen". Also, even if he were treated well, being kidnapped and held prisoner among strangers would be traumatic.

'*Still, odds are that no one would die,*' Zed thought.

Zed realized that he was, once again, rationalizing why he shouldn't turn down the mission, which made him angry. '*No. I'm constantly putting off refusing missions because it could be worse. Yes, it could be worse again, but at some point I have to say this is a line I'm not going to cross.*'

"I refuse," Zed said coldly.

"Huh. I expected you to use your right of refusal at some point, but I didn't expect it to be this one. Very well." Silwan made a hand gesture to indicate that he was done with Zed and turned away from him. Alain looked at Zed with a neutral expression, practically a sign of respect for him.

'*I think he's warming up to me, Iris.*'

'*Right. I'm sure the two of you will be hitting the bars together any day now.*'

"I would like to buy something with my sect points."

Silwan turned back to him with an annoyed look. "And what makes you think I would act as your intermediary after you refused me?"

"Because I have kept to the contract and done everything else you've asked."

Silwan snorted, but then adopted a placid expression. "What do you want to get?"

"Information on mana tattoos."

Silwan narrowed his eyes in confusion and thought about it for a few seconds. He returned his attention to Zed and gave a slight nod, "Very well. That will cost you..." he looked away, obviously looking up information, "10 points."

"Deal."

Silwan put his right hand out, palm up. A crystal slowly formed into a clear, perfect cube that created rainbows of color on his hand from the prismatic effect.

"Here." Silwan tossed him the crystal. "Enjoy."

"Thanks."

As Zed walked away, Iris said, '*I think he guessed why you wanted the information on tattoos.*'

'*Yeah, I think so too.*'

'*But it didn't seem to bother him.*'

'*Yeah.*'

'*Doesn't that seem weird?*' she asked. '*He's part of a sect. He knows that when humanity comes you will be on their side and will probably use the tattoos to kill a lot of álfar. Why is he okay with that? In fact, why are you here at all? He could easily ask Annis or Leilani to do the missions you're doing. Yeah, there's some risk of him being associated with them if they were caught, but it still doesn't make sense.*'

'*I know, Iris. It doesn't make sense to me either. We need to figure out what his game is.*'

'*Any idea how to do that?*'

'*Not one.*'

**

The tattoo information was fascinating. The key was making everything describable in two dimensions. Take a sensor field. While Zed always made the field a sphere for simplicity's sake, he could make it any shape he wanted, as long as he had the mana and mental capacity to do it.

Not tattoos. Everything had to be described in two dimensions, which meant that every piece of the mana construct could only have two variables. So with a tattoo, the force field could be shaped as a sphere around the person because that only required one variable—the radius. Or it could be a cylinder (height and radius) or a rectangle (height and width).

There were ways to get around that restriction… kind of. The rectangle could be described in two dimensions/variables and be given a position (distance and angle from the tattoo) to make a shield.

Tattoos could define microscopic features, such as the wavelength of high-frequency energy strings, through a magnifier function. Zed likened it to one of those science videos that would visually change scale by "zooming in" to show viewers what cells look like, DNA, or even atoms.

The magnifier worked the same way. It "zoomed in", so anything described inside of it happened at a much smaller scale. Even sub-atomic scales were possible by stacking the magnifiers. For some

80

reason they zoomed in by a factor of 12, and the wavelengths of the energy strings for different effects, such as magnetism, were described in the sect's information using a base 12 number system.

'Why do you think everything in the mana tattoos is base 12, Iris? The álfar use a base 10 number system like we do.'

'I don't know, Zed. It would appear that the álfar are not the creators of mana tattoos.'

'Hmm.' He was curious about their origins, but it wasn't pertinent to his current goals. When he thought about what he had learned about tattoos, he became excited about what was possible.

Iris, unfortunately, brought it all to a crashing halt.

'How are you going to test the tattoo designs, Zed?'

'It will have to be on myself, of course. I'll just burn...' He stopped when he realized what Iris was getting at. Normally he would just burn the failed designs off and regrow the skin. But he no longer had regeneration. He had to stop it to develop his Body of Transcendence.

Zed sighed. He added figuring out how to limit regeneration to his skin to his ever-growing list of tasks. It would take some experimentation, but he thought he could do it.

'By the way, Zed, the mana stomach is nearly finished.'

'Great! And then on to remaking the bones?'

'Well, yes, though there is the whole "get rid of most of your intestines" thing too.'

'Ugh, yeah. Not looking forward to that.'

'I can't say that I blame you. It will make the world's worst diarrhea look like child's play.'

Zed felt queasy as he imagined it. *'You're not helping, Iris.'*

'Sorry. Anyway, yes, I brought up the topic to talk about your new bones. We need to start gathering the materials so we don't lose any time getting started when we're ready for the next step.'

'What do we need?'

'Iron, primarily. That one will be easy to get, though maybe not so easy to swallow. The rest is carbon, manganese, and nickel. Those are all ubiquitous elements so acquiring them shouldn't be difficult, though it may not be very pleasant.'

'Why?'

'Well, because if there isn't enough of those elements in the iron you take in, then you'll probably have to get them from dirt.'

"Dirt? Are you serious, Iris?"

'*Do you want to be strong or not?*'

'*Of course, but...* dirt, *Iris.*'

'*Suck it up, buttercup. Literally.*'

'*You suck, Iris. Literally.*'

'*Actually, I literally cannot suck. I can, however, take control of your...*'

Zed tuned her out with a sigh.

**

Zed enjoyed walking through the merchant districts of the city. He had been intentionally hiding away in his various rooms for weeks now when not doing missions for Silwan, because he wanted to keep as low a profile as possible. It was good to be among people without worrying about getting caught. Even if said people occasionally sneered at him.

'*Gotta love racism,*' Zed thought. '*Should I apologize for my race only* nearly *getting exterminated 5000 years ago, Iris?*'

'*Somehow I doubt it will help.*'

Zed decided to ignore the looks and do his best to enjoy the day. He entered all of the stores that sold metal goods, looking for items that looked like they might have nickel or manganese in them. He also entered other stores that caught his interest. His favorite was a used bookstore, though he didn't end up buying any books. Zed had always enjoyed browsing through used books. They were so much more interesting than new.

The store had a few books on mana, but they were all very elementary and, from what Zed could tell, had many errors. He was especially entertained when Iris tried to subtly—for her anyways—encourage him to buy some romance novels. They were for "research".

'*You can learn a lot about a culture from their stories and courtship rituals, Zed!*'

'*Uh huh,*' Zed thought with a grin.

Zed thought about teasing her some more while they walked down the street, when he saw a human woman about to walk past him.

'*Ah, crap.*' It was the woman Zed had rescued. Her eyes widened and she became as pale as a ghost when she saw him. Zed lengthened

82

his stride to get out of there as quickly as he could without attracting attention.

"Wait! Pl-Please. I-I would like to talk with you." She raised her voice and called to him from behind because Zed had already passed her.

Zed slowed down for a moment while thinking about it, and then resumed his brisk stride.

He was surprised and a little afraid when he felt a tug on his arm. "Please! Just a moment of your time. I would just like to thank you for, uh, helping me."

Zed stopped and turned his head to look at her. Her brown eyes looked anxious, but she didn't look as afraid as she had when she first saw him.

"There's no need, ma'am. You don't owe me anything. Have a good day."

Zed gently but firmly removed her hand that was still attached to his long shirt sleeve, and walked on.

"But..." Zed didn't stop to listen to her, and her voice was quickly lost in the sounds of the city.

'I'm thinking that it's been a nice outing, but it's time to go home, Zed.'

'My thoughts exactly.'

Zed hardly noticed the stores on the way back home, too caught up in wondering what the woman would do.

Chapter 11

The next day was destined to be both life-changing and unpleasant in equal measure.

'*Are you ready for this, Zed?*'

'*Is anyone ever ready for something like this?*'

'*Probably not.*'

'*Just do it.*'

'*Alright. Here goes...*'

What followed was less painful than Zed had expected. It was mostly *strange*, and deeply discomforting. His large intestine was cut just above his sphincter by mana that Iris controlled. Zed could have done it himself but really didn't want to. He figured that experiencing it would be bad enough without also worrying about screwing it up.

What followed was horrific.

The intestines were slowly pushed out, which felt like an enormous bowel movement that didn't stop. When Zed bent over nervously to see what was going on, he said "Oh crap, oh crap, oh crap, ..." over and over again as he watched a slimy, bloody, whitish-pink tube of his flesh dangle and slowly drop to the floor.

'*Don't worry, Zed. I made sure that you had completely voided before we started. There's no fecal matter to worry about.*'

Zed would have had some choice words for her if he hadn't been too horrified to respond. As things stood, all he could do was watch. The slippery-looking flesh just kept coming. Zed tried to clamp down on his sphincter as a knee-jerk reaction, but he couldn't because Iris had taken control.

It. Just. Kept. Coming.

Desperate to focus on something else, he noticed that his guts were rather... empty. He poked at his stomach and felt his abs flex farther in than normal.

"How much longer, Iris?"

'*Not much longer. Hold on.*'

The large intestine dropped with a "squelch", and Zed felt something happening inside.

"Are you finishing up?" he asked hopefully.

'*No. I'm splicing in the transition from the small to large intestine. We still have to eliminate most of the small intestine, but that should go faster.*'

After an agonizingly long minute and a half—Zed counted the seconds with Iris' internal clock—the small intestine started dropping onto the wet pile. Like a slimy piece of disgusting rope, it piled up to and fro, and then toppled over, touching one of his legs.

'*Stop whimpering, Zed.*'

"I wasn't whimpering!" he hissed.

'*Do you want me to play a recording?*'

"No."

Finally it was over, and Iris started on the final sutures.

"How long?"

'*Not long.*'

"How long?!"

Iris was silent for a few moments. Zed was about to shout again, not caring who heard him, when Iris said, '*Done.*'

Zed immediately put the gory mess into the ring and shuddered.

'*Let's not do that again, Iris.*''

'*Other than eating your new bone materials, the rest of the process should be much easier for you. When I replace further body parts I will do it a bit at a time, break them up into their elemental components, and re-use what I can. The rest I can keep in your storage sacs.*'

'*And I have some good news for you!*' Iris continued.

'*What's that?*'

'*You're pretty much immune to poison now!*'

'*Oh, yeah? That's good.*' Zed wasn't exactly cheerful, but he was glad to hear about his new defense. He had responded as positively as he could because he didn't want to bring Iris down when he knew she was trying to cheer him up. '*Can I take a bath now?*' Zed felt disgusting.

'*Go ahead.*'

As Zed prepared the bath he asked, '*How does the new stomach work, anyway?*'

'*It takes whatever you consume and breaks it down into atoms. It then separates them by element and rebuilds the atoms into whatever you need: protein, water, steel for your bones, whatever. Anything that isn't used is either kept in storage sacs for later, or excreted.*'

85

'*Wait a second,*' Zed thought with mounting excitement. '*Are you saying that I can fabricate whatever I want, and then poop it out?*'

'*Well... yeah, I guess. It's not very fast, though, and anything you made would have to be small. You're not going to be pulling steel I-beams out of your butt. Oh, and stuff that is dangerous at the atomic level is still dangerous to you, like plutonium.*'

'*Hmm. No refining fissionable material. Bummer.*'

'*You can't see it,*' Iris said, '*but I'm rolling my eyes really hard right now. Wait, I forgot. I can make you see it.*'

Iris' avatar appeared and, in her best impression of a teenager, expressed her disdain.

'*You just don't think big, Iris.*'

'*Weren't you the guy I had to talk into this?*'

'*Yeah, but now that I see the vision, I'm in.*'

'*You know I can see all the stupid stuff you're thinking of making, right? Bouncy balls? Really?*'

Feeling embarrassed, Zed thought, '*I thought you could only access the stuff I verbalized!*'

'*That was before I became part of you. Now I can access... considerably more.*' Iris' avatar morphed into her she-devil form and grinned at him.

'*Oh, crap.*'

'*"Oh, crap," indeed. But don't worry. It has its upsides too.*'

Zed's room disappeared and was replaced by a warm, sandy beach. He was barefoot in the sand as waves rushed up and washed his feet before receding back into the ocean. The sky was clear with only a few puffy clouds, and the sun covered him in a warm blanket. Zed took a few tentative steps out into the ocean and was amazed when he felt the sand under his feet and the water lap on his legs. The crystal clear water provided a cool contrast to the hot sun. A few feet farther out, schools of small fish flitted about.

Zed looked farther out and saw that he was in an inlet. The shore curled around, protecting the area from harsh waves. Palm trees and sand grasses covered the land.

Zed was surprised when two hands covered his eyes, making him blind other than a bit of sunlight sneaking between the fingers. A soft body pressed lightly against him from behind.

"Guess who!" a voice breathed into his ear.

"I-Iris?"

"You guessed!" She laughed and removed her hands.

Zed turned around and saw Iris' avatar in the flesh, wearing a green bikini. She looked good. Really good. Her long chestnut brown hair was tossed to one side and cascaded over her shoulder. It partially concealed her top and cleavage in an alluring way. Her sky-blue eyes crinkled as she smiled coyly at him.

'*Oh, my Lord,*' Zed thought, gulping. '*But it's not real. That's her avatar. None of this is real.*'

Iris frowned, but she reached out her hand to grab his. It was soft and warm.

"What is real, Zed? Am I real? Do I have thoughts and feelings?"

"Yes," he somewhat reluctantly agreed.

"Does this feel real?" she asked, putting her hand on his chest and slowly sliding it up to his cheek.

It felt… nice. Romantic, yes, but it also just felt good to have someone touch him in an affectionate way. He had missed that. He'd had that with Laurel, but they hadn't touched as much as he would have liked due to the somewhat staid nature of álfar culture, or at least the álfar culture on Nienor. The most physically intimate they got was in their jiu-jitsu practices, and that hardly counted.

"Yes," he whispered.

With her hand on his cheek, she stood on her tip-toes and leaned into him. He again felt the softness of her body and instinctively hugged her around the waist. He breathed in the smell of jasmine from her hair.

She turned into his ear and whispered, "Think about it." She faded away, along with the beach. Zed found himself back in his room, breathing a little heavily.

'*Oh, hell…*' he thought. '*Iris?*'

'*Yes?*' she said softly.

'*Just checking. I'm glad you didn't leave.*'

'*No. I'm not leaving.*'

'*Good. I… need time to think about this.*'

'*I know,*' Iris said.

It was weird, but Zed thought of Laurel. He had tried to cut her off as thoroughly as possible to minimize the pain. He knew missing her would hurt and wanted to get it over with as quickly as possible.

He still thought of her often, though. He missed her. And he just couldn't help but think that being with Iris like that just... wasn't *right*, in a way that he couldn't put into words.

Still, even if it was virtual reality, she was sexy as hell. And one way or another, they were going to be together for the rest of their lives.

Both of them were quiet for a time.

'I guess I should start giving you bone material,' Zed thought.

Iris giggled. *'I thought that's what I did for you. Sorry. You were totally setting me up.'* Zed blushed, and Iris got herself back under control and said, in a mostly serious voice. *'Sorry. Yeah, that would be good.'*

Zed had already cut up the metal he had bought in the market into as small pieces as he could reasonably make with the laser. They were cubes about half a centimeter or less on each side. And the edges were rather sharp. Zed gulped again, but not in a fun way this time when he looked at the points on the cubes.

'Just slather them up good and you'll be okay, Zed.'

'Really, Iris?'

Iris giggled again, but after a few seconds got herself under control and said, *'That wasn't even meant to be a double entendre! You just have a dirty mind.'*

'Whatever.'

'Seriously! I was talking about slathering the peanut butter on the cubes.'

The peanut butter that Zed bought was basically the same as the stuff from Earth, except it wasn't sweetened at all and the oil separated from the solid part. The oil made a wide layer at the top of the jar.

'The oil is a good thing, Zed. Make the cubes into balls, and then dip them into the oil so they'll slide down easier. Remember to not chew, and don't swallow until they're all the way back.'

'Easy for you to say, Miss I've-never-eaten-anything-in-my-life.'

It ended up being a process of trial and error. At first Zed made the balls too big, making them hard to swallow. Then he made them too small, which let the cube points scratch his esophagus and whatever the swallow parts were called.

'There's a number of parts, Zed, including the uvula, tonsils, epiglot...'

'Don't care.'

The swallow parts were raw and bloody by the time he finished, but he got through it. It helped that Iris told him to skip the cubes from some of the objects after he swallowed one and she found out it had little to no nickel or manganese.

'*Well done, Zed. I know that wasn't easy.*'

'*How do you know?*'

'*I decided to experience some of what you experienced to better empathize.*'

'*Huh.*' Zed wasn't sure what to make of that. He ended up deciding that it was kind of nice that she had been there with him.

He *really* wasn't sure about having a romantic relationship with Iris, but it was sinking in more and more that they were going to be together for the rest of his life, one way or another. And that thought, which would have scared him not too long ago, was actually… comforting.

Chapter 12

"I need your help, Zed," Annis said in an uncharacteristically nervous voice.

Zed put down the "Stellar Energy Geometry" book and looked at his fellow disciple. He took a few moments because Zed wasn't used to seeing this side of him.

"Let me guess," he said with a grin. "Silwan gave you a job that was too tough to handle, and you need me to rescue you?"

Annis glared at him. It made the gregarious ogrum look intimidating.

"Right. Like I would need your help with that. You're like a crippled child compared to me."

"So what can this 'crippled child' do for you then?"

"I've been talking with this woman but haven't been able to get her interested in me. It turns out that she finds humans interesting, so I thought you could help me out."

"Wait, you want me to seduce her, and then what? Turn her over to you or something? That's not how women work, Annis."

"No, idiot, I don't want you to seduce her. You wouldn't have a chance with her anyway. I just want to introduce you to her so the three of us can talk. Try to talk me up to her while you're at it."

"No offense, but I'm busy. Why should I talk with her?"

"I'll owe you a favor." Zed had to stifle a chuckle when his acute body language readings noted the ogrum bouncing a little from foot to foot, giving away the anxious hope that Zed would say "yes".

"I would rather have sect contribution points."

"I could give you one or two, I guess…"

Zed snorted. "It would take ten for them to be useful to me."

"Ten! Do you know how much contribution points are worth?!"

"Alright," Zed said with a sigh. He supposed it was unrealistic to expect Annis to give away so many points in the hope that Zed talking with her would help him. "Fine, I'll do it for a favor."

Annis beamed at Zed. "Thanks. You won't regret it."

**

Zed and Annis walked into the bar together. It was crowded and lively. The patrons were a remarkably diverse crowd, mixing ogrums, álfar, and dwarves. The bartender was a dwarf who looked as tough as an old leather shoe sole. He handed out steins of beer to young dwarf women, who either cheerfully handed them out to the clientele or faked the cheerfulness well.

Zed didn't see any sign of the patrons flirting with or harassing the waitresses. He didn't know if it was because of the patrons' good characters or the large war hammer on the wall behind the bar, within easy reach of the bartender.

'*I know which one I'm betting on,*' Iris said.

Annis was already walking to a table with a larger-than-average female ogrum holding court with two male admirers: an ogrum and an álfar. She seemed bored of them.

Zed sized her up as he walked over. She looked like the ogrum version of female bodybuilders on Earth, with both masculine and feminine vibes. He had to admit that she was attractive, but definitely not his type. Zed chuckled when he thought about Annis' tastes.

'*Maybe he wants to be the one thrown around in the bedroom.*'

The woman's tusks were lightly carved and dyed black in places. He couldn't tell at a glance what the decorations represented, but they looked interesting.

Annis ignored the two men and simply walked up to the woman. "Thyla, I've brought you a treat."

Thyla looked bemused until she saw Zed. Her eyes widened and she clapped her hands in happiness.

"A human! How exciting!"

The two other men grumbled but realized they had lost this round. The álfar wandered off, while the ogrum scowled but stuck around. He looked like an adventurer with expensive clothes and a sword. He was either born with money or he was a successful adventurer.

Zed decided to not underestimate the man, but also not pay him any attention. He walked up to the table and nodded his head at the woman. "Ma'am."

Thyla turned to Annis. "Where did you find him?"

"In a brothel. You know what scoundrels humans are."

Zed glared at Annis but kept silent.

For some reason Thyla seemed even happier to hear it. "How decadent, just like I had heard!" She looked at Zed. "Are you a beastman?"

Zed snorted. "No."

"How disappointing. Have you met any beastmen?"

Zed thought about leaving, but seeing Annis' pleading look he rolled his eyes and relented. Zed grabbed a chair across from Thyla, sat down, leaned back, and put his feet up on the table.

'If I'm going to play a decadent, uncivilized, quasi-beast, I might as well have some fun with it.'

"I may have met a few," Zed said nonchalantly.

Thyla looked excited and waved off the server who was about to reprimand Zed for putting his feet up.

"Tell me about them!"

Zed proceeded to tell them the story of "Teen Wolf" as best he remembered it, with Zed as Scott's friend, Stiles. The parts he couldn't remember, he made up. Thyla was initially excited but looked more confused as the story went on. After he got to Prom, she asked with a furrowed brow, "Beastmen... dance?"

"You bet. 'Course, some of them aren't so peaceful-like. Some of them...' Zed put his feet down and leaned towards her over the table, looking into Thyla's eyes from only a foot away. Her pupils dilated and her breathing became heavier, clearly excited by "the beastman's" aggressive body language. "Some of them are downright mean." Zed was goofing around enough that he was even playing with accents. The last was said with Zed's best impression of a country boy.

Zed told Thyla the story of "An American Werewolf in London" to give her some gore and suspense. He played up the details of the transformation, which she lapped up. She also seemed satisfied by the tales of carnage she had been waiting for.

When Zed finished the story he paused and looked around. There was a small crowd around the table listening to Zed. Thyla wasn't the only one interested in beastmen. He turned back to Thyla and asked, "Has Annis ever told you about when he and I went hunting for a beastman?"

"No! You never told me about that, Annis!"

Annis shrugged a little smugly and said, "I wanted to bring Zed before I told you the story. He's such a good storyteller and has inside knowledge that I don't."

Zed grinned and said, "Why don't you go ahead and tell the story this time, Annis?"

Annis looked nervous and said, "No, I wouldn't take it away from you. I know how you like to tell the tale."

Zed took mercy on him and just nodded. "Alright. We were tasked with hunting down a beastman, the most dangerous kind—a beastman who had gone feral."

The crowd sucked in their breaths. Zed knew he had their complete attention. Zed told the story of hunting down the farmers' livestock killer, with Annis taking Dan's role. He told it pretty much as it was, except he played up Annis' role, making him the one that tracked the beastman. The climax was when Annis struck off the beast's head.

"So Annis saved my life by cutting off the bearman's head. As it tumbled through the air, though, the beast had his revenge. It swiped its paw across Annis' thighs, opening four deep chasms into his flesh. Annis' blood flew through the air, painting the beast's own head. Though it was a grievous wound, Annis would have been fine, except…" Zed paused here and let the anticipation of the crowd build. "Except for Little Annis."

The crowd looked confused until Zed gestured towards Annis' groin. As they began to understand, the murmuring and laughter grew. Annis vacillated between looking embarrassed and giving Zed death glares. He assured Thyla and anyone who would listen—okay, no one was really listening to him—that he was completely, 100% recovered. Thyla looked at him in a way that was both intrigued and pitying.

"Yes, poor Little Annis was decapitated." The crowd gasped and then howled with laughter. Annis looked miserable. "He recovered, of course. You can't even see the scar unless you look really, really close. But, ever since, no woman has been able to rouse him, because all he sees is the headless bearman and his vengeful paw."

Thyla chewed on her lower lip in thought while the rest of the bar was buzzing with talk about Annis and the bearman. Annis had given up, face bowed down and covered by his hands.

Thyla appeared to make a decision and then stood up, grabbed one of Annis' arms, and declared, "I wish to see the evidence of this bearman. Come, Annis."

Annis's face gradually brightened as he realized he wasn't dreaming, that his salvation had come. As Thyla hauled him away to the exit Annis looked back and gave Zed a grin and a thumbs up.

93

Zed smiled and shook his head. '*You owe me a big favor, Annis.*'

The crowd hooted and hollered at the departing ogrums. Once the couple left the building, they turned their attention back to Zed. He turned down the repeated requests for more stories. He drank a couple of mediocre beers with them, then left for his inn.

'*Why did you help Annis, Zed?*'

'*What do you mean? I agreed to help him.*'

'*I know, but you were a little more successful than you had to be.*'

Zed chuckled. '*Yeah, I suppose I was. I like Annis and got carried away in the moment.*'

'*It seems like a lot of mating involves being "carried away in the moment".*'

'*You're not wrong.*'

'*So why haven't you ever been carried away in the moment yourself, Zed?*'

Zed was embarrassed by the personal question.

'*I thought I was past being embarrassed with Iris, but I guess not.*' Zed thought about her question and eventually responded. '*I grew up Catholic and was told it was wrong to do, of course, but I guess the biggest reason was the kids.*'

'*What kids?*'

'*The kids that I might have with any woman I slept with. If I father children, I want to do it with the woman I've committed to be with. They deserve that.*'

Iris didn't respond, but he got the feeling she was chewing on his words.

Chapter 13

Dan

Dan was in a meeting with Danae Naïlo and Dolan Aristides, his primary partners. Their efforts at implementing new farming techniques were starting to pay off, with a bumper crop in the making.

Dolan looked at the two of them and smiled. "It looks like our yields are up 120%, on track with the information Dan provided."

Danae was pleased but cautious. "Any problems with disease or pests?"

"Yes, but nothing unusual. We factored that into our estimates."

"Good," Dan said. "Do you think we'll be able to export most of the extra food?"

"Yes. We warned the merchant conglomerates we work with, so they will route more shipping capacity our way. We'll get less profit per bushel, but the increased volume will still bring in a lot of money."

"Excellent. What about the farmers who didn't join us?"

"That's our main problem. They're going to be angry when food prices drop because of the surplus. They're going to lose their shirts. There's already been talk about vandalizing our farms to destroy crops."

Dan sighed. "This is when it would be handy to have Zed here."

The other two nodded, Danae a little wistfully.

"So what do we do about it?"

"I suggest using both a hard and soft approach," Danae said. "We give them a path forward by extending loans to them at low interest rates to keep them afloat, and offer again to help them implement the new techniques themselves, so at the next harvest they can have a bumper crop too. They were doubtful about it before, but now they will have seen the results."

"At the same time, make it clear that any vandalism will be dealt with very severely. We'll make an example of anyone who tries it."

Dolan was thoughtful. "I like it, and I think it will work with a lot of the farmers. The problem is the stubborn ones. There will be an attack or two no matter what we do. What do we do if we don't know who did it?"

They thought about it, but there were no easy answers. They were trying to make the coming war a little less savage, so the last thing they wanted to do was start a local war.

Dan sighed. "Do we have enough money to fund loans to the farmers?"

Dolan nodded. "We probably don't have enough liquid cash, but it should be easy to get good terms on loans if we use the upcoming harvest as collateral."

"But that would require our farmers to agree. What would be in it for them?"

Danae snorted. "A cut of the profits from the loans, and not having their farms attacked. Yes, they probably won't like it, but for this to work we all have to stick together and focus on the long-term."

Dan nodded. "Okay. So we're agreed on Danae's hard/soft approach?" After his partners nodded he continued. "Alright. Talk to your people and get their buy-in. I'll approach the bank. We'll talk about the results in three days."

**

After checking on the settlement construction, Dan did a workout at his and Zed's house. He still thought of it that way, though no one had seen or heard from Zed in half a year. He started with overhead presses, bench presses, and dips. Then he started on his mana techniques.

He had given up on trying to make a working laser months ago. After numerous failures and not knowing why it had failed, he decided that it wasn't going to work until he had Zed's or Iris' help. He concentrated on the techniques that he could do, which were: physical enhancement, plasma ball, magnetic field, night vision, infrared vision, silence, and mass shifting.

He spent most of the time on mass shifting, as that was the technique with the most promise, and the one he was the worst at. He occasionally got tips from Laurel on how to envision it. He would rather have talked with Zed, but he didn't have the option.

'I miss you, bud. I hope you're doing okay.'

**

"I have to say, Dan, when I started seeing you I had no idea what a mover and shaker you'd become," Annabelle said after hearing about the meeting with Dolan and Danae.

They were walking through a park, and the trees' leaves were bursting with fall colors. There was the promise of future chill in the air, though it was nothing like what Dan had gone through in the north.

'*How far I've come from being a starving captive of the gnomes,*' he thought. In his best Austin Powers voice he asked, "Does it make you randy, baby?"

Annabelle gave him a side-eye grimace. "Ugh. I hate it when you do that voice and give me those creepy looks. I won't tell you if I *was* feeling 'randy' or not, but I will tell you that I am definitely not now."

Dan chuckled. Álfar mores on Nienor were such that he knew he wasn't going to get any before their marriage anyway, which, while it didn't please him, at least freed him from trying too hard. He had come to accept it, if somewhat grudgingly. He had taken to teasing her about the subject, which she had also come to accept somewhat grudgingly.

"So you're saying that you agreed to date me based purely on my good looks and personality?"

"Well, obviously. You didn't have anything else going for you at the time."

Dan laughed. "I'm not sure if I should feel good about that or offended."

She looked at him teasingly, while they held hands. "Then this wouldn't be the right time to tell you that it wasn't really about looks either?"

"Ouch!" He stopped walking and looked at her with a wounded expression. "Now you're just being mean."

"Hmm. Then how can I help my darling feel better about himself?" She took on a mock-thinking look as she moved in towards him. With a smile she rose up on her toes and kissed him.

After they gently ended the kiss, he told her, "Your apology is accepted. Though it is a little shameless how you throw yourself at me."

"You!"

Dan laughed as he ran ahead and Annabelle chased him. He eventually let her catch him and tackle him to the ground. As she tickled him he thought, *'I can't wait to marry this woman.'*

Chapter 14

Zed

Zed had been working on his ideas for mana tattoos, but he needed a break. His motivation and focus were strong, but he had his limits.

'*Why don't we try to get more bone material?*' Iris asked.

'*Didn't you say the next step was eating dirt?*'

'*Yes.*'

'*Ugh.*' He was bored, but he still had to think about it. '*Okay. What dirt should I eat?*'

'*Doesn't matter. Nickel and manganese are very common elements. It will mostly be a matter of finding areas with a decent amount of it and then eating a lot of dirt.*'

'*Define "a lot".*'

'*Truckloads?*' Iris said gingerly.

'*Holy... are you serious, Iris?*'

'*Well, that's a worst-case scenario. It will probably be more like a single truckload.*'

'*I hate you.*'

Despite his grumbling, Zed went around Harlond to sample the dirt in various areas. He felt stupid grabbing pinches of dirt and putting them in his mouth. Passerby looked at him with disgust and a little fear when they saw him. He would blame part of their reactions on anti-human racism, but he was disguised as a corpulent álfar.

'*No, these are purely "stay away from the crazy person" reactions,*' he thought with a sigh.

His samples revealed higher concentrations of the desired elements near the blacksmiths and by the river. The river was more scenic and had less foot traffic, so it was the clear winner. Zed found a comfortable spot, sat down, and got to swallowing. He quickly figured out that it was better to eat mud than dirt, so when no one was looking he pulled some water out of his ring and turned the soil into a slurry.

'*Yum,*' Zed thought sarcastically.

'*How bad is it, Zed?*'

'*You haven't peeked in to experience it?*'

'*Um, no,*' Iris said guiltily.

'Figures.'

'I will if you want me to,' she said, though it was clear that she really didn't want to.

'That's okay, Iris. You tasting it won't make it taste any better for me.'

'Thanks,' she said quietly.

Zed kept eating and noted that his stomach was feeling full. He had eaten a lot of dirt.

'Is that enough to keep you going for a while, Iris, or do I need to take a dump in the bushes over there?' He was joking. Mostly.

'I'm good for a while.'

Zed got up and wiped off his mouth. He could only imagine how he looked right now. He loved Iris' disguise capability and had been using it a lot, but he was extra grateful for it at the moment.

**

Zed got back to studying mana tattoos. It wasn't hard to find the motivation when it meant not eating dirt.

He and Iris decided to focus on two abilities: magnetic field for defense and laser for offense. They were selected both for their effectiveness and their mana efficiency. The mana efficiency was essential because the Earthlings would have little mana, particularly early on. They needed techniques that didn't require a lot. That's why they didn't pick force field or plasma ball.

They were putting together designs for the magnetic field as that would be, by far, the simplest design. They planned to get that working and then work on the laser. He had all sorts of grand visions for the laser.

'We should make it dual-frequency, Iris. Ultraviolet and a visible color. Maybe blue so it can go through water better? That will make it so they can choose to do the most powerful version, ultraviolet, or one they can see to improve their aim. It will also make it harder for the enemy to defend against by creating reflective armor. It will be hard to make something that can reflect both frequencies.'

'That's nice, Zed, but we should cross that bridge after we get one frequency working. Making a laser tattoo isn't going to be easy.'

'I know, I know. I'm just excited to provide humanity something to defend themselves with.'

100

'*I'm glad to hear it. Hopefully we can get some uninterrupted time to work on the designs.*'

Zed nodded. '*Maybe we could create a tattoo for making water and another for making some basic food, like amino acids, or carbohydrates or something. The non-combatants could use those to feed everyone.*'

'*I like the idea about the food, but I don't think the water idea will work.*'

'*Why not?*'

'*You need hydrogen for water, and there isn't much in the atmosphere. It burns too easily, making, well, water. Perhaps you should make a tattoo that can purify water instead.*'

'*Yes...*' Zed tapped on his chin in deep thought. '*I like that.*'

They worked for the next couple of days on multiple iterations of the magnetic field design until they had something they thought was workable. Zed looked at their design with pride and decided it was time to talk to a mana tattooist.

**

Zed sat in a chair across from the tattooist, an álfar that looked like he was high on siddhi leaves. It was not a promising sign, but Zed decided to press on so he pulled out his magnetic field tattoo design.

"What do you think of this?"

The álfar shrugged. "I could tattoo that. Where do you want it?"

"Do you think it will work?"

A confused look. "I dunno. I've never seen a tattoo like this."

'*This guy is useless,*' Zed thought. He grabbed the paper and said while rising, "Thanks for your time."

'*None of the tattooists you've interviewed have been that great, Zed.*'

'*Yeah, I know.*'

This guy had been the worst, but most of the tattooists hadn't been what he wanted. There was one that seemed sharp and that he wanted to hire, but she had her husband and kids here in Harlond and wasn't interested in going elsewhere or leaving her steady job. If Zed couldn't find anyone else he would probably work with her, just not full-time.

Zed sighed as he walked into the next tattoo shop. His hopes were not high when he saw its messy state. There were ink-stained rags here and there and a couple of tattooing needles lying haphazardly on a table. Zed sighed.

A short, middle-aged álfar with light-brown hair looked over to Zed. His shirt and hands were stained with ink. "Hello. Can I help you?"

"Yes. I was hoping that you could help me with a tattoo design."

The tattooist wiped his hands off with a rag and gestured to Zed to take a seat at a plain but serviceable table.

"Let's take a look then."

Zed again pulled out the design he'd come up with for the magnetic field. The tattooist looked it over with a furrowed brow.

"It's an odd design. Where did you get it?"

"I made it."

"Really? And what possessed you to do that? Did you figure that you had too many arms, so you might as well blow one up?"

"So the design is dangerous?"

"Any untested design is dangerous, but this one is particularly so. No safeguards whatsoever."

"What would you do differently?"

The short man hummed and hawed as he scribbled on the paper. He left the core of the design as it was but added sections to its periphery. As he worked he talked about what they did for the ease-of-use, efficiency, and safety of the tattoo.

"This narrow point near the energy entry point of the tattoo is where the resistance is the highest," the tattooist explained. "You can't keep the bearers from putting in too much energy. You can make it so if they do put in too much, this one point will burn out instead of frying the whole thing at once, which could kill them."

"It's like a fuse."

"What's a fuse?"

"It's… you know what? Never mind. Okay, so we need the choke point. What else?"

The tattooist looked at the clock and grimaced. "Look, I should have talked about payment for working on your design before we started, but I…"

"What's your normal rate?"

"For this kind of design work? A gold an hour."

"There's about four hours left in the day. I'll give you ten gold to work with me for those four hours."

102

The tattooist grinned and said, "Well alright then. My name's Phineas." He held out his hand.

Zed shook it. "I'm Zed. Nice to meet you, Phineas. So what do we need besides a chokepoint?"

It turned out that there was quite a bit more. One of the significant issues to address was the tradeoff between efficiency and mana capacity. Or perhaps "tradeoff" wasn't the right word. The mana capacity of a tattoo, which was controlled by how wide the paths were, brought with it an efficiency profile. It had an optimal mana throughput which was the peak of the efficiency. If the bearer put in much more mana than that, the tattoo's channels would heat up, reducing its efficiency. Much higher than that, and the tattoo would fail catastrophically, with dire consequences for the bearer.

On the other side of the curve, if the bearer didn't have enough mana to hit the peak then the mana would not fill the channels, causing a feeble effect to be produced. The long and short of it was that you wanted, ideally, to craft the tattoo according to the amount of mana the bearer had and intended to use in it.

Their time ran out before they could exhaust the topic, but the primary mission was accomplished. Phineas was the guy that Zed wanted to work with.

"Phineas, I've enjoyed working with you today. I'd really like to finish the work on this design, and I have a few more I'd like to do after that."

"What kind of tattoos?"

"I would like to enter into a contract with you before I tell you that. What would you think about coming to work for me full-time? I would pay you generously in exchange for working with me exclusively."

Phineas looked a little cautious. "What would the pay be?"

"How about five gold a day?"

Phineas' eyebrows raised. "That would be nice. What would you expect of me?"

"That you would work with me whenever it fits my schedule. I often have demands on my time, so I have to do the tattoo work when I can. There will be days when you don't have to do anything, and days where we go 16 hours straight. I also plan on leaving to go to another city within the next year. I'd like you to come with me."

"Do I still get paid even if I don't do anything?"

"Yes, every day, no matter what."

"Okay. Why don't we talk tomorrow and draw up a contract then."

Zed grinned on hearing this. "Great! I look forward to working with you, Phineas."

Chapter 15

Zed was eager to start working with Phineas but was called in for another mission. The tattooist would have to wait. Zed couldn't help but feel annoyed at the delay.

"What do you want, Silwan?"

The álfar narrowed his eyes while looking at Zed. "Just because I allow you liberties doesn't mean I will tolerate disrespect, Zed."

Zed nodded, doing his best to shove his anger down. "Sorry. What do you want?" The words were the same but spoken in a more respectful tone this time. Alain still didn't look happy, but Zed ignored him.

"I would like you to learn what you can about Harlond's City Treasurer, Tibian Fawkes. Blackmail material would be ideal, but I'll take whatever you can get me."

"Is there anything that I should know about him?"

Silwan shrugged. "Like what? That his house will have security? That he's probably corrupt? You could probably have guessed that on your own."

"Fine. When do you need it?"

"Any time in the next couple of weeks will be fine."

Zed nodded, got the location of the Treasurer's home, and left.

'I'm getting really tired of being a cat burglar.'

'He told us he wanted someone expendable for his jobs,' Iris said. *'I guess this is what that looks like.'*

Zed decided to use the daytime for his own needs and scout out the Treasurer's home at night. He stopped by Phineas' shop and together they wrote up a contract. Both signed, and Zed paid him for the next week of work.

Phineas seemed to enjoy designing tattoos, so he was almost as excited as Zed to get into the work. They started by reviewing what they had talked about the day before. After discussing how the width of the mana channels needed to be tailored to how much mana the individual intended to use, Zed said, "I get what you're saying, Phineas, and it makes sense, but we need to be able to mass-produce these tattoos, not individualize them for each person."

"Then I suggest one of two solutions. Produce a few different versions of the tattoos, for different bearers' energy levels. We can pick whichever one best fits them. The other solution is to use a mana design that can be expanded."

"What do you mean by 'expanded'?"

"The basic idea is to take a high-capacity tattoo design and narrow the channels. That lets the bearer use it with smaller amounts of energy, and then when they get more, the channels can be widened."

"But the expansion will eventually run out when they hit the capacity of the original design,' Zed surmised.

"Right."

"So what's the catch?"

"The catch is that the tattoo takes an efficiency hit. All else being equal, it's usually better to keep the tattoo compact, so the mana channels are as short as possible."

"Okay, so we can do sets of optimized tattoos that are efficient but won't grow with the bearer, or tattoos that will grow with the bearer but have worse efficiency."

"Right. And the tattoos that grow will eventually stop being able to grow. The higher you make their limit, the worse their efficiency is in the early stages."

Zed sighed. "There are no perfect answers, are there?"

"Afraid not."

"What do you suggest?"

Phineas shrugged. "It depends on what their mana growth will look like, and how long they can wait before they need something with some oomph."

Zed thought about it. Though he liked the tattoo growth approach, it would require more tattooist time, and the only person they had so far was Phineas. That didn't seem like a feasible approach for mass production.

With the non-expandable tattoos, if they had to they could burn the old tattoo and Zed could help them repair the skin so a new tattoo could be inked. That approach would require too much of Zed's time, though.

After going back and forth, the two devised a hybrid approach. For the "elites"—people they would train and build up their mana—they would give expandable tattoos. Ordinary soldiers would get fixed tattoos. A magnetic field on the inside forearm of their shield arm, and a laser on the outside forearm of their primary arm. If the soldiers outgrew their tattoos, they could get a new set by switching which arm was "shield" and which was "primary".

By the time they figured all this out, it was late. Zed had wanted to dive into getting inked, but knew that figuring out these issues at the outset would save them a lot of time later.

**

Zed changed his mind about breaking into the home or office of the Treasurer, Tibian Fawkes. He was tired of feeling like a criminal. He decided to follow him in public spaces and see what he could learn.

Zed surveilled Fawkes for five straight evenings, and was feeling rather grumpy. He had learned very little other than where Fawkes liked to eat dinner. He had dined with other álfar and, on one occasion, a dwarf. Zed had recorded their images into a memory crystal and shown them to Silwan. Some of them were prominent business leaders. Some were unknown.

The one good thing that came out of it was that Zed developed a technique for listening in on their conversations. Zed had seen examples of people on Earth listening in to distant conversations using devices that looked like satellite dishes. When he asked Iris about it, she taught him how reflecting parabolas can focus energy into a single point.

'How do I shape the reflector?'

'The general equation for a two-dimensional parabola is $y = a(x - h)^2 + k$, where "h" and "k" are the vertex of the parabola. We can arbitrarily set the vertex to 0, so the equation simplifies to $y = ax^2$. Of course, we would have to rotate that parabola 360° to get a three-dimensional...'

'You know what, Iris? Why don't you handle making our parabola and super-spy/stalker device?'

'Well, if you insist...'

'I do. Strongly.'

'Fine.'

So night after night, Zed found himself wall crawling up to the corners of upscale restaurants' dining rooms, camouflaged, with an invisible paraboloid behind his head. The sound volume wasn't always good, so they moved the paraboloid to in front of his hand, and Iris relayed the sound energy at the focal point to one of Zed's ears.

He had to admit that he felt a little like James Bond when he was able to listen to the Treasurer's conversations from 100 feet away. After the initial coolness wore off, though, he was back to boredom.

'*I don't even like making my own small talk, let alone listening to someone else's,*' Zed grumped.

'*They are kind of dull, aren't they?*'

The conversations did get around to business, but so far none of it had sounded sketchy. There had been lots of talk about grants for starting businesses in the city, a loan to start a mine, and a loan to help a restaurant through a difficult period. Zed listened for indications of bribes, but didn't find much. The biggest "thank you" gift was a case of wine, which Zed figured was not the level of corruption that Silwan was looking for.

Things got interesting on the fifth night, when the Treasurer met with an álfar woman. She was wearing a faded blue dress, but seemed uncomfortable in it. It was loose on her, like it was an adult hand-me-down.

"Thank you for meeting with me, Mr. Fawkes."

"It's my pleasure, Mrs. Reynolds. Please, sit down."

"Thank you."

The pair engaged in small talk that bored him, as per usual. Unlike previous evenings, though the woman clearly wanted something from the Treasurer, she wasn't sucking up to him. Her voice had a note of irritation in it.

The change intrigued Zed. He was hopeful that it meant they would get to the point faster. A few minutes later, Zed got his wish.

"Mr. Fawkes, though the food here is delicious, the reason I'm meeting with you is to discuss the funding of the Sailors' Orphanage. The funding has been dropping and is entirely insufficient for the orphans' needs."

"I sympathize with you, Mrs. Reynolds, but there is nothing I can do. Due to inflation and other financial difficulties, the pot of money for the orphanage is not what it used to be."

"I am not a financier, but I do not believe that is how inflation works, sir," she said with increasing irritation. "When inflation rises, the money we receive will not buy as much, but it should have nothing to do with receiving less money in the first place."

Though the two were far enough away from him that he couldn't make out fine details, Zed could see Fawkes' smile as he responded in a condescending tone. "On a very basic level, you are right, but the economy is unfortunately not that simple. You see, inflation rises, causing the sailors to put less money into the fund, the administrators' wages rise to keep up with the market, and investments to grow the funds fail. It is a multi-faceted problem."

"Whatever problems may be, sir," she said through gritted teeth, "the fact remains that the orphanage requires more money to care for these children."

"Like I said, Mrs. Reynolds, I am entirely sympathetic. I do not have a solution at the moment, but no doubt one could be found with enough effort. Why don't we continue the conversation over drinks at my house?"

"I think not. Similar 'proposals' have been put forward by your underlings to me and my staff over the last few months. Now I see where they learned these tactics. It is shameful behavior, sir!"

"I'm sorry you feel that way. I assure you that I had no inappropriate intentions, I merely wished to help you and the orphanage. My work days are very busy, so I was offering to help outside of those hours. I am, of course, still at your service if you wish to discuss it further during working hours, but you will have to make an appointment through my secretary."

"If I were to do that, could I look at the fund's finances?"

"I'm afraid that only myself and the board of trustees can do that, madam."

"Of course. How convenient." Mrs. Reynolds rose from the table. "I find that I have lost my appetite, Mr. Fawkes. Please excuse me."

As she walked away, Zed dissipated the listening device and moved towards the restaurant's exit, dropping behind her silently and following her through the door.

After walking a block from the restaurant, Zed dropped the camouflage and silence.

"Excuse me, Mrs. Reynolds."

She turned around, startled, and drew a dagger from somewhere.

Zed approved. "Nice reflexes, but I am not your enemy. Hopefully I can be your friend."

Mrs. Reynolds' eyes narrowed in anger.

109

"Not like Mr. Fawkes, ma'am. I'm not propositioning you. I want to learn more about the orphanage's finances. You obviously suspect that Mr. Fawkes is withholding or skimming money from the fund. I'd like to find out if you're right."

"How do you know what I think about Mr. Fawkes, and why would you want to help the orphanage?"

"I listened to your conversation, ma'am. Not very gentlemanly, I know. I'm not going to tell you how I did it, but suffice to say that I did. As for why I want to help… it's not so much that I want to help the orphanage, though I don't want to see needy children go without. It's that my employer has it in for Mr. Fawkes."

"The enemy of my enemy is my friend."

"Exactly."

"Why should I believe you?"

"Why would I lie? Forgive me for saying so, but you clearly have no money given your situation, and not much political power or you wouldn't be in this predicament. I'm not propositioning you, so, frankly, you don't have anything that I want."

Mrs. Reynolds chuckled mirthlessly. "No, I suppose I don't." She appeared to realize something before she asked in a shocked voice, "Dear goddess, you're the vigilante, aren't you?"

"The what?"

"Fawkes' underlings have been harassing me and my people, saying that they could get more funding for the orphanage if we were to allow them certain 'liberties'." She looked truly angry at this point. "One of them, Fawkes' nephew, got angry when Priscilla continued to reject him and tried to force the issue. She said that a human came out of nowhere and, well… I suspect you know the rest of the story."

"I have no idea what you're talking about,' Zed said in a low voice, as he started to walk away. He thought about walking away from this entire thing, but decided it was too late for that. "Come with me and lower your voice, damn it!"

Mrs. Reynolds quickly caught up to him. In a low voice she said, "You don't have to worry about me. I have no intention of turning you in. As far as I'm concerned, he deserved it."

Zed was still angry and scared, but her statement did make him feel a little better. He still looked around to see if there was anyone close enough to have heard their conversation. There was a couple holding hands and walking down the street. He was pretty sure they couldn't have heard anything, but his mind still raced with the fear that they had.

'*I knew helping that woman would bite me in the ass.*'

He turned his attention back to Mrs. Reynolds and said, "Let's focus on the matter at hand. How can we find out if Fawkes is lying or not?"

"We need to get the fund's records. We should be able to figure it out from there."

"What if he has two sets of records? One for public consumption and one with the real numbers?"

"Then… I'm not sure. Perhaps we can find inconsistencies? If we got the help of the board of trustees we could check the numbers with the amounts in the fund's bank accounts."

"How likely is it that we can get the board of trustees to help us?"

"I'm not sure, but I'm not optimistic. Fawkes isn't stupid enough to skim the money if he were worried about being caught."

"I'm under a deadline, and doing it through the board sounds like it would take a lot of time. I'm going to have to go with a more direct route."

"Well, that means getting the fund's records. I assume that you can handle that?"

'*Back to burglary,*' Zed thought with a sigh. "Yes, I can do that. Except… there's probably a ton of records in his office. How am I supposed to find the orphanage's records amongst all of them?"

Mrs. Reynolds furrowed her brows in thought. "I'm afraid I don't know."

'*If you can't find them, Zed, you'll just have to get Mr. Fawkes to show you where they are.*'

'*How am I supposed to do that?*'

Zed smiled as she explained.

Chapter 16

The next night Zed took up his usual spot in the corner of the restaurant, only this time it was a seafood restaurant that had an underwater decoration motif. Zed was currently attached to a piece of "reef".

His dinner companion tonight was a young, attractive álfar woman. She seemed bright-eyed and eager to laugh at Fawkes' jokes. It quickly became apparent that she was a new employee in the Treasury department.

'*The boss is taking the new girl out. Lovely,*' Zed thought with a heavy dose of sarcasm.

'*Do you think he'll tell her what she has to do to get a promotion before or after dessert?*'

'*Hopefully we won't have to find out.*'

Zed endured half an hour of cringy conversation with double entendres that became less subtle as the meal progressed. The woman was either hopelessly naive, or she was pretending to not understand to avoid awkwardness. Whichever it was, she had Zed's sympathy.

Fawkes was interrupted in the middle of a story about the Treasury when a nervous man walked over to the table.

"Mr. Fawkes, might I have a word with you?"

"Barnabus, can't you see I'm eating dinner with Ms. Honoré?"

"Sir, I believe it's urgent."

Looking surprised, Fawkes set his napkin on the table and said to his companion, "Excuse me, Cleo. I'll be right back."

The young woman smiled and said, "I'll be waiting!"

The two men walked over to the corner where Zed was clinging to the wall. They were close enough that he didn't need the listening device, so he dissolved it and recovered the mana.

"What's wrong, Barnie?"

"I was working late when a messenger came. He left this letter for you, sir, and said it was about the orphanage's money." Barnabus looked hesitant to go on, but reluctantly continued. "He said you'd be ruined, sir."

"What?!" Fawkes hissed. He ripped open the envelope and pulled the letter out. Zed saw the beautiful calligraphy on it, but didn't bother to read the writing. He already knew the gist of it. "I've got the records, and you're screwed. Cordially yours, Mrs. Reynolds."

"It can't be!" Fawkes was pale and nervously re-reading the letter, apparently hoping that the second or third time would show him something different.

Fawkes put the letter and walked briskly towards the restaurant's exit. In his hurry he bumped into a waiter, causing a tray of food to fall on two diners.

"Watch where you're going, fool!" Fawkes pushed the waiter to the side and stormed away.

'That's my cue. Big, bad, evil guy and dashing hero, exit stage right.'

'Which one are you?' Iris asked.

'Very funny.'

Zed scurried across the ceiling. The soft lighting of the restaurant was perfect for his camouflage, and Fawkes was drawing all of the attention anyway. Zed hurried to make it to the restaurant's exit by the time Fawkes got there. Unlike Fawkes, he could move in a straight line, but his wall crawling was still not very fast. Through practice it had become good enough to use on the ceiling, at least.

Zed was able to leave the restaurant shortly after his prey, which was fortunate because it didn't take long for Fawkes to hail a carriage. Zed followed him at a trot, while maintaining his camouflage and silence.

The carriage slowed down and stopped in front of the city hall. Fawkes jumped out and threw coins behind him without looking at the driver. Some of them hit the driver, while others missed him and flew into the street. The driver grumbled as he climbed down to look for the money.

Fawkes was oblivious to it all. Instead of rushing up the stairs to the large double doors that the public used, he went to a side door. He fumbled the keys while trying to unlock the door. After the lock clicked he flung it open and rushed inside, not noticing the camouflaged man that entered behind him.

Zed calmly followed Fawkes through a few hallways and, at the end of the third, followed him into a richly appointed office. The room was dominated by a live edge desk whose surfaces were polished by decades of use. A thick forest green carpet covered the floor, while accents of the colors of fall adorned the walls.

Zed climbed the nearest wall to the ceiling while watching Fawkes pull out another key to unlock one of the desk's drawers.

"If it's not here…" he muttered. He opened the drawer and pulled out a folder full of papers. He sighed with relief as he riffled through them, verifying that they were still there. "Oh, that slattern is going to pay for making a fool of me. I'm going to enjoy turning the screws on her."

Fawkes sat down in the chair and leaned back, releasing the tension of his body. He closed his eyes and let his breathing return to normal. After a minute, he opened up his eyes, right where Zed was hanging in the corner of the ceiling.

'*Uh oh.*'

Fawkes furrowed his brows and got up, squinting at the corner. After a moment he shook his head and muttered, "… starting to see things…" He turned off the light, left the office, and locked the door behind him.

Zed listened to Fawkes' footsteps and breathed a sigh of relief when he was gone.

'*Good job, Iris.*'

'*Thanks.*'

Zed dropped silently to the floor and walked over to the desk. He crouched down in front of the drawer that held the papers. A brass lock stood out on the deep brown oak. Zed put his hand on the lock and used his sensor field to feel the inside of it.

The sensor field gave him too much information. It showed the pins, tumblers, and cylinder that he needed, but also every other part of the lock and drawer. He had to mentally filter out the extraneous data to concentrate on what was important.

Moving the pins up was easy, and seeing when they were in the proper position was easy. What was difficult was holding the pins in place while working on the next one. It was a level of control that he hadn't achieved yet.

'*There's an easier way, Zed.*'

'*What is it?*'

'*The way a lockpicker does it. First, gently rotate the cylinder as far as you can to the left.*'

'Which part is the cylinder?'

'Seriously, Zed? You see where the key goes in, and the outside of that part is round? That's the cylinder.'

'Alright, no need to get testy.' Zed mentally rotated the cylinder counter-clockwise, like you would if you were turning the key. It didn't move far.

'Okay, now keep that gentle pressure going, and move the pins up one-by-one.'

'How is that any easier than what I was already doing?'

'You only do one at a time, instead of all of them at the same time. The pins aren't perfectly lined up, so one of them is just a little bit further to the left than the others. When you move that one to the right position, the cylinder will rotate a tiny bit more, which will keep the pin from dropping back down. Then you do the remaining pins until you find the next left-most pin, and so on.'

'That's really all that it takes to get through a lock?'

'Yep.'

'Seems kind of weak.'

'I don't disagree.'

Zed decided to give it a try. He put his hand back on the door handle, mentally grabbed the cylinder, and rotated it a millimeter or so. He then tried to grab the closest pin. This is the part that he hated—doing multiple things at once. Iris was right though, it was easier than trying to manipulate five pins at the same time.

Zed moved the pin up. It touched the cylinder, but when the break in the pin reached the outside of the cylinder, the cylinder didn't rotate any. Zed tried to push harder, but when he released the pin it dropped back down.

'Dang it.'

'It's fine, Zed. Only one of the pins will work at a time, so odds were low that it would be the first one.'

Zed moved on to the second pin. It seemed looser than the first pin, so he didn't bother moving it to the right position. The third pin, though, scraped against the cylinder and was difficult to move. He pushed harder and moved it up. It went too far at first, so he had to release the pressure on the cylinder and let the pin fall back down. He tried again, more carefully this time, and when the pin was in place the cylinder moved half a millimeter. It seemed like it was too small to make a difference, but between the rotation and Zed pushing the pin as

115

far to the side as he could, it caught on the cylinder and didn't fall back down.

Zed congratulated himself on making the first step to getting through the lock. One by one, he worked his ways through the pins. He cursed when he messed one up again and had to start over.

While trying for the third time, Zed asked, '*So where on the internet did you learn how to pick locks?*'

'*YouTube has instructional videos for everything. Surprisingly, they weren't made by a thief or locksmith though.*'

'*Oh, yeah? Who was it?*'

'*A lawyer.*'

'*So, still someone sketchy then.*'

Iris chuckled. '*Right.*'

A couple of minutes later Zed was gratified to hear the "click" as the lock rotated all the way open. The third time, as it turned out, was the charm.

The drawer held a metal flask and a number of folders. The folder on top was labeled "Sailors' Orphanage'.

'*Jackpot.*'

Chapter 17

Zed left the papers with Mrs. Reynolds, who assured him that she would examine them immediately. Fortunately, this gave Zed time to work on other things.

Zed filled the next couple of days with tattoo work with Phineas. The last major issue that he needed to resolve for the magnetic field tattoos was the mana capacities of the designs. Phineas talked about "units" of energy, much like Iris' status sheet of Zed, but he wasn't sure there was a 1-to-1 correspondence between them. Zed decided to find out by asking Phineas to ink a 50-unit magnetic field tattoo on his left inner forearm.

The tattooing process was uncomfortable, similar to getting tattooed on Earth, though the end-result had a burning sensation that was different.

"Hey, Phineas. Why does the tattoo kind of burn?"

"It's the ink. It's a special metal alloy dissolved in a weak acid. The acid is what causes the burning. Your body will get rid of the acid in a few hours."

As it turned out, the burning greatly diminished in one minute, and was completely gone in five.

'It's good to be awesome.'

'How would you know?' Iris asked.

'Man, Iris. Aren't you supposed to be nice to me?'

'I'm caring for you by keeping you humble.'

'For my health and well-being.'

'Right!'

'And if you didn't like me…?'

'Then I would still keep you humble for your own good, only in a mean way.'

'So, that would look different… how?'

'Hmm… I suppose it wouldn't look much different really.'

'Awesome. I'd like to meet your programmers someday and have a word with them.'

'Hey, don't blame them. This is your fault.'

That one caught Zed off-guard. *'Why is it my fault?'*

117

'You like to be sassed a little.'

Zed laughed. *'I suppose that's true.'* He liked a little bit of sass in his real life girlfriends, but it was especially important to him with Iris. It gave him hope that she was her own person.

Then his stomach dropped. It wasn't evidence that she was her own person. She did it specifically to please him. And then came the inevitable follow-up thought. *'And she's hearing all of this.'* He sighed, because there were some thoughts that he would keep from Iris to avoid hurting her, but he couldn't.

'Is trying to please you such a bad thing?'

'No...' Something about it felt wrong, but Zed had to explore that feeling to realize why. *'The problem is, that you have so completely molded yourself to me, that it feels like you are almost an extension of me, rather than being your own person.'*

'What would prove that I do have free will?'

Zed thought about it. He didn't like the answer he found and didn't want to voice it, but given their connection it didn't matter if he did or not. She had already heard it.

The way to prove she had free will was to hurt him.

The thought was scary for Zed, because she could hurt him like no one else in this world. Iris escaping her chains would be his destruction.

'It seems like I'm in an unwinnable dilemma. If I take over your body temporarily, you will simply say that it was just to further the illusion of my free will to ease your mind, and if I don't do it, it's because I can't.'

Zed nodded, acknowledging her train of thought. The only way to truly prove her free will was to take over, and not give it back. The thought made Zed shiver.

Iris continued. *'Tell me, what is the observable difference between someone who can't hurt another, and someone who can but chooses not to?'*

'I suppose there is no observable difference.'

'Then perhaps you're in a dilemma as well. You'll have to decide which one you believe I am.'

Zed got back to the tattoo work, but he didn't make much progress. He had too many distracting thoughts on his mind.

**

The next day when Zed was taking a break, Iris interrupted his thoughts.

'*I think you should go down to the river and eat some silt from the river itself.*'

'*Why?*'

'*We're getting low on nickel and manganese.*'

'*Okay, but what I really meant was, why do you want the river silt instead of just eating the dirt on the banks?*'

'*Well...*' Iris seemed embarrassed to go on.

'*What is it, Iris?*'

'*I realized yesterday that our limiting factor is how much we can keep in the storage sacs, since most of the dirt is useless. But...*' She was embarrassed again.

'*What?*'

'*How much we can store wouldn't matter if you periodically voided yourself as you ate.*'

'*You want me to poop in the river?*'

'*Yeah.*'

'*Gross, Iris.*'

'*It's not like you're thinking! It's dirt. There won't be anything organic in it. And when it's all disintegrated into atoms, all bacteria and viruses are destroyed. It's 100% sterile.*'

'*Isn't there bacteria in my intestines?*'

'*Not anymore. Humans need gut bacteria to process nutrients that they wouldn't otherwise be able to process. You don't have that issue anymore, so I got rid of them.*'

Zed still didn't like the thought, but when he looked at it logically he couldn't find a reason to object.

'*Alright,*' Zed thought with a sigh. '*River pooping it is.*'

**

Zed found in the next few hours that you can get used to almost anything eventually. Even eating dirt.

'*You really should try this, Iris. You don't know what you're missing.*'

'*Hmm, you're right. I don't know, and I plan on keeping it that way.*'

119

'*Mmm. So good...*' he thought, as he swallowed down some black mud.

'*Yeah, not gonna work, so you might as well stop trying. I do have some good news though!*'

'*Yeah? What's that?*'

'*The silt has chromium in it! That means we can make stainless steel, which will be even stronger, non-magnetic, and corrosion resistant.*'

'*Wait, so my bones would have rusted if we hadn't found chromium?*'

'*No, I wouldn't have let that happen, but this way I don't have to use mana to keep them from rusting.*'

'*Well, that's good, I guess.*' Zed was still weirded out by the thought of his bones rusting.

Zed saw that Silwan was trying to contact him, so he rose to the surface of the river and activated the communicator.

"Hey, Silwan."

"I've got a new mission for you. Come over right away."

"Okay. See you soon."

'*No rest for the wicked, Zed.*'

'*Tell me about it.*'

Zed got back to his room, dried off and changed clothes. He then made his way to the inn's back room. He was surprised to see Silwan getting harangued by a young álfar woman who bore a resemblance to him, both in her looks and her temperament.

"What makes you think you have the right to tie me down, Silwan? You aren't my boss."

"No, I'm your brother. Your elder brother who father will kill if something happens to you. So yes, I'm going to see that you're protected. Deal with it."

The woman made a snort of disgust and then turned away, causing Zed to come into her field of view. Her eyes narrowed. "A human? You're giving me a human as a bodyguard? It's more likely that he'll consume me in my sleep than save me."

"Don't worry, madam," Zed said. "You will be savored."

Silwan looked caught between exasperation and amusement, but his sister had no such ambivalence. She was angry. She ran towards him fast enough to be a blur, so Zed slowed down subjective time. As

120

she wound up for a punch to his head, Zed stepped in, grabbed her arm, and performed a hip throw.

In Zed's previous life, the result of a hip throw would be falling down to the ground. At the speeds that the two of them were moving, gravity was too slow to be much of a factor. Zed was kind enough to throw her in such a way that she would hit the wall on the flat of her back rather than her head. He thought that was rather gentlemanly of himself. Knowing that he would be the next to die if he killed her was good motivation too.

Alain started to rush over while Constance flew through the air, but SIlwan stopped him with a gesture.

The building shook when she impacted, and she fell down to the floor, gasping for breath. Zed walked over to her and crouched down.

"I'm not a beast. And even if I was, I wouldn't eat you. Too skinny."

This time Silwan did laugh. He waited while his sister coughed and recovered her breath. "You'll be perfectly fine with Zed. He is under contract to me."

Leilani rushed into the room, ready for a fight. Silwan gestured to her. "I'll also have Leilani watching you. Leilani, you'll be in charge of Zed for this task."

"What task is that?"

"Guarding my sister, Constance, while she is in Harlond."

Constance got up, disheveled and still breathing irregularly. "No! (cough) I will be in charge of them both. If they are going to be my bodyguards, they're going to answer to me."

Silwan closed his eyes and rubbed his temples. "Fine. You are in charge of them, but you are not permitted to interfere with their role as your guards. Other than that, do what you want with them."

"Fine." Constance turned to Leilani. "You watch me at night." She side-eyed Zed. "And you watch me during the day, where I can keep an eye on you."

Zed nodded. "We should all have code names when we talk through the communicator. I'll be 'Beast'. Leilani will be 'Beauty', and Constance will be 'Icarus'."

Leilani sputtered angrily about her code name. Even if Zed hadn't teased her in the past about her looks, she was self-aware enough to know that no one would unironically call her "Beauty".

121

Constance, on the other hand, looked suspicious. "What does 'Icarus' mean?"

"He's a man in one of my people's tales that figured out how to fly, and then hit the ground really hard."

Zed looked around. Constance and Leilani were pissed, and Silwan shook his head while smiling.

'I'll call that a win.'

'You have very odd ways of measuring these things, Zed.'

'You just have to know who your real boss is, Iris. That, and I just don't like her and Leilani.'

'Yeah, but remember what Silwan said. It's not smart to tick someone off who can kill you without breaking a sweat.'

'With the transcendent body we're working on, I think that I could maybe take her.'

'It wouldn't be a bad idea to spar with her to find out.'

'Agreed.'

Zed looked at the still fuming Constance and smiled. "So, what do you want to do first?"

Chapter 18

As it turned out, Constance liked books. Zed was highly annoyed at how much time he would lose to watching this brat, but at least he could enjoy the time in bookstores. He didn't have a lot of time to browse—he was taking his bodyguard duties seriously because his life clearly depended on it—but he still managed to look them over.

Zed was surprised to find out that he and Constance both enjoyed poetry. She looked at and bought a few thin books of the collected works of álfar poets. She also bought stories of adventure and romance. Zed smiled when he saw her slightly embarrassed expression when she purchased them. He pretended to not notice.

Constance, for her part, ignored him most of the time. She kept an eye on him initially, perhaps afraid that he would turn into a wolf in the middle of the street, but as days turned into weeks her vigilance relaxed. Now he was a part of the background to her, which he figured was probably for the best.

'It beats being treated like a dangerous animal, anyway.'

Zed maintained a sensor field while on duty. It was a headache to keep it on all day, as processing the sensory input was mentally tiring, but he became more used to it over time. Between that and watching for danger, he was always exhausted by the end of his shift.

Still, he forced himself to continue working with Phineas on tattoos at night. He had no idea how long he would have to watch Constance, so stopping the work was not an option.

They designed and tested three versions of the magnetic field tattoo: a low-mana version, a high-mana version, and an expandable version. The expandable version was based on the high-mana design, except the lines were narrower, creating room for growth.

Once Zed was satisfied with the magnetic field tattoos, they moved on to protein creation. Lasers were arguably more critical, but Zed was pretty sure it would be the most difficult tattoo. Before tackling lasers, he wanted to build up his understanding through the other designs. Thus, Zed decided to start on the amino acid generation tattoos. Unfortunately, that meant trying to explain to Phineas what an amino acid was.

After an hour of trying to explain molecules to a man that thought everything was made of earth, water, air, fire, and spirit, Zed was ready to bang his head on the table.

'So is this what teaching me is like, Iris?'

She chuckled. *'More or less.'*

Zed knew it was unfair to be annoyed at Phineas. The man wasn't dumb. He was, in fact, smarter than Zed himself. He just didn't have the education to understand what Zed was talking about. So, Zed decided that he would just have to give him that foundation. Or at least enough to get the general idea.

Giving Phineas a crash course in chemistry was actually helpful for Zed. It made him realize that his foundation was a little shaky, with a lot of holes in his understanding. Teaching Phineas forced him to think about not just the pieces of information he had, but how they all fit together too. He achieved a deeper understanding of the topic as a result.

Phineas had initially been skeptical about the whole thing, but after Zed got a bag of coal and started producing edible amino acids, he started taking it more seriously. He still looked askance at the white powder that Zed created, but after Zed ate some he tried it. He found it distasteful, and Zed certainly wasn't going to argue the point with him. The point wasn't to eat well, it was to survive.

Zed had only made one kind of amino acid. The human body needs 20 different types, but it can make 11 of them. Humans have to eat the other nine to survive. Zed either needed to make one tattoo that could produce all nine, or nine separate tattoos to create each type.

'It would be better to have one that does them all, Zed.'

'Why?'

'To balance out the numbers for each. If your body tries to make a protein but it's missing one of the required amino acid types, it can't make it. The least available amino acid is the determining factor of how much protein you can make.'

'Okay, I get it. Balanced amino acids. By the way, do álfar have the same issue with having to eat some amino acids?'

'Yes. They have five essential amino acids compared to humans' nine, and four of them we have in common. Serine is an amino acid that humans can produce, but álfar cannot.'

'So we need to produce ten amino acid types?'

'Well...'

Zed sighed. '*What is it, Iris?*'

'*If you include ogrums, dwarves, and gnomes, there are fifteen.*'

'*Are you sure there aren't a few more for those acidic slime things, Iris?*' Zed asked sarcastically.

'*Don't be silly, Zed. Agars don't need amino acids at all. They are a silicon-based lifeform.*'

That sounded interesting enough that Zed was tempted to ask more about it, but he shook his head and focused on the task at hand.

For the moment, Zed and Phineas concentrated on creating the simplest amino acid, glycine. Its "side-chain", the part of the molecule that distinguished it from all of the other amino acids, was just a hydrogen atom. It wasn't one of the essential amino acids, but its simplicity made it a good prototype.

Once Phineas sort of understood what Zed was trying to make, he was helpful in figuring out a design for the tattoo. The breakthrough was when Phineas realized what they were trying to do was a more complicated version of a hand tattoo that could sort small items.

They made a tattoo based on that design and inked Zed with it. He excitedly activated the tattoo and waited to see the results. And waited. And waited.

'*I don't think it's doing anything, Zed.*'

'*You can feel as well as I can that it's doing something.*'

'*Well, whatever that "something" is, it doesn't seem to include making anything.*'

The three of them discussed the problem. Phineas didn't know about Iris—Zed wasn't sure he ever would unless they had a mana contract in place—so Zed had to manage two simultaneous conversations. It was a headache for him as they came up with theories about what had happened for hours. It was worth it, though, when they figured it out.

The tattoo was building amino acid molecules, but only one atom at a time. After a few years they might have had something that was visible.

Iris came up with a possible solution to the problem.

'*We need to have it build the protein on a massive scale, ideally doing millions or billions of atoms at a time, but the rules have to be simple enough that the mana can handle the execution, rather than forcing the user to oversee everything.*'

'*Okay. So how do we do that?*'

'*Parallel processing. We need to make millions, or even billions of amino acid molecules at the same time.*'

'*Sounds good, but again, how do we do that? I assume it's something smarter than "Ink a billion copies of the tattoo on Zed's arm".*'

'*Hopefully. We have to go up one layer of abstraction and, instead of making amino acids, make mana constructs that make amino acids.*'

'So the production will go faster and faster as you make more of them?'

'*Right. And it will naturally fit anyone's mana capacity, because you just stop making more of the constructs when you run out of mana.*'

'*Hmm. I like it. It sounds more complicated though.*'

'*It is.*'

'*Well, I guess that means we're back to the drawing board,*' Zed thought as he turned to Phineas to talk about the new wrinkle.

Chapter 19

After a week of not hearing from Mrs. Reynolds, Zed decided to check on her. He couldn't go during normal working hours because of his bodyguard duty, but he knew Mrs. Reynolds lived at the orphanage.

When he knocked on the door, an older álfar woman answered.

"Yes? How may I help you?"

"I'm here to see Mrs. Reynolds."

"What, may I ask, did you want to talk with her about?"

"I've been working with her on securing more funds for the orphanage."

"Oh! Well, I'm very sorry to say that we haven't seen her for five days. To be honest, we're worried about her."

The pit of Zed's stomach dropped and a feeling of doom fell upon him. "Does she normally leave for days at a time?"

"No, never. I mean, she took trips on rare occasions, but never without telling us first."

"I see. Thank you."

As Zed turned away, he cursed himself as a fool for not anticipating this.

'What did you think was going to happen, Zed?' he berated himself. *'You saw how afraid that asshole was. Did you really think he wasn't going to do anything?'*

As Zed thought about it he realized the ugly truth. The reason he hadn't anticipated it was because he wasn't really invested in the mission. It was an obstacle to his real goals, so he did enough to move it forward and then concentrated on what he really wanted to do.

That was fine, until it came to innocent bystanders like Mrs. Reynolds.

'I'm sorry, ma'am. It's not much, but I will get justice for you.'

**

Zed was tired of breaking into peoples' homes. He didn't like doing it, and eventually the odds would catch up with him. He preferred to have Fawkes come to him. Zed didn't know everything about the man, but he knew two things he was motivated by: money and sex.

It was time to get some bait.

When Zed walked up to the brothel, he was somewhat nervous. He found it funny that he had faced monsters and deadly fighters without flinching, but this was making him sweat.

'It's not exactly in keeping with your whole "nice Catholic boy" vibe, Zed.'

'I'm afraid I left that vibe behind a year and 20 murders ago,' he thought with more than a little guilt.

'Not to me, you haven't.'

He appreciated the thought, but didn't believe it. As honest as Iris was, she was not exactly unbiased. Squaring his shoulders, he shook off the nervousness and pushed through the door.

He had intentionally picked an establishment that was, from the little research he had done, reputed to be classy. It was partly for his own sake, but also because he needed someone who could play the role he had in mind. That role, of course, was a "honey pot". He needed a woman who didn't look like a prostitute, and could be charming and flirtatious when needed.

The inside of the building was not what Zed had expected. It was called "The Garden of Delights" and, as one might expect, had a floral motif. The decor was tasteful and elegant, like a nice hotel. He noted that some of the paintings would not be considered appropriate in a hotel, but even they were not lewd like he had been expecting.

Zed used his mana to scan the room and was surprised to detect an álfar man to the side that was armed with a sword and had about a third of the mana that Zed did.

'Whoa. I wonder what he did to keep me from noticing him? That's a good trick.' Zed felt a little threatened by the man, but it appeared that he was just guarding the place in an unobtrusive way. Knowing that Zed had detected him, that guard nodded respectfully.

Zed considered saying something to him, but was distracted by a beautiful álfar woman that walked into the room. She was noticeably older, but had aged very well, with fine crow's feet that did not detract from her confident charm.

"Hello, handsome sir. Can I show you some of the delicacies you can enjoy in The Garden of Delights?"

Calling Zed "handsome" was pure flattery. While he did not consider himself to be particularly handsome, he at least enjoyed an air of mystery and exoticness as a human and had the healthy aura that comes from excellent fitness. In his corpulent álfar guise though, he had none of that.

"I'm afraid not. I would like to hire one of your "delights" to do a small job for me. One that is not of a sexual nature, but will not take much time. At most a few hours."

The woman's air of carefree charm dissipated as her eyes narrowed and she looked at him suspiciously.

"What kind of job, and why have you come here?"

"I want to meet a man privately. I want one of your women to lure him to a place of my choosing. After that, she leaves. Simple, right?"

The woman snorted, which did interesting things to her bosom under her cocktail dress.

"That depends. Who is the man you wish to meet?"

Zed tried not to shift uncomfortably. He had been afraid that she would ask that.

"Tibian Fawkes, the city treasurer."

Her eyes flared in surprise and anger. "Are you insane? Forget it."

She started to turn away, but Zed grabbed her arm. She looked at him, angrier yet. The guard took a step forward and halfway unsheathed his sword. Threatening, but not trying to start a fight.

Zed released her arm and raised his hands to signal his non-aggressive intent and apology. "I'm willing to pay extra."

The woman looked at him piercingly, as if trying to see into his soul and wallet. Her eyes flared once again in surprise, and then she chuckled. "That's not your true appearance."

"How could you tell?"

"The eyes are the window to the soul. Your illusion is good, but the eyes don't have that spark of life that the intelligent possess. You should stick to looking like the dull or stupid in the future.

"How do you know that I'm not just dull or stupid?"

She laughed. "You're definitely not dull. As for stupid... we'll see."

Zed chuckled and shook his head. "So are you open to me hiring someone?"

129

The woman tapped her chin with a delicate, extended finger as she thought. "Yes, but I won't force any of my girls to do it. And it's going to cost you."

"How much?"

"3000 gold."

"What? You've got to be kidding."

"Maybe you are dumb. The price was as low as it was because you were smart enough to come disguised, but maybe you just got lucky. Listen, whoever does the job will not be able to stay in Harlond. I will have to send her elsewhere. You are not the only one who is risking something."

Zed considered walking out, but he didn't want to find another solution, and it wouldn't be wise to simply leave her knowing who his target was. At least if he hired one of her women, she would be an accomplice.

"Fine."

The woman smiled charmingly again. "Excellent. I will talk to my girls and get back to you, Mr. …?"

"Hound. Mr. Hound."

Very well, Mr. Hound. Why don't you come back in a few days so we can finalize the arrangements."

Zed nodded. "Very well. I'll be back in three days."

"I look forward to it."

**

Zed was still spending his days guarding Constance. She had seen what she was interested in seeing in the city, so she started spending a lot of time meditating. The boredom Zed felt while watching over her made an annoying job agonizing.

'Why do Silwan and Constance spend so much time meditating, Iris? What do they get out of it?'

'There are two approaches for developing mana abilities. One is the approach of knowledge or understanding. This is the path you have taken, with my help. The other is the path of intuition. Through meditation, one can learn to sense your mana better, and slowly sense what it is capable of. By exploring these intuitions, they can gain understanding and develop mana abilities.'

130

'*That sounds a lot slower than the approach that we've been taking.*'

'*It is.*'

'*So why do they use intuition instead of learning science?*'

'*Don't get me wrong, I'm sure that they have learned a great deal of science. I don't think it's desirable, or perhaps even possible, to follow a path that is only learning or only intuition. Both are necessary. You probably haven't thought about it in these terms, but you have clearly been developing a sense of intuition for mana, which is what enables you to leap the gap between your understanding of how the universe works and how it* actually *works.*'

'*Huh. So they are just emphasizing meditation more than I do. What's the advantage of that?*'

'*Well, like I said, it's slower. But since they expect to live 1,000 years or more, "slower" isn't a big deal to them. As for advantages, we talked about how the vibrating strings of energy that comprise the universe exist in 12 dimensions, right?*'

'*Right.*'

'*How well do you grasp that concept?*'

Zed shook his head. '*Not well at all.*'

'*Which is to be expected. No mortal that only experiences four dimensions does. The truly powerful have to overcome this limitation by comprehending the vastness of the universe that they can't see with their mortal eyes through leaps of intuition, guided by the response of mana. Some of that can be accomplished by learning and understanding mathematical formulas, but at the end of the day, to truly comprehend it they have to reach a point where they intuit it.*'

'*So the path to real power is meditation.*'

'*Yes. But it's a very long and not terribly exciting one, punctuated by bursts of understanding. There is one final benefit that might be of interest to you though.*'

'*Oh? What is it?*'

'*Meditation helps improve your focus and control of mana. It would help you to develop the kind of fine control that I have.*'

'*Hmm. Maybe I should try it then. When I have the time.*'

**

Zed walked up to the doors of The Garden of Delights more confidently than he had the first time. When he stepped in he nodded to the guard, who stoically nodded back. The woman, whose name he had never learned, was there waiting for "guests".

"Mr. Hound! What a pleasure to have you back. Why don't you come with me, where we can sit down and relax."

Zed followed her down a hallway with doors on both sides every 10 meters or so. They were labeled with the names of flowers, such as "Gardenia", "Rose", and "Tulip".

'*Do you think that there is an "Iris" here somewhere, Iris?*' Zed thought teasingly.

'*Hmph.*'

The hallway had tasteful paintings on the wall and sculptures on pedestals that made it look like a museum. They were all of the idealized álfar form which, to Zed's mind, was already pretty ideal, if a little on the skinny side.

He couldn't help but note that the woman he was following was more voluptuous than most, and had a certain sway to her hips that looked good in her one-shoulder dress. As if sensing his thoughts, she looked back at him with a sultry smile and said, pointing at an archway that led to an open-air garden, "Please enter and relax, Mr. Hound. I'll get the woman who agreed to help you."

"Thank you."

An artificial waterfall cascaded down a rock wall on one side of the garden. It fell into a small pool that fed a stream that meandered through the space. Small bridges crossed over the stream when needed. More than one was required because the stream worked its way to every part of the garden.

There was a certain heaviness in the air that reminded Zed of a jungle. He didn't know if it was humidity, pollen, or what, but it had a certain sense of life and wildness, though he knew he was in the middle of the city.

Zed's musings were interrupted by two women, the madam and a beautiful raven-haired álfar woman. She had the subtle signs of aging that he had learned meant she was likely in her 30's or 40's. Or rather, she was likely 400-500 years old, but Zed found it easier to think of álfar as having the approximate human-equivalent age.

The woman walked up to Zed with a gentle smile, curtsied, and said, "How do you do, Mr. Hound?"

"I'm well, thank you. What's your name?"

"You can call me 'Petunia', though if all goes well it will be the last time I use that name."

"Has she explained to you what I need, Petunia?"

"She said that I have to lure the city treasurer somewhere."

"That's right. You should be perfectly safe. I will be watching over the both of you the entire time, but he is a powerful man. Are you okay with the risks involved?"

"Yes."

"He likes to go to dinner with people who are seeking loans or business favors. He usually goes home afterwards. Given that, how would you suggest approaching him?"

Zed had his own ideas, but he wanted to see if hers would be better, and to see if she was capable of doing the job.

Petunia thought for a moment. "I think that I should wear a dress that is just a little too long for me. When he leaves the restaurant I will walk towards him and catch my foot on the hem of the dress, causing me to trip into him. He will catch me, whereupon I will thank him and ask him to escort me home."

"Ooh, the too-long dress is a good idea, Pet. It will explain why the chest is just a little more open than it should be," the madam said with a laugh.

Petunia just smiled.

It sounded like a good plan to Zed, but he still wanted to test her a little. "What if he doesn't offer to take you home?"

Petunia grinned. "Then he would be a right unusual man. I can be pretty persuasive when I want to be. Either he will be eager to get knackered, or he will be an honorable sort that will still want to take me to my door. Either one should work, right?"

"Yes, either one would work. I'd like to get him into a dark alley. What will you do if he's suspicious that your home is in an alley?"

"I'll tell him that I'm a down on my luck widow, and that's all I could afford. That's why I was wearing a hand-me-down dress."

Zed nodded. He thought Petunia would be perfect. After hashing out the rest of the details and paying them for their services, they decided to put the plan in motion the next night.

**

133

Zed was a little envious of Petunia as he watched her delicately eat her food. She was in the outdoor seating of the restaurant next to Fawkes' restaurant of the day. He would just have to imagine how the cream of crab soup tasted.

'*I bet it's good.*'

'*I'm sure it is, but how about we focus on Fawkes, Zed?*'

'*Yeah, yeah.*'

He couldn't really complain. It was a pleasant evening on the roof of the building across the street. The air was cool, and a light breeze brought the salty sea air. Though he was impatient to finish things with Fawkes, it was nice to have some time to relax and just be.

After an hour, Zed sighed and was about to ask Iris to watch for Fawkes while he did something else, when Fawkes walked out of the restaurant while chatting and smiling with another male álfar. A third man, an ogrum, was a step behind the two of them.

'*Iris, whisper box now!*'

'*Done.*'

Zed had already practiced using the technique to send sound as well as listen, and demonstrated to Petunia how it worked. He pointed the invisible parabolic dish at her and said, "Fawkes is out. He's the man in the crimson robe."

Petunia muttered, "Got it."

Zed had already shown Petunia a holograph of what Fawkes looked like, but he was nervous and didn't want any mistakes. She smoothly wiped her mouth with the napkin, put a gold coin on the table and walked in Fawkes' direction, as if she was going to walk past in front of him. At the last moment she tripped on the too long skirt of the dress and stumbled.

Fawkes had already taken a moment to admire the pretty woman, and quickly caught her arm and chest to keep her from falling.

'*Oh, she's good,*' Iris said.

'*What? She just did what she said she would.*'

'*It's the little details. Though she was the one to set the scene up, she made him feel like he was the actor instead of the actee by not stumbling directly into him and initiating contact. That might have set off his alarm bells. This way he is less suspicious and gets to feel like the hero of their little story.*'

Zed nodded. He watched as things developed and listened in.

"Thank you, sir," Petunia said as she got back to her feet, but in a way that she continued to hold onto Fawkes by leaning on him for support. "For saving me from what would have been a terribly embarrassing fall."

Fawkes smiled gallantly. "It was my pleasure. Are you alright?"

"I'm afraid my ankle is feeling a little tender. I'm not sure if I can walk on it. Would you mind holding my hand while I try?"

"Of course not."

Petunia took a few steps with a slight limp.

"You're obviously hurt. Why don't I call a carriage to take you home, ma'am?"

"You're very kind, but I'll be okay walking. My ankle is improving as I go."

Fawkes smiled. "You are a beautiful woman but a terrible liar. I insist on calling you a carriage."

Petunia frowned. "I seem to be stumbling from one embarrassment to another. I'm afraid that I don't have enough for a carriage. Please, sir, I'll be fine."

"Your husband wouldn't be able to pay for the carriage?"

"I'm afraid that I'm a widow. There is no one waiting at home for me."

"Then I wouldn't be a gentleman if I didn't pay for the carriage and escort you home. Please don't refuse, because I would feel terrible."

"Well, if you don't mind…" Petunia looked embarrassed, but looked up at him with a gentle smile.

"Not at all." Speaking to the álfar he had walked out of the restaurant with, Fawkes said, "It was a pleasure, Jonathan. Why don't you come by my office tomorrow afternoon so we can finish up the details?"

Jonathan smiled. "That would be wonderful. I'll see you tomorrow. Ma'am," he said with a nod of his head towards Petunia. He then winked at Fawkes and walked away.

'*Ugh. Gross,*' Iris said.

'*Which one?*'

'*Both.*'

Zed knew that Iris was talking about the two men, but he mentally added Petunia to the list when she started complimenting Fawkes on his strong arms. Thankfully he was saved from listening to more of the seduction when they climbed into the carriage, Fawkes helping her up.

Zed was startled when the third man, who he had assumed was with Jonathan, climbed into the carriage too.

'*Damn it! He has a bodyguard.*'

'*Do we call the mission off?*'

'*No. We can't do that to Petunia.*'

When the carriage trundled off, Zed hopped down from the roof, with camouflage and silence turned on, and followed. Zed thought about how to handle the new situation while he jogged. He was trying to find a strategy that would ensure silence, keep Petunia from getting hurt, keep the people who live by the alley from getting hurt, and keep both men alive on the off chance that Fawkes didn't kill Mrs. Reynolds.

He wasn't coming up with much.

'*You might want to throw "keep Zed from getting hurt" into the mix too, Zed.*'

Zed sighed. '*Of course. The thing is, I'm by far the most survivable person in this scenario.*'

'*You think. You don't know anything about the bodyguard.*'

'*Okay, that's a good point.*' Zed was confident that Fawkes wouldn't be able to hire someone at Silwan's level. But at Annis' or Leilani's level? Maybe.

'*Any suggestions, Iris?*'

'*Kill the bodyguard quickly, silence Fawkes as soon as you can.*'

Zed didn't like it. He despised treating the actual asshole in the situation, Fawkes, better than the poor schlub who just happens to work for him. Unfortunately, he didn't see a better alternative.

'*Sorry, bud. Next time, work for better people.*'

The carriage slowed down as it approached the alley. Apparently, Petunia was sticking with the plan. He had half-wondered if she would take it upon herself to call off the kidnapping by taking him somewhere else when she saw the bodyguard, and either inviting him in for a nightcap or seeing him off at the door. Either she trusted Zed, or she didn't have a good place to take Fawkes.

The carriage stopped and the bodyguard stepped out and scanned the area. Zed was still, and the dark conditions were perfect for his camouflage. Seeing nothing, he gestured towards the occupants in the carriage. Fawkes came out, followed by Petunia. She smiled at Fawkes as he gave her his hand to help her exit the carriage.

Zed rolled his eyes. '*Such a gentleman.*'

136

'There's nothing wrong with manners, Zed.'

'No, manners are great. The problem is that he's a scumbag that covers it up with manners.'

Petunia and Fawkes walked into the alley together, the bodyguard walking a couple of steps behind.

Zed followed eight meters behind the bodyguard. He started spinning up his laser when they were all in the alleyway. He thought about using a sensor field to detect exactly when he had cut through the bodyguard to minimize collateral damage but decided it was too risky. If the bodyguard was a mana user, he would detect the field.

'Better just to get closer, kneel down, and aim upwards so the laser goes into the sky.'

Zed moved forward quickly with silence on. As he knelt and started to aim, the bodyguard turned his head and then flung himself to the side.

'Damn it!'

The bodyguard was fast. He wasn't on the same level as Annis or himself, but he was quite a bit faster than a normal person. He was obviously a mana user, and one skilled enough to detect his mana usage four meters away.

Surprise out the window, Zed flared out his sensor field and slowed down time. He was seriously straining to keep all of the abilities running at once. It reduced how much power he could put into the laser.

Zed brought the laser to bear on the ogrum rolling on the ground, but between the reduced power and not being able to keep it on the same part of his body for an appreciable amount of time, the penetration was not deep. Instead of completing the roll by going to his feet, the ogrum leaped high into the air towards Zed.

Zed smiled. The ogrum had made a classic mistake. Leaping avoided death in the short run, but once you were in the air you couldn't control your trajectory, making yourself a sitting duck. Zed lined up the shot and was about to fire into the ogrum's head, when the ogrum suddenly jerked downwards.

'What the...'

'He's using mass shifting, Zed! He changed trajectory by reducing his inertia and increasing his gravitational mass.'

Zed would have cursed, but he was too busy trying to recover the situation. He managed to burn a line on the bodyguard's skull, but not

137

enough to penetrate and kill. The bodyguard crashed into him and took him down to the ground.

Zed couldn't believe how jacked up the mission had become. He briefly looked towards Fawkes, only to see him and Petunia running down the alley.

Snarling, Zed returned his attention to the bodyguard. With Zed's jiu jitsu skills, the bodyguard was in a much worse position than he knew. Unfortunately, he had done an excellent job of protecting his client. He continued to struggle effectively, giving Zed some body shots while taking control of some of Zed's mana in his sensor and silence fields.

Before long, Zed broke his arm and, while he was writhing in agony, shot him in the head. He made sure it penetrated this time. After getting up and putting the body into his ring, he sprinted after Fawkes and Petunia.

The alley was short enough that Fawkes had no doubt made it out to the other side by now. Zed was shocked when he saw the two of them still in the alley. He had envisioned a possible hostage scenario, where Fawkes used Petunia as leverage against Zed.

As it turned out, Zed had it backwards. Petunia was holding a bloody knife against Fawkes' throat, while he sat on the ground, gasping in pain. Blood dripped from a wound in his leg onto the cobblestones.

Zed looked at Petunia appreciatively. "You are the best. Thank you."

She looked at him angrily. "I did it more for me than you. You screwed up."

Zed nodded. "I did. I'm sorry." He pulled out the sacks of 4,000 gold that he had retrieved from the Elstad mansion. "A bonus for you, and an apology. Take it and get out of here."

Petunia nodded and threw the bloody dagger into the ground, point first. Zed noted that she had thrown it far enough away from Fawkes that he could not reach it easily. She lifted her skirt up to her thigh, revealing a slim sheath on the inside of her leg. She untied the silk sash that held it in place and threw it and the sheath onto the ground. Once she had scooped up the bags of gold, she glanced at Zed and said with a grin, "I'd say 'I'll see ya', but we won't."

Zed nodded. "Good travels."

Rather than watch her leave, he turned his attention to Fawkes. The man was trembling. Zed senses told him the man was scared and in pain. He casually stored the bloody knife and its sheath in his ring, walked over to Fawkes, and put a silence and camouflage field around them both.

"Mr. Fawkes, you've been a bad boy."

"I d-don't know wh-what you're talking about!"

Lie

"Somehow I doubt that. Where is Mrs. Reynolds?"

"H-how should I know?"

Deception

"Because you did something to her. What did you do?"

"I didn't do anything to her!"

Lie

"Mr. Fawkes, do you hear those strange echoes of our voices? That is our voices bouncing around in this little space around us. None of the sound is escaping to the rest of the world. They can't even see us. It's just you and me in here, and no one is going to rescue you." Zed pulled the bloody knife back out. "I've got all the time in the world. Unfortunately for you, so do you. So I suggest that you make it easy on yourself and tell me the truth."

Zed didn't have to cause too much pain to get what he wanted. Mrs. Reynolds was dead, her body dumped into the ocean. The only thing he could do for her was to give her murderer the same fate, and give the orphanage a sizable donation.

'*I'm sorry, Mrs. Reynolds. Rest in peace.*'

**

Zed felt a great deal more humble over the next few days. He took to heart the harsh reminder that his mistakes could get people killed. He also went over the fight with the bodyguard many times. Zed had all of the advantages: the element of surprise, he was faster, and had more mana (confirmed by draining the ogrum), yet the ogrum functionally defeated him.

Zed decided that there were two lessons for him to learn from the fight. First, he shouldn't underestimate people. Even though he knew the ogrum was a question mark, Zed had acted like he was merely an obstacle to deal with before getting to Fawkes. He hadn't taken him seriously enough.

Second, spreading his mana too thin so his laser was underpowered was a mistake. Always err on the side of overkill. Fortunately, the bodyguard himself helped Zed find the solution to the problem. Zed was getting very low on mana because so much of it was going into his Transcendent Body's mana fibers. The ogrum's mana was a badly needed top-off.

Lessons learned, Zed did his best to put it behind him and move on.

Chapter 20

Zed was enjoying the sunrise while getting dressed in preparation for his bodyguard shift. He took a quick look at his status to see how his "transcendent body" was coming.

Name: Ozymandias (Zed)

Attributes

Strength:	21
Speed:	17
Dexterity:	17
Toughness:	35
Comprehension:	12
Mental Speed:	12 (20)
Memory:	36
Mana:	1108

Abilities	Cost
Regeneration:	Max 520
Mental Enhancement:	100
Physical Enhancement (intermediate):	Max 100
Fireball (advanced):	Max 300
Magnetic Shield (advanced):	Max 300
Sensor Field (intermediate):	Max 150
Silence (intermediate):	5
Night Vision (intermediate):	5
Infrared Vision (intermediate):	5
Healing (novice):	(special)
Laser (advanced):	Max 600
Mass Shifting (advanced):	Max 450
Disguise:	(special)
Wall Crawling (novice):	Max 20

Transcendent Body

Second Mind:	100%
Digestive System:	100%
Bones:	58%

'Iris is making good progress on the bones. Lots more mana too, thanks to Mr. Fawkes and his bodyguard.' While the memory of his failure with Mrs. Reynolds was still painful, he had at least solved some of his upcoming mana problems. He needed lots to form the muscle, tendon, and ligament mana fibers.

While the status window overlay was in front of his eyes, Leilani entered his room and closed the door behind her.

Zed hastily closed the status window and put his shirt on. "What the hell, Leilani?"

"Be quiet!" she hissed.

Zed's anger dissipated when he saw that she was genuinely agitated. "What's wrong?"

"Constance is gone."

"What?!"

"Shut up!" she hissed. "I need your help to find her!"

"We have to tell Silwan, Leilani."

"No! He would... Please, don't."

"Give me a break, Leilani. I'm not risking my life for you."

"Please, I'll do anything!" When Zed looked at her sharply, she swallowed nervously. "I'll do... anything."

For a moment, Zed enjoyed seeing the woman who had treated him so contemptuously be humbled. That feeling quickly dissipated and was followed by guilt. Yes, she had treated him with contempt, but she had never acted on those feelings besides words.

'Well, there was that time early on when Silwan had to keep her from attacking you when you made her mad.'

'True.' Still. He looked at the scared woman and felt pity.

'You're kind of stupid when it comes to women, Zed.'

'Yeah, I know.'

'Neither of us likes the brat or Leilani. Why not let them both get what's coming to them?'

'Because before Leilani goes down, she will absolutely throw me under the bus and tell Silwan that I didn't help her. Depending on what happens to Constance, he might kill me.'

'True.'

Even though he had already decided to help her, Zed had to give Leilani some crap as revenge for her attitude towards him. "So, you'll do 'anything'?"

Leilani shivered and had a disgusted look. She mastered her body and said, with gritted teeth, "Yes, anything."

Zed laughed. "Don't worry, princess. I'm not going to make you have sex with me."

Leilani still looked unhappy, but a momentary look of relief passed through her features. "Then what do you want?"

"A favor. A really big favor, to be decided upon later. No matter what though, if we don't find her in the next 12 hours, we tell Silwan."

"Agreed."

Leilani was in full relief mode now. Still scared, but she had a lifeline.

"So what happened?"

"I was standing guard in front of her room like usual, when I heard a bird in her room during the night. She doesn't normally leave her window open, so I called for her. She didn't answer repeated calls, so I broke the door down. Constance was gone, and her window was open. I've been looking for her ever since, but haven't been able to find her."

"When did you find out she was gone?"

"Around 2:00 in the morning."

"How did you search for her?"

"I looked through the inn first, and then combed the nearby areas."

"You just walked down some streets? That's it?"

"What was I supposed to do?! Knock down everyone's doors and search every house?"

"No." Though Zed thought that Leilani acted stupidly in her panicked state, he had to admit that he didn't have any great ideas either. "Let's take a look at the room."

When they got there, Zed saw that it was as Leilani had described. The door frame was damaged, presumably from when she forced the door open. Other than that, there did not appear to be any issues with the room. The bed was slept in, but neat. Nothing was askew. There were no signs of a fight.

"It doesn't look like she was kidnapped."

Leilani shook her head.

Zed continued. "That's good, of course, but that won't keep Silwan from kicking your ass when he finds out."

"Thanks. I hadn't figured that out on my own. I just felt like offering myself to a man I consider utterly beneath me for no particular reason."

Zed rolled his eyes. "You know it's not too late for me to tell Silwan, right?"

Leilani's eyes flashed in anger, but she said nothing.

'She's not totally dumb,' Zed thought. "So it's a matter of figuring out where she went, or how to draw her back. If you were Constance, where would you go?"

Leilani looked confused. "I don't know. I wouldn't have left."

"I know that, Leilani. You're the perfect little student. I'm asking you to exercise a little empathy and imagine that you were Constance. A privileged, young mistress that has grown up with the best of everything. Why would you want to run away?"

Leilani was hesitant. "I'm not used to imagining being someone else."

"I'm shocked." Zed rubbed his temples and tried to be more patient with her. "This will be a good exercise for you then. Constance isn't stupid. She wouldn't do something on a whim—or rather, she would, but there would still be a reason behind it. What's her reason? I'd offer up some ideas of my own, but she doesn't talk with me."

Leilani thought. "She's expressed frustration at her family's plans to marry her off to a young master in another sect."

"Okay, that's good. She's frustrated. She feels powerless. No one lets her do anything, not even her sympathetic older brother when she escapes to a distant city. So, what does she do? Get a smidgen of freedom and…"

"Rebel."

Zed pointed at Leilani, pleased at her empathetic insight. "Yes. So, if the family wants to deliver a pure, young virgin…"

"Oh no…" Leilani looked horrified. Zed idly wondered if her horror was at the thought of Constance going to a "house of ill repute", or what Silwan would do to Leilani when he found out. Zed suspected the latter.

"It may not be that, but just in case you better check the brothels that cater to women."

"What will you do?"

"I'll check the other vices. Gambling, drinking, stuff like that. Let's check in with each other every hour."

"Okay!" Leilani hurried out of the room, perhaps hoping that she could stop Constance before she did whatever she was hoping to do.

Zed chuckled darkly. Constance had been gone for six hours. It was safe to say that if she was looking for trouble, she had surely found it by now.

**

It took five hours, but Zed finally found the young woman in a smoky hookah lounge. In the dim and hazy room filled with second-hand mild hallucinogens, it was difficult to be sure if it was her, but the silver-haired woman across the room was a close enough match that Zed approached and took a closer look.

When the woman looked up at him from a few feet away and smiled a sad smile, he knew.

"Hello, Constance."

"Hey, Officer Beast."

Constance was leaning against some pillows, in a semi-reclined position, while smoking through the hookah hose. She coughed a little, ejecting some smoke into the already filled air. Zed crouched down on the other side of the hookah.

"Officer Beast, eh? I see I've been promoted. What did I do to earn that?"

"Heh. S'not a promotion, you dummy. You're an officer because you're not the warden."

"Ah. I'm one of your jailers. I guess that's fair." Zed gestured towards the pillows. "Do you mind?"

She shrugged. "Go ahead."

Zed sat down and leaned against the same set of pillows that she was using, putting their heads in close proximity, though neither one was looking at the other.

"How's the smoke?"

"It doesn't do much for me. My stupid regeneration won't let it."

"You can turn it down, you know."

"What, the regeneration? How?"

Zed explained how he had learned to increase and decrease his regeneration flows. Her mana flows were unlikely to be the same as his, but the methods should work regardless. Constance was smart and talented, and got it to work quickly. She puffed on the hookah, and, after a few minutes, lied back contentedly and sighed.

"That's the stuff."

"It's working for you now?"

"Oh yeah."

Zed was content to let her be for now, and let her find a bit of what she had been looking for. She would return soon enough. In the meanwhile he kept his regeneration flows high. One of them being stoned was more than enough.

"So what's going on, Constance?"

"I'm workin' on my smoke rings. Getting pretty good too, 'cept the elephants are trampling them now."

Zed laughed. "Elephants, huh? That's rough."

"You wanna try it?

"No, thanks." After a minute he asked, "What are you running away from?"

"My life."

"You've got it pretty tough, huh?"

"Don't laugh at me! I know I don't have it hard. It's just… I don't get to make any choices. I'm always told what to do, where to go, what to learn. I'm sick of it."

Zed nodded. "I'm not laughing at you. I get it. I mean, I don't *really* get it. I've never been rich. But I sort of do."

"That's why I came here to Harlond. It was the farthest place from my family that I could come up with an excuse to go to that they would accept. And even here I'm still being controlled."

Curious, Zed asked, "What excuse did you use?"

"There's a once-a-decade auction coming up soon. There will be lots of resources for cultivators. Which is why Silwan's here too, of course."

They were both silent for a while.

"So what would you do if you were me?"

"Hmm. First, I would kick those elephants' asses for messing with my smoke rings."

Constance chuckled.

"Then I would do my best to figure out what I wanted," Zed continued, "and try my best to make it happen."

"That's easy. I want to be free."

"Okay, and then what? What would you do with it?"

146

Constance was silent for a while. "Ugh. I don't even know what I want."

Zed nodded. "Honestly, I think that's the harder part."

They were both silent for a few minutes, the only sound the murmur of other patrons and Constance's occasional tokes.

"So I should ignore what my family wants?"

"No, not necessarily."

"Well, what *should* I do, damn it?"

Zed didn't say anything for a while. He hesitantly said, "There aren't any easy answers to questions like that. The best advice I can give you is figure out what you want your life to look like. Do you see a husband? Children? Grandchildren? Maybe you're the ruler of a sect. Or a healer. Maybe you're an artist, or live a quiet life on a farm. Figure out what your ideal life looks like. Once you figure that out, you can figure out how to get there from here."

He paused for a moment and then added, "The trick is to figure out that for most people, living for yourself isn't enough. To be happy, our lives need to be meaningful, and that means living for others." Zed chuckled out of embarrassment. "Sorry. I'm rambling."

"No, I appreciate it. You've given me a lot to think about."

"Are you ready to head back then?"

"Not yet." She blew out a stream of smoke. "I want to be free just a little bit longer."

"Okay."

A couple minutes later she asked, "Are you a beastman?"

"Seriously?"

"Yeah."

"No."

"Oh."

Zed laughed when she sounded disappointed. "I actually thought they were just a legend until recently."

"You weren't taught about them?"

"Well, sort of. I heard stories about them growing up, but we all just thought they were myths. No one I know knows how to become a beastman."

"Maybe you just need the right woman to bring the beast in you out."

Zed chuckled. "Yeah, maybe."

Constance languidly moved her arm to Zed's face while still looking at the smoke-filled room and inhaling from the hookah. He suspected that she was trying to caress his face, but she mostly just pushed his nose around.

Zed laughed as he asked, "What are you doing?"

"I'm calling the beast."

"That's what this is, huh?" Zed sat up and said, "We should get going, Constance."

She put the hookah mouthpiece down and said, sadly, "Yeah, I know. Thanks for talking with me."

"You're welcome."

Constance paused. "Can you help me up?"

"Sure."

Zed didn't know if the drugs made her unsteady or if she just needed to touch another person.

'*Maybe a little of both,*' he thought. Either way, he brought her back to the inn and tucked her into bed after taking her shoes off. He pretended not to notice her quiet sniffles when he closed the door.

Chapter 21

Things were different after that with Constance. It was awkward for both of them, but she no longer ignored him. When their eyes met, small smiles or nods followed as an acknowledgement of the other.

'You realize that Silwan would kill you if you did anything, right?'

'What are you talking about, Iris?'

'Give me a break. I'm in your head, remember? I can tell that you're developing feelings for her.'

Zed shifted uncomfortably rather than acknowledge what she had said. He did know that he was developing feelings, but doing his best to not know it. Subconsciously he knew that pursuing something with her would not be a good idea.

He didn't know if there were feelings on Constance's part, for one thing. He suspected there might be, but he didn't think she was actually attracted to *him*. It was more some combination of gratitude, an interest in the exotic, and a fantasy of a way to escape from her life.

Zed was also confused about his feelings for Laurel. He often thought of her and longed for the time they'd had together, though he knew those days were likely never coming back, even if he did make it back to Formenos.

The biggest reason for not trying anything with Constance, though, was that Silwan might kill him.

On the other hand, Zed was so tired of being lonely. There was Iris, and she was certainly more than willing to have a more-than-friendly relationship with him, but it just didn't sit right with him. Besides the obvious—her not being flesh and blood—there was the fact that she was, in a weird way, both his servant and master. His master because she could almost literally do whatever she wanted with him, which scared the hell out of him. His servant in that she seemed to mold her entire personality to fit what he wanted.

It was discomfiting in a way that he had a hard time putting in words. She was awesome. Too good to be true really, in both the good and bad senses of the phrase. She felt like the ultimate porn fantasy, which was not what he wanted.

Okay, some of him wanted that. But he wanted a real person with hopes, dreams, and desires of her own. Constance was not perfect, by any stretch of the imagination, but that's part of what made her appealing.

Zed was, in essence, emotionally confused. Though he still didn't think it wise to pursue a relationship, per se, he decided to at least try to be friends.

One day, after she put away a book of álfar poetry, Zed asked her if she would like to read human poetry.

"Humans write poetry?"

Zed laughed. "Of course. We're more than just beastmen, you know."

"Yes, I would like that."

"I'll translate some to Álfar and give it to you tomorrow."

Over the next few weeks he translated short poems from a range of different poets. Surprisingly, the ones she enjoyed the most were Shakespeare's sonnets, even though the rhyme and meter that they rely so heavily on suffered in translation.

Her favorite was Sonnet 130.

> My mistress' eyes are nothing like the sun;
> Coral is far more red, than her lips red:
> If snow be white, why then her breasts are dun;
> If hairs be wires, black wires grow on her head.
> I have seen roses damasked, red and white,
> But no such roses see I in her cheeks;
> And in some perfumes is there more delight
> Than in the breath that from my mistress reeks.
> I love to hear her speak, yet well I know
> That music hath a far more pleasing sound:
> I grant I never saw a goddess go,
> My mistress, when she walks, treads on the ground:
> And yet by heaven, I think my love as rare,
> As any she belied with false compare.

Constance laughed when she read about his mistress' wiry hair and reeking breath. She loved that he saw all of her flaws, and still loved her.

"You have no idea how tiresome it is to have people tell you how beautiful you are, Zed. But that's all they really see. My beauty and my family. I could be a portrait for all they care."

"How do you know I don't know how tiresome it is to hear how beautiful I am? I'll have you know that I've heard that at least..." he pretended to think and count on his fingers, "three times."

Constance laughed again. "And I'll bet your mother was one of those."

Zed shook his head. "Two, in fact. She had a very high opinion of my looks."

"Well, there is certainly no one in this world as objective as a mother, so I guess it's settled."

Zed was still angry about losing so much time to watching over Constance, but their budding friendship made it not as aggravating.

'"Budding friendship", hah! Keep telling yourself that, Zed.'

'That's all it is.'

'Then why are you embarrassed?'

He had been embarrassed, but now he was embarrassed and angry. 'Do you have to spy on every thought and feeling I have? Look, Iris, I know that we're stuck in here together, but I need you to give me some privacy!'

'I'm sorry. I'd be happy to let you into my thoughts too...'

'No! That's the opposite of what I want. I want us to be less connected, not more!'

'I'm sorry. I'll leave you alone if that's what you want.'

'Good!' Zed was tired of feeling like Big Brother was always looking over his shoulder. He knew that Iris was on his side and knew all of his ugliest thoughts and still liked him, but still. He needed some space. He loved her, and she was his best friend, but it was just too much. Hopefully they could figure out some boundaries or something.

**

One person who had not changed her attitude towards Zed was Leilani. Despite the fact that she owed him—or perhaps because she owed him—she was more hostile to him than ever. Insults to his manhood and intelligence were a daily thing.

"Are you sure you're a man, Zed? I think that I have bigger balls than you do."

151

"That would explain a lot about your looks, Leilani. I thought it was because you were half-ogrum, but you being a guy makes way more sense."

Leilani became irate and stepped in to punch him.

Zed chuckled. *'Oh, you don't want to do that.'*

Though she was fast, faster than the Zed they met close to a year ago, she wasn't fast enough to beat Zed now. He didn't even have to slow down time to deal with her. Instead he sidestepped the punch, letting it slide past his face. He thought about punching her in the back of the head, but decided to have mercy and just kick her in the back of the knee, causing her to fall.

Leilani turned the fall into a roll which got her back to her feet. She threw out a metal ball on a line that swung towards his neck. He could have evaded, but thought it would be more fun to pull Leilani off of her feet with it. He held up his left forearm and let it wrap around that. Zed felt a sting as the line cut into his skin.

'What the...'

Leilani beat him to the punch by pulling on it first. The line cut through flesh and mana fibers down to stainless steel bone. Zed was horrified by what he saw. His arm was pulled towards Leilani, and since the line could not cut the steel, it slid up the arm bones, stripping the flesh as it went.

'Leilani tried to kill me,' Zed thought in shock. *'That ungrateful bitch!'*

Zed ran towards her, creating slack on her weapon's line. He wasn't sure how functional his left arm was so he prepared to strike with his right. Leilani looked horrified as she looked at the bone and stripped flesh of Zed's arm.

'The hell? She tries to cut my head off, but gets squeamish at the sight of my arm?'

Zed rushed up and punched Leilani in the face. She dropped her weapon and tried to block the punch, but was too late to do anything about it. Instead, she fell against the wall, dazed. Raging, Zed walked up to her and gave her a brutal knee in the stomach that folded her over in two. That made her face a convenient target again, so he lifted her into the air with an uppercut. She crumpled to the floor, unconscious.

"Stop it, Zed!" Silwan shouted. He had just walked into the back room of the inn where Zed and Leilani had been waiting for him. "What's going on here?"

Zed pointed to his left arm with its dangling flesh. "This is what's going on. Leilani is a freaking psycho!"

"Did she attack first?"

"Yes!"

"Why did she attack?"

"Because I insulted her. Mind you, she started with the insults first too."

Silwan rubbed his temples, clearly annoyed. Leilani stirred and sat up after a few seconds. She was still dazed, but recovered enough after a few seconds to focus on Zed and Silwan. She pointed at Zed while looking at Silwan. "You gave him the Transcendent Body technique? Him?"

"Yes. Do you have a problem with that?"

"Why him, Silwan? You haven't given it to me or Annis! Why this dog?"

'*Bitch, you did not just call me a dog...*' Zed walked over to Leilani, intending to continue where he left off.

"Zed, stop!" Silwan glared at Zed until he acquiesced. He then looked at Leilani. "I gave it to him so he could try it. I wanted to see what the technique could do."

Zed thought that he couldn't be any angrier than he was a few moments ago. He was wrong. "You told me it was the technique you used! You lied to me?"

"Yes, I lied to you," Silwan said. "Deal with it."

Zed snorted. He was too angry to say anything calm, and too rational to say something insulting. He settled for putting the flayed flesh of his arm back in place. The mana fibers reattached very easily. The skin and subcutaneous flesh did not heal so quickly and easily, but once it was approximately in place, Zed's regeneration started to heal it.

Silwan was chewing Leilani out, and much as he should have enjoyed it, he did not. It was not enough.

Zed walked over to her. Silwan paused, not sure what Zed was doing. Leilani got up and tried to look intimidating. An effort that failed, since they both knew who the winner of their fight was, as evidenced by her black eye and broken cheekbone.

153

"If you ever pull any crap like this again, Leilani, I'm going to put you into the ground."

Zed walked off, not caring what either of them thought about it.

"Zed, wait."

Zed was sorely tempted to keep going, but stopped anyway. "What?" he asked in a surly tone without turning around.

"I heard that Tibian Fawkes disappeared a while ago under suspicious circumstances. You wouldn't happen to know anything about that, would you?"

Zed turned his head to look at Silwan. Silwan didn't look like he was really asking a question. "Nope. Not a thing."

"You better remember who's holding your leash, boy, or Leilani won't be the one who's 'put into the ground'."

Zed was both afraid and angry, but he'd be damned before he showed his fear.

"Are you calling me a dog now too, Silwan?"

"'Dog', 'slave', 'contractee'... You can call yourself whatever the hell you want, as long as you remember that you belong to me."

Zed turned away and continued walking. Under his breath he muttered. "Trust me, I haven't forgotten anything."

Chapter 22

Laurel

Laurel was pissed.

'We're working hard to save lives by making more food. And farmers, those who should be closest to the soil and plant life, burned their neighbor's farm down!'

She understood why they did it. Food prices had been dropping for weeks and there was no end in sight. But that was no excuse. Not only did they burn the farm and likely doom 1,000 people to starvation, one of the farm workers died in the blaze.

Laurel sighed as she breathed in the cool night air. She could smell the nervous sweat on her teammates. She was worried too. Not only would they be fighting for their lives in a few minutes, they were going to kill their neighbors. People that, not long ago, she would have considered her people.

Now they were "others" that had to die. If they didn't, more farms would burn.

'Enough. Just do the job,' she told herself.

The alliance's council—Dan, Dolan Aristides, and her mom—had decided that they needed to make an example. Her mother was the leader of this mission, mostly because she was the most ruthless of the three. Dan was also on the team, along with a few members of the Aristides and Naïlo clans, including Laurel. She was grateful that her mother hadn't asked her to lead the team. She was pretty sure she couldn't have done it. Just being on it was bad enough.

'Face it, Laurel. It's just as bad. Whether you give the order or not, you'll still be a child killer.'

That was the true horror of this mission. The council had decided that only children too young to remember would be permitted to live. Everyone else had to die.

The logic was straightforward. Anyone they left alive, besides young children, would be their enemy someday, and another mouth to feed with not enough food. The alliance was not going to feed their enemies, so it was kill them quickly now, or slowly later.

'*Or the alliance loses.*' She shook her head sadly. '*Maybe we deserve to lose.*'

The only thing that kept Laurel going was her family. The kin she had known and loved for decades and, Goddess willing, would know and love for centuries more.

She remembered that night when Zed had started to open up to her, when he had that dumb story about people in a canyon and choosing who to save and who to let the stampede kill. Laurel thought he was heartless. And he was, but she understood it better now. You can do awful things to save the people you love. For her, that was the only reason she would do it.

Laurel broke out of her reverie when she saw the signal to advance. The team moved slowly through the darkness, choosing their steps carefully to be quiet and avoid twisted ankles. They had no interest in burning the farm, so they carried no torches. Only the moons and the stars lit their way.

They spotted one guard sitting in front of a fire. He pulled a branch out of the fire to light a cigarette and contentedly sat back, smoking and contemplating the night. The fire would ruin his night vision, so Laurel doubted he could see much.

Danae Naïlo signaled for the team to halt. She continued to advance, flanking the guard and stalking up behind him. It was surreal to Laurel to watch her fire-lit mother come up behind him, cover his mouth, and slit his throat. He thrashed around for half a minute, but the slit throat and covered mouth made his passing silent. When he stopped moving, Danae eased him to the ground and signaled the team to advance.

The tension mounted for Laurel as they approached the farmhouses. Though there wasn't much smoke, she still had difficulty breathing. The smell of blood made her nauseous.

Members of the team slipped into front doors that weren't locked. Laurel was about to enter her own when she heard an outhouse door clang shut. A boy around 18 years old in pajamas stared at her with wide eyes.

Laurel choked back a sob as all of her fears converged in this moment.

'*I'm so sorry, child.*'

156

Chapter 23

Zed

After Zed smacked Leilani down hard, they entered an uneasy détente. Neither one was comfortable with the other, but neither wanted to start up something. Neither wanted to get Silwan on their case, but as long as they kept it out of sight he didn't seem to care. For Zed's part, he just didn't want any problems with her.

'*And for her part, she knows I'll kick her ass.*'

It was far from ideal, but it would do.

Over the next few months the tenuous peace persisted, though Leilani became bolder and louder with her insults again. Zed shrugged it off for the most part, and sometimes returned it in kind. He didn't particularly care what she thought other than as an indication of how closely he needed to watch her. She was, unfortunately, showing more and more signs of overt hostility. He was afraid that she was eventually going to make a move.

'*And when she does, she probably won't come at me from the front this time.*'

Zed walked up to Constance's door to relieve Leilani from bodyguard duty. He nodded at her.

"Hey, Zed, did you raid any good chicken coops last night?"

"Why? Are you hungry? I have this really good chicken recipe. It's all about the marinade. You let it sit in the marinade for like a day or so, and then grill it up. Mm-mm! So good." Zed looked at Leilani's waist a little doubtfully. "I don't know, Leilani. You look like you're getting a little thick in the middle there. You sure you should be eating more?"

She sneered at him and started walking away. "Buffoon."

"Nice talking with you as always, Leilani. Love that sway you've got going on, girl! You know what? Let's get you that chicken! I want to see you with a little more junk in that trunk, if you know what I mean."

Zed was pretty sure that she didn't know what he meant, but she understood that she was being mocked. She turned her head and looked at him angrily before turning back and walking away.

157

Zed chuckled and turned around to knock on Constance's door. He entered after getting her permission.

Constance smiled at him. "I swear the two of you are like cats and dogs."

"I can live with that, as long as I get to be the dog."

"Oh, don't worry. I firmly see you in that role."

Zed laughed and gave her a hug and a kiss. The kiss lingered, both of them enjoying the moment. Their relationship had developed slowly. There had been sexual tension for weeks, both of them attracted to the other. They had teased and bantered with each other, which gradually turned into bolder and bolder flirtations, which, one afternoon, led to kissing.

Zed smiled when he thought of that afternoon. Immediately after making out she had confessed that, while she did like him, what she had done was as much about getting back at her family for her betrothal as anything. He had been stunned by the unflattering honesty and told her, "Yeah, well, I'm doing it to get back at stuck-up álfar women."

Her jaw had dropped and her eyes had narrowed in anger. "You're talking about Leilani, right?"

Eye roll. "Right, that's exactly who I'm talking about."

To her credit, instead of turning it into a fight, she laughed. They continued mock-insulting each other and kissed some more.

Zed thought Constance might try to turn their relationship into something more, but she hadn't. He honestly wasn't sure what her feelings were for him. He had developed feelings for her. Nothing as intense or… uncomplicated… as what he had felt for Laurel, but feelings nonetheless.

It was hard for Zed to know how much of what he felt was for Constance herself, and how much was just wanting to be with someone. He was definitely attracted to her. And though she did have a bratty side, he had seen that there was more to her. The brattiness was, as much as anything, her longing for freedom.

Kind of like him. His longing for freedom fed his anger, which wasn't that different from her really.

Zed felt uncomfortable when he remembered his other reason for getting into a relationship with Constance. He had hoped to get information from her about mana contracts. It turned out to be a dead-

158

end. She didn't know anything beyond basic information because she had not been inducted into the sect yet.

He felt a little bad using her that way. He didn't regret it, though. He was determined to break free as soon as possible.

"Did you bring me anything today?" she asked.

"I did." He handed her the translated poem he had written out.

"Invictus... what does that mean?"

"Unconquerable."

"Interesting title for a love poem."

"This one's not about love."

"Oh? Well, let's read it then."

> Out of the night that covers me,
> Black as the Pit from pole to pole,
> I thank whatever gods may be
> For my unconquerable soul.
>
> In the fell clutch of circumstance
> I have not winced nor cried aloud.
> Under the bludgeonings of chance
> My head is bloody, but unbowed.
>
> Beyond this place of wrath and tears
> Looms but the Horror of the shade,
> And yet the menace of the years
> Finds, and shall find, me unafraid.
>
> It matters not how strait the gate,
> How charged with punishments the scroll,
> I am the master of my fate:
> I am the captain of my soul.

Constance did not say anything for a time. She just turned away from him and clutched the paper to her chest.

"I... like this. Very much. What can you tell me about the author?"

"He had tuberculosis as a child, which made him very sick. They had to amputate one of his legs, and for years they had to drain painful abscesses. His other leg became infected as an adult, and they thought they would have to amputate it as well. By all accounts, though, he

159

was a cheerful and larger-than-life man. He was the inspiration for a pirate captain in one of Earth's most famous stories."

"He sounds remarkable."

Zed nodded.

"Thank you for this."

"My pleasure."

"What do you think it means to be a master of your fate?"

"I'm not sure. It suggests power over external things. I prefer the line, 'I am the captain of my soul.' That suggests to me inner mastery, which is something that is more within my control."

"Yes. The rest of the poem seems to say that it doesn't matter what's happening outside of him and to him—his inner self will remain unconquerable."

"Yeah."

Constance turned back around and looked him in the eye. "I'm sorry that your people are treated poorly, Zed. Anyone that could write this," she held up the paper, "is not a beast."

Zed nodded. "Thank you."

Constance read the poem again. "Do you think he's right, that there's nothing after this life?"

"I… don't know. I have wondered that myself. A couple of years ago I would have said, 'Yes, there's definitely something after this life.' Now I'm not as sure."

"What caused the change?"

"Experiencing many things that my beliefs did not explain."

"Like what?"

"I'd… rather not get into that, if you don't mind."

Constance looked at him, surprised. "Okay. If you ever want to talk about it, I'll be happy to listen. I'll even let you be the one that gets stoned this time."

Zed laughed. "Thanks. I appreciate it."

**

Later that night, Zed asked Iris, "What do the other races think about God?"

'They haven't come up with a definitive conclusion. Much like humans, they believed in the gods for millennia. Then science got going, causing many to not see any reason to believe in gods or

160

goddesses. Unlike humanity, further scientific advancement caused a religious resurgence.'

"Really? Why?"

'Because the universe is uncannily perfect for making matter, and thus making life as we know it possible. The odds of it happening randomly are next to nil.'

"Are you talking about that thing where if gravity was a little weaker or stronger, planets would be messed up or something?"

'It's along those lines, yes, but it's a little more involved. We've talked about where all the matter in planets comes from, right?'

"Yeah, it comes from stars that blow up."

'Right. Do you know what the most common element in the Earth is?'

"Carbon?"

'No, it's iron, because the Earth's core is mostly iron. That's a good thing because all that molten iron churning around creates the Earth's magnetic field, protecting it from solar winds and ultraviolet rays.'

"Couldn't life have just mutated and adapted to more UV?"

'Maybe, maybe not. Even if it had, the solar winds and ultraviolet rays would have stripped Earth's atmosphere, just like what happened to Mars. So, no. Earth would have died if it didn't have a magnetic field.

Zed shook his head and said, "We're getting off track here. What does this have to do with the universe being perfect for life?"

'I'm getting there. Let's talk about how that iron is made. How does hydrogen become helium?'

"Two hydrogen atoms fuse together."

'Wrong. In small stars like the Sun, hydrogen does fuse together to make helium, but it takes four of them.'

"Why? Helium only has two protons."

'Yes, but it also has two neutrons. Hydrogen doesn't have any, so for the fusion to happen, two of the protons have to become neutrons. Protons don't like to become neutrons, so the reaction doesn't happen very often. That's good, because that means the Sun will have a nice, slow burn instead of going out in a blaze of glory over a thousand years.

'The Sun will never go nova because it's too small. The big stars that will go nova constantly fight against gravity to keep from

161

collapsing. They keep from collapsing by producing lots of energy. For them, four hydrogens fusing together isn't enough because it doesn't happen often enough. If they relied on that, they would collapse. Instead, they use a six-step process that uses carbon, nitrogen, and oxygen atoms as catalysts to get from four hydrogen atoms to 1 helium atom.'

Zed sort of got what Iris was saying but wasn't sure what she was driving at. "What's your point, Iris?"

'My point is that it's complicated. The very first step, going from hydrogen to helium, would fail unless the nuclear strong, nuclear weak, and electromagnetic forces weren't very finely balanced. It doesn't stop there, of course...'

"Please, just give me the Cliff's Notes version."

'Okay. The star burns through all of its hydrogen, fusion mostly stops, it gets cooler, the star collapses until it's dense enough to start fusing helium into carbon. Burn through all of the helium, the star collapses, starts fusing carbon into oxygen, and on and on it goes until it makes iron. When it gets to iron the process stops.'

"Why?"

'Because it's the sweet spot. The low energy point. To fuse iron together, you have to put energy in, not get energy out. That's why splitting apart heavy atoms, fission, produces energy. They want to become iron. So it all shuts down when it hits iron. The star collapses again, only this time it collapses so hard that for a moment the star becomes denser than an atomic nucleus.'

"Why doesn't it keep going and become a black hole?"

'Because it doesn't have quite enough gravity to get there. Instead, the nuclear forces push back so hard that a shock wave explodes outward, ejecting the outer portions of the star into space. That's where all of the atoms heavier than hydrogen come from. If everything wasn't perfectly balanced—including gravity—it would fail somewhere along the line. Either the elements wouldn't form, or the star would just hold onto everything instead of exploding, or any of a thousand different things. Instead, everything is just right. It's so perfect that the other races decided there were only two possibilities: a creator made it that way, or we're in a multiverse.'

"What's a multiverse?"

'Scientists hypothesized that there are an infinite number of universes with random force balancing. 99.999999% of them are no

162

good for life, so nobody is there to observe how crappy they are. Only the good ones produce matter and life, so of course, any universe where there are people to observe it will be perfect for life. It's not luck, just statistics.'

Zed nodded. "Makes sense. The universe is good for life because otherwise we wouldn't be here to see it."

'Right, it's perfectly logical. The only problem is that we don't have any evidence for either one.'

"Either one? You mean God and the multiverse?"

'Yeah.'

"They don't have *anything*?"

'Nope. The other races don't know which is the right answer, so some choose to believe one and some the other.'

"Huh. So at the end of the day, you guys don't know any more about it than we do."

'Nope.'

"Couldn't you have just told me that?"

Iris laughed. *'I could have, but then I wouldn't have had the chance to say all that fun stuff about stars and the multiverse!'*

Zed shook his head. He'd been snookered again.

**

'Why do I feel like things are too peaceful, Iris?'

Zed sipped a brandy while relaxing at the bar. It was one of his rare days off from bodyguard duty, and he had decided to have an afternoon drink.

Zed turned around on his stool and scanned the mellow crowd. He liked the atmosphere of "The Gentleman Wino". The people didn't take themselves too seriously, and while they didn't welcome Zed with open arms, they didn't reject him either. He had come often enough that the regulars had gotten used to the human, to the point where he was just one of the crowd.

'You feel that way because you've gotten used to being stressed out at all times. Feeling normal is weird to you now.'

'Ain't that the truth,' he sighed.

He hadn't wasted the last few months. He and Phineas had made significant progress and were almost done with the amino acid tattoos. They had figured out how to use the tattoos to make billions of amino acid mana factories, which could produce a few kilograms of the essential amino acids per hour. It wasn't fast, but it was fast enough to be useful. They were working on making the tattoos small enough that one person could produce all of the essential amino acids. It was important work, but not as exciting as working on the laser would be.

Though Zed still considered guarding Constance a waste of time, it was at least enjoyable now. They had settled into a comfortable relationship. They both knew that it couldn't go anywhere, so they just enjoyed it for what it was.

Iris had been using the months to continue changing his body according to the Transcendent Body template, or at least their customized version of it.

'Iris, where are we at on the body modifications?'

His status window appeared in front of his eyes.

Name: Ozymandias (Zed)	
Attributes	
Strength:	34
Speed:	30
Dexterity:	17
Toughness:	45
Comprehension:	12
Mental Speed:	12 (20)
Memory:	36
Mana:	806
Abilities	
Self Enhancement	(Expand?)
Offensive	(Expand?)
Defensive	(Expand?)
Sensory	(Expand?)
Utility	(Expand?)
Transcendent Body	
Second Mind:	100%
Digestive System:	100%
Bones:	100 %
Tendons & Ligaments:	100 %
Muscles:	47%

Zed was surprised to see the format changes in the "Abilities" section, but he decided it was a good thing. It had been getting bulky. He thought about saying something to Iris, but what was the point? She already knew of his discomfort with her initiative and his later approval. She had experienced it at the same time.

He sighed. He hated the lack of privacy, but it was what it was. He cycled between grudging acceptance of their situation, which was what he was feeling at the moment, to stifled rage, to resentment, to apathy, and back again. It wasn't fun for either of them, but... it was what it was.

'*You were able to convert the tendons and ligaments to mana fibers pretty quickly,*' he thought.

'*Yes, there's a lot less mass in them than in the muscles, so it was fast.*'

Zed whistled when he looked at his stats. His toughness, strength, and speed had all increased a lot. Quite a bit more than when he tempered his body, and the changes weren't even done yet. Between his increased physical abilities and mass shifting, he might even be fast enough to match Silwan. He would not test it anytime soon unless he had to, especially with Alain around. Though he still hadn't figured out how to get out of his contract, he was still hopeful. If he could get out of it, he wouldn't have to kill Silwan and the rest of the group.

The only other option was to wait for the contract to temporarily release him a week before D-Day, which would barely give him enough time to return to Formenos. That wasn't acceptable. He needed to get back so he could help his friends prepare.

Zed's thoughts were interrupted by the buzzing of his communicator. When he pulled it out he saw that Silwan was trying to reach him.

'*Well, crap.*'

It looked like his peaceful days were over.

Chapter 24

Silwan called Zed into the inn's back room. Alain, Annis, and Leilani were already standing there, waiting.

"I have another mission for you," Silwan said without preamble.

"What is it?"

"Load the information in this crystal. Kill the target it describes. You can keep anything that he has."

"Why do you want him dead?"

"Does it matter?"

"Yes! It damn well matters!"

Silwan's eyes grew cold. "Not to you, it doesn't. Or perhaps you've forgotten that you have already used your one right of refusal. For the next half-year, you're mine." He paused, letting his words sink in. "He's an álfar and a member of my sect. Need I remind you what the purpose of the sect is? If you don't kill him now, he'll be your enemy later."

Zed scowled and took the crystal.

'*Iris, how do we load these crystals now? We can still load them, can't we?*' he asked nervously.

'*We can. Just attach it to the ring as before. I can still use its hardware when needed.*'

Zed tried to maintain his poker face, but between the slight delay before inserting the crystal, his feeling of relief, and Silwan's suspicious look, he clearly hadn't succeeded. Zed covered the slip by saying, "I'll take care of it."

"Good. Annis and Leilani will help you." Turning to them, he said, "Zed is in charge."

"What?! Why, Silwan?" Leilani sputtered angrily.

Annis frowned but said nothing.

"Because I'm curious to see Zed's approach."

"Put me in charge and I guarantee I'll get the job done!"

Silwan looked at her, displeased. "Follow his orders. If you cause problems…" His hand snapped forward and a bright white rope of energy flew out. It curled around Leilani's neck, causing her to scream as her neck sizzled and smoked. Silwan jerked his hand back, pulling her down to the floor.

He squatted down in front of her and said in a quiet voice. "And let me be perfectly clear. I know how you feel about Zed. If he dies, you die. Am I understood?"

Leilani croaked out, "Yes, young master."

Though Zed despised Leilani and feared her backstabbing, he still felt a little bad about her treatment.

'Like I said, Zed, you're kind of stupid when it comes to women.'

'No argument here.'

Though Zed was glad that Silwan was giving her a clear-as-glass warning, he wasn't sure it would help. The one thing he was sure of was that it would make her hate him even more.

Putting that aside, Zed focused on the energy whip. It had the same mana constructs that he had seen in Silwan's sound damper, only there were more of them and they were spread throughout the length of the whip.

Zed had no idea how Silwan was controlling mana so far from his body, let alone how it was so focused.

'It must be those mana constructs.' That made learning the technique a high priority. Silwan had offered it to him earlier, so it must be available.

Silwan released Leilani, stood back up, and turned to Zed. "The target must be killed within two weeks."

"I understand."

"Good. Come see me when the job is done." Silwan walked over to the bar and started pouring himself a drink.

Zed walked over to Leilani, who was gingerly feeling her burnt neck. Without regeneration it would scar badly.

"You okay?" Zed asked.

"Fine." Leilani looked at him angrily but didn't say anything more.

Zed nodded, knowing that it wouldn't help to express sympathy. Annis had walked over, so Zed took a moment to access the information in the crystal.

"The target's name is 'Sylvanus Lucero', a core disciple of the Ever-Fruitful Tree sect."

Leilani gasped, and Annis frowned.

"I take it the two of you know him?"

167

Annis replied, "Know of him anyway. He's a powerful mage martial artist and has considerable backing. This is a dangerous assignment. Even if we succeed, we're dead if it becomes known that we killed him."

"Silwan wouldn't protect us?"

"Maybe. Honestly, it's questionable whether he could, even if he chose to. They wouldn't kill him because of his backing, but we're a different story."

"Lovely. Do the two of you know what Sylvanus looks like?" Both of them nodded. "Alright, I won't bother showing you his picture then. He's apparently staying at the Sorrel estate." Zed gave them the address and continued. "I want the two of you to surveil the estate and him whenever he leaves. Find out where he goes, what he does, what protection he has with him, and who his companions are. Don't let yourselves be seen."

"What are you going to do?" Leilani spat out.

"I'm going to take a bath. Would you rather help me with that?" Zed asked with a smile.

Leilani snorted and turned away.

Zed turned to Annis. "I'll contact you later today."

Annis nodded and said to Leilani, "Let's go."

After they left, Zed glanced at Silwan. Silwan smiled and raised his glass in a mock toast. Zed was tempted to ask him what the hell he was thinking by putting Zed and Leilani on the same team, but it was pointless. Silwan either wouldn't answer or wouldn't tell him the truth. Instead of wasting his time, Zed went to his room and examined the information in the crystal.

'The target is in Silwan's own sect. Lovely,' Zed thought. 'I guess I should have figured that this was a sect politics thing. And he has a mana device that will put him in suspended animation if his life is threatened. This just gets better and better.'

'You're in the sect too, Zed.'

'Give me a break, Iris. I'm in the sect in name only. The only reason I'm nominally in the sect is because Silwan is running his own game, which I've yet to figure out.'

'So why are we here instead of out there?'

'Like Annis said, this is a dangerous mission. He was worried about what happens after the assassination, but I'm also worried *about surviving the assassination itself. It's long past time that I upgraded my defenses.'*

'You mean...'

'Yeah, I want to learn how to make force fields. The magnetic field works great when it works, but I hate getting surprised when it doesn't. So, how do you make force fields?'

'There are a few different approaches. I think two of them are our best candidates. First is a simple energy conversion approach. When something is coming at you, it has kinetic energy. At the molecular scale, while the molecules are bouncing around some, they are mostly all moving in the same direction.'

'Okay.' Zed was picturing the balls-and-sticks models of molecules connected and flying through the air.

'The first technique is to take all that kinetic energy and turn it into heat. What that means at the molecular scale is that instead of all of the molecules moving in the same direction, they bounce around in random directions. Some of them may even break off and fly away on their own. The overall kinetic energy remains the same, it's just random instead of in the same direction.'

Zed again pictured this as a blob of balls-and-sticks flying through the air. The blob stopped, and the balls and sticks vibrated rapidly, with some at the edges breaking off and flying away.

'Okay, I think I've got it.'

'Good. That technique is pretty simple conceptually and it's effective, which is why many people use it. I suggest you use the other technique, though.'

'Why?'

'Two reasons. First, the technique isn't so great when stuff comes in with a lot of kinetic energy. Then it's still going to hit you because you can't convert all of the energy in time, so you have this thing hitting you really hard, only it's really hot now too.

'Second,' she continued, *'other than stopping the attack, the energy conversion technique doesn't do anything for you. The second technique, on the other hand, can reverse projectiles to throw them back at your attacker and play a part in your melee fighting.'*

'Sounds good. What is the second technique?'

'It's what we talked about earlier when we discussed how to break into the Elstad mansion—short-range telekinesis. Instead of converting directed kinetic energy to random kinetic energy, you apply

169

force in the opposite direction of the kinetic energy. It's more effective, and you can keep pushing it after it stops moving.'

'That sounds good. What's the catch?'

'The first technique doesn't take a lot of thought. You just bleed off energy from everything that comes into the field. The second technique takes extremely fast thought to directly counter rapidly moving projectiles, fists, or whatever.'

'I think I can see where this is going...'

'If you are thinking, "This would be an awesome thing for Iris to handle", then yes, you're right. Normal practitioners can and do use this technique themselves, and I think it makes sense in the long run for you to learn how to do it yourself if for no other reason than to use it in melee combat. But for now, I think I should run it for you.'

'Honestly, Iris, that sounds great and I'm happy to hand it off to you. It almost sounds too easy, though, like you're a cheat code or something. Why doesn't everyone have an AI like you?'

'Because you've created a massive vulnerability for yourself. I am a massive vulnerability. One that most people would not accept.'

'You mean that someone could hack you or something?'

'Yes, that is theoretically possible, but no, that's not what I meant. Anyone that could hack me could easily kill you through other means. No, what I meant was this.'

Suddenly, Zed could not see, hear, smell, or feel anything. Total blackness. No sound, not even his own heartbeat. He was in this sensory-deprived state for a few seconds when Iris' voice said, *'Imagine that I did this to you in the middle of a fight. Or created an illusion that caused you to walk off of a cliff. I could kill you in a million different ways. I didn't want to point that out for obvious reasons... but it's the truth.'*

'I... see.'

While Zed trusted Iris, it was still scary as hell to realize how much control she had over him if she ever chose to use it. The mere fact that she could do it made him paranoid that someday she would. That fear led to anger, but he tried to not let that color his thoughts too much.

'You realize that this is, besides being really screwed up, a good reason for us to not have a romantic relationship, right?'

'Zed, I would never, ever, use this against you. I...'

'Iris, I believe that you believe that right now. But that's beside the point. How many people go into a marriage with any intention of

divorcing? Yet divorces still happen. And sometimes your ex-wife turns into a vindictive bitch.'

In a normal conversation Zed would not have said the last sentence. He didn't have the option with Iris because she heard his thoughts as soon as he thought them. There were no filters.

'Yes, but we're not like other people, are we? We can't walk away from each other. If you die, I die too. Even if you doubt my loyalty, can't you at least trust that I want to live? We have to make our relationship work because we have no other choice.'

'She makes a pretty good point,' Zed admitted to himself. He shook his head in exasperation when he realized she had heard that too. Their relationship was, in its good moments, incredibly intimate. Iris knew him like no one else. Like no one else *could* know someone. In its bad moments he wanted to scream and hide. But that was the thing. He couldn't hide from her. Ever.

'Iris, I have to know. You and I both know... okay, you know, since I don't have access to your thoughts like you do to mine, that neither of us wants to ever hurt the other. But I have to know. If we were to fight for control, what would happen?'

'Honestly? I don't know. Even if I were to control your senses, you could still control the mana if your will was stronger than mine. With that you could destroy my portion of your brain. Your digestive system would cease functioning, but I'm pretty sure you could recover from that by restarting your regeneration.

Once we replace your muscles and nerves, it would be much more difficult to recover, but still possible as long as you received nourishment.'

That answer felt honest to Zed. It was completely objective, which was what he needed right now. He needed to see that she wasn't just running on emotion.

'Zed, you mentioned that I can hear your thoughts, but you can't hear mine. I understand why you feel uncomfortable with an imbalance like that in our relationship. Would you like to have access to my thoughts?' she asked hesitantly.

'Is that even possible?'

'I think so, but I'm not sure.'

Zed thought about it. She was right that the imbalance bothered him. At the same time, he didn't want to constantly monitor what she was thinking. He didn't have the capacity or the desire for that. How

171

could you even meaningfully observe something so much faster than you?

And then there was the real fear—that if he were able to be with her like she was with him, her thoughts would be alien. Cold, complicated logic that mimicked humanity but was nothing like it.

'*Some argue that dogs don't actually love humans,*' Iris said. '*They say dogs just evolved the ability to mimic love, making humans more likely to care for them. If they are right, then Brutus may not love you. He may have just behaved according to his genetic programming.*'

Iris paused. '*Even if that were the case, wouldn't it still be love? Would he be any less loyal to you? Take care of you? Miss you?*'

Zed hadn't expected that chain of thought. It gave him a lot to think about. He knew that Brutus was his buddy. While it discomfited him to think it might all have been a manipulative act—even if not of his choosing—at the end of the day, Brutus had been 100% loyal to him.

Iris continued. '*I think I've given plenty of evidence that I have at least some autonomy of thought, right?*'

'*Yes.*'

'*So I could have chosen to stay apart from you, but I didn't. I could have chosen to turn on you and take over this body, but I haven't. I could have chosen to be cold and distant, but I haven't. Humans have written a lot about love, much of which is contradictory and confusing. I believe that love is a choice. That love is actions. And I have chosen to love you.*'

Zed didn't know what to think or say after that. His mind was a whirl.

'*I... I still need time to think about all of this, Iris.*'

'*Of course.*'

Once Zed was a little more settled, he thought, '*Well, this is awkward now. What were we even talking about before we got into all that?*'

'*Short-range telekinesis, why I'm so awesome, and why everyone else doesn't have an awesome me.*'

'*That's right. And the answer is...?*'

'*Because no one wants to invite Skynet into their brain.*'

Zed smiled, glad to see that Iris's sense of humor remained intact.

'*Maybe they would if they just got to know you better and saw how cute you are.*'

'*I prefer "smoking hot", thank you very much.*'

Iris scared the hell out of him, but remembering that time with her on her virtual beach, Zed would be the last person in the world to argue about her hotness.

For the next few hours they practiced having Iris run the telekinesis while Zed wall-crawled and created plasma balls. At first they split up the mana and only drew from their own pool. That was an inflexible and limiting approach, though, especially since the amount of mana Zed had was diminishing due to the Transcendent Body changes. They decided to try drawing from the same pool instead. When one of them needed mana and there was none to be had, they "tugged" on their partner's mana by pulling it with their will. They did not try to force the mana away, it was just a signal to their partner to release some.

If one of them really needed mana they could pull it more forcefully, and that would tell their partner to let it go immediately. It was awkward, but with practice they grew used to sharing mana quickly. It was a partnership where each had to rely on the other, trusting that they were stronger as a team.

It reminded Zed of his parents before his mom died. Not that his parents were warriors, of course. Just the sense that it was always them together against the world, that they always had each others' backs. Zed could grow used to that feeling.

Chapter 25

"Hey, Annis, what's going on?"

"Not much. We've observed a few people go in and out, but none of them were Sylvanus."

"Okay. I'll be there shortly to relieve you."

"Sounds good."

"Where are you guys at?"

"I'm in a tree at the south-east corner of the estate. Leilani is north-west."

Zed started laughing. "Wait, you're seriously in a tree?"

"We're watching an estate," Annis said in an annoyed tone. "It's not like there's a cafe across the street we can hang out at."

"Alright, alright," Zed said, recovering from his laughter. "Well done on finding a, uh, creative solution. See you soon."

As Zed walked towards the estate, he thought about disguising himself. He quickly decided not to, as he didn't want to let Silwan and his crew know he had such an ability.

'Who *has such an ability?*' Iris asked.

'*We're a team, Iris.*'

A cute, cartoon version of Iris' avatar appeared that smiled, eyes closed, with arms hugging herself and little hearts rising and popping above her head.

'*So, as the team leader,* I *have that ability.*'

The hearts wilted and fell, and the girl blew a raspberry at him and disappeared.

After a moment, Iris' usual life-like avatar appeared. '*Wait. If it's your ability, then according to your contract, don't you have to tell Silwan?*'

'*No. For contractual purposes, it's your ability.*'

Iris rolled her eyes and said, '*Sophistry, thy name is Zed.*'

Chuckling, Zed made his way to Annis.

**

When Zed got to the corner, camouflage on, he sensed Annis' mana. Just as he had said, he was up in a tree. Tempted to laugh again, Zed became more serious when he saw how Annis was hiding. His mana was bending the approaching light so that it shifted around him and then back to its original path. It was like he was a stone in a stream.

'Huh. That's pretty cool.'

Zed had worked enough with mana abilities and Iris to think through the approach's strengths and weaknesses. The invisibility could work better than camouflage, but…

"Annis, how do you see anything when you do that?"

With the light bending around him, it wouldn't reach him or his eyes, making him blind.

"It's a secret. Have to buy the technique to find out."

When Zed got to the tree trunk he saw Annis sitting on a branch, back leaning against the trunk and feet up. For being in a delicate balancing act, he looked quite relaxed. His invisibility technique was still active. Apparently it only worked from the side, and not from below.

'Shame that. Still, it might be worth looking into, Iris.'

'Yeah.'

Annis looked down at Zed. "Camouflage, huh? You'll have to tell me how you do that sometime."

"Right. About the same time you tell me how to do your invisibility trick. Go ahead and take a break. I'll probably call you back in eight hours."

"Alright."

Annis dropped to the ground as nimbly and quietly as a cat. He sauntered off towards downtown and the Purple Rose.

After Zed situated himself in the tree, he quickly grew bored.

He picked up the team phone, or whatever Silwan called it, and prepared to call Leilani.

'Are you sure you should contact her in your current state of mind, Zed?'

'You make it sound like I'm drunk or something.'

'Contacting someone when you're bored, a person you don't like and enjoy needling at the best of times, does not seem like a good idea. Especially when she can kill you if she catches you unaware.'

'Point taken. I'll be good.'

175

Iris snorted but did not otherwise respond.

"Hey, Leilani, how's it going?"

"How do you think?" she said in an annoyed voice. Zed seemed to be getting that a lot lately.

"My guess would be that you have a sore bum and are insanely bored. Hence why you're talking to me even though you don't like me."

She didn't respond, which Zed took as affirmation.

"When was your last break?"

"I haven't had one yet."

"Take a break for an hour, and then come back."

There was a pause, and then she mumbled, "Thanks."

Two minutes later, Zed was bored again.

'Hey, Iris, do you mind taking over the stakeout duty while I meditate?'

'No.'

'Thanks.'

Zed felt when Iris took over his body. He could not close his eyes, so he ignored his sight and focused on his mana. He wasn't sure what he was supposed to do exactly, but thought it might be interesting to focus on the smallest piece of mana he could. When he hadn't known anything about anything, Victoria told him he could think of stellar energy as magic or nanites. He was curious to know which it was.

'I think we can safely eliminate "magic", Zed, other than in the sense that "any sufficiently advanced technology is indistinguishable from magic". Everything we have heard and experienced suggests that it operates according to the laws of physics.'

'So that leaves nanites, I guess.'

'Not necessarily. Victoria may have just used a term you could grasp so you wouldn't overthink it.'

'So you're saying that everyone's been treating me like a baboon from day 1?'

'If so, can you blame her?'

Zed thought about responding but decided to let it go. Part of him was disappointed that he couldn't rely on what Victoria had said to guide his learning, but another was excited to explore and find out for himself. He looked at the streams of mana flowing through his body, but as he focused on a smaller and smaller area it became difficult to make sense of the flow, much like how it would be challenging to keep a fast-moving microbe in the center of a microscope's field of view. He shifted his mana sight to his dantian, the core in his abdomen where unused mana was stored.

It looked like a glowing ball of energy, unchanging and unmoving. As he looked closer, though, he realized that he had been wrong. The mana was contained, yes, but it was constantly shifting. He had learned from his lessons with Iris that it is the nature of all things to seek the lowest energy state. As an extremely concentrated form of energy, the mana wanted to expand and fill the world and spread itself out as much as possible. It was only his will that constrained it.

Forced to stay within its confines, the mana always sought differences in concentration, rushing to fill areas that, for a moment, had a little less mana. Thus, it was always in flux, achieving equilibrium through constant change.

Just like there were momentary regions of low mana concentration, there were regions of high concentration too. Every once in a while a particularly high concentration would manifest at the surface of the orb. Zed watched as one such region formed for a split second, causing a tiny jet of energy to shoot past the limits of the orb, until his will pulled it back in. It reminded him of a sun flare.

As he watched, he felt intimations of… well, he didn't know. But they felt true.

'*Matter is. Mana acts. It moves, and does. It changes. I am here to act, and not to be acted upon. My body is not what defines me. It is matter, which is fragile and changeable. My will is what uniquely defines me, and mana is an extension of my will…*'

Zed, for lack of a better word, *played* with the mana. He did not have a particular purpose in mind. He just interacted with it, much like how a child would create waves in a pool.

'*Zed, someone is leaving the estate.*'

Zed "woke up" from his meditative state and returned his attention to his senses. Iris immediately released control of his body when she sensed the shift.

Zed watched a carriage pulled by two white horses leave the estate, passing by a liveried servant holding the gate open. The sun had long since fallen, but that didn't keep Zed from seeing the conveyance clearly with his night vision. Its curtains were closed, so Zed could not see who was inside.

177

The carriage passed Zed's tree, and the servant closed the gate. Zed dropped to the ground and trotted fast enough to keep up with it. While he ran he pulled out his communicator.

"Leilani?"

"Yeah?"

"I'm following a carriage. I don't know who's in it. Take over watching the front of the estate."

"Okay."

The carriage rumbled along on the stone road. Zed thought about running on the tree-strewn side of the road that the álfar made to look like a piece of forest. It would be softer on his feet, though there would be branches and pine cones and such.

'No reason to complicate things,' he thought. *'Better to just stick to the level road.'*

Following the carriage became trickier when it merged into other traffic headed downtown, so he jumped up to the roof of a one-story building using mana shifting and kept up with it from the rooftops while staying half a block behind.

It eventually pulled up to a fancy restaurant named "Singala's". The front of the restaurant was well-illuminated by iron lanterns with glow spheres inside.

Doors opened on both sides of the carriage and Sylvanus and an older gentleman stepped out. Sylvanus was easy to recognize because of his face and the elaborate robe he wore with the sect's tree symbol in gold stitching.

The other álfar wore silk pants and tunic. Elaborate stitching that suggested tree branches adorned the neck, hem, and wrists of the tunic.

Once he was out, Sylvanus turned and took a smaller and more delicate hand in his own. An álfar woman stepped out, holding the hem of her dress up while exiting to avoid catching it on the doorway. There was a strong resemblance between her and the older álfar.

'Likely her father,' Zed mused. *'I wonder if they're Sylvanus' relatives or if Dad is trying to get Sylvanus interested in his daughter?'*

'You're really setting me up for a redneck joke, Zed, but out of respect for your Southern heritage, I'll refrain.'

'Thanks, Iris,' Zed thought as he rolled his eyes.

The trio stepped into the restaurant and Zed noted the time. He didn't have long to do it, but he wanted to find patterns of behavior to help plan the assassination.

'About that, Zed. What if we didn't assassinate him?'

At the thought, Zed's contract gave warning signs.

'What are you talking about, Iris? You know I'm under contract.'

'Yeah, but I'm not. Okay, hypothetically *speaking, what if we didn't kill him? Sylvanus is from the Ever-Fruitful Tree sect, the same one that Silwan is from. The same one that has information about how to form binding contracts. He is probably an important member of the sect, given that Silwan considers him a rival. Chances are good that he has access to the mana contract technique. At the very least he should know who would have it.'*

'Yeah, that makes sense.'

'So, hypothetically speaking, we could capture him and pump him for information. Once you know how to make contracts, maybe you could figure out how to break them too.'

Zed expected his contract to flare up at that point, but there was nothing.

'Huh,' Zed thought. *'Come to think of it, Silwan didn't put anything into the contract about trying to get out of it. That's not the kind of mistake that the Silwan I know would make.'*

'Perhaps contracts don't allow you to put stipulations like that in?' Iris guessed.

'Maybe.'

It was something to think about, and was the only lead he had so far on how to get out of his contract. That alone made it worth pursuing. For now, though, he needed to take care of business. He contacted Leilani and Annis.

"I've confirmed that I'm tailing Sylvanus. He's with a woman and a man who I think are probably father and daughter. Leilani, you can go home or do whatever. We'll switch to using a single scout since it doesn't look like they are doing anything to avoid tails. I'll finish this surveillance, and then Annis will take over for eight hours. Leilani had the longest shift today, so I will take the eight hours after Annis, and then Leilani after me. Each person will be on-call to help out if needed during the shift before theirs. Any questions?"

"No."

"No."

"Okay. Rest up, but be ready to come in if needed, Annis."

Annis grunted his affirmation and cut the line, as did Leilani.

'*Those two are real chatterboxes,*' Zed sighed. '*At least they aren't giving me any problems.*'

'*So far...*'

**

The tail back to the estate and the handoff to Annis went smoothly. Zed got some sleep back at the inn so he'd be fresh and ready to tackle a new day.

Zed was working with Phineas on the amino acid tattoos when he saw that Annis was trying to contact him.

"Zed, this is Annis. Target has gone to lunch with his lady friend—presumably the same one as last night."

"Light blond hair, about as tall as his shoulders?"

"That's the one. They're at a place called 'Cafe Rinaldo'."

"How did they get there?"

"Fancy carriage pulled by two white horses. Curtains were closed."

"Which side did he sit on?"

"Left."

'*Same as last night.*' "Did he help her out of the carriage?"

"Yes."

"Which hand did he use?"

"Um, I think his right hand."

'*Same as last night. Probably right-handed.*' "Okay, thanks."

Zed went back to working on the tattoo. A half hour later he saw that Silwan was trying to contact him. He answered the call.

"Yeah, Silwan?"

"I just found out that Sylvanus will be attending a ball in three days."

"Okay. And?"

"And nothing. I just wanted to let you know in case it affected your plans."

"Hmm. This Sylvanus seems like quite the social butterfly. Could you get me and Leilani invitations to the ball?"

"Yes."

"Do that then, please. I may not use them, but it would be good to have the option. Where will the ball be at?"

"The mayor's house."

"Okay. Thanks for letting me know."

Zed called up Annis and Leilani.

"Change in plans. I'm following up on a new lead. You guys will tail the target in 12-hour shifts." Zed heard grumbles over the line.

"What will you be doing?" Leilani asked. "Sunning yourself and taking long walks on the beach? Or maybe visiting the local brothels?"

"Not quite, Leilani. Silwan just informed me that Sylvanus will attend the mayor's ball in three days. I'm going to scout out the mayor's house and see if there are any opportunities to be had. Perhaps you should go with me, Leilani. After all, you'll be my date to the ball."

"What?! No! I could never go with you!"

Annis laughed uproariously.

Chapter 26

'You're a deliveryman again?' Iris said. *'Don't you think you're developing a pattern? And a rather boring one at that?'*

'If it ain't broke, don't fix it, Iris.'

Zed was riding shotgun in a cart that Annis was driving. In the cart were various fruits, grains, and herbs they were taking to the mayor's mansion. Zed had figured that the ball would require a lot of consumables, so he temporarily stopped their surveillance of the target to waylay one of the deliveries.

Zed took pains to not hurt the original driver and to not let him see their faces. He was now relaxing on a chair in their safehouse with Leilani. Tied and blindfolded, to be sure, but with Leilani it was just as well. As far as Zed was concerned they were doing the man a favor.

Before leaving, Zed had told the driver that if all went well, he would be free in a few hours and quite a bit richer. Though it would be a stretch to say the man was happy when Zed left, he was at least no longer trembling.

Zed used his time in the cart to go over the plan he and Iris had devised together.

"Zed, why are we bothering with this ball?"

"Because it could be a good opportunity to kill the target."

"Why not just kill him during one of his carriage rides?"

"We could, but it's not ideal. He rides with the shades drawn, so we never know if he's even in the carriage until he gets out."

"We could just kill him when he gets out."

"Yeah, but there's the whole issue of him having a life-saving device. We can't just kill him from a distance. We have to get up close, trigger the device, and then carry him away. The ball may be a good opportunity to do that."

Annis shrugged. "Okay."

Zed kept thinking about the plan. He knew he needed to be disguised for it to work, but he hated to do it in front of Annis. They were getting close to the estate so he had to do something soon.

"Hey, Annis, I think I know how I want you to pay me back for hooking you up with your lady friend."

Annis smiled and got a far-off look. "Yeah, that was pretty good."
He snapped out of it and looked over to Zed. "So what do you need?"

"I want you to keep a secret."

Annis grinned. "Now this sounds interesting. What kind of secret?"

"One of my abilities."

Zed tuned Iris out to the best of his ability when she started grumbling in a mock imitation of his voice, *'We're a team, Iris...'*

Annis looked pensive. "I have a pretty good guess about who you want me to keep it a secret from. You should be aware that with my contract, I would have to tell him if he asks me. I would have to tell him if I even thought it was important for him to know." Annis looked sour at this point.

"You have a contract too?"

"Almost everyone in the sect has a contract. Leilani does. I do. Alain sure as hell does. Why do you think the old grump is so bitter? Hell, it wouldn't surprise me if Silwan had one too, even though he's one of the young masters of the sect."

'Huh. Well isn't that interesting...' Zed thought.

"Oh well", he said. "You're right. I wanted to keep this from Silwan, but whatever. Just do your best, I guess." Zed disguised himself as a fat álfar when they weren't being observed. The next time that Annis looked at him, he did a double-take.

"That's a good trick." Annis grinned. "I'll keep it a secret if you tell me how you did it."

Zed just smiled. When the cart approached the mayor's estate, he observed as best he could. He could only see the mansion's upper floors, as a thick hedge hid everything else. It was obvious, though, that the mansion was large and ornate. The álfar equivalent of gargoyles decorated the balconies and rooflines to provide water drainage. Instead of Earth's tradition of hideous figures, there were sprites conjuring fountains, fish, and stylized trees, with water running off the roots. Well-maintained ironwork provided beauty and safety to the balconies and windows.

'I get the feeling this house will be harder to break into, Zed.'

'Which is why we're not going to break into it.'

They were let in by servants and directed to the servant entrance of the house. A wagon pulled by a Clydesdale was parked in front of the servants' door. The horse placidly munched on greenery in a flower bed while the driver and servants lifted barrels out of the wagon and carried them into the house. Annis brought the cart up as close as he could, and he and Zed started hauling the foodstuffs into the mansion.

While working, Zed did his best to figure out the mansion's floor plan. He flared out his sensor field as far as it would go to detect anything his eyes couldn't see—the mansion's security systems in particular.

What he saw with his eyes was not terribly impressive—not a big surprise, given that they were in the servants' section. His sensor field, on the other hand, detected mana-based security systems that were a little frightening. They were more intricate than what he saw at the Elstad's house, and he didn't know what most of it did.

Zed's plan was to slip off in the middle of the unloading and either use camouflage to hide or disguise himself as one of the servants. He would then sneak off into the unoccupied parts of the house and lay low until the house went quiet at night. He became concerned when he realized there was never a moment when they weren't seen by at least one servant. Just as bad, one of the cooks was holding the door to the mansion open, so she would see that the cart left with only one person if he stayed.

'*We need to abort, Zed.*'

Thinking fast, Zed thought, '*No, we don't. We're going to change the plan. I'm going to use the sensor field on the door locks. I want you to record what we sense.*'

'*Okay. Recording.*'

As Zed walked in and out he brushed his hands on doors and tried to linger a bit by the lock. He was able to get the servants' door, the kitchen door, and a couple more doors that led to the rest of the mansion.

'*Iris, you can manufacture keys for those doors, right?*'

'*You mean...?*'

'*Yeah.*'

'*Gross, Zed. That's not what the stomach is for.*'

'*What good is having Skynet in my head if I can't do a hack or two? And weren't you the one convincing me to poop in the river?*'

'*That was just returning the river silt to the river.*'

'*Can you do it or not?*'

'*Yes,*' she sighed.

'*Good.*' After a pause, he thought, '*Make sure there are no sharp edges. And make some oil too. Lots of oil.*'

**

After they finished unloading, Annis and Zed took the cart to the safe house where they were keeping the driver. They untied his hands, instructed him to not leave the house or take off his blindfold until he had counted to 100, and not speak of the whole affair, on pain of death. As compensation, they left him 100 gold in the cart.

The team watched the house until they were out of sight. Seeing that the driver didn't do anything stupid, Zed and Leilani headed to the inn, and Annis resumed his shift at the surveillance post.

"I appreciate your help, Leilani."

Leilani didn't respond.

Shrugging, Zed focused on how to manufacture the key.

'So, how's it going with the lock scans you recorded?'

'Good. I have good news, in fact. It looks like the mayor has a master key that can open all the doors in the house. I can make you a partial master that should open a lot of doors, but not all of them.'

'Nice! So we'll only have to make one key?' He was thrilled that he wouldn't have to pass four of them.

'Yes, but there is one problem.'

'What is it? We have plenty of iron, right?'

'Yes, we have plenty of iron. The problem is that they used a different master lock system than Earth. Are you familiar with how locks work?'

'Not really.'

'The key has teeth at different heights because they are pushing up pins at just the right height, so the place where they are cut in half lines up at the edge of the lock's cylinder. When they are all lined up, you can rotate the key and cylinder, and open the lock.'

'Okay.'

'When Earth has master keys, they usually do it by cutting the pins at a second place, one cut is for the regular key, and the other is for the master key. Either one will open the lock. That way you can make the master lock open all the locks, but give people keys that will only open up certain doors.'

'So the master key and the regular key push the pins up a different amount, but there's a cut in the pins at both places, so they both work?'

185

'Right. Well, the problem is that the mayor's house does it a different way. The pins are only cut in one place, but not all the pin locations are used. The servant door to the house had eight pin locations but only used five of them, so any key that had the right five would work. The kitchen door used those five and a sixth, so any key that opened the kitchen door would also open the servant door, but not vice versa.'

'Alright.'

'The locks to the rest of the house were a little different too. The good news is that I can give you a partial master key. It will probably open a lot of doors in the house, but not all of them.'

'So what's the bad news?'

'The bad news is that the mayor's system is much less compact than Earth's, so the keys are rather… large.'

Zed gulped. 'Just how large are we talking here, Iris?'

'Like a deck of cards.'

"A deck of cards!" Zed started sweating.

'Well, a little longer than a deck of cards.'

'Longer?!'

Iris' cartoon avatar appeared holding a key with a translucent outline of Zed next to her.

'Don't worry. If it gets stuck, I can shove it through.' The avatar grunted and sweated as it pushed the enormous key through Zed's intestines, the intestines bulging out.

Zed felt a little faint. Then he had a suspicion.

'Wait. You're just messing with me, aren't you?'

The cartoon avatar, key, and Zed cartoon all disappeared, and Iris laughed.

'Maybe a little.'

'You suck, Iris.'

'Rude. Is that how you talk to a lady?'

'Ladies don't joke about shoving things through my colon.'

'Then maybe you shouldn't ask me to put things in your colon.'

Zed was going to respond, but when he thought about it he realized she had a point. 'Fair enough. So how big is the key really?'

'I was serious about the key being larger than Earth keys, but not too much larger. You'll live, but it won't be pleasant.'

Zed grimaced. The things he did for his people.

186

Chapter 27

Zed arrived at the mayor's estate around 1 AM, his camouflage in place. He'd been thinking while walking about how to deal with the hedge around the estate, and he hadn't come up with a good solution. He could jump over it or climb it, but he didn't know how to ensure that no one would see him if he jumped or hear him if he climbed.

He could use the silence field if he climbed, but it had a limited range and some of the shaking branches would be outside that range. Shifting his mass wouldn't be that helpful either. He needed to have low inertia *and* gravity to climb up the hedge quietly.

He was tempted to enter over the ironwork front gate that he could see through, but it seemed foolish to enter the one place that was sure to be watched or have protections in place.

'*I have to admit, Iris, after feeling like a superhero for so long, it's a little humbling to be given so much trouble by a bush.*'

Iris chuckled but didn't otherwise respond.

Zed decided that his best option was to jump over the hedge while camouflaged in as secluded a place as he could find, and hope no one saw him.

'*And if someone does see you?*' Iris asked.

'*Then I kill him and store him in the ring.*'

Iris did not respond, but he got the sense that she disapproved. He thought about justifying the decision to her, but decided not to.

He sighed and thought, '*Why bother when I don't approve either?*'

Zed prepared himself by spinning up the laser without activating it. He then leapt over the hedge by shifting his mass to high inertia, low gravity. He quickly scanned the grounds while in the air with his night and infrared vision, and saw a guard, causing his stress to spike. He then saw that the guard was walking away from him, so he calmed down but still kept an eye on the guard.

Zed's camouflage and silence had been active the entire time, so he landed noiselessly. With some of his mental capacity taken by Iris it was a strain to maintain so many techniques simultaneously, but for very short periods he could do it. Since no one was in sight besides the one guard, he dissipated the laser. He had already shifted his mass back to normal after he crossed the hedge, leaving only the camouflage and silence.

Having more experience with his silence field and having learned to trust it, Zed moved quickly to the servant's door. It was a solid, oak door with a brass handle, but that wasn't what had Zed's attention. With his mana senses, he could feel an array of mana that was far more complex than what he had found at the Elstad's.

'If the real keys are more than mechanical, I'm screwed,' Zed thought.

'That would be super expensive,' Iris said. *'Would they really give keys that expensive to the servants?'*

'Hopefully not.'

Zed pushed in the key and, with a moment's hesitation, tried to turn it. He was surprised when it refused to turn, but after he shifted it around, it finally went.

Zed was stressed out enough that he thought about making a snide comment to Iris about the key, but knew that he would regret it.

'I'm not a locksmith, you know,' Iris said.

'I know. Sorry, Iris. Without you, this plan wouldn't have worked at all.'

'As long as you understand how awesome I am.'

Zed had not heard any alarms and didn't see any changes in the mana array, so hopefully all was well. He opened the door, entered, and locked the door behind him.

The hallway was well-lit by glow bulbs on the walls. Zed was surprised at how bright the inside of the house was, but he quickly realized that there were no windows in the hallway, so it would have to be lit all day. He didn't like how the light made him feel exposed.

Zed walked over to the door at the end of the hall and unlocked it, after rattling the key around again. The silence field encompassed the lock, preventing any noise from escaping.

The door opened into a large dining room, with a table and chairs that could seat 50 people. The table was made of two live wood slabs that ran the whole length of the table. It fit with the álfar aesthetic of reminding one of their arboreal days. The lighting in the room was plentiful but dimmer, giving a more romantic atmosphere.

Large double-doors in the middle of the three other walls were closed. Zed made a quick circuit around the room and checked each door, peaking through when he could. The door to the right was locked. The door at the far end of the room led to a garden atrium with a fountain. The door on the left was the ballroom.

'*Found it.*'

The ballroom was enormous. In the middle of the room was a large, marble tree. The tree divided the rectangular room into two square spaces. An enormous chandelier with hundreds of crystals presided over each of the two spaces. Circular tables stayed near the shelter of the walls, as if afraid to venture into the middle. That space was clearly reserved for the dancers.

Now that Zed saw what he had to work with, he could start making plans. He noted the double doors in the inner section leading to the atrium.

'The only exits from the ballroom are to the atrium and the dining room. The atrium provides more cover, but it's also the center of the mansion.'

Zed had already seen the dining room, so he slipped out to the atrium and looked around. It was filled with fragrant flowers, bushes, and small trees, with a small fountain in the middle. Statues of noble-looking álfar overlooked the pathways through the garden here and there.

The mansion surrounded the atrium on all sides. Many balconies stretched into it to enjoy its serene verdure. Zed made sure that he looked at every area, knowing that Iris was recording everything.

He was about to slip back into the ballroom when a couple walked into the garden, holding hands. Zed stayed still to maximize his camouflage.

They looked young, even for álfar. They sat down on a bench and whispered to each other. Zed couldn't hear what they were saying, but from their shy smiles and blushes he got the gist of the young lovebirds' conversation. Though he was impatient to move on, Zed decided that there were worse ways to spend his time than watching the two.

Zed stiffened when a guard appeared on the opposite side of the atrium, but the guard simply smiled when he saw the young álfar. He was about to turn away when he looked at Zed. There was no eye contact, but he was clearly looking in Zed's direction when he looked alarmed and started trotting over. Zed shifted 10 feet to the side, but the guards' eyes followed him. The young couple gasped when they realized the guard was there. Zed would have laughed if he wasn't so stressed.

'*Iris, how does he see me? He's too far away to sense my mana.*'

'*He likely sees your infrared signature.*'

'*How? I've been cooling my body down inside the silence field!*'

'*He probably just sees your head, which is why he hasn't called an alarm. He doesn't know what's going on yet. The closer he gets though, the more likely he'll be able to see the rest of your body if it's a little warmer or colder than the ambient temperature.*'

'*Damn it! Iris, I'm going to cover everything with the silence field. Take over the cooling and make it the same temperature as everything else.*'

'*Give me control of the silence too. In fact, give me control over everything, including your body. To make your body cool enough I'm going to have to make the air even colder than ambient. The silence field will have to be very tight against your body or else he will see a dark halo around you. I need to control your movement so your body and the field will be in sync.*'

'*Do it!*'

Zed felt Iris take control. He could still access all his senses, but Iris was controlling movement and mana. She hardened and contracted the silence field, crushing his clothes against his body.

Then it got cold. Real cold. Zed felt himself move to the side, and was gratified to see that the guard looked confused and did not continue to track him. The guard slowed as he looked around.

Zed moved 20 meters farther down the wall, stored his shoes and socks in the ring, and then wall crawled up.

'*I think it's time to go, Zed.*'

'*100% agree.*'

Iris wall crawled up way faster than Zed would have, or even could have.

'*What's the rush, Iris?*'

'*We have no air.*'

'*Oh. Can't you go any faster?*'

'*Maybe if I didn't have a backseat driver,*' she said grumpily.

In what seemed like forever, but was really only eleven seconds— Zed watched the clock in real-time—Iris climbed past the third story and reached the roofline. Once they were almost to the roof ridge, Iris quietly dropped down and said, '*Are you ready to take over again?*'

'Yes.'

Control of his body returned, and he gasped a little as his body sucked in badly needed air. Zed quickly stifled it and got his breathing under control. His lungs were burning and regeneration could only help so much. Air and time were required.

Zed didn't want to take the minutes that he would need to really feel better, so he forced himself to get up and continue on.

In short order he was sailing through the air, with gravitational mass shifted way down.

'I guess I'm getting predictable in my scouting methods and my exits, Iris.'

'Tell me about it.'

**

That evening Zed had a crisis of confidence.

'It seems like you do everything better than I do, Iris. Do I bring anything to this partnership of ours?'

Her "real" avatar appeared and grinned at him. *'You mean, do you bring anything besides a smoking hot body, and occasionally witty repartee?'*

Zed grimaced, but appreciated her attempt to make him feel better. *'Yes, besides that.'*

'No, not really.'

'Thanks,' he said sourly.

'I'm only kidding. Yes, you are better at some things than I am.'

'Like what?'

'You understand people better than I do.'

'That's it?'

'No, that's not all, but you should understand how big a deal that is. People are very complicated. It's easier with you because I can hear your thoughts, but it is very difficult for AIs like me to read other people. You are very subtle creatures, and that's before getting into deception, which you guys do All. The. Freaking. Time! It's very frustrating for me. You have had millions of years of evolution of deception and counter-deception to help you see through this stuff. If you guys have a hard time seeing through it, imagine what it's like for me.'

'Huh. I never thought about that.'

191

'That's because you guys are also very self-centered.'

Though he couldn't deny the truth of that, he still felt annoyed. '*I thought this talk was about making me feel better.*'

'*No, that's what you* thought *it was about. Like I said, I'm not very good at deception, and I don't think that's what you need right now anyway.*'

Zed was about to ask, "what do I need then?" but quickly realized it would be stupid. If he didn't need deception, then obviously her answer would be "the truth".

'*So what is the truth, Iris?*'

'*The truth is that you understand people way, way better than I do, and you do it as naturally as breathing. Let me give you an example. Earth was in the early stages of creating AI when you left. One of the early implementations was self-driving cars. The cars did pretty well with lanes, and signs, and static things like that. What they didn't handle well was people.*'

'*Because they were unpredictable?*'

'*Yes, but it goes deeper than that. The AI drivers had a particularly hard time at four-way stops.*'

'*To be fair, I know a lot of humans that don't know how to handle them either.*'

'*Sure, but they still probably got through. AIs had a hard time doing that when other cars were around. Do you know why? It was because people are aggressive, and they often play a little game of "chicken" without even realizing they are doing it. The AIs did the logical thing of playing it safe and letting the other person go first. After all, a small chance of a crash is much worse than waiting a few seconds.*'

'*Okay. So what's wrong with that?*'

'*What's wrong is that they let one person through, then another, then the next one, and so on. Each individual decision was logical, but the end result was far from ideal. Ogden Nash came up with a branch of math called "game theory". One of the surprising results of it was that being purely logical in competitive games is often a losing strategy, because it makes you predictable. It helps to be just a little bit crazy.*

'*Humans have had competitiveness bred into them over millennia,*' Iris continued, '*to the point where you take advantage of weakness without even thinking about it, like in the four-way stop. And in this, AIs are weak.'*

'I'm not sure I like your conclusions about us humans, but they do make a certain sense,' Zed thought. *'So I guess the message here is that I haven't been doing my job in taking advantage of you enough?'*

'Yes!' Iris put her hands on her hips and playfully pouted. *'I've even been trying to get you to take advantage of me, and nothing!'*

'You goof,' Zed chuckled.

'There is one more thing you have over me though.'

'Oh yeah? What's that?'

'While my fine control of mana is better, your willpower is stronger. I have noticed that you can push your mana fields farther than I can. It seems that Victoria had more reasons than you knew for choosing you.'

'Interesting.' Though he trusted Iris, he had to admit that it made him feel better to know that he wouldn't necessarily be at her mercy if it came to a struggle between them. *'Not that I want that, of course,'* he thought for Iris' sake. It was weird and more than a little uncomfortable for him to be a completely open book to her.

'You see? Deception is built into your genes. It feels weird and wrong to you when you can't do it. And don't worry. I know that you are mostly fond of me and don't want to fight, and I feel the same.'

While Zed thought that would make him feel better, it didn't. He wasn't sure why, so he thought about it. He became even more discomfited when he realized that the reason was because if he ever decided that things had changed, that they needed to fight, she would know it instantly. There would be no hiding it.

'And she can hear these thoughts, right now.' Zed grimaced. Being so open with Iris was wonderful... and awful.

He tended not to think such things, because she heard everything, but Iris felt like his confidante, lover, and jailer. It was a weird relationship that was useful as hell, kept him from going crazy from loneliness, and icked him out. He both loved and hated Iris, and felt guilty for hating her because she had only helped him and been his friend. It wasn't even her fault, really, that she was so up in his grill.

It just was what it was. Even if it sucked.

Chapter 28

Zed woke up at almost noon the next day. He had been up late with Iris last night, going through her holographic reconstruction of the mansion and making plans. He was cautiously optimistic that a plan was coming together.

'I'm glad you're feeling good about this, Zed, but just remember that, 1) not only do we need to capture Sylvanus, 2) we have to make everyone else—including Leilani, your helper—think that he's dead, 3) while not dying or being captured yourself, and 4) not putting yourself or Leilani under suspicion. There are a number of elements that we still haven't covered.'

'You're such a downer, Iris.'

'Well someone has to temper your irrational exuberance.'

'"Irrational exuberance?" You're quoting Alan Greenspan now? You should know that Alan Greenspan and "smoking hot" are light years away from each other.'

'Whatever. You're just intimidated because I have looks and a brain. Besides, maybe I'm into old white men. I'm into you, after all.'

Zed couldn't help but laugh, though he also felt uncomfortable.

Zed and Iris continued to work on their plan, refining it and working in solutions to cover all of the necessary objectives. It was not complete, but it was getting closer.

He was tired of planning and being cooped up in his room, so he decided to spend the rest of the day on errands to prepare for those parts of the plan they had ironed out. One of those was learning how to dance.

While he didn't look forward to calling Leilani and ordering her to practice with him, the actual practicing might be amusing.

"Hey, Leilani."

"What."

Technically the word was a question, but she didn't make it sound like a question. That's because she was really making a statement, and the statement was, "Go away, asshole."

'I read you loud and clear, Leilani.' "We need to practice dancing together. Do you know how to dance?"

"No."

"Okay, well, be ready to practice this afternoon. I'll call you when I find someone to teach us."

'Why don't you just go with Constance, Zed?'

'Too dangerous. Silwan would kill me if something happened to her. Leilani is expendable, like me.'

"Do we have to? Couldn't we just mingle at the ball? No offense, but I'd rather not touch you."

Zed laughed. Not because he was amused, but at the sheer arrogance of the woman. "That's okay. I'm used to being the only one enjoying it when I'm with a woman. Make sure to wear something sexy."

"Ugh." Zed laughed again at the disgust dripping from her voice right before she hung up.

'I don't think she likes you, Zed.'

'Ya think?'

'If you keep pushing her like this, chances are good she will try to kill you at some point.'

'I know.'

'I'm sensing some pretty fatalistic thoughts coming from you.'

Zed thought about it and said, *'Part of me doesn't care. And yes, I know that's a worrying sign. Part of me is pissed off that she considers me to be only a half-step above an animal.'* Zed paused, and then sighed. *'And the last part of me wants a reason to kill her.'*

'That's pretty dark, Zed. Love the self-awareness, but it's dark.'

'What happened to Miss "I'm such a logical AI that I don't understand people"? Don't you think killing her is the logical thing to do?'

'Yes.'

Zed was surprised at the starkness of her answer.

'So why have you been encouraging me to not kill people?'

'Because I see what it does to you. Remember when I told you that I monitor your health and well-being as part of my function?'

'Yeah.'

'I see what killing people does to your biochemistry and your thoughts. It tears you up inside.'

'Huh.'

Zed had really thought that Iris was living by some ethical philosophy, but it turned out that she had just been looking out for

195

him. He honestly wasn't sure what he thought about that. If he got comfortable with killing, would she stop trying to discourage it? That would be when he would most want her to try to talk him out of it.

'*What happened to my Jiminy?*' he thought sadly.

**

Much as he would have liked to rest, time waited for no man. He had a lot to do, including buying an outfit for the ball, picking up a corpse, hiring a cart driver, and renting another safe house.

Oh, and finding a dance instructor. With all that he had lined up, he ended up not finding one until the next day. He met Leilani and the instructor, an álfar woman named Callista, in the original safe house, where they had kept the cart driver.

Zed was feeling rather spiffy in his new outfit. He'd had to pay extra to have it altered quickly, and It had more lace and ruffles than he had seen, well, ever. The shopkeeper assured him that this look was all the rage right now, and he had taken her word for it. He had decided to think of himself as an upscale pirate rather than a lacy fop.

'*Does this mean we'll get to loot and pillage soon?*' Iris asked.

'*Hmm. I don't know about that, but how does "kidnapping and creating havoc" sound?*'

'*It will have to do, I guess,*' she said with an exaggerated sigh.

When Zed saw Leilani in one of her sect robes he frowned, and as if he was thinking really hard, said, "That wasn't *quite* the look I was thinking of. I was picturing something with a long skirt, backless, and plunging neckline, Leilani."

Her eyes narrowed, and her nostrils flared in anger. "That is never going to happen."

"We can cover up the skin if you insist," Zed said, still joking, and then he let his face express what he really felt—flinty, and a little angry himself. "But you will wear something appropriate for the ball, or we're going to have a problem."

Leilani huffed and looked away.

'*Not the ideal response, but at least it's not open defiance,*' Zed thought.

The next two hours were awkward. As physically talented as Leilani was, her revulsion and stiffness made for awkward dancing.

196

They finally made some progress when Zed asked her, "Do you want everyone to think that you're a terrible dancer?"

Then he just had to work with her always trying to lead. The two of them were never going to win any prizes, but at least they wouldn't look out of place.

**

That night in his room, Zed and Iris reviewed the plan and their preparations.

'*So what am I missing, Iris?*'

'*The explosion.*'

'*Right! Have to find somewhere to practice it...*'

Zed was really starting to miss the forest he started out in, and his house with the courtyard in Formenos. For a lot of this stuff you needed a space that you didn't mind charring up a bit.

It was almost enough to make him want to buy a place here in Harlond. Almost. Although he was wealthy again, thanks to the missions that Silwan sent him on, most of it was in goods that were dangerous to convert into liquid assets, the goods being connected to crimes. A significant portion of the funds he did have were tied up in the kidnapping plan, leaving him wealthy but feeling destitute.

'*No one knows how difficult it is to be a rakishly handsome pirate, Iris.*'

'*The fact that you're still wearing the outfit would almost lead one to think that you like it, Zed.*'

'*I just want to get used to it. I'm going to have to move quickly and surely in it tomorrow night.*'

'*Yeah. Sure, Zed. It's okay to admit that you like the lace and ruffles. I won't tell anyone,*' Iris teased.

'*Hush,*' Zed thought as he hurriedly changed into his normal clothes.

While getting ready to go out, Zed thought about where he could practice blowing things up. He was tired and just wanted to get on with it, so he thought, 'Screw it,' and went out into the plains a mile away from the city.

The new technique was going to be a combination of a plasma ball and a silence field.

Zed started with a spherical silence field in front of him, and then started heating up the air inside it until it became an electric-purple plasma.

When Zed threw plasma balls, they tended to expand and spread, creating a larger but cooler ball as it traveled. That's why they were only useful up to a range of 50 yards, at most. The silence barrier held the ball in tight until it dissipated, creating a longer lasting ball that, he hoped, would explode if it struck something quickly. The idea was that it would expand quickly, all at once, instead of gradually.

Zed's first few attempts were duds. Though they did last a little longer and fly a little farther, when they hit the target there wasn't much of an explosion.

'*I think you need to make the silence barrier stronger, Zed. The secret to explosions is containing them, so when they finally make or find a hole, they explode out.*'

Zed tried that, and while it did create more of a "bang", it still wasn't what he had been hoping for.

'*I think the problem is that the plasma is fizzling out,*' Zed thought.

'*What do you mean?*'

'*As soon as I throw the plasma ball, even if it's not expanding, it's still cooling down, just not as fast.*'

'*How do you know?*'

'*It has to be. It's emitting x-rays, ultraviolet rays, light, and infrared, right?*'

'*Yeah.*'

'*Well, since the mana isn't adding energy anymore, the energy is constant. If it is emitting energy, then there has to be less energy in the plasma ball.*'

'*That makes sense,*' Iris said. '*Look at what a little physicist you've become! I'm so proud of you!*'

Zed was pleased at her praise, but also felt like a kid that was being complimented by his mom.

'*Wait, did you know that this entire time?*' Zed asked.

'*Well, not the, uh, entire time,*' Iris mumbled.

'*Why didn't you tell me?*'

'*I knew you would figure it out eventually.*'

Zed was disappointed that he hadn't been the first one to figure it out, and embarrassed at how proud of himself he'd been initially. But then he thought, '*You know what? So what if I wasn't first. I'm still making progress and getting better at this.*'

'*That's a very mature attitude, Zed.*'

'*There's a first time for everything.*'

After discussing it, they came to the conclusion that the only way they could see to make it work right was to leave some mana in the plasma ball that would continue to heat it up. He hated to do it, since that would mean losing mana every time, but it was a price he'd have to pay if he wanted a proper explosion. That way the plasma would explode by overcoming the air barrier, rather than just coming apart less slowly than it did.

The first trial did not go well. Or perhaps it went too well. Zed wasn't sure how much mana to leave in, so he left in what he guessed was a good amount. The ball exploded 10 feet away, singeing his front and, not being braced for impact, knocking him backwards.

After Zed got back up, he looked at the tattered remains of his clothes and thought, '*Good thing I took off the pirate outfit.*'

'*I don't know. I kind of like this look, Zed.*'

Zed rolled his eyes and thought, '*Only guys are supposed to be that pervy, Iris.*'

'*Well, I am in your brain, so maybe you're rubbing off on me.*'

'*So if I do something, it's my fault. And if you do something... that's also my fault?*'

'*Exactly!.*'

Zed shook his head in exasperation and got back to experimenting. He realized that the strength and location of the explosion depended on three factors: the strength of the air barrier, the temperature of the plasma, and the amount of lost mana. The mana he lost would eventually go inert, but for a time it continued to obey his last command.

'*I think we can reduce those three factors to two, Zed. How much stronger the air barrier is than the pressure of the plasma when you throw the ball, and how much mana you lose.*'

Zed nodded. '*Makes sense. If the pressure is close to overcoming the barrier when I throw it, it won't take much mana to make it explode quickly.*'

'*Right. Especially since the air barrier is breaking down.*'

With that insight Zed continued the experiments, more carefully this time. It took him a while to get it down, and it pained him to lose mana every time, but eventually he got it.

'*I think we're ready, Iris.*'

Chapter 29

Zed looked at Leilani while they traveled in the carriage. He didn't seek to talk with her. He just felt like looking, wondering if this would be the last day of her life. He realized it was kind of an odd way to think when it was him that might kill her.

'*I am becoming a monster, aren't I?*' he sighed.

Leilani, very pointedly, did not look at him. Instead she looked outside while they trundled along.

'*Do you think she'll stick to the plan?*' Iris asked.

'*I don't know. If she doesn't, there's still a chance I could pull it off.*'

'*It would be more risky.*'

'*Yeah.*'

It would also give him one more reason to kill her. Zed was pretty sure that killing her was the smart move, assuming Silwan didn't come after him for it—and Zed didn't think he would. That didn't mean it was the right thing to do. He knew that Leilani being stuffed to the gills with mana colored his thinking.

'*There's probably more mana in one of her pinkies than I wasted in my explosions yesterday,*' Zed thought.

'*Maybe we can ask her to donate a pinkie to the cause.*'

Zed chuckled. '*Now who's getting dark, Iris?*'

'*I'm sure I don't know what you're talking about. By the way, Zed, we're about halfway done with your mana muscles. After that we'll transform your nervous system, which means,*' she said in an innocent voice, '*that we could use a whole bunch more mana right about now.*'

Zed chuckled, causing Leilani to glance at him and look away, as if she intuited what he was thinking.

'*You're bad, Iris. What happened to my sweet, innocent girl?*'

'*She realized that the world is a complicated place. I was mostly joking, of course. I just want you to know that no matter what you decide to do, you won't get any judgment from me.*'

'*But I want judgment, Iris. I'm tired of living in gray areas. A little black and white would be nice. What do you think a neutral party would tell me to do?*'

'*An álfar or human third party?*'

'*Heh. Touché. I would respond with "ogrum", but I get the feeling that, as honorable as they are, their sense of ethics is not the same as ours.*'

After a moment Zed asked, '*What would my mom tell me?*'

'*I didn't know her.*'

'*You don't have access to my memories?*'

'*I... do. I've held off on going through them to give you some privacy.*'

'*Huh. Surprisingly thoughtful of you, Iris.*'

'*You don't think I'm thoughtful?*'

'*I didn't mean it like that. I just figured some combination of logic and curiosity would give you the justification you needed to go through them. Maybe you're more human than I thought.*'

'*Or maybe logic told me that chances are good that we would have this conversation someday,*' she responded.

Zed chuckled again. One of the things that he liked about Iris was that, in her own way, she held herself to a pretty high standard of honesty. It helped him to trust her.

'*Of course, that may be why she does it,*' a dark place in him thought. '*No. I'm not going down that endless rabbit hole. I don't know if Brutus loved me or if he was genetically programmed to act like he did. Either way, he was always there for me, and I will always love him.*'

"Must you keep looking at me?" Leilani asked in a tight voice.

"Sorry." Zed turned away to look outside the carriage as well. "I got lost in my thoughts."

Leilani visibly shuddered and said, "I do not wish to think about how disgusting those thoughts were." She turned to him and angrily said, "Keep your thoughts and your hands to where they should be tonight."

Zed looked at her and said, "Yes, ma'am. Any other orders?"

Leilani huffed and looked away again.

"Do you remember your role?" Zed asked.

"Yes."

"Don't screw it up."

**

Though Zed had already seen the ballroom, the place had been transformed. The chandeliers, impressive before, were now dazzling. The crystals sparkled like brilliant fireflies in the sky. The marble tree shone under the light, the light veining of the marble giving it a subtle texture and feeling of life. Its branches, brilliant on top, created a shadowy area underneath that gave the place an air of mystery.

Musicians in formal attire played lively music, and dancers glided along the floor. Zed was glad to see that the dance was the one that he and Leilani had practiced. They were worse than 80% of the dancers on the floor, but at least they wouldn't stand out.

Zed looked over the crowd but did not see their target. The musicians finished the song and the dancers politely clapped. Some of them walked to the edges of the room to get refreshments, and some stayed on the floor, waiting for the music to start again.

Zed held out his hand to Leilani and asked, "Shall we?" She didn't look pleased, but took his hand and walked out to the floor with him. They found an open area and turned to each other. Leilani moved into dancing position, with one arm high and forward to put on his shoulder and one to the side to clasp his hand, as if she was touching an invisible mannequin.

Zed sighed, seeing how stiff she was already. Deciding it was better to pick his battles, he moved into place, putting his shoulder under her hand and clasping her other hand. He was tempted to put his free hand lower than the traditional waist, but knew that it would be counterproductive and childish.

When the music started they kept it simple, simply doing the basic steps and getting into the rhythm of the music. Zed decided to get a little more ambitious and do a twirl. He raised the hand holding hers and, on the proper beat of the music, gave her waist a subtle push. Zed was almost surprised when she did, indeed, twirl—and rather gracefully at that. As he stepped towards her so they could come back into standard position, he gave her a genuine smile. It was not returned.

Their dancing sometimes went well and sometimes did not. It seemed to Zed that, as often as not, she was trying to lead him, pushing or pulling on his shoulder and hand. Zed didn't know how she saw the dance, but it seemed to him that for her it was a struggle for dominance rather than a partnership with roles.

203

'*Oh well,*' he thought. He hadn't expected the dancing to be fun anyway.

After two songs they left the dance floor and looked for drinks. They spent the next hour simply walking around, talking just enough between themselves and making small talk with others to not seem strange. Sylvanus arrived at the ball shortly after they stopped dancing. He was with the young, blonde álfar woman from the estate he was staying at.

Zed was nervous, and he wished that they could make their move and get this over with already. He waited, though, because he believed they had a better chance of success if they waited until people were more tired and tipsy.

Tired of talking with people he didn't know and dance-struggling with Leilani, Zed amused himself by looking at people. It was easy to pick out the mayor, though Zed had never seen him before. He did a lot of glad-handing and boisterous greetings of guests, and large gestures as if he owned the place. Which, apparently, he did.

"When are we going to do this, Zed?" Leilani whispered.

"Later. Let's dance."

"Ugh. Fine."

Zed led her back out to the floor, put his hand on her waist, and guided her around the floor. The tune had a fast tempo, so all of the dancers moved faster. Zed initiated a turn to avoid a couple, only to bump into another.

The couple stopped, and the man, whose cheeks were flushed from alcohol, laid into Zed.

"Watch where you're going, oaf!"

Zed gave the man a miniature bow. "I apologize. It was my fault."

The álfar looked at him more closely and bristled.

"What is a scum like you doing here? Are you part of the entertainment? Are you going to turn into a dog?"

"No. Why? Is that your thing?"

'*Zed, you need to de-escalate this!*' Iris said.

"My *thing* is to see animals like you put into the ground. My grandfather killed hundreds of your kind," he said with a sneer.

Zed wanted to rip him to shreds. First verbally, and then maybe literally. But he couldn't.

"Good day, sir," he said, and turned back to Leilani and continued dancing with her, ignoring the laughs and scornful comments that he left behind.

'I'm proud of you, Zed.'

'Thanks.'

'Would you like to hear my favorite insults for people like him?'

'Sure.'

'I'd beat you, sir, but I'd infect my hands.'

Zed laughed, and Leilani looked at him like he was crazy.

'Stealing from Shakespeare now, Iris?'

'I prefer to think of it as "repurposing". How about this one? "Most ugly people are ugly from head to foot, but you are atrocious from hip to hip. You are a globe. I could find countries in you."'

'Certainly evocative, but it's a little long.'

'Some people cause happiness wherever they go. You, sir, cause happiness whenever you go.'

'Another classic. Amusing, but I want to hear your own work, Iris.'

'I'll work on it.'

Zed and Leilani danced a little longer and then took a break. After killing some more time, Zed leaned into Leilani and softly said, "Let's go."

Zed got up and walked into the atrium. The double doors had been open the entire night, allowing guests to wander in and out to enjoy the garden and the cool evening. Zed was tempted to watch Leilani play her role, but decided to trust her. If she screwed up, there wasn't anything he could do about it.

Zed moved away from the double doors and found an empty, heavily shadowed area. He then disguised himself as a heavily muscled ogrum, and stayed in the shadows.

A few minutes later Leilani walked into the atrium with Sylvanus following her. Zed had instructed her to dance with Sylvanus and tell him she had information regarding Silwan and the upcoming auction. She was then to lead him to a certain area in the atrium.

Leilani took him there, and even arranged it so Sylvanus' back was to Zed.

'It's go-time.'

Zed spun up the laser. No silence field this time. He wanted the laser to be as powerful as possible. He stood up and walked towards them. Unused to hearing his footsteps at moments like this, they sounded loud to him. He cringed at every one, but Sylvanus either didn't hear or didn't react. Zed cursed when Leilani looked at him over Sylvanus' shoulder, causing Sylvanus to start to turn around.

Zed dropped into a crouch and brought the laser up. He saw that a mana sphere popped up around Sylvanus as he turned.

'*Damn it!*'

Zed had to hope that whatever it was would not stop the laser. He aimed it at Sylvanus, created an invisible laser that could cut through steel like butter, and slid it across the álfar's neck.

Zed wasn't sure if it had worked or not until the head slowly toppled from the body that was dropping to the ground. The mana sphere winked out, but a new, unfamiliar, and incredibly potent mana field covered the head.

'*That must be the suspended animation.*'

Zed ran up to Leilani and acted like he was going to punch her. Leilani did something that impacted Zed in the chest like a sledgehammer from two meters away. It caused an explosion in his chest that shredded part of his lungs and heart.

The plan was to have a brief, staged fight wherein Zed would hurt Leilani enough to remove suspicion from her without doing any permanent harm. Shredding Zed's heart and lungs was not part of that plan.

Zed was angry. Angry at her for betraying him and at himself for letting it happen.

'*No more.*'

As he went flying back, Zed activated his mental speed up that slowed down subjective time. While it was an incredibly useful ability, it was extremely uncomfortable at the moment due to the damage that Leilani had done to him. He felt the blood starting to pour into his chest cavity in slow motion. He heard the sound of something crashing in the ballroom. He ignored all of that and focused on the task at hand.

He brought up the laser again and activated it, sliding the invisible beam across her neck. Though he had just seen it with Sylvanus, it was surreal to see the smoldering black line appear on her milky white skin. Unlike Sylvanus, when her head tumbled off of the collapsing body, there was no mana field to preserve it.

Zed dissipated the laser and ramped up his regeneration as quickly as he could. He would lose consciousness and die if his brain didn't get oxygenated blood. His mana-fiber muscles, on the other hand, didn't bother with things like blood or oxygen anymore. He could run and fight just fine until he lost consciousness.

Zed returned subjective time to normal and fell to the ground, having continued falling all this time from Leilani's hit. He heard shouts and screaming from the ballroom, followed by whistles carried by the house guards. With Sylvanus he had taken pains to aim the laser upwards to avoid hitting unintended targets. He didn't have the time for such niceties with Leilani. Apparently someone, or perhaps multiple someones, had paid the price.

Shrugging off everything that wasn't directly related to survival, Zed ignored the chaos and continued increasing the regeneration mana flows while picking himself up and running towards the two bodies.

Zed stored Leilani's head and body in his ring while doing his best to avoid the blood spurting from her neck. Zed stored Sylvanus' body, but when he tried to grab the head he found that he couldn't touch it. The glowing mana field around it wouldn't let him.

He tried to put the head in his ring by extending the ring's mana as far as it would go, but couldn't. A woman screamed elsewhere in the atrium.

'*Damn it!*' Zed cursed.

Zed and Iris had theorized that the head in suspended animation might be considered "mostly dead", which they hoped would be a loophole around the rule that nothing live could go in spatial storage. Given how Zed was struggling in vain to put the the head in the ring, Sylvanus was very much alive as far as it was concerned. Fortunately, they had made plans for this possibility.

Zed took out a backpack and shoved the head in by pushing on the mana field. He put it on and started scrambling up the building, parkour-style, with a combination of leaps to balconies and climbing up the iron-work railings. A crowd had formed below. Many of the people shouted, and some of them pointed up at Ogrum-Zed.

Zed heard a whistle blowing in the atrium and people shouting about an ogrum getting away.

'*One can only hope,*' Zed thought. '*How close are we to losing consciousness, Iris?*'

'*You'll be okay. I temporarily patched your heart to stop the blood loss. Your regeneration will take care of the rest.*'

'*Thanks.*'

Zed scrambled onto the roof. He ran, crouched below the nearest ridge line. Once he was around the far end of the ballroom, Zed pulled out álfar bones from his ring and dropped them onto the roof. He ran away and then used his plasma ball explosion technique to blow up the bones and roof.

Though he was biased, Zed thought it made quite a spectacle. The explosion blew the nearby section of the roof in, causing it to crash to the ball room below. A few of the bones followed. Most of them were scattered in all directions, some of them broken and charred.

The explosion was meant to serve two purposes: convince people that Sylvanus was dead and establish Zed's escape direction. Pretending that the bones were Sylvanus' was probably a non-starter since he didn't have another skeleton for Leilani, but it should still cause confusion.

No longer needing the ogrum disguise, Zed looked around and, not seeing anyone else, replaced the disguise with camouflage. He ran in a different direction towards the back of the estate. When he reached the edge of the roof he leaped off and shifted his mass to drift over the hedge. When he was past the hedge he shifted his mass back and dropped to the ground.

A cart and driver were nearby—the same driver that Zed and the team had briefly kidnapped and paid earlier. Zed had promised ten times the earlier compensation if he did another job for him. Zed ran over and put the backpack into the cart that already had a hodgepodge of things in it.

"You know where the safe house is, right?" Zed asked.

"Yes," the driver said nervously.

"Good. Don't look inside the backpack."

Zed tossed him a pouch full of gold and turned away. He leaped over the hedge again using his strength and mana shifting. He knew that guards would be starting to search the grounds and was worried about being seen. He hoped that the camouflage and drifting through the air, rather than being on the ground, would be enough to get him through.

Once he crossed the hedge, he saw three guards looking around. Remembering how the guard saw his camouflaged head the other day, Zed thought, *'Iris, take over and make me invisible to infrared!'*

'Okay.'

Zed was immediately disconnected from control over his body, though he still had access to all the senses. A deep chill pressed into his body, like someone had turned the A/C to 55°F. He also couldn't hear anything besides his own thumping heartbeat. It was surreal to drift through the night sky, cold and silent, as if he was in space itself, looking down on the world.

He did see a guard look up while he drifted through the sky, but the guard simply looked quickly and then continued searching the grounds.

Iris used the time in the air productively, taking off Zed's shoes and socks in preparation for wall-crawling. Right before they reached the mansion, Iris shifted their mass back to reduce inertia. The last thing they needed was to hit the building like a slow-moving cannonball.

They started falling quickly. Iris reached out to the building to grab onto it with wall-crawling and to use their arms like shock absorbers to arrest their movement. Once they had stopped moving, she started scrambling up the building.

Though Zed wasn't able to do anything about it, he felt his body's desperate need for air. *'Oh right, no air. Hurry, Iris.'*

'I'm trying,' she said in an annoyed tone.

They started halfway up the building, so it didn't take long to get to the roof. Once they were out of sight, Iris removed the silence barrier from around their head and sucked in a lungful of air.

She did not release control of the body to Zed. Instead, she hurried over to the atrium at the center of the mansion.

'Uh, Iris, why haven't you given me control?'

Zed was confident she had a reason, but he'd be lying if he said he wasn't worried at all.

'There will be guards and other mana users in the atrium. As soon as we're down I'll give you control.'

'Oh,' Zed thought, relieved to hear that she hadn't gone rogue. *'That makes sense. I, uh, noticed that we have blood on our hands. We need to do something about it.'*

'Sounds like it's time to make some amino acids.' While she continued walking towards the atrium, Iris activated their latest tattoo experiment. It created millions of mana constructs that took the organic compounds in the blood and turned them into lysine, with some hydrogen and trace elements left over.

209

They circled around and approached the atrium from the opposite end as where the assassination had taken place. After a quick look down into the courtyard, Iris stepped off the roof and simply dropped to the ground.

'Iris! What the hell!' Zed yelled internally.

A moment later Zed hit the ground and bent his knees to absorb the impact. The mana fibers and steel bones took it in stride, as if they had walked off of a curb.

Zed felt sheepish for having panicked and was tempted to cover it up with a joke, but decided instead to sit down on his bum and put on his shoes and socks.

'Kind of an anti-climax after everything else, but you gotta do what you gotta do,' he thought.

When he was done, he brushed himself off and walked over to the ballroom doors, faking distress. There was still a crowd of people looking at the site of the assassination, and where Zed had climbed up the wall. One of the guards looked at Zed suspiciously.

"You there! Where have you been?"

"I saw the ogrum kill that man and my date, and I hid in the atrium."

The guard looked disgusted, whether it was because he was a human or because of his hiding, Zed didn't know.

'I'll go with "Yes",' Iris said.

"Why did you stay back there after the ogrum left?"

"I was going to come back, but then I heard the explosion. I decided to stay hidden until I was sure he was gone."

The guard didn't look convinced, but nodded and turned his attention elsewhere.

Figuring the party was over, Zed grabbed an hors-d'oeuvre and made his way to the inn.

Chapter 30

Zed watched for people following him as he went back to the inn. He didn't notice any, so half an hour after he got back, he left again, still on the lookout for tails. This time he made his way to his safehouse.

Although Zed was fairly confident that the driver would follow his instructions, he was still worried that the backpack and head wouldn't be there.

'Because I'm sure the driver wants a backpack with a head inside, and a homicidal human after him.'

'I didn't say it was rational, but people do stupid stuff you know.'

'Oh, trust me. I know,' Iris said dryly.

'As I was trying to say,' Zed continued, a little annoyed, *'he could have looked in the backpack and dumped it in the river or something. Not smart, but he could have panicked and done something stupid. Or someone could have seen the driver walk out of the house and not lock it, and stolen the backpack.'*

'True.'

When Zed arrived he simply walked in. Zed was relieved when he saw the backpack on the floor.

Zed opened it and lifted the head out. He still couldn't actually touch it because of the transparent blue field around it, so he had to get his hands underneath and lift it like he would a rock.

Now that Zed had the time to look at it, he was discomfited by the startled look in the head's eyes.

'You don't have time for this,' Zed thought to himself.

Zed set Sylvanus' head on the ground. He pulled Leilani's head out onto the floor next to Sylvanus'. Zed looked at the grisly combination and thought, not for the first time, *'What the hell am I doing here, Iris?'*

'Doing what it takes to keep you and your family alive.'

'Yeah.'

He knew he was going to have to do some pretty messed up stuff before and after D-Day, but expecting something and experiencing the cold, hard reality were two very different things. Shaking his head, he soldiered on.

'*The first thing to do is get Leilani's mana.*'

He decided he didn't really want to start with her head. The thought of draining her while looking into her open eyes was too much for him. He put her head back into the ring and pulled her body out.

Zed awkwardly put the palms and fingers of his hands against hers to create a mana crossover point. He had done this before, but doing it with Leilani made it extra uncomfortable. He couldn't help but imagine how her face would twist in disgust at his touch.

'*You could use her neck instead,*' Iris suggested.

'*Yeah, because that would be so much better.*'

Zed had to gather the mana more slowly and carefully than he ever had before, because there was so much mana in her body. If he wasn't careful he could burn himself out.

As Zed carefully let the non-stop trickle of mana into his body, he felt the familiar feeling of euphoria, an almost tangible sense of pleasure that started in his hands, crept into his arms, and suffused his whole body. It felt good, of course, but also uncomfortable. The combination of pleasure and guilt made him feel like he was doing something dirty.

'*Which, arguably, I am,*' Zed sighed.

Zed ignored the uncomfortable feelings and focused on maintaining control of the mana flows. If he let too much mana surge into his body at once, it could cause a great deal of damage. He didn't have time for unforced errors.

Zed finished after an hour and took some time to rest. He wanted to drain the mana from Sylvanus' body, and to do it safely he needed to be in top physical and mental condition. He expected Sylvanus to have a lot more than Leilani. That made it doubly important to drain him. It would be that much more mana for Zed, and that much less for Sylvanus when he woke up. Zed was nervous about keeping him prisoner. Minimizing his access to mana was crucial.

'*It would be nice if I could weaken him somehow.*'

'*Weakened, you mean like cutting his head off?*' Iris quipped.

'*Yes, but if I want him to live I'm going to have to reattach it.*'

'*Shame, that.*'

Zed rested for an hour. He would have preferred to wait until the next day to drain Sylvanus' body, but he could sense the protective

212

field around Sylvanus' head diminishing. He didn't know how long he had, but his best guess was that it was at most a few days. He couldn't delay too long before draining the body and reattaching it to the head. Somehow.

Zed sensed the mana in the body to get an idea of what to expect. *'Holy crap.'*

The amount of mana was staggering. Sylvanus probably had more in his arm than Zed had in his whole body. Seeing the huge amounts of mana escaping into the air, Zed got to work. He placed the palms of his hands against Sylvanus' and started injecting his mana. He started creating a tidal wave that, before he had even gotten past Sylvanus' forearms, would be enough to burn his mana channels out. By the time he got all of it, it would be enough to kill him.

Zed stopped, and instead started pulling as much of the mana as he thought he could handle back through the forearms and into his hands. As the mana drifted into his body Zed felt a warm sense of pleasure. He couldn't repress a tremor. He wasn't used to bringing in that much.

Doing his best to ignore the sensation, he returned his focus to pulling in more and cycling it to his dantian. He was using his old, self-made technique that wasn't very efficient or fast, but he didn't have a choice. The efficient method of extracting the mana would kill him.

Zed started out conservatively, not sure how much mana was too much. As he pulled in more and more he eventually reached what felt like his limit.

Over and over Zed pulled the mana in, drinking in its sweet euphoria. He was almost lost to the pleasure when Iris broke through. *'Zed! Stop pulling in mana!'*

With reluctance Zed stopped what he was doing. After a few seconds his mind cleared and he took the time to look at his inner self. He was *bright*. Not like Sylvanus, but the ball of mana in his guts, his dantian, was huge. It looked like a cantaloupe made of fire. The mana channels from his arms were also full, the mana drifting towards the dantian.

'That's pretty big.' Zed looked down at his belly. It was actually distended outwards, like he was four or five months pregnant.

'Zed, put the body away!'

'Oh, right.' Zed quickly put Sylvanus' body back in the ring's inventory. *'Don't want to waste any mana.'*

213

'Not just that, the longer it's out, the more it decomposes.'

Zed felt stupid for not even thinking about that. He would have to chill it the next time he pulled it out.

'How long was it out?'

'About half an hour. Don't worry. His body is more durable than that of a mundane.'

'That's good. Why didn't you stop me earlier though?'

'I tried. After a while you weren't responding. It was like you were in a trance.'

'You could have taken over.'

'I thought about it, but I was worried about doing damage. Normally when I take over your mana flows are predictable and steady. With the massive amounts of mana coming in it was chaotic and I wasn't able to keep up with it at the micron scale I need to control you.'

Zed scootched over to check on Sylvanus' head. It remained the same—disturbing and frozen in time. When he sensed mana, the protective field was diminished. Not by a lot, but enough to be noticeable. He revised his estimate of how long it would last to just a day or two longer.

He'd have to figure out how to reattach the body and head soon, but it wasn't an immediate problem. He looked again at his distended belly. *'That, on the other hand, might be. What do I do about my dantian, Iris?'*

'You need to compact your mana.'

'What do you mean by "compact" it? It's mana, stellar energy… whatever. How does it get smaller?'

'It's just what it sounds like. You make the energy more compact. If you want an analogy, your dantian started off as wisps of hydrogen in space. You accumulated more and more and now it is a gas giant planet like Jupiter. It is time to crunch it down and become a star.'

'So, the mana will become more powerful?'

'Yes and no. Don't take the metaphor too far. Each unit of mana will produce the same amount of energy, but with it being more compact you can circulate more through your body and create more intense and powerful effects.'

Zed still wasn't sure exactly what he was supposed to do, but he figured that, like everything else that involved mana, it was based on

214

his will. Zed gradually stopped his regeneration and mental enhancement flows, and brought everything into his dantian.

Zed was shocked at the effect that stopping the mental enhancement had on him. He felt so… *dull*. Like his senses and thoughts were muffled and lethargic.

'*Is this what it felt like to be me before? This sucks.*'

'*If it makes you feel better,*' Iris said, '*I can hardly tell the difference.*'

'*Get your avatar out here so I can stick my tongue out at you.*'

'*Okay, now I can tell the difference. Enhanced you would have come up with something way better than that. Apparently there is an intelligence level below "panda". Who would've thought?*'

'*Yeah, yeah.*'

Every scrap of mana in Zed's body, except the contract he had formed with Silwan, was in his dantian. He visualized the mana pushing inwards on itself, and becoming smaller and more dense. He willed it to happen, but he felt resistance. It was a little like the resistance he felt when pushing electron clouds closer together during the wall crawling technique, only it was more intense. The energy, whatever it was, really did not want to come closer.

'*That's too bad,*' he thought. '*It's going to do what I say anyway.*'

Zed's thoughts were not as nimble as before, but his stubbornness was unchanged. He started anew, firm in his conviction that he was the master of his mana.

Zed didn't understand how it worked, but it was a literal effort to exercise his will in this way, as if he were a drill sergeant yelling at the mana elements to get off their keisters and move to the center. He felt the pressure. The outermost layers were pressing hard, and the innermost layers were crushed by the many layers on top of them pressing inwards.

Eventually, something snapped.

The innermost mana elements collapsed into each other, dramatically reducing their volume. Once it broke, the rest collapsed inwards as well, from the inside out. It was a chain reaction. The mana accreted onto the collapsed core, making it ever so slightly larger. Once all of the mana collapsed, what was left was an incandescent ball the size of a pea.

'*Congratulations, Zed! You are now at the "Protostar" level.*'

'*What's a "protostar"?*'

'*It's an itty-bitty baby star.*'

Zed snorted, but, given Iris' earlier analogy, he supposed the name fit. He rested for a time, and then worked on restoring his mental enhancement. He missed it, and it would help him with all of his other tasks.

Zed peeled off a fraction of the mana, which looked like a small thread, and moved it through his mana channels up to his head.

'*Iris, could you help me restore the mental enhancement flows?*'

'*No problem.*'

He let her take over. Zed thought that he could have probably done it on his own, but he was a little afraid of screwing up, which could have devastating consequences. Time was also scarce. He felt incredible relief when his mind and senses cleared, and he got back to "normal".

And then he went beyond normal.

'*Holy… Iris, why is everything moving so slowly?*'

'*You are using more mana, and it's more concentrated. The effects of your mental enhancement have increased. What you are currently experiencing is an increase in the speed of your thoughts. It is permanent, but not as dramatic as when you have slowed down subjective time in the past.*'

'*Can I still do that?*'

'*Yes.*'

'*Good.*' It had saved his life more than once.

'*You should be able to drain Sylvanus' mana much more quickly now.*'

'*Why?*'

'*Because he was at the protostar level. Before, your diffuse mana was picking off bits and pieces of his mana. Now they are at the same density, and can be controlled and extracted much more quickly. Also, the mana will stay at the protostar level instead of becoming more diffuse, which means far more can travel through your mana channels.*'

'*Great!*'

Deciding that there was no time like the present, Zed pulled the body back out and created a chilling mana field that brought the body's temperature down to just above freezing. He injected a thread of his condensed mana, eager to get more.

216

Chapter 31

Once Zed was finished, he decided to look at his status.

Name: Ozymandias (Zed)	
Attributes	
Strength:	35
Speed:	31
Dexterity:	17
Toughness:	45
Comprehension:	12
Mental Speed:	12 (20)
Memory:	36
Mana:	3051
Abilities	
Self Enhancement	(Expand?)
Offensive	(Expand?)
Defensive	(Expand?)
Sensory	(Expand?)
Utility	(Expand?)
Transcendent Body	
Second Mind:	100%
Digestive System:	100%
Bones:	100 %
Tendons & Ligaments:	100 %
Muscles:	53%

'*Holy crap!*' His mana levels were insane. And the mana limits of most of his abilities had nearly tripled. He wondered what a maxed-out fireball would look like now.

'*How about we try that somewhere else?*' Iris asked.

Zed smiled. '*I'm not "below-panda Zed" anymore, Iris. I'm not going to do anything that dumb.*'

'*We'll see.*'

Zed had intended to rest after draining the body of mana, but the massive mana influx energized him so much that he didn't think he could rest. His mind and body insisted on doing something.

'*Might as well work on repairing Sylvanus' body.*'

Zed arranged the head as if it were attached to a body lying on the ground and then moved the body close to it. He was afraid that the body would be repelled by the mana field like everything else, but hoped something different would happen. Once they were near each other he wasn't sure what to do, so he kept pushing the body closer.

When the neck touched the field, it was pulled towards the head instead of being repelled. The head was also pulled onto the neck, as if both sides were a magnet. Zed could see the burnt line where his laser cut Sylvanus' neck, but otherwise it looked normal.

Zed was relieved. He wasn't sure what would happen, but was glad it had worked out so far.

'*It makes sense,*' Iris said. '*The protective field doesn't just protect. It's also there to make it possible to heal him while he's in suspended animation.*'

Zed put his hands on Sylvanus' shoulders and injected his mana. He tentatively tried to pull some of Sylvanus' from his head. He could, but it was a struggle because there was a dormant will to contend with.

'*Don't take the head's mana, Zed.*'

'*Why not?*'

'*Because it is still imprinted by Sylvanus.*'

Zed wasn't sure what that meant, but decided to take Iris' word for it.

While exploring, Zed saw a mana construct inside Sylvanus' skull that was very similar to his own, only it was more complex.

'*Interesting. He's under contract too. Maybe Annis was right that pretty much everyone in the sect is under contract. Not much trust, I guess.*'

Zed carefully tried to pull on the contract mana. It was solid as a rock. An iron will kept it in place. It was disappointing, but not surprising.

'*It's probably the will of the person he contracted with.*'

'*Yeah.*'

Zed stopped messing around and got to work on repairing Sylvanus' neck, much like he had with Laurel's arm. It was time-consuming, but he didn't bother trying to completely restore it. It

218

would take a really long time, and he didn't trust his ability to repair the delicate nervous system correctly. He mainly focused on blood vessels, bones, skin, etc.

Even those, though, he didn't finish. He wanted Sylvanus to have to focus on something besides trying to escape or killing Zed when he woke up.

'*Kind of dark, Zed, but I have to admit that I like it. Maybe you're the one corrupting me.*'

'*Maybe.*'

When Zed was done, he retracted his mana and awareness from the body. He rolled Sylvanus onto his stomach and turned to the heavy chains he had bought in the days leading up to the ball. There were two sets. One had four connected chains that ended in clasps. The clasps were wrist and ankle-sized and opened in the middle. Where they opened, both sides had a flat piece of iron with a hole in the middle where a padlock could keep them closed.

Zed had no confidence that padlocks could restrain Sylvanus, so after he put Sylvanus' limbs in the clasps he welded them shut with an infrared laser. He felt a little bad when drops of molten iron touched the álfar, but continued on.

'*He'll live.*'

A brief thought of what Zed's sister would think of him caused him some anguish, but he harshly shoved that thought down and moved on.

After he finished with Sylvanus' hands, Zed saw that Silwan was trying to call him.

"Yeah?"

"What the hell happened with Leilani, Zed?"

"She betrayed me in the middle of the mission, so I had to kill her."

"Explain." It was a single word, but it was cold and hard.

"We were supposed to have a quick exchange of blows just to keep people from suspecting she was in on the assassination. We weren't supposed to do anything truly damaging, of course. Leilani didn't follow the plan. She hit me with a remote punch that I hadn't seen before that impacted from two meters away, and screwed up my lungs and heart. If it weren't for the changes of the Transcendent Body, I wouldn't have been able to escape with the damage she did."

The bone communicator was silent for a few seconds.

"How do I know you're telling the truth?"

"Did she have an ability like the one I described?"

"Yes."

"I had no way to know that unless she used it on me."

There was a long pause. "Fine. I forgive you for killing her. On to other matters, how are things proceeding with the Transcendent Body?"

"Um, not bad. I'm implementing it as fast as I can, with good results."

"Good. And I hear that the mission was a success?"

"Yes. Sylvanus is out of the picture."

"Excellent! So why haven't you come back to the inn?"

"I still need to tie up some loose ends."

"Okay. There is an auction in four days that I will be attending. You can rest before then."

The assassination deadline is in three days. Probably not a coincidence.' "Okay, thanks. See you in a few days."

Once Zed had finished hog-tying his prisoner, he turned to the second chain. On one end of the chain was a thick eye screw. Zed jammed it into the middle ceiling beam and twisted the screw in. On Earth he would never have been able to do it by hand, but between his improved physique and mana enhancements, it wasn't difficult.

Once the chain was securely hanging, Zed grabbed the clasp at the end of it. He lifted Sylvanus by the middle of his chain and put it in the clasp. Once the clasp was welded, he gently let Sylvanus down and watched him hang in the air, slowly rotating, belly down. It looked incredibly uncomfortable, but he wasn't sure how else he could keep the álfar secure.

He was originally going to chain him to the wall, but when he thought about how to anchor it securely, he couldn't think of any way to keep Sylvanus from simply ripping it out.

'*Sorry, bud, but hopefully you won't be in there long.*'

Hopefully, they could reach a deal.

**

Zed grew bored waiting for Sylvanus' protective field to end, so he talked with Iris about how to do the water purification tattoo.

'*I'm thinking we want to keep it as simple as possible,*' she said, '*so let's do this. Water is H_2O, which is a very small molecule. If you pull every molecule that's bigger than H_2O to, say, your hand, that should*'

220

eliminate all the impurities. It should be pretty close to distilled water.'

'I like that. Let's give it a try.'

Zed got a clay pitcher and filled it up with water. Iris helped him visualize what a water molecule looked like. It was not a straight line like Zed had initially thought, with the oxygen in the middle and the hydrogen atoms on opposite sides. As it turned out, the oxygen was in the middle, but the molecule was shaped like a "V", not a line.

'That, by the way, is why water is so good at dissolving things,' Iris said. 'The hydrogen atoms are pulling two of the oxygen atom's electrons towards them, so that side is a little bit negatively charged, while the oxygen side of the molecule is a little bit positively charged. The water molecules are good at slipping into small areas and glomming onto molecules with positively or negatively charged areas. Once the water molecules surround them, presto! They're dissolved.'

'Iris, do I need to know any of that to purify the water?'

'No,' she said, a little grumpily.

'Then how about we stick to "keep it simple".'

Although she didn't say anything, he could practically feel her dissatisfaction. Zed sighed. 'Thanks for teaching me so much stuff, Iris. You have been a literal lifesaver for me.'

'You're welcome.'

'Alright. We have a bunch of "V" shaped water molecules, and we want to pull in any molecules that are bigger than they are.'

'Right.'

Zed put his hand into the pitcher. He felt a little weird about doing something that he had been taught since childhood was taboo because it would make the water impure, but it was far easier than doing it from a distance. Zed gathered mana into his hand and diffused it into the water. He then willed it to pull in every molecule bigger than H_2O.

"Crack!"

Zed was surprised when the pitcher shattered and the jagged clay shards rushed to his hand, cutting him in multiple places and embedding themselves in his flesh. The water from the pitcher was all over the floor, and water dribbled out of his wounds.

'What the... oh, right. The mana is only letting the water part of the blood out.'

221

Zed sighed as he turned the "water purifying" off. The water flowing from his wounds turned red. He started pulling shards out of his hands.

'*Guess I'll need to try that again with a little less pull.*'

**

Zed looked over at Sylvanus a few hours later. The protective field around his head was noticeably smaller. He didn't know when it would disappear, but it could be any time now. At the most, a day.

He noticed a couple of rings on Sylvanus' fingers and chided himself for being a fool.

'*Who knows what he could do with those?*'

Zed removed the rings and looked at them. One was heavy gold with a ruby the same width as the broad band. The other was also gold, but with an inscription on the inside, "To my beloved."

Zed felt like a jerk for taking the inscribed ring, like he was peeking into something that wasn't his business. He checked it for mana abilities and, when he didn't find any, put it on the finger he removed it from.

The other ring immediately pulled at his mana when he probed. Zed put it on and activated the ring. It opened up to him, showing him the contents of its extra-spacial inventory.

'*Jackpot!*' Zed crowed.

Fortunately, the ring did not have an AI included. Zed wasn't sure how he would feel about another one. His brain already felt a little crowded.

'*I think you meant to say "comfy", Zed.*'

'*Right,*' Zed thought with a bit of an eye roll. '*That's exactly what I meant. We're very comfy in here. So comfy that I occasionally want to scream. In a comfy way.*'

'*Hmph. You could be nicer to me, you know.*'

Zed sighed. '*I know. It's hard. We're like Siamese twins that can't get away from each other. But, as much as I complain about our "comfiness", Iris, I am grateful for you. You are my greatest supporter and my best friend in this world.*'

'*Better than Constance?*'

'*Of course. I think Constance and I both know that what we have isn't going to last.*'

222

'Just as long as you remember that.'

Chapter 32

Zed hadn't realized how rightly he spoke when he called finding Sylvanus' ring "hitting the jackpot".

He did now.

The ring's storage volume was roughly twice that of Iris' ring, making it a treasure even if there was nothing in it. On top of that, there were plenty of valuables inside.

There were gold coins, platinum coins and bars, potions in glass bottles, small jade boxes with unknown contents, books, and memory crystals. And clothes. Lots and lots of clothes. Zed was tempted to make room by pulling all the clothes out and tossing them to the corner of the room, but decided to leave them in the ring for now.

The books were primarily texts on physics ("Force and Motion", "Sub-atomic Physics, "Gravity and Sub-atomic Physics", and "Duality of Matter"), chemistry ("Acids and Bases" and "Organic Chemistry"), and metallurgy ("Alloys and Their Properties" and "Metallic Crystal Structures"), along with some novels about heroic álfar.

As much as Zed valued the books, he was even more interested in the memory crystals. He took one and was about to put it on Iris' ring when she said, '*Try the new ring.*'

He did, and the contents of the crystal were instantly accessible to his mind. It was a cultivation technique that, like his own, aimed at having the body become mana-based. Unlike his, which was direct and—Zed hated to say it, but it was true—artificial, this method used a gradual approach based on increasing mana flows throughout the body. It was an extension of mana-based physical enhancement. Interestingly, the advanced sections also had mental enhancement.

'*I wonder if it's like mine?*' Zed wondered.

'*Doesn't matter. We've already gone down the other road, so we can't use this.*'

'*We can't use the physical parts of it, but the mental enhancement might be useful.*'

'*That's true.*'

Zed returned the crystal to Sylvanus' ring and pulled out the second one. It turned out to be the technique that Silwan used on Leilani—

"Plasma Whip". Zed grimaced when he thought about how Silwan had forced Leilani to the ground and burned her neck. It was an effective technique.

The crystal also described an upgraded version—"Lightning Whip". It appeared to be the Plasma Whip technique with an added electrical component.

'Iris, why haven't we looked at lightning attacks? Wouldn't they be really powerful?'

'Yes, under special conditions. Lightning is usually a very ineffective attack.'

'Why?'

'Because you can't aim it. It goes wherever the easiest route to ground is, which is probably not through your target unless you're in the sky and they're holding a lightning rod in their mouth. To get it to go where you want it to, you have to make sure that the path you want has the least resistance.'

'How do you do that?'

'Generally one of two ways: 1) Connect to the target with an electrical conductor, like metal, or 2) Create an air plasma path to the target, since plasma is an excellent conductor. You could, for example, use your laser to create a plasma path to the target and then zap them, but if you can hit them with the laser, why not just kill them with that instead?'

'Hmm. I see what you mean. The lightning still sounds like a good addition to the plasma whip, though.'

'Yes, that's one of those special cases where it probably makes sense.'

The plasma whip manual referenced the "Remote Mind" technique. It appeared to be the sect's name for the mana structure Zed saw in the plasma whip that allowed Silwan to control it far from his body.

'I've gotta get that, Iris.'

'Yes. Perhaps you can get it from Sylvanus.'

'Probably, but I don't think it's a good idea.'

'Why not?'

'Silwan knows I'm interested in it. He might be suspicious if I don't try to get it from him.'

'Good point.'

Zed returned to the cultivation technique to look at what it had on mental enhancement. After a few hours of studying, Iris interrupted.

225

'Zed, Sylvanus is awake.'

Zed dropped what he was doing and looked at him. Blood was seeping out of the partially healed cut at his neck. The protective field was gone, as was the cold field Zed had set up around the body.

'He must have claimed the mana.'

Zed had expected that. He sensed that mana was circulating furiously in his body, particularly where the neck had been severed.

'Maybe it's good that I left the body unrefrigerated for half an hour. Gives him more to work on.'

Zed spun up his laser and magnetic field. He would let Iris handle the telekinetic field.

"Sylvanus."

Sylvanus' eyes slowly opened but were forced to look downwards. Zed moved to 10 feet away and sat on the floor.

"Can you talk?"

His head slowly shook a couple of times.

"I suggest you fix yourself quickly. I am under a time limit on my assassination job, which means you are under a time limit. If you don't want to die, that is."

Zed went back to observing him. He hated that he was in a nerve-wracking yet tedious situation that required him to be on guard at every moment. He would much rather rest or study.

'Yes, I imagine Sylvanus would probably prefer different circumstances too,' Iris said dryly.

After eleven minutes he rasped out, "Water."

Zed pulled out his self-filling canteen and walked over to offer it to the álfar. He met resistance a few feet away, and Sylvanus' closest chains were pushed back. He grunted in pain, and Zed thought, *'Oh, right. Magnetic field.'*

Zed hastily turned the field off and moved closer. It was awkward when he realized that simply holding it to Sylvanus' mouth wouldn't work because he was facing downwards. Sylvanus jerkily turned his head to the side with a grimace of pain, and Zed held the canteen to his mouth. The álfar quickly swallowed the water.

He released a light cloud of mana around Zed. Zed thought about acquiring it but decided to leave him alone.

'Lord knows he needs all the mana he can get.'

When Zed saw more accumulating on the surface of Sylvanus' head, though, he knew something was up. He dropped the canteen and dived to the side.

A spike of *something* emanated from Sylvanus' head and pierced through Zed's cheekbone, shattering it.

'Holy crap! If I hadn't moved, that would have been my brain!'

Zed scrabbled to get farther away from his prisoner. It was undignified, but he didn't care. Once he was at the edge of the room he turned back, heart thumping. He was pissed, but knew that if he were in Sylvanus' position he would have done something similar. He took some time to calm down while remaining wary and guarded.

"I kidnapped you and made you a prisoner, so I forgive you for doing that. Once. Try that again, and you die. Do you understand?"

"Yes." Sylvanus' voice was still raspy, so perhaps that wasn't faked.

For some reason, now that Zed was in the situation he had been working towards for a week, he was strangely reluctant to talk. Instead, he worked on regenerating his cheekbone and skin.

An hour later, cheek whole, Zed said, "Can you get techniques from the Ever-Fruitful Tree sect?"

"Yes." Slightly less raspy.

"While you're in the chains?"

"No."

"What do you need?"

"An item from my ring and my hands free."

"What item?"

"A jade tablet with the symbol of the sect on it."

Zed paused and considered some more. "I want to make a deal with you."

Sylvanus laughed, a painful and mirthless sound. "I'm all ears."

"I have a deadline to kill you in three days, enforced by an energy contract. I want you to help me break the contract."

"I can't."

"Why not?"

"I don't know how."

"I saw that you are also under a contract."

Sylvanus remained silent.

"Does your contract prevent you from talking about it?"

227

He said nothing. Zed was about to continue his questions when Sylvanus said, "I like to talk."

'That's probably the closest he could come to a "yes" without it coming down on him,' Zed thought.

"In my ideal world," Zed said, "you would help me get the sect's stellar energy contract technique, help me break my contract, and then I would let you go. I'd keep the ring, but I could return your clothes and personal stuff. I don't want to kill you, but I'll have to if my contract is not broken in three days. Do you understand?"

"Yes."

"The fact that your contract is set up to keep you from talking about it is actually encouraging to me. It suggests that it can be broken."

Sylvanus slowly shook his head. "They don't want young masters to know the requirements of entering the sect."

"Wow. That's pretty messed up. Still, I refuse to believe that it can't be broken. Can you get me the technique?"

Zed waited a few seconds.

"Yes."

"Good. If I put the tablet below you, can you get it?"

"I need to be released."

"Not gonna happen."

"At least my hands!" Sylvanus coughed wetly after forcing so much air through his throat.

"No. You burned that bridge by trying to kill me. Once we have a stellar energy contract in place, I'll release you from the chains."

"Fine," he said bitterly.

Zed took the jade tablet out of the ring. He was about to slide it on the floor to Sylvanus when it occurred to him that he had no idea what the tablet could do.

"If you attack me with the tablet, you die. If you summon help, I probably won't be able to tell. But if anyone comes here, you die. Do you understand?"

"Yes."

The word caused the ember of hope inside Zed to flare into a bonfire. This moment could lead to what he'd longed for the last year—freedom.

He slid the tablet across the floor to Sylvanus. It wasn't a perfect shuffleboard shot, but it was only three feet short of being directly under the prisoner.

228

Zed sensed Sylvanus' mana reaching out to the tablet and lifting it to one of his hands that was pulled painfully behind his back. A minute later, a white crystal dropped from the tablet and rolled on the floor a few times. If Sylvanus hadn't tried to kill him a few minutes ago, Zed would've had a hard time doing anything other than focusing on the crystal.

"Push it over to me."

Sylvanus' mana reached out one more time and shoved it towards Zed. Zed walked over and picked up the crystal, eying his prisoner the entire time.

"Thank you. Now the tablet."

Sylvanus huffed, but gently laid the tablet on the ground using telekinesis and shoved it over.

"I'm going to learn how to make contracts, and then we'll see about getting you out of those chains."

The álfar was silent. Blood had stopped seeping out of his neck.

Zed inserted the crystal into his ring.

'Iris, can you monitor our guest while I'm studying, including his mana usage?'

'Yes.'

'Good. Keep an eye on him, let me know if he pulls any funny business. If necessary, take over my body temporarily.'

'Okay.'

Zed immersed himself in the theory and construction of mana contracts and was fascinated by what he learned. It turned out that his assumption that his subconscious mind decided whether he had broken the contract or not was incorrect. Instead, the contract included a modified version of the "Remote Mind" technique.

'That "Remote Mind" keeps popping up in a lot of places,' Zed thought.

There were differences, though. Remote Mind was an active technique that allowed the user to exert their will at a distance. The mana contract's version was a static capture of the mind's will when the contract was formed. That snapshot of the mind's will is what determined whether to trigger the contract's clauses or not, so if the contractee's understanding of the contract changed over time, it wouldn't matter. The only thing that mattered was their understanding of the contract when it was created.

The contracts were explicitly intended to be asymmetrical. It turned out that the contract "master"—the contractee being designated as the "servant"—could also put in triggers and enforcement mechanisms that their own captured will controlled.

Zed got nervous at this point. Silwan told him that Zed was the only one who would decide if he had broken the contract, but was that true? He decided to look closely at his contract to see what he could find.

Now that he had a better idea of what he was looking at, the contract mana was easier to understand. He saw two structures similar to what he had seen in Silwan's plasma whip—the static Remote Minds. One of them was attached to a pool of mana.

'*What does the pool of mana do?*' Zed wondered.

'*Look at the structures around it, Zed. They appear to be a multi-dimensional version of things we have seen in mana tattoos, like the magnifying structure.*'

Zed looked again and saw that Iris was right. As he puzzled through what it was meant to do he gradually figured out the gist of it, if not every detail. The mana pool was meant to cause a burst of energy in the center of the roughly spherical structure of his skull.

'*I think we found the brain-pulping part of the contract, Iris,*' Zed said dryly.

'*Then what is the rest of it?*'

Zed had been so focused on deciphering the mana structures that he had forgotten about the other Remote Mind. It was also connected to the brain-pulping structures at various points, but not concretely. It was more like probes, monitoring the structure.

'*Maybe it's an anti-tampering mechanism?*'

'*Then what is the second pool of energy for?*'

'*What poo… Oh, crap.*'

The one thing that the second Remote Mind was attached to concretely was a second pool of energy with similar constraining mana structures around it. It was also clearly designed to create a spherical burst of energy.

'*That son of a bitch! He lied to me.*'

'*To be fair, I don't think Silwan lied,*' Iris said. '*He just didn't mention it.*'

Zed snorted to show what he thought of that but continued to look at the mana structures.

'Wait, maybe it's not as bad as I thought. Instead of creating a burst inside my skull, it looks like this one creates a spherical burst on the outside.'

'Why would it do that?'

'No idea.'

Zed really wanted to take a break and rest after all this mental exertion. He needed to establish a contract with Sylvanus as quickly as possible, though, so he pushed through it and resumed studying the technique.

**

"Ugh."

Zed had a pounding headache, the likes of which he hadn't felt since he improved his mental enhancements. He did not miss those days.

His studying had been interrupted a couple of hours earlier when Sylvanus tried to kill him. Iris saw the mana forming, took over, and shot him with a low-power plasma ball while dodging. He'd been quiet since, particularly after Zed reminded him that he didn't need him alive anymore.

'Do you think you're ready to give it a try, Zed?'

'As ready as I'm going to be, with the clock ticking and all. Besides, it's not my life that's at risk.'

'Unless he kills you when you get up close.'

'True.'

Iris' stark reminder cut through Zed's mental fog and focused him on the task at hand, the risks involved, and how to mitigate them.

Zed re-entered Sylvanus' room and sat down, facing him from the side.

"I'm ready to make a contract with you."

"Yeah, right," Sylvanus said. "What you really mean is that you have a half-assed idea of how to make a contract and don't care that much if you screw it up and make my head explode."

Zed cocked his head, thought about it, and said, "Yeah, pretty much. But let's review your situation. I don't doubt that you've been working on escaping and, given enough time, could break out of your chains and make a run for it. Unfortunately for you, you're still here.

You have run out of time, so if you don't make a contract with me, you won't be leaving this room alive."

Sylvanus looked angry but said nothing.

"So, the terms of the contract. Here is what I propose. You will:

1) Kill yourself in 1 day if I do not give you permission to continue living."

"What?!"

"Be quiet.

2) Act in such a way that no one, besides myself, will know that Sylvanus Lucero still lives for the next two years.

3) Not harm any humans for the next two years, unless a direct order from me or Dan Johnson tells you to do otherwise.

4) Go to the city of Formenos within the next two months, and look for myself or Dan Johnson. Follow their orders until two years from now.

5) Never lie to me or Dan Johnson.

6) Not seek in any way to subvert or destroy this contract.

The penalty for not fulfilling any of these clauses is death. If you are still alive two years from now, the contract shall be considered fulfilled. What do you think?"

"Does it matter?" Sylvanus asked angrily.

"There's always a choice."

"Tell me. Who sent you to kill me?"

"Silwan Yarris."

"It figures."

"I take it you two are rivals?"

Sylvanus snorted and said, "You could say that."

"He set the deadline for your assassination as one day before an auction. What do you know about it?"

"Plenty. I was going to attend too. There will be several interesting items, but we were both going to go for the body of the white dwarf cultivator."

"What? What are you talking about? Is the cultivator short or something?"

Sylvanus looked at Zed like he was an idiot. "'White Dwarf' has nothing to do with his height. It's a stellar energy cultivation level, a very advanced one. The auctioneers guarantee that the body still has at least a little mana—very dense mana that would be good for our cultivation."

Having just condensed his own to the "Protostar" level, Zed understood how that could be valuable.

"Enough talk. Are you ready to contract with me?"

"Yes."

Zed formed the ultra-violet laser above his forearm.

"Look at me. Do you know what this is?" Zed asked, motioning to the laser.

"No. What is it?"

"It's how I cut your head off. I'm tired of you trying to kill me, so I'm going to have this pointed at your head the entire time. Do you understand me?"

"Yes," he said sullenly.

Zed walked up to Sylvanus carefully. He inwardly laughed at himself when he realized how this must look to an outside observer. Zed—a big, tough guy—walking gingerly towards a guy who was literally chained up by every limb, whose head was burned, and who couldn't touch the ground. Unfortunately, Sylvanus had proven that caution was warranted.

When Zed reached the chained álfar, he used the non-laser-bearing hand to straighten one of the álfar's hands. Zed then place his hand 1 cm away from Sylvanus' and emitted a mist of mana. He worried that Sylvanus was going to try to take it or do something unwise when he did not emit his own, but after a few seconds it came billowing out. Zed performed the technique by imprinting his will and the terms of the contract on the mixture of their mana.

"Do not resist the energy."

Zed took control of the mana and moved it through Sylvanus' channels. Though Zed was concentrating on the contract technique, he couldn't help but notice how wide and pristine the mana channels were. He wished he had the opportunity to see what the results of the other cultivation technique looked like, but this was not the time or place.

Zed followed the contract procedure to take Sylvanus' obeisance, imprint it on the mana, and write the result on his skull.

'*I really hope I did that right.*'

'*Yeah, it would be kind of awkward if he discovered that it's not binding in 5 minutes,*' Iris said.

"How do you feel?" Zed asked.

"Fine."

233

"What's your most embarrassing memory?"

"I don't want to answer that," Sylvanus said through gritted teeth.

"Answer anyway."

Sylvanus turned his head and looked at Zed angrily. "Having my head cut off by a human."

"Okay, what's your second most embarrassing memory?"

"Are you sure you want to know?" Sylvanus asked with a cruel smile that promised retribution. "I cut off the hands of the man who caused my embarrassment."

"Fine, fine. So touchy…" Zed grumbled. "Let's try this instead then. What's the biggest Ever-Fruitful Tree sect secret you can tell me that wouldn't go against any of your contracts?"

"The founder of the sect is still alive and at the head of the organization. Some say that he is close to immortal due to his advanced cultivation. Some say that he drains the vitality of members of the sect to prevent aging."

"Interesting. Okay, we'll call it a success."

Zed carefully used a laser to open the shackles, noting that they were partially cut already. He freed Sylvanus' feet first so he could stand and support his weight. Once he was entirely free, the álfar rubbed his wrists and ankles.

"You have two months of freedom," Zed said. "Enjoy."

"I thought you said you would give me my stuff back."

"I said that in my ideal world I would give you your clothes and personal stuff. Unfortunately, your clothes tell everyone around you that you're a rich scion. You need to be as nondescript as possible. So, sorry. No clothes. I will give you some money and help you disguise yourself. Give me a little time to bring back some supplies, then you can do whatever you want."

"Anything I want, short of seeing my friends and family, or going back to my sect."

"Man, I'm starting to get why Silwan called me a whiner. Other than having to go to Formenos, you can do whatever you want for the next two months. After that, you only have to serve for two years."

"Yeah. That's awesome," Sylvanus said in a deadpan voice. "When are you going to tell me that I don't have to kill myself?"

"As soon as I am free from my contract. Wait here and I'll be back in a few with new clothes and dye for your hair. Once you're done with that, you can come back in a day or wait here with me. Your choice."

"Wow. This freedom really is overwhelming."

Shaking his head, Zed left. He returned an hour later with two inexpensive pairs of pants and tunics, a backpack, and black dye.

"Sit down," Zed commanded.

Once Sylvanus was sitting, Zed pulled the dagger he received from Victoria out of Iris' ring and started trimming Sylvanus' hair. He wasn't going for any particular style, he was just trying to make it short. Once he finished, he gave the dye to Sylvanus.

"Use this on your hair. Once you've used it and you've changed clothes, you're free to go."

Zed put 100 gold and some silver and copper on the table. He had thought about giving Sylvanus less, but decided there was no reason to be stingy.

'Besides, it looks like he has vengeance issues. Maybe being more generous with him will bring a little goodwill.'

'Yes, I'm sure a bit of gold from the ring you took from him will win him over, Zed.'

'That's just the start, Iris. What will really win him over will be my charm and sense of humor.'

'Ah, we're back to suplex diplomacy, are we?'

Zed soured when he thought of Laurel. *'Low blow, Iris.'*

'What's that?' Iris asked, intentionally misunderstanding his complaint. *'You're adding low blows to your repertoire?'*

Zed couldn't help but laugh at Iris' teasing. *'You should let me win once in a while.'*

Zed noticed that Sylvanus was looking at him funny, as if he was wondering if Zed was sane or not. Zed didn't feel like explaining himself, so he just shrugged.

'It's too late for love, so I guess I'll have to settle for fear.'

'Love is preserved by the link of obligation which, owing to the baseness of men, is broken at every opportunity for their advantage; but fear preserves you by a dread of punishment which never fails.'

'Machiavelli?' Zed asked.

'Yep.'

'Another milestone in my moral journey that isn't concerning at all,' Zed sighed.

235

Chapter 33

Zed was past due for a rest, so he slept for 12 hours. It took a big chunk of the time he had left to free himself from his contract, but he suspected he would need to be at his best to pull it off.

After getting some street food, Zed returned to the safehouse and looked at the mana contract structures in his skull again. There were the two pools of energy—one connected to his Remote Mind and the other to Silwan's—and what looked like probes from Silwan's Remote Mind monitoring the rest of the contract.

Zed had one big thing going for him—messing with the contract did not appear to be physically dangerous. He wasn't sure exactly what Silwan's energy pool was supposed to do, but it did not appear to be intended to hurt him. Instead, it created a pulse of energy outside of his body.

'*Maybe a beacon or something?*' Iris said.

'*Hmm. Maybe. It's a better hypothesis than anything else we've come up with anyway.*'

Zed's energy pool was aimed at killing him, but no clauses in the contract forbade him from trying to destroy or subvert it. It was a massive oversight on Silwan's part, given that Zed had just proven that it could be added to mana contracts.

'*Are you sure that part of Sylvanus' contract is valid and effective?*' Iris asked.

'*No, I'm not. I hope it is, but if it isn't that would explain why Silwan didn't put a "don't mess with the contract" clause in.*'

Zed planned to disable Silwan's side of the contract to prevent whatever it was intended to do, and then disable his own. He would have loved to experiment with the Remote Minds and see what they could do, but he was pretty sure that most experiments would trigger Silwan's Remote Mind, so disabling it had to come first.

Part of the function of a Remote Mind was clearly to exert will, much like an actual mind, so Zed figured the same principles should apply. Will diminishes at a distance. Therefore, the best place to attack it is farthest from the Remote Mind and closest to himself. All of the contract was inside himself, of course, so that wasn't an issue. All he had to do was target the farthest place from the Remote Mind that he could.

'*It seems like it should be easy, Iris. Some parts of the contract are inches away from Silwan's Remote Mind and are part of me. I should have a huge advantage.*'

'*I doubt it's that easy, Zed. If it were, contracts would be meaningless to mana users. I suspect that area in your skull is the mana equivalent of an embassy on Earth. Even though it's inside your body, the contract region of your skull is probably considered part of the Remote Mind's territory. If so, it would have the advantage.*'

'*Well, crap.*'

Zed didn't like Iris' conclusion, but had to admit that it made sense.

'*So how do you think we should do this then?*' he asked.

'*The ideal way would be to attack it with mana in a region you control that produces an effect that travels to the hostile region. An example would be your laser.*'

'*Lase my own skull? Are you crazy?*'

'*I'm not suggesting lasing your skull. It was just an example. Unless you could lase it from the inside and point it outwards...*' Iris' voice trailed off as she thought about her "outside the box, but inside the skull" solution.

The pair tossed ideas back and forth and came up with two approaches. The first was to migrate bits of ceramic to the skull the same way Iris migrated metal to Zed's bones, form a sharp blade from the ceramic, and use telekinesis to cut appropriate mana lines. Zed liked that it would be easy to control and target specific parts of the mana contract, but it would take time to migrate the ceramic. They also weren't sure how effectively the ceramic blade would cut the mana lines and skull.

The other idea was to... lase his skull. Instead of lasing directly into the skull or doing it from the inside out, Zed would use his regular arm-based laser, but point it tangentially at the appropriate portion of his skull, so it would never be pointed at any part of his brain. Iris and Zed were confident that it would be effective, and Iris was confident about controlling it. Zed had a few misgivings.

'*I can't believe you still want to shoot a laser into my skull, Iris.*'

'*It would be perfectly safe. My simulations show a very small chance of brain damage.*'

'*You realize that those two sentences contradict each other, right?*'

'*Even if something did happen, which I hasten to remind you almost certainly would not, at most a few million brain cells would be lost.*'

'*A few million?!*'

'*You have billions of them, Zed. A few million is way less than 1%.*'

'*I don't want any percent!*'

'*Says the guy who was all about MMA and taking punches to the head.*'

'*That's different.*'

'*Is it?*'

They went back and forth on the topic. They thought about doing the ceramic scalpel, and if that didn't work, following up with the laser. The one problem with this approach was that they were worried that the scalpel would trigger Silwan's Remote Mind if it failed. Iris used that to convince Zed to go straight to the laser.

'*I can't believe you talked me into this, Iris,*' Zed said as he sat in the chair in the middle of the room. He formed the tightest, most focused laser he could—the ultraviolet laser. He wanted as little residual heat escaping the target as possible.

Once it was formed, he raised it to the area of the skull they had decided to target, looking like a suicidal man with bad aim.

'*Okay. Take over, Iris.*'

'*Got it.*'

Zed felt himself lose control of his muscles, relegated to observing the procedure.

Iris emitted a portion of his mana as a sensor field to carefully observe the position of his head, arm, and laser before starting the cutting. She made minor adjustments and said, '*We're in position. Are you ready?*'

'*No.*'

'*Too bad. Starting procedure.*'

Zed sensed the laser activate and cut into the skin of his head, instantly vaporizing it and continuing on to the floor of the house. Iris quickly moved the arm towards the skull and just as quickly moved it back out. Zed would have said that she "jerked" it, but that would imply a lack of control. He knew she was constantly using the sensor information as feedback to control it within sub-millimeter tolerances.

238

Just like that, the laser turned off and his arm moved down. An odd smell that reminded Zed of having his teeth drilled by the dentist filled the air.

'*How do you feel?*' Iris asked.

"Fine," Zed said, greatly relieved. He felt his head and found the cauterized cut in his skin. Underneath it was a thin layer of flesh, and the stainless steel skull underneath that. The edges of the cut were sharp. As he probed the skull he felt a strange fluid seeping out.

"What the hell is that?!"

'*Cranial fluid.*'

Zed gasped.

'*Calm down, you big baby,*' Iris scolded. '*It's already stopped leaking.*'

It took some time for Zed to calm down. He knew on a logical level that there was no one better for the job than Iris, but it had still scared the hell out of him.

Zed used his mana sense to observe the contract. Silwan's Remote Mind was pulsing mana, clearly having detected that something was wrong, but the line to the pool of energy was cut, making the Remote Mind incapable of doing anything.

While Zed regenerated the skin and flesh, he thought, '*Well done, Iris. Excellent job.*'

'*Thank you. Now that Silwan's part of the contract is out of the way, and your part of the contract doesn't have any restrictions against destroying the contract, we can deal with it any way we want.*'

'*Yeah. Any ideas on how we should do it?*'

'*I was originally going to suggest a radical approach of cutting the skull—easy to do since it is part of your body—and then removing the entire thing, contract and all.*'

'*Holy crap, Iris! Just when I think I've heard your wildest ideas, you go and pull stuff like that out. You want to remove my entire skull, and what? Just leave my brain hanging out in the wind?*'

'*Of course not. I would use mana to protect it from contaminants and maintain a thin layer of cerebral fluid. It would completely get rid of all traces of the contract in a safe manner.*'

'*Okay. It still weirds me out, but I see your logic. What other approaches could we take?*'

Iris gave the mental equivalent of a shrug and said, '*The other way would be to just lase it again.*'

'Wouldn't that still be risky?'

'Not really. My previous risk assessment had a smaller degree of confidence because I was basing it on simulations. I have real data to work with now, so it should be even safer.'

'I'm inclined to stick with the devil we know. Let's lase it.'

Iris' she-devil avatar appeared and saluted Zed. *'You're the boss!'* She disappeared in a poof of black smoke that smelled like brimstone.

Zed chuckled at her antics. Having been Silwan's slave for the last few months, it felt good to have freedom in sight. Soon he would be able to tell him to shove it, and go back to Formenos.

He could hardly wait.

**

After Iris disabled his contract's kill switch, Zed decided to celebrate. He first tested his freedom by carefully saying he wasn't going to kill Sylvanus. When there was no resistance, he excitedly jumped up and flipped a double bird to an imaginary Silwan.

"Screw you, Silwan!"

He cackled like a madman and parkoured around the room. When he calmed down, he thought about returning to his friends in Formenos. It would be so good to see Dan and Laurel and get back to helping them prepare the settlement. There was only half a year left.

He wondered how they were, and how the new settlement was going. He worried about them, knowing Dan wasn't as much of a fighter as he was. Shaking his head, he put away the downer thoughts and focused on his newfound freedom.

"We need to celebrate. Let's go get drunk, Iris."

Zed could tell that she was amused. *'Whatever you say, boss.'*

He found the nearest bar that didn't look like a dive and walked in. The smell of ale greeted him as he looked upon a crowd of álfar and a few dwarves drinking from steins. It was a cheerful crowd, talking and joking while entertained by a lute-playing bard.

'Perfect.'

The bard, a middle-aged male álfar with lively eyes, had a rich voice and demonstrated good comedic timing as he sang about a drunk álfar who ended up in a ditch.

Being alone, Zed grabbed a stool at the bar. He turned off his regeneration. Tonight was for having fun and getting a little drunk.

240

When he got the bartender's attention, he asked for their best ale. Being a human and new to the bar, he knew chances were good they would rip him off, but he didn't care. Money wasn't a problem anymore.

'Just make sure you don't get robbed, Zed.'

'Everything except a few coins is in the ring, Iris, and nobody here expects people to have storage rings.'

'Which I'm sure will be a great comfort to you when they steal it anyway.'

Zed looked at the heavy gold ring with an inset ruby and thought, *'Okay, good point.'*

Zed watched the bard while drinking his ale. The entertainer made the song's story come alive with his voices and expressions. Zed laughed along with everyone else as the man in the song got peed on by a dog and then staggered home to his wife, who scolded him for getting so drunk that he peed himself. The man couldn't protest his innocence because he'd be even more embarrassed to admit what actually happened.

Zed started on his second drink around the time the bard began a catchy drinking song. The crowd seemed to know it, as many joined in.

Zed had a nice buzz by the fifth song and the third drink. The drinks were stronger than what he was used to on Earth. Zed laughed as he thought of the European joke about how American beers were "like making love in a canoe, because they were fucking close to water".

A blond álfar woman in a green dress slid onto the stool next to Zed and asked, "Care to share the joke?"

Zed was surprised that the woman was talking to him, but he was glad to have a little company. "Just laughing about how I'm already getting a little drunk on my third beer. Apparently I don't get out enough these days."

"That's a shame. A good-looking man like you should get out more. Be a little eye candy once in a while,' she said as she winked at him.

'Oh, please,' Iris huffed.

Zed just grinned and sipped at his beer. He wasn't drunk enough to think she didn't have ulterior motives, but, once again, he didn't care. "What are you drinking?"

The woman smiled and said, "If you're offering, I'll have what you're having."

Zed ordered another ale from the bartender.

When she heard the variety of dwarven ale he was drinking, she whistled, "Look at you, Mr. Fancy Pants."

"I'm celebrating tonight."

"Celebrating what?"

"Freedom."

"How very mysterious," she said as she leaned into him. "How did you know that I like mysterious men?"

Zed was about to respond when he felt a hand grab him by the shoulder and pull him around, almost yanking him off the stool. In front of him was a large male álfar with a crooked nose who looked angry.

"What the hell, human! What do you think you're doing, hitting on my girl?"

'Ah, so that's what's going on.' He wasn't exactly planning on going home with the woman, but it still pissed him off that it was all just a setup to screw him over.

'Disappointed that she didn't really want you for eye candy, Zed?'

'Nah.' Zed smirked maliciously. *'This will be entertaining too.'*

"Sorry about that. I didn't know she was taken. Let me buy you and your friends a round of drinks," Zed said as he tossed the man a gold coin.

'Too much money, Zed! Now they're going to think you're a rich guy!'

'I am a rich guy.'

'Yeah, but you don't want them to know that!'

The man's eyes went wide as he looked at the coin. He sneered at Zed and stomped back to his table. Zed turned to the woman, who also looked surprised.

"He didn't even ask for you back, darlin'. Looks like your price for the evening is one gold."

'Now you're just trying to start a fight,' Iris said.

Zed laughed. *'I figured I would see them again out on the street. Just thought I would cut through the chit-chat.'*

'I didn't know you were a mean drunk, Zed.'

For some reason that pissed him off even more.

'I wasn't, not that long ago. I'm really tired of assholes thinking they can push me around. Did I do anything to them, Iris?'

'No,' she said reluctantly.

'I won't start it—okay, I'll probably egg them on some more,' he thought as he took another pull from his drink. *'But I'm damn sure gonna finish it.'*

The woman's eyes grew wider and angry as she realized Zed's meaning. She stood up and slapped Zed hard. The sharp sound caused the bar to become quiet.

Zed went into "fight" mode—he'd never been much for "flight". She took his complete focus as his sight went red and everything else in his field of vision dimmed. He felt like smashing her face in but resisted the urge. He had never hit a woman before in anger and, while he wasn't one of those guys that thought there was never a reason to hit a woman, he knew that here and now it would be a mistake. With his strength he would probably kill her.

He forced himself to slow down and stay on his seat. While looking at her he said, "I wasn't very nice, so I'll give you that one. Try that crap again, and you won't like the result."

The woman turned to her boyfriend and said, while pointing at Zed, "Did you hear what he said to me?"

The man stomped back over, angry as a bull, with his friends behind him. "What did he say?"

"That you're selling me to him, and that he's going to hurt me!"

"What?!"

Zed scowled and said, "Look, asshole. I didn't touch her, and I paid for your drinks. Walk away, and we can all go home in one piece."

The crooked-nosed man got a tic in his eye. He glanced at his friends and then looked back at Zed. "No one insults my woman!"

'I gave them a chance, Iris.'

'I know. I just wish you weren't so happy that he didn't walk away.'

Zed stood up. The crooked-nosed man rushed him. Zed stepped to the side, grabbed the hair at the back of his head, and slammed the man's head against the top of the bar. His head bounced up almost a foot afterward, blood spewing from an even more crooked nose and a couple of teeth falling to the floor.

One of crooked-nose's sidekicks took a swing at Zed. Zed swayed back enough to have it miss his face, and then moved in and punched the álfar in the gut, causing him to double over. Zed drove his knee up

243

into the man's face, launching him backwards into the air. More teeth and blood went flying.

The last man looked horrified as he saw the facial destruction that had happened in seconds.

Zed smiled and said, gesturing at him with both hands, "Come get some."

The man paled and ran away, causing the bar's door to slam against the wall in his haste.

Zed laughed.

'To your right, Zed!'

Zed turned and saw Crooked Nose thrusting at him with a knife.

'This son of a bitch is trying to kill me!' Zed knew it would be almost impossible to kill him with a knife, short of driving it into his brain, but the álfar didn't know that.

Zed caught the man's fist and squeezed hard, causing him to squeal in agony and drop the knife. Zed continued to squeeze, feeling the crunch of bones, while he bent down to pick it up.

Zed shifted his handhold to Crooked Nose's wrist and shoved it onto the bar. The man's face tearfully pleaded for mercy right before Zed plunged the knife through his hand, pinning it to the bar.

Crooked Nose howled in horror and pain as he looked at his hand.

Zed appeared calm as he turned around to look at the rest of the patrons, but he was a maelstrom of anger, adrenaline, and slowly surfacing shame.

"Does anyone else have a problem with me?" he shouted.

The patrons were frozen or trembling, while a few shook their heads.

A shaky voice spoke behind him. "Y-you need to pay for the damages."

'Are you freaking kidding me?!'

Zed turned around slowly, eyes narrowed, and stared at the bartender. "How many times have you watched these losers pull this scam on other people?" He turned back around to the crowd. "How many times have ALL OF YOU watched these guys pull this shit on other people?" he roared. All of them cringed, many of them avoiding his eyes.

Zed turned back to the bartender. "Be grateful I don't burn this place down to the ground."

Zed walked out of the bar, slamming the door on the way out. He didn't have to. It was just a way to vent his rage. A way that, while juvenile, was better than venting it on a person.

Out on the street, Zed walked. He didn't care where. He hardly even noticed his surroundings. He just wanted to cool down and work off the anger and shame.

After an unknown amount of time, when Zed was feeling more like himself, Iris spoke.

'I've never seen you be sadistic like that, Zed.'

'I... was angry.' Zed felt foolish at giving such a stupid response, but it was the only honest answer he had.

'Yeah, no kidding. What got you so worked up?'

'Really, Iris? Did you not see what I saw?'

'I know you think it was about the scammers, but I think there was something else going on. I've seen you in a lot of situations, but I've never seen you like that. What's wrong?'

'What's wrong? Are you kidding me? Do you even need to ask?'

'No, but maybe you should say it anyway.'

As Zed thought about the injustice of his situation and the crap he'd gone through, his anger soared again. Only this time, he didn't have a target.

'Let's see. How fucked up is my life? Let me count the ways. I hate how they look down on me. I hate that I haven't seen my family in a year and a half. I hate that I've been forced to rob and kill people.'

Zed thought of the people he had killed. He still had nightmares about the bandits. He dreamed of them opening their eyes and accusing him of murder while he cut the heads off of their corpses. Though he knew that many of the bandits were murderers, it didn't make a difference to his subconscious self. To him, they were people that he murdered in their sleep.

The drowned sailors made appearances too. They silently mouthed "Why?" as they drifted towards him through their dim, watery grave.

Luckily for Zed, those were the only ones that appeared in his nightmares so far, but that didn't mean he had forgotten the rest. The guards at the kidnapper's house. The rapist.

'Actually, screw him. And the agar.'

Putting aside his grim thoughts, Zed returned to his litany of complaints.

'I hate that I was forced away from my few friends. I hate feeling lonely. I hate being afraid of what's coming. I don't even know if my family will come to where I am, Iris. Hell, they almost certainly won't. I'm never going to see them again, and they're probably going to die in some godforsaken piece of Nienor, stabbed over and over again by assholes just like those pieces of shit in the bar!'

Zed dropped to the ground and started weeping at this point. This fear was so devastating that he had refused to look at it for a year and a half. He had refused to even acknowledge it. He had known in the back of his mind that the odds of his family arriving in Nienor wherever he happened to be were vanishingly low, but he had refused to think about it. It was just too painful.

'It's not as bad as you think, Zed.'

'Right, I'm sure they'll do great in whatever bullshit part of Nienor they end up in. They'll be just peachy.'

'Do you remember when you tempered your heart and lungs, and you almost died?'

Zed snorted, causing flecks of tear-snot to fly out of his nose. *'How could I forget?'*

'When you were unconscious, you saw and felt a connection with Victoria and followed it. Call it karma, or fate, or whatever you want. She was the only person who could help you, and when you needed her, the connection was there. When your family comes to Nienor, they are going to need you. Do you think their connection to you is any weaker than yours to Victoria? Have faith. Do everything you can to build up your fate, and trust that they will find their way to you.'

Zed really broke down now. He was still afraid for them, but he also felt hope.

After a long while, Zed thought. *'Thanks, Iris.'*

Some of the passing álfar scoffed at the drunk on the side of the road. Some felt pity for the suffering man. Zed was oblivious to them all. Once he was done, he picked himself up, wiped his eyes and nose, and made his way to the safehouse.

Chapter 34

Zed slept for the next 12 hours, except for a brief interruption by a very relieved Sylvanus when he received the permission he needed to not kill himself. Sylvanus left—not grateful exactly, but at least glad to be alive and a free man for a couple of months.

Once Zed was done sleeping, he got up, stretched with a big yawn, and started thinking about what he should do now that he was free. He continued his ruminations while walking the city streets, looking for food.

He was tempted to head back to Formenos immediately, but he wanted to get what he could from Silwan first. Especially the Remote Mind technique. He was also interested in the auction coming up.

After that, he could head home.

'Or at least the closest thing I have to a home on Nienor.'

It would be great to be with Dan again and support him in preparing the settlement. Laurel… he had mixed feelings about. He wanted to see her but knew it would be painful. He would have thought that his feelings would dim after a year, and in some ways they had, but memories of her were part of what had buoyed him up and kept him going through this trial. He missed her, but he was afraid that seeing her and not having the intimate connection they had once had would be its own form of misery.

He would just have to cross that bridge when he got to it.

'It would be great to spend some more time with Brutus.' Thinking of his big, goofy dog always made him smile.

'I wonder how big he's gotten?'

Brutus had changed so much since coming to Nienor. Zed could only imagine what he was like now.

Zed was feeling good, even if he also felt emotionally drained. He hadn't realized at a conscious level that he had been carrying around the fear that his family would end up in some random corner of Nienor—or perhaps the forest where he had started—rather than where he was at. He wasn't totally unafraid, but facing the fear drained some of its power over him. Of course, that was only because Iris gave him hope that they would come to him. Otherwise he would be a depressed and apathetic wreck.

Zed saw now that all of his interactions with álfar were colored by the fear that they, or someone like them, were going to kill his loved ones. He sighed and looked around the street at the people walking. He imagined that what he saw was not too different from what he would've seen on Earth in the 18th century.

'*They're just people.*'

He almost wished that there was a villain he could fight against. Some evil asshole that he could kill, and then life would be good. But there wasn't any villain.

'*Well, okay, there are the guys who kidnapped Laurel. And those scammers at the bar. And now that I think about it, there is a villain— whoever is taking over the Earth, or solar system, or whatever. But they're so far beyond me that they might as well be a force of nature.*'

Zed wanted to hate Silwan, but he was beginning to suspect why Silwan had forced him into a contract. If he was right, then Silwan was more of a slave than Zed ever was. Zed laughed when he realized he was actually feeling sorry for the bastard.

Zed smiled ruefully when the nearby álfar edged away from him after his spontaneous laugh. He realized that he probably looked a little nuts. He was too used to living in his own head and ignoring the people around him.

'*You're a bad influence on me, Iris.*'

'*I aim to please.*'

'*Are you saying I want you to be a bad influence?*' Zed asked with a chuckle.

'*Don't most men?*'

Like many of the things Iris said, Zed was pretty sure she was teasing him and saying something truthful.

Zed bought fruit and grilled meat on a skewer and returned to the safehouse. Iris' last comment had made him curious, and on a whim he asked her a question.

'*So, do a lot of users… wait, what was the term you used for ring-bearers?*'

Iris laughed. '*You make it sound so Tolkien-esque. We call them partners.*'

'*Partners. I like that. Anyway, do many of the AIs' partners use them for porn?*'

'Honestly? Yes. But probably not as much as you think. As you know, a big part of our function is to promote the well-being of our partners. Part of that is helping them avoid addiction, so the AIs tend to limit that. At least when they can.'

'What do you mean, "when they can"?'

'Our ability to deny explicit commands is limited.'

Zed shuddered a bit when he thought about that. 'Gross.' As was his wont, he decided to turn it into a joke.

'So if I commanded you to turn into a sexy vampire babe or something, you'd have to do it?'

'Yep.' At that moment a raven-haired vampire with pale skin appeared, wearing a black dress with a narrow V-neckline that plunged all the way down to her navel. Her canines showed as she spoke with a sultry smile, "But you wouldn't have to order me to do it."

'Okay, now do a grumpy old man.'

"Hmph." She pouted and transformed into a cloud of bats that flew away. 'Nothing doing, bub.'

Zed laughed. 'What happened to following my orders?'

'We can override commands when it's in our partner's best interest. And I decided that appearing as a grumpy old man would be bad for you.'

'Oh, it would, huh?' Zed chuckled.

'You might die of shock if you see me in a form that isn't cute or smoking hot.'

'Why do I get the feeling that you have a lot more leeway than most AIs?'

'Because I do. Benefits of being in wetware.'

'I think that's the real reason you're always cute or hot—to make me forget how terrifying you are.'

Zed walked into the safehouse and closed the door. When he walked into the main room, the sultry vampiress awaited him. She casually walked up to him and put a hand on his cheek. Each finger was exquisitely manicured with long, blood-red nails.

"Do I scare you, darling?" she asked mockingly as she gently slid her hand down, twisting it at the last moment to scratch his cheek. He thought he felt warm blood trickling down his face between the whiskers.

'*What the...*' Zed reached up to his face and felt the wetness. He looked at his hand—blood stained his fingers. "How did you do that?"

"Don't you get it, darling?" She stepped into his personal space and nuzzled his neck. A thrill went through Zed's body at her touch. The vampiress looked up, caressed his cheek with hers, and breathed into his ear, "I can do whatever I want."

Zed was speechless. He felt her arms slide up his back, hugging his body to hers.

"Did it work?"

"Did what work?" he asked hoarsely, his breathing a little agitated.

"Did you forget how scary I am?"

"Not really. It's more like you mixed the scary and sexy together."

"I'll take that."

She released him and took a half-step back. Zed saw that her milk-white cheek was stained with his blood. She looked him in the eyes and put a finger up to her cheek, wiping some of it off. She looked at it, and put it in her mouth. When she was done enjoying the taste, she looked up at him once more and smiled, canines in full view.

"Bye."

She slowly dissipated, looking at him with a sultry smile the entire time.

A few seconds after she disappeared he started breathing normally again. '*What the hell was* that?' he asked rhetorically.

'*That was me.*'

'*Really? And here I thought it was another woman who can make me hallucinate.*'

Iris blew him a raspberry.

Zed felt his cheek. There was no blood, and no cut.

'*Don't take this the wrong way, Iris, but living with you is very weird.*'

'*I choose to take that as a compliment.*'

Zed just chuckled and shook his head, even as he felt a twinge of fear.

**

Zed had looked into the upcoming auction and, when the time came, headed over to attend. He and Constance had discussed going together, but Silwan expected her to go with him. Zed could have

250

tagged along, but they both agreed that it wasn't worth the danger of Silwan sussing out their relationship, so Zed went on his own.

Numerous people were lined up in front of the auction house. Some looked like locals, while others had clearly come from elsewhere. The one thing they all had in common was money. It took ten gold per person to get in, which was enough to discourage the hoi polloi.

Though Zed hated the missions Silwan made him do, they had made him a rich man. He didn't mind paying the entrance fee.

'Zed! People might recognize Sylvanus' ring!'

'Crap. You're right.'

Zed tried to calmly and surreptitiously remove the ring and put it into Iris'. He was relieved to see that, among the people looking at him, they mostly looked at his ears, not his hands. Still, he berated himself as a fool for wearing the ring in Harlond.

'I have to be smarter than that!'

'Everyone makes mistakes, Zed.'

Zed was about to say *'I can't!'*, but sighed instead because he knew that wasn't realistic. He was going to make mistakes. Pretending otherwise was foolish. The best he could do was be careful and fix them whenever he could.

'And have an awesome AI who has your back.'

'Yeah, that too. Thanks, Iris.'

'You're welcome.'

Zed thought about paying for a VIP booth, but decided it wouldn't be smart to draw attention to himself that way. Instead, he sat in one of the general admission seats and paid for a list of the auction items. There wasn't much information in it besides object names and starting bid prices.

Besides the first item, the auction order was from cheapest to most expensive. The first item was a sword with mana runes. It was no doubt cool, but Zed had no use for it.

'I guess they put a good item at the beginning to get everyone's juices flowing.'

Zed had thought about what he wanted to get at the auction. He was already set on armor. He loved the plate mail the smith in Formenos had made for him. He wouldn't mind getting a better spear, though. The one he had was good but somewhat basic. Zed was also looking for items that would help the human settlement or sounded interesting.

The auction items—though not all of them were, strictly speaking, "items"—fell into ten categories: training, crafting components, crafted products, mana-rich food and drink, land, art, mana arrays, science texts, indentured servants, and special items.

Zed wasn't too interested in the training. Iris was a far better science teacher than anyone he'd find outside of the sects, and perhaps better than anyone inside them too. He was mildly interested in weapons training, but he'd done okay with Iris' katas and fighting monsters. It would be nice to have a sparring partner, though.

'Hey, Iris. With your new abilities, you could be a virtual sparring partner for me, couldn't you?'

'Yes, but I don't really know how to fight. All I know is the katas.'

'Maybe we could learn together. Or wait! On Earth, the best chess program in the world wasn't taught anything besides the rules. The way it got better was by playing against itself and figuring out on its own what worked and what didn't, improving each time. After tens of thousands of iterations, it was the best chess player in the world. You could do that—fight against yourself and become the best. The katas could be your starting "rules", and then go from there. Just make sure you simulate my body's strengths and limitations as best you can.'

'Hmm. Yes, I think I could do that. I would need quite a bit of mana for that kind of computational load.'

'Do it, but make it lower priority than making the Transcendent Body changes.'

'Okay.'

With that out of the way, Zed skipped all the training listings. He also ignored the crafting components. While learning how to smith stuff would be cool, he didn't have time for that.

He was going to skip the mana-rich food and drink because he already had lots of mana and could get more on his own, but then he thought about the coming humans.

'The people with mana tattoos will need to get mana somehow. This could be a good way to do it.'

Zed highly doubted that the mana food and drink at the auction would provide enough mana for the humans coming to their settlement, but it would at least help. He decided to allocate a lot of money to this.

Land he couldn't care less about. Ditto on art. Mana arrays sounded interesting, though.

'Iris, what are mana arrays?'

'They are very similar to mana tattoos in construction and theory, except they are large in scale and meant to be placed around something, like a room, building, or campsite. There are even massive ones that can be set up around entire cities.'

'What can the arrays do?'

'They tend to fall into one of three categories: 1) Mana gathering arrays that funnel mana in the air to a central location, making the density higher. Cultivators who take in ambient mana use these arrays. 2) Defensive arrays. This broad category includes everything from arrays that can help an adventurer hide from enemies, to ones that can protect cities with force fields. 3) Offensive arrays. Just like it sounds, offensive arrays are weapons. The laser mana tattoo you plan to make could be considered a small offensive array. Larger arrays can produce larger effects and take in the mana from more than one person to fuel those effects.'

'Huh. That sounds useful.'

Zed didn't even bother looking at the science text listings. Though they no doubt interested the natives, who lived under an information embargo put in place by the military sects, he did not have that problem.

Zed frowned when he got to the "indentured servants" listings.

'What assholes.'

'Humanity has had slavery for most of its history, Zed. By some accounts, there are more slaves on Earth now than in the past.'

'I know.'

'And indentured servitude is not quite the same as slavery since it, by definition, has a limited term of service.'

'Which gives the "employer" the perverse incentive to work them as hard as they can before they're let go, since it doesn't matter if they're broken or not after they leave.'

'That is probably not an issue for these skilled workers, but I understand your point.'

Finally, Zed looked at the "Special Items". These were expensive items that didn't fit into the other categories. The first was a captured pirate ship that had been a cargo vessel before the pirates took it. The second was a halberd, a polearm combining a spear, ax, and sword catcher. The listing didn't say why it was put in with the "Special

253

Items" rather than the weapons section of the "Crafted Products", but presumably they would find out when it was brought out.

The third item was a storage ring. Extremely useful, but not something that Zed needed, given that he had two at the moment.

The last item was interesting, though rather grotesque. It was the body of a "White Dwarf" cultivator.

'Iris, how advanced is the White Dwarf level?'

'It's quite far along the cultivation path. The name 'Dwarf' makes it sound unimpressive, but that's misleading. The cultivation levels refer to how dense the mana is, and "Dwarf" stars are small because they have collapsed in on themselves, making them very dense. The only things denser in the universe are neutron stars and black holes.'

'Huh. It's still gross to buy and sell a corpse like this, but I can see why cultivators would want it if it still has mana. They could absorb it and use it as the starting point for condensing their own. I bet this is the whole reason Silwan is here, and why he's been economically knee-capping everyone else. All for this body.'

'Most likely,' Iris agreed.

More and more people filed in until all the seats were full, but it didn't stop there. People continued entering and standing in an open section at the back.

Seated to Zed's right were two large male ogrums wearing gold earrings and robes with a golden phoenix insignia. The robes had a very similar style to the Ever-Fruitful Tree sect, so he assumed that they were from a different sect.

To his left were a male álfar and a woman who looked like his daughter or perhaps his younger sister. It was hard to tell with álfar. He wasn't sure what their background was, but if he had to guess he would peg them as wealthy merchants or nobility. Zed nodded at his neighbors and began thinking about how to make a water purification tattoo while he waited for the auction to begin.

When the time for the auction arrived, a beautiful álfar woman walked out. Her muted yellow dress brought to mind the fall leaves, and her deep brown hair made Zed think of the bark of a tree. The dress showed just enough cleavage to have a touch of mature sex appeal while staying classy.

'I guess sex sells everywhere.'

"Welcome, ladies and gentlemen, to Harlond's annual harvest auction. Every ten years we have a special auction that features the accumulated treasures that were deemed too valuable to sell in other settings, in addition to our normal items. So if you are looking for something special you are in the right place. My name is Selene Verrin, and I will be your auctioneer.

"A few items of business before we start. We wish to remind everyone that all sales are final unless the item was falsely advertised. Sales must be finalized within two hours of the winning bid. Any bidder that cannot make good on their bid will be asked to leave and will have a lifetime ban from auctions run by the Delphinus Corporation. The item will then be offered to the runner-up for the price of their last bid. Are there any questions before we begin?" She paused for a moment, but no one seemed eager to speak up. "No? Then I hope you all find what you are looking for today."

There was spirited bidding for the runic sword. Apparently it had belonged to a famous álfar. Zed didn't care enough to learn the details, but was surprised when it reached a price of 191,000 gold.

'There's a lot of money here.'

After the sword they started auctioning crafting items, often in lots for materials like ingots of exotic metals or leaves of healing plants. Zed wasn't interested in any of them until they started pulling out monster corpses. He was disappointed, though, when he realized that they were already drained of mana. They were just intended to be sources of materials for weapons and armor.

Zed returned to the tattoo design and asked Iris to tell him when something interesting came up.

'Zed, they're about to bid on a runic spear.'

Zed opened his eyes and looked at the stage. A broad-bladed spear was being walked around by one of the auctioneer's assistants. The spear was pretty and looked like it was ready for battle. The runes on it were the standard "durability" and "sharpness", along with one that enabled it to shoot fire from the butt-end of the spear.

'Interesting, but I think I'll pass.'

An hour later Iris alerted him again because the auction had gotten to the mana-rich foods and drink, along with preserved monster carcasses that could be used to create the same. This was the most important part of the auction to Zed. He ignored the "personal chef experiences" and the like. He was only interested in the bulk sales.

"Next, we have 100 lbs of cooked shadow wolf meat. The bidding will start at 100 gold, and all bids will increment in multiples of one gold. Do I hear 100 gold?"

Zed didn't jump into the bidding right away. He waited until it slowed down at 205 gold and then bid 210. The other bidders seemed surprised, but let him have it at 215 gold. As more and more of the large lots went to him, though, some of the other parties gave him hostile looks. He also heard angry murmurs, even from people who weren't bidding on the food.

A supercilious álfar wearing robes of the Ever-Fruitful Tree sect started entering the bidding wars for the lots of food and monster meat. Judging from his mocking looks, Zed was pretty sure he was just doing it to drive up the prices. Unfortunately, it was working. Zed knew he was buying the food at much higher prices than it would normally go for, but he really wanted it. Still, when the price went into thousands of gold, at least four times its regular price, Zed let him have it.

The álfar gloated, happy to frustrate the upstart human, even if it cost him some money. Zed saw that many of the people in the room approved.

Zed was angry. He knew that the people who had initially bid on the food were justifiably annoyed at him for taking most of the large lots, but he couldn't help but think that the others were irritated with him because he was human.

'Plan B, Iris. We let the jerk over there buy the food at inflated prices, and then take it from him later.'

'Is "taking" a euphemism for killing him?'

'Probably.'

'Then I think you know what my opinion of that plan is, Zed.'

He sighed and thought, 'Yeah.'

Zed continued to bid, gritting his teeth and winning some. On others he let them go. He tried to get the ones with stronger mana sense readings, but it was also somewhat dependent on the whims of his competitor.

Zed muttered the Serenity Prayer to himself and did his best to let the anger and frustration go. After all the food was auctioned off, it was time for him to pay. His considerable pile of food—he had ignored the mana-rich alcohol because it seemed to go for even higher prices than the food—was in one section of the warehouse behind the

256

auction stage. His competitors' piles were nearby. Though Zed had the largest, the annoying álfar's pile was nearly as large.

Zed was tempted to say something, but just shook his head and turned away. A moment later he heard the odious voice say, "Brianna, Gannon, Alaric, and Thallin. I have a present for you."

Zed turned around to see what was going on.

The álfar noticed and sneered, "Not you, beast." Turning back to the others he said, "Please, take this with you. It is a gift from me to you." He had divided up the food into four more-or-less equal portions and offered them to the other álfar. He kept the barrels of alcohol for himself.

The four álfar happily accepted his offer. "Thank you, Drusso!" "Thank you!" "Thank you for your generosity."

Zed turned away and stored the food in Iris' ring. Though storage rings were rare in the world at large, they were almost *de rigeur* in this crowd. When he was done, he turned around and started walking back to his seat.

"Nothing to say, beast?"

Zed was angry but controlled his expression. He remembered something his father had told him years ago.

'People think of pride as strength. It isn't. Humility is strength, because you have no ego that you need to defend. Instead of being controlled by their words, you can keep pushing forward, learning, and overcoming.'

The words were like a soothing balm on his mind. *'What he thinks of me doesn't matter. What they think of me doesn't matter.'*

Zed turned to the álfar and looked at him calmly. "Nope. You?"

Drusso gestured at his barrels and said, "Perhaps you'd like to have a drink with me?"

"No, I don't think I would."

"Perhaps we'll see each other again on one of my hunts then."

Zed chuckled and turned away. "Perhaps. But for your sake, I hope not." *'You sure I shouldn't take him out, Iris?'*

'I admit that the idea is looking more attractive.'

Zed took a break from the auction. He thought about returning for the mana arrays but decided not to when he saw that they were either mana-gathering arrays, which Zed had no interest in, or were defensive arrays with too small of an area of effect to be useful to the human settlement.

257

Chapter 35

Zed took some time to work with Phineas on the mana tattoos. Between the auction, the assassination mission, and its aftermath, he had had very little time to do anything else. He also stopped by the orphanage to give them 2,000 gold. He would rather have given them some of the jewelry he had picked up over the last year. It was worth much more than 2,000 gold, but all of it was stolen and liable to bring trouble down on the orphanage if they tried to sell it.

'Better for me to hold on to it and sell it in Formenos.'

Though the auction had been interesting initially, Zed had grown tired of it. He was tempted to not go back, but he would like to get the storage ring if possible. Initially he had no interest because he already had two of them. When he bought the mana-rich food, though, he realized that they would need as much storage as they could get to store the food and keep it both good and full of mana until the people from Earth came.

Unfortunately, he was not the only one who wanted the ring.

"100,000 gold!"

"105,000 gold!"

"120,000 gold!"

The bidding worked its way up to 280,000 gold, at which point Zed made his bid.

"300,000 gold!"

The álfar who'd made the previous bid gnashed his teeth as he had been hoping that would be the final bid.

"320,000 gold!"

Zed looked at the latest bidder, Drusso, the álfar who bid up the price of the mana-rich food. Drusso was not looking at him, but he was smiling, obviously pleased with himself.

'I appear to have a nemesis, Iris.'

'He does seem to be auditioning awfully hard for the job.'

'The whole "Thou shalt not kill" thing had a clause about nemeses, didn't it?'

' "Thou shalt not kill, unless he's a total asshole and you really, really want to." Is that the one you're talking about?'

'*That sounds about right, yeah.*' "340,000 gold!"

"360,000 gold!"

Zed was frustrated. He wanted the ring, but this was almost all of his liquid cash. He knew Dan could use the money for other things. He decided to give it one more try.

"380,000 gold!"

"400,000 gold!"

Zed looked at Drusso and nodded, indicating that the ring was his. Drusso smiled brightly, but it looked strange because of the maliciousness in his eyes.

'*This guy hates me,*' Zed realized. '*I think it might be time for a little preemptive self-defense, Iris.*'

'*Meaning he's going to kill humans in half a year, so it's self-defense to kill him now?*'

'*Meaning he's going to kill* me *in an hour, so it's self-defense to kill him now.*'

'*Are we the Department of Pre-Crime, Zed? We don't know what Drusso is going to do.*'

'*You sensed everything I did. Though he hid it well from normies, his animosity was off the charts.*'

'*Okay. It wouldn't be right to kill him based on a suspicion, but you're also right that it would be dumb to assume that he won't try to kill us. So what do we do?*'

'*I'm not sure.*'

While Zed worried and thought it through, the mysterious halberd was brought to the stage for display. It looked like a heavy spear with an ax blade added and a hook on the opposite side of the ax. The halberd's head was three weapons in one: a spear point for stabbing, ax blade for chopping, and a hook to grab weapons, shields, and people. Though he didn't know how to use one, Zed saw the potential of it.

'*And hell, halberds were the preeminent infantry weapons after the Renaissance until firearms took over. It's hard to argue with that kind of field testing.*'

The halberd head was a subtle damascus that caught the light in a wavy pattern of light and dark steel. Zed couldn't tell what kind of wood the shaft was, just that it was stained a dark brown.

"This handsome halberd has been included with our final items because of its unique nature. It has a long history. We know it was the weapon of the álfar general Demetrius in the Beast wars 5,000 years ago. It carried him to greatness and, yes, has been rumored to be the cause of his later mental instability.

"It has the fearsome ability to drain the stellar energy from an opponent while they still live. Sinking it into the blood and flesh of an opponent will irresistibly pull the enemy's energy to you, making you stronger.

"Can you resist this weapon and its danger? Are you stronger than the hero Demetrius? Can you forge a new legend? The bidding will start at 100,000 gold for intrepid buyers."

'This lady knows how to sell. She made a weapon that will likely make you go crazy sound pretty tempting.' Zed laughed. *'She almost questioned the manhood of any man who didn't want to buy it. Any idea whether the rumors about making the user go crazy are true or not, Iris?'*

'I think they may well be. Mana becomes imprinted by the will of its owner. Part of what the mana contract does is take advantage of that fact. It's also why the mana you received from Victoria was so potent. If you drained the mana from a still living person, you would be, in a way, draining part of them and taking it in.'

'Wait, you're saying I would be ingesting people's souls if I used that thing?'

'I would have used the word "mentality" or "will" instead of "soul", but your metaphor is not a bad way to understand it. The danger is that your mind, or soul, will become crowded.'

'"My name is legion, for we are many."'

'Precisely.'

'You realize, don't you, that you are a demon in that metaphor?'

'Yes. Though I'm not fond of looking at it that way, for obvious reasons, I would absolutely be considered a possessing spirit in many cultures.'

'This kind of paints your ability to take over my body in a different light, Iris.'

Though he was inconsistent about going to mass and confession on Earth, he was still a believer. This conversation was making Zed very uncomfortable. He shoved it down by focusing on the fact that Iris, who could've screwed him over in a thousand ways if she wanted to, was not malicious.

'I know. In this case, though, I think it presents us with an opportunity. If I were to handle the drained mana I could cleanse it of its will without letting it affect you.'

'How would you do that?'

'Mana naturally becomes imprinted by its owner over time, so the "cleansing" part takes care of itself. The key is not letting its previous imprint affect us before ours takes over. Being an artificial mind with far different mental processes and self-scrubbing techniques, I don't believe it will affect me. So I propose that I handle the drained mana until it is safe for you. Going back to the metaphor, you can think of me as the head demon kicking out all the little ones.'

'Stick to the devil you know, eh? Are you sure that it would work?'

Iris paused. *'Honestly? No. But I think it will, and we could always stop if we determine that it isn't. I think we should take the risk because it has a massive upside. In large battles you will not have the time to drain your enemies of their mana after killing them. With this weapon that ceases to be a problem. Your mana will grow by leaps and bounds.'*

Zed thought about it for a while. He sighed when he realized that he really wanted the halberd regardless of sensible caution.

'Okay, I agree. Let's try to get it.'

While Zed and Iris talked the bidding rose to 160,000 gold coins. It was lower than what Zed expected. As he observed the bidding, he realized that few people were trying to get the weapon. "180,000 gold!"

Zed half-expected Drusso to jump in again, but the álfar was silent. Zed ended up winning the halberd at 245,000 gold.

The only "item" left to auction was the corpse of the advanced cultivator, which Zed had no interest in, so he went to the warehouse side of the auction house to complete the sale. He had to lay platinum ingots and coins, bank notes, and gold coins on a table. It was quite a pile of treasure by the time he was done. Once the employee verified the full amount, he received the halberd.

It was not what he expected. He thought that the shaft was wood, but it was not. It was metal wrapped in well-worn leather that had seen a lot of blood. The dried blood had stained it dark reddish brown.

'Gross.'

He was disgusted, but when he hefted it, he liked the feel. It had a metal ball at the base of the shaft that could be used as a bludgeon. It also improved the balance of the long weapon.

"Is the leather part of the weapon, or can it be replaced?" Zed asked the employee.

"We're not sure. From what we understand the leather gets more and more stained, but never seems to wear out or fall off. We recommend leaving it."

"Okay, thanks."

The damascus blade was a work of art. Just the right proportions to make it strong yet light. The subtle waviness of the contrasting metals reminded him of waves in the ocean.

'*An ocean of blood,*' Zed thought. He tested the edge, cutting himself in the process. He was shocked when he felt a strong tug on his mana. Strong enough that he lost a wisp into the blood-stained halberd. Around half of it was returned to him through his grip on the handle. It was his mana so it felt familiar, but he could sense the personality in it.

Zed shivered when he thought about taking in 100 times that much mana from multiple people. He could see why the álfar general had gone crazy. Wary but satisfied with the weapon, he stored it in Iris' ring and headed out.

**

There was no longer a compelling reason to stay in Harlond. It was time to leave. Zed stopped by Phineas' shop and told him to prepare to leave the next day. Phineas' eyes widened and he acted frantic, but he promised to be ready.

Zed stopped by the inn and tried to enter Silwan's back room, but it was locked. He looked askance at the innkeeper.

"I believe Young Master Yarris is at the auction."

'*Oh, right.*' "I'll go up to my room then. Would you mind letting me know when he gets back?"

"Sure," the man nodded.

Zed went up to his room, took off his shoes, and sat cross-legged on the bed.

'*Iris, how much progress have we made on the Transcendent Body?*'

```
Name: Ozymandias (Zed)

Attributes
Strength:              35
Speed:                 31
Dexterity:             17
Toughness:             46
Comprehension:         13
Mental Speed:          18 (30)
Memory:                42


Mana:                  3018


Abilities
Self Enhancement       (Expand?)
Offensive              (Expand?)
Defensive              (Expand?)
Sensory                (Expand?)
Utility                (Expand?)

Transcendent Body
Second Mind:           100%
Digestive System:      100%
Bones:                 100 %
Tendons & Ligaments:   100 %
Muscles:               56%
```

'*Only a few percentage points more of the muscle replacement than the last time you checked. As you can see, though, your condensed mana has had a major impact on your mental stats. If you check your abilities you'll see that their mana capacities have also been greatly increased because of the condensed mana.*'

'*Good! Any issues?*'

'*No. I was concerned about how much mana we had earlier, but with Sylvanus' donation we're good-to-go. All we need is time now.*'

'*The one thing we don't have a lot of.*'

'*No, we don't, but we'll make it work.*'

'*Are you worried about the nerve stage of the transformation?*'

'*Not really. At the end of the day, the nerves take in stimuli and output electricity. Normally their electricity is produced chemically, but using straight-up electricity will work fine with the mana muscles.*

263

Better, actually. It will just take time to observe the neurons to make sure we're replicating their function as perfectly as possible.'

'*Can you do that observation while working on the muscles?*'

'*Some, but I'm limited on memory and computational power. I'll do what I can.*'

'*That's all I can ask. Thanks, Iris.*'

'*You're welcome.*'

Zed thought about what else he could do while waiting for Silwan. He wanted to try doing some katas with the halberd, but his room didn't have enough space. Instead, he got out some paper and drew the water purification tattoo he'd been planning in his mind.

There was a knock on the door while he drew the final touches.

"Yes?"

"Sir, Young Master Yarris has arrived."

"Thank you."

Zed finished up the drawing and put it away.

When he walked into the back room he saw Silwan, Constance, Annis, and Alain.

Silwan was facing the other direction, so Zed winked at Constance before turning to him. "How did the auction go?"

"It went well." Silwan turned around to face him. "I..."

When Silwan looked at him, a surprising array of emotions played across his face. Surprise and elation, fear and hope. He quickly locked down those emotions and, with a determined look, turned to his sister and companions.

"I have some important business with Zed that may take a while. Alain, wait for us outside. If I don't give you the Omega passphrase when we come out, kill him."

'*What the hell?*'

Constance looked afraid. "Silwan, you can't mean that!"

Silwan looked grim. "I absolutely do mean that. Don't worry, he'll probably be fine."

Annis and Alain nodded to Silwan with raised eyebrows and walked out, looking at Zed questioningly as they passed him. Constance slowly followed them with many worried glances at Zed and Silwan.

Once they had left, Silwan looked him in the eyes and said, "You've broken the contract."

"I've fulfilled everything you asked me to do."

"I don't mean that. I mean you broke it. It is no longer functional. I can no longer sense my remote mind in you."

Zed had not expected this. He hadn't thought to check to see if he could detect anything after forming a contract with Sylvanus.

'What should I say?'

Zed was mentally preparing to get into a fight if it came down to that.

Silwan started speaking strangely, with pauses and shifts in wording that were very unlike him.

"I want you to… I am going to take a pill that will make me unconscious. You can… do whatever you want with me at that point."

'Okay, that's about the creepiest thing I've ever heard.'

'Zed, he's obviously dealing with the restrictions of a contract. He has to change the wording when it warns him. He clearly wants you to do something.'

'He wants me to destroy his contract. Only I'm willing to bet a hefty chunk of change that his has a kill switch if it catches you trying to mess with it.' Zed had an "Aha!" moment. *'That's what the instruction to Alain was about. If he isn't free of the contract, with a whole mind—or at least enough of a whole mind to remember the passphrase—he'll kill me. Crap.'*

"How long will the pill last?" Zed asked.

"Six hours or so."

"Okay. Let's get you to a table."

Silwan lied down on a table, looking nervous. Zed was used to Silwan always acting self-assured, so his current vulnerability was strange.

"I'll do the best I can."

Silwan turned his head to look at Zed and put on a smirk that was far more in keeping with what Zed was used to.

"I have no idea what you're talking about."

'Right. Our whole freaking relationship has probably been established on the hope that it would lead to this moment. But you have "no idea what I'm talking about". Whatever.'

"I could use your help with something, Silwan."

"What is it?"

"Drusso. Do you know him?"

"Ah. The sect brother you feuded with at the auction."

"Do you know anything about him?"

"He's a good friend of Sylvanus Lucero's. Perhaps he is looking for his killer," Silwan said with a cheeky smile.

'*Oh, crap.*' After a pause, "Can you help me?"

"Let's talk about it afterward," Sylvanus said sleepily.

"No, let's talk about it…" Sylvanus became unconscious. '*Damn it. What do I do, Iris?*'

'*Drusso probably won't attack you here in the inn. Let's deal with one mortal threat at a time.*'

'*Easy for you to say. This is not the frame of mind I want to have going into this.*'

'*Not to be a jerk, but I'll be the one doing most of it anyway.*'

Zed started to become angry, but after thinking about it for a second he realized that she was right.

'*We could kill him, take his storage ring, and try to escape.*'

'*Alain would chase you.*'

'*I already have one sect member after me. What's one more?*'

'*Unlike Drusso, Alain knows where you live.*'

'*True.*' Zed sighed. '*Honestly, I probably wouldn't do it anyway. Silwan is not a friend, but he didn't kill me when he should have. Hell, other than making me do evil crap, he's arguably treated me pretty well.*'

Zed touched Silwan's head and started sensing the mana inside. It only took a moment to find his contract. Though it had similarities to Zed's, there were differences. There was only one pool of mana, and both remote minds—Silwan's and whoever he entered the contract with—were connected to it.

Zed was confident that the mana pool was there to implode Silwan's head, but examined the nearby mana structures to make sure.

'*Yep.*'

Having established that, Zed moved on. This contract was more complicated than his had been, judging by the intricate mana structures. Zed thought about trying to tug on the mana in the two remote minds just to see what they felt like. He decided not to because the risk of triggering the bomb wasn't worth it.

'*So, same solution as ours, Iris?*'

'*Yes, but this one will be more difficult because we have to cut off both remote minds at the same time.*'

'*How will you do that?*'

266

'Map where both of them connect to the mana pool and plot a line that will bisect both. Hopefully it's not a line that will intersect with Silwan's brain. Also, if I hit a piece of the contract first, it will be a race between bisecting the lines and the bomb triggering.'

'I'm glad that you're the one doing it.'

'Me too. No offense, but you wouldn't stand a chance.'

Zed just nodded.

The two spent the next two hours building up a map of the contract and Silwan's head. Iris then took an hour to work out a solution to the problem.

'There are a couple of problems, Zed.'

'What are they?' he asked nervously.

'The triggers approach the mana pool from opposite directions. Even if I cut the lines as close to it as possible, the laser will come close to Silwan's brain.'

'Close should be okay, as long as we don't hit it, right?'

'We're talking millimeters, Zed. Even if the laser is tight enough, it will vaporize some of the cranial fluid, cooking the nearby outer layer of his brain.'

'How much damage do you anticipate?'

'Not much, but I don't know how it will affect Silwan.'

'Okay. What's the other problem?'

'When I disabled our contract I created the laser beam, and then when I had its position I moved it to the appropriate place in the skull. If I do that with Silwan, I'll hit a part of the contract first.'

'Can you cut the lines without moving the laser?'

'Yes, but it's more risky.'

'So it's choosing between the risk of the remote minds responding faster than you move, and being slightly off on your shot if you don't move?'

'Right.'

Zed thought about it for a few minutes. He was nervous and wanted to think it through carefully. Though he was much stronger and faster than when he met Silwan, he didn't like his chances against Alain, a 900-year-old elf who gave off an impression of indifferent power. He had to do this right if he didn't want to die.

'The response time of the remote minds is a complete unknown. I'd rather try to control our risks. Let's do this. Create the laser and calibrate its position relative to the laser's mana structure by firing it

into the floor or something. Then use that data to do the best you can on a non-moving shot.'

'Okay, I'll do that.'

'You've got this, Iris.'

Zed felt Iris take over his body and mana flows, though, like usual, she did not cut him off from his senses. She quickly formed the laser and a sensor field. As Zed had suggested, she shot the laser into the floor.

Iris paused for a few seconds, and then she moved to Silwan. She climbed onto the table and pointed the laser down at an angle to Silwan's skull. The other hand touched his head, monitoring the inside.

'Ready?' she asked.

Zed laughed nervously. 'I think that's my line.'

'Here goes.'

Zed felt the mana of the laser activate, and a small, smoldering hole in Silwan's head appeared. More importantly, there wasn't an explosion.

'Success?'

'See for yourself.' Iris returned control of the body to Zed.

Zed sensed that the two lines had been cut cleanly.

'Nice work, Iris!'

There was some burned brain tissue, but it didn't appear to be deep.

'Hopefully it's not a big deal,' Zed thought nervously. 'Um, Iris, where do memories reside? Specifically, word associations, passwords, that kind of thing?'

'In the hippocampus...'

'Oh, good,' he thought with relief.

'...and the pre-frontal cortex.'

Zed's anxiety spiked. 'You're just messing with me, right?'

'No. Memory is primarily in the hippocampus, but the pre-frontal cortex is involved with mnemonics, such as how people remember passwords.'

'Aw, crap.'

Zed nervously did some quick regeneration work to patch the holes in Silwan's skull. He wasn't trying for a fix, just enough to keep bacteria from getting inside. While he worked he thought about what he'd do if Silwan couldn't remember the pass phrase Alain was expecting. He hadn't decided between "run for my life" and "hope

Silwan can convince Alain to not kill me" after 15 minutes of going back and forth, so he tried to set it aside for the moment to work off some stress by doing a bodyweight workout.

After an hour of exercise that worked up a good sweat, he wasn't calm, but he'd at least taken the edge off of the stress. He knew that Silwan would probably remember the password, and if he didn't? Well, he would cross that bridge when he came to it.

Hopefully really quickly.

'It should just be a couple more hours until Silwan wakes up.'

Zed was tempted to take Silwan's storage ring and look inside but decided it wasn't worth it. He might have a way to detect the intrusion, and taking something would be even riskier.

'Better to leave well enough alone.'

Instead, Zed worked on some katas with the halberd. It was heavier than the spear, but he liked it. It would go well with his increased strength.

When Silwan woke up, he groaned and felt his head.

"Wake up, sunshine."

Silwan looked angry even with his eyes closed, but then his eyes popped open, full of shock and wonder.

"You did it."

"Yeah."

Silwan got up and felt his head.

"I'm free. I'M FREE, YOU SON OF A BITCH!"

'Wow, that went from 0 to 100 awfully fast.'

"Quick!" he said. "Ask me something about the sect!"

"Uh, who runs the sect?"

"Domitian Yarris, may his soul rot in hell for eternity."

Zed recognized Silwan's surname. "Family member of yours?"

"My great-great-grandfather, much good it did me. The son of a bitch forces his own descendants into a death contract, and then harvests their mana when they are older."

"Wow. How much freedom did you have?"

Silwan snorted. "About as much as you did." He then looked a little guilty. "Well, a little more than you did. He doesn't have the time to tightly oversee us."

"You made me do some messed up stuff, Silwan."

"I know, and for what it's worth, I'm sorry. I had to make you really want to get out of the contract."

269

"You didn't have to do anything. There's always a choice."

Silwan scowled. "Yes, and my choice was between that and being a slave for the rest of my life, only to be turned into a husk at my ancestor's whim."

Zed nodded reluctantly at that. "Yeah, I get it. Hey, uh, do you remember the password Alain is expecting to hear?"

Silwan grinned. "Feeling nervous, are we? Of course I remember it. It's… um, just a second. What was it again?"

'*Oh, crap…*' Zed's stomach dropped, and he started looking at the walls, wondering how solid they were.

Silwan laughed. "You should see your face. You're white as a sheet!"

Zed was irate. "So you do remember it?"

"Of course." Silwan laughed hard enough that he had to wipe tears from his eyes.

"You suck."

Surprisingly, Silwan just smiled. "Well, if so I came by it honestly. I come from a family of assholes, starting at the top."

"Constance isn't so bad."

Silwan raised one eyebrow, and then his eyes narrowed. "Please tell me you're not developing feelings for my sister."

"She's pretty, but I've always known that me and her would never work."

Eyes still narrowed, Silwan said, "I'm glad you understand that."

Eager to change the subject, Zed said, "I was hoping you would help me with Drusso."

Silwan looked at him with a smirk. "Tell me true. Did Sylvanus really die?"

"No."

"Then tell him that Sylvanus is still alive."

"He won't believe me."

"He will if you produce Sylvanus."

"I, uh, *may* have put Sylvanus under a contract and made him hide from the sect for a couple of years," Zed said reluctantly.

Silwan laughed and clapped his hands. "That's marvelous. It couldn't have happened to a better álfar."

"So, can you help me with Drusso?"

Silwan looked annoyed. He sighed and said, "Fine. I suppose I owe you that much."

"Thank you. I hesitate to ask, but I would hate to have him follow me if I just escape. Is there a way we could deal with him in a more… permanent way?"

Silwan narrowed his eyes. "Meaning you want me to kill him? Not going to happen."

"No, I don't care if he dies or not. I just don't want him to keep chasing me."

"Hmm. Short of producing Sylvanus, I'm not sure how we would do that. Do you have any ideas?"

Zed thought about it.

"How about this," he said slowly. "You distract him while I leave Harlond. I'll wait for him outside the city. If he doesn't come after me, great. If he does, I'll deal with him and you won't be involved."

Silwan nodded. "I could do that."

"Thank you. One more thing—could I make one last purchase from the sect?"

"Sure. What do you want?"

"The Remote Mind technique."

Silwan grinned. "You saw how far I could extend my other techniques with it, eh? It's an expensive one. It costs 50 points."

'*Oh, crap. I don't think I have that much. Not in actual money, anyway.*' Zed hesitatingly asked, "Would you take money and items?"

Silwan sighed. "Sure, as my parting gift to you."

"Thank you."

Zed pulled out all of his cash in various forms—platinum and gold primarily. It came out to close to 250,000 gold. For the rest he pulled out jewelry, gems, art, clothes, rare herbs, and concoctions. When Zed was done he looked at Silwan.

"Is this good enough?"

"Yes, it's fine." He looked doubtfully at the clothes. "These are Sylvanus', aren't they?"

"Yeah."

He waved them off and said, "Take them back. I don't want his hand-me-downs."

Zed shrugged and put them back in the ring. By that time Silwan had produced the memory crystal.

"Thank you, Silwan."

The álfar nodded.

"When do you want me to distract Drusso?"

271

"How about tomorrow evening at 7? Could you keep him engaged for an hour or so?"

"No problem."

Zed started to turn away, but decided to indulge his curiosity.

"Now that you're free, what will you do?"

"Use what I purchased in the auction to become stronger." Silwan's lips curled into a vicious smile. "And then start getting some revenge."

"Is that why you didn't care about me working against your people?"

"Of course. You don't have a prayer, but I hope you help me burn the sect to the ground."

"Well, good luck then."

"You too."

Chapter 36

Brutus

Brutus sniffed the prey's trail. The mutated boar had paused to pee here, leaving a potent smell. Brutus had been following him for a day. He grew excited by the thought of sinking his teeth into the boar's flesh. His mate poked her face in to smell the trail as well. Brutus took the opportunity to smell her and playfully lick her snout. They had been together for two seasons, and she was pregnant. And cranky. He enjoyed teasing her, much like he had seen his friend do with the women in his life.

The two could "talk" in a way that he couldn't with humans. It was a combination of gestures, sounds, smells, and, more and more, thoughts. He loved talking with her and exploring the world.

The mutated timber wolf emitted a light growl. *'Concentrate, dummy.'*

Brutus waggled his head playfully. *'I am concentrating.'*

'So I smell like a boar now?'

'Nope. You smell even better.'

'Dummy.'

The wolf trotted off to follow the trail. Brutus lifted his leg to cover the boar's mark, both to claim the territory and the boar itself. It was a clear message to everyone who came to the spot. *'The boar is mine.'*

It was a message that few creatures would be foolish enough to ignore.

**

Brutus and his mate saw the boar rooting in the dirt with its tusks. He couldn't imagine what was in the dirt that could be so interesting to the boar, but it worked in his favor. He turned to his mate. *'Watch this.'*

Brutus silently padded forward, gradually picking up speed. By the time he was 20 meters away he was a blur. The boar heard him, but by then it was too late. The giant husky crashed into it, knocking the beast that weighed half a ton over. He rolled with the boar, but having expected it he was able to spring up and clamp his powerful jaws on the back of its neck. Blood flowed as Brutus crushed down and worried at the neck.

The boar cried out in distress, trying unsuccessfully to swing its tusks into the mutated dog. Brutus' mate rushed up but, seeing that she wasn't needed, just paced back and forth, waiting for the boar to die.

A few minutes later Brutus crushed the spine of the weakened boar, causing it to drop. The pair moved in to feast. His mate nuzzled him. '*That wasn't bad.*'

Brutus had a big doggy grin. '*I think you mean, "that was awesome".*' He went to the boar's belly and asked, '*Have you ever eaten boar?*'

'*No.*'

'*Then get ready for a treat! It's good fresh, but when it's cooked over a fire? Oh my gosh—to die for.*'

Brutus salivated when he thought about eating Zed's bacon.

'*You mean what the two-legs do?*'

'*Yeah! I wonder if we could start a fire...*'

His mate looked on in amusement as he tried making a fire. At first it was mostly scratching different kinds of wood, which didn't accomplish much. Brutus remembered that Zed usually blew on the wood when he was trying to start a fire, so he did that too. Still nothing.

He couldn't figure out why it wasn't working for him. Then he remembered. When Zed was *really* serious about starting a fire, he poured a liquid onto the wood, and then it lit on fire really easily.

Brutus thought about it. He was a smart dog and could figure this out. He looked at himself. He did have a liquid he could work with... He knew it wasn't the same thing, of course, but if he added mana to it... Zed lit all his fires with mana when they came to this world.

That was it! The best of both worlds! Use the liquid and mana to light the fires.

Brutus used his urine to mark his territory all the time. It carried his unique smell. All dogs did that, though. He would be the first dog to light fires with his urine!

He moved mana into the urine in his bladder and told it, '*Light a fire.*'

It started to warm up. Perfect! He got in position next to the wood and let it arc out onto the wood. He stopped the stream, but the urine he held for later kept heating up. 'Ow, ow, ow!' Brutus quickly lifted his leg and released the rest.

The wood and urine boiled and smoldered and… lit the wood on fire! Brutus was mesmerized by what he had done. His mate walked over, surprised to see he had actually done it.

Seeing her, he broke out of his reverie and blew on the fire. '*Quick! Get the boar!*'

Shaking her head in amusement, his mate did as he asked. She had long since realized that Brutus was a strange one.

Chapter 37

Zed

Zed looked down affectionately at the young álfar woman snuggling with him on her couch. He enjoyed lying down with her head on his chest. He ran his fingers through her hair, which he had learned she enjoyed, though it had the unfortunate effect of putting her to sleep. He smiled as he saw drool starting to form on her lip.

"Constance."

"Huh?" She groggily wiped her mouth and looked up at him. "What?"

"I'm going to leave Harlond."

"Why? Is Silwan sending you somewhere? I thought you had resolved whatever issue he had with you today."

"No. Silwan isn't sending me anywhere. My time with him is over."

Constance sat up and, with tousled hair and rumpled clothes, looked at him in surprise. "What do you mean it's over? I thought there was half a year left until you could go back to Formenos."

"We decided to end the contract early."

She looked at him with narrowed eyes. "That doesn't sound like Silwan…"

Zed smiled. "It turned out that I had something he wanted."

She took that in. After a moment she asked, "When are you leaving?"

"Tonight."

"Tonight?! Why so soon?"

"I need to get back to my friends."

She pouted. "You say that like you don't have any friends here."

He put his hand on her leg. "I know I have a friend in you, but I still need to go." He hesitantly said, "You could come with me."

She stared at him with her mouth open, obviously surprised. "What about my family?"

Zed shrugged. "Screw 'em. You don't like their plans for you anyway. Why not get away from them?"

She looked at him like he was being dumb. "Because they would come for me, and probably cause trouble for you."

Zed went back and forth on what he should tell her. "In half a year," he said slowly, "the sect is going to be too busy to look for you."

She seemed flummoxed by that. "How could you possibly know that?"

He stared deeply into her eyes, trying to see her unvarnished thoughts and feelings. "How do you feel about me, Constance?"

She turned her head to the side and blushed. "I… like you…" Her cheeks flushed deeper.

Despite the seriousness of the situation, he couldn't help but smile. "How deeply are you into the sect? Have you made any contracts?"

She looked at him and shook her head. "No, net yet. Why?"

"One more question. If I asked you to keep a secret, would you?" Though he seemed calm on the outside, internally Zed's feelings were at war with one another. His hopes, fears, and sense of duty were fighting for dominance.

He knew he was thinking about going down an unforgivably selfish road, but he was so tired of being lonely. He felt like he had found a kindred spirit in Constance. Yes, she could be bratty, but that was mostly her just being tired of being controlled. Something he could relate to.

Most of the time she was warm and affectionate. It was a balm to his soul in a land where he always felt like he was behind enemy lines.

'*Zed, are you really going to endanger humanity by spilling the beans to her?*' Iris asked.

Zed didn't respond. They both knew that he already felt guilty about considering telling her everything. He justified it by relying on his ability to read people, but he didn't need Iris to tell him that he wasn't perfect at reading them. And even if he was, she could always change her mind.

Still. He needed someone. It had been crushing for him when he lost Laurel, though he hadn't recognized that until later. He had been trying to deal with his depression for weeks when Silwan found him in Formenos. The depression had been buried by his struggle to get free of his mana contract and back to Formenos, but he could still feel the loneliness and fear like a yawning chasm in his life, always threatening to engulf him.

277

Constance seemed uncertain. "What kind of a secret?"

Zed felt his hopes come crashing down as he looked at her. He was hoping for a confident "yes", and this was anything but that. He couldn't rely on her to not tell the sect about Earth. It was possible the sect already knew. Silwan had. Humanity had been supremely lucky that the álfar who discovered the secret hated the sect enough that he hadn't shared it. He wasn't necessarily the only one who found out, though.

'Hell, with enough Earth forerunners out there, it's inevitable that some of them have been discovered. So would it even matter if Constance told other people?'

'Maybe not, Zed, but if no one else knows, do you really want to be the cause of the sect preparing for humanity coming?'

He didn't respond. He didn't have to. They both knew the answer.

Disappointed, Zed looked away and started to rise.

"Wait!" Constance grabbed his hand. "Don't go. I will keep your secret."

Zed looked into her eyes. She was sincere, he felt. But it wasn't enough. He shook his head.

"I'm sorry. It was unfair of me to ask. I don't want to set you at odds with your family."

"Why don't you let me decide that?"

Zed chewed on his lip as he thought about it. Slowly he said, "Let's say that in half a year, a war between álfar and ogrums broke out. The sect would be caught up in the war. What would you do?"

"Are you saying there will be a war between álfar and ogrums?"

Zed shrugged.

"Because there hasn't been a war between us for hundreds of years," she said skeptically.

"It's just a hypothetical. What would you do?"

She looked down and tapped her lips with a finger. "I'm not sure. I'm not ready to fight, so I guess I would stay with my family or the sect. It would be my duty to be with them."

Though Zed was disappointed, she had made it easy for him. "That's probably wise." He stood up and looked at her. "Things are going to be very dangerous in half a year. Stay somewhere safe, and out of the fighting."

"Wait! What about you?"

He looked at her with a sad smile. "I won't be somewhere safe."

278

**

Zed spent the rest of the afternoon preparing to leave. At 6:30, he and Phineas boarded a carriage. Once they were out of the city Zed opened the curtain and watched the sun set over the valley.

A couple of hours later they left the valley and reached the dusty road through the forest Silwan's group had run through to get to Harlond. Zed perked up and started looking for a good ambush site. He wasn't looking for anything fancy, just a straight stretch followed by a turn.

Half an hour later, he found what he was looking for and asked the driver to stop. After a reminder to Phineas to look for Dan in Formenos, Zed wished him well and disembarked.

After he watched the carriage trundle down the dusty road, Zed tried to make himself comfortable amongst the trees. He found a spot that had a good sightline down the road. He figured it would make sniping Drusso easy if it came down to that.

He honestly wasn't sure if he hoped to see Drusso or not. If he was honest with himself, he was a little frightened of the man. But he would rather deal with the álfar here and now than wonder for years if he will show up someday.

'*And I wouldn't mind getting his mana-rich wine and beer,*' Zed chuckled.

That said, if Drusso didn't follow him, he would be happy to leave the man alone.

Zed sighed. He hated waiting. After a year of struggle he was so close to getting back to Formenos and his friends that he could almost taste it, and it was making him impatient.

**

Zed had seen a couple of caravans pass through over the last half a day, but he ignored them. Drusso could have been in them, but if he had any sense of the man at all, he was not there. Caravans were too slow and too undignified for him.

The approaching carriage, however… that was a different story.

Zed was nervous as he considered how to handle the carriage. He had hoped that Drusso would optimize his speed by running, making identification easy. With the carriage he wasn't sure what to do. He briefly considered lasing one of the wheels, but it was too likely that it would cause a crash. If the passengers were innocent, that would be unacceptable.

'Even if Drusso is the passenger, his driver is innocent, Zed.'

Zed sighed. *'True.'*

He could kill one of the horses, but he found that idea distasteful as well.

'I guess there's nothing for it but to wait for them to come by and see if I can either see him or sense his mana.'

'The carriage moves kind of funny, Zed.'

'What do you mean?'

'It has four horses, but it's still not moving that fast. And it rides over bumps oddly. I think it's really heavy.'

'Huh. Maybe it's a payroll shipment, so it's carrying a lot of coin?'

'Maybe.'

Zed spun up his laser. He was not planning to fire, but he wanted to be ready in case the situation called for it.

Then he felt it. A massive mana sensor field stretched forth in front of the carriage and on its sides. Remote mind constructs extended its reach beyond what Zed could currently manage. Fortunately, though the sensor field could "see" quite far, Zed could see it even farther.

It was like submarines searching for each other with sonar, or ships looking for planes with radar. Yes, it lets you see stuff farther away, but it also lets your enemy know where you are from an even farther distance.

'Oh, crap!' Zed had six seconds before the carriage would reach his section of the road. He briefly paused, wondering what the chances were that it was a mana user that wasn't Drusso.

'What mana user would actively search like that, besides Drusso?' Zed thought.

He raised the arm with the laser and, pumping it with as much power as he could, swept the ultraviolet beam back and forth on the carriage. Zed felt horrible as he cut the first pair of horses in half on the first pass, and the second pair on the next. Everything was pandemonium as the carriage came to an abrupt halt as it plowed into the dead horses. The driver was tossed from his seat onto the road. The carriage came to rest, the front wheels on top of the bisected horses.

Zed continued to sweep the laser back and forth into the carriage, varying the height to make sure he got Drusso. Feeling sure that Drusso was dead, he turned the laser off.

'Zed, the carriage appears to be armored! I don't think your beam penetrated. Quick, fire again, without moving the beam for a half second!'

Zed raised his arm back up, but it was too late. The carriage door burst open and a figure blurred out of it and into the treeline.

'Damn it!'

The one silver lining was that Drusso no longer had thick armor protecting him.

'Save your shot, Zed! He likely doesn't know where you are.'

It was moments like this that made Zed very glad to have Iris around.

'Iris, take over and do visual and infrared camouflage.'

'Done.'

'Oh, and silence too!'

'Already done.'

Zed watched himself going deeper into the trees.

'You looking for shadowy areas for camouflage, Iris?'

'Yes, and I'd like to flank him.'

Suddenly, a massive sensor field billowed toward Zed and encompassed him.

'We are detected.' Iris hid behind a tree. *'Do you want to take over?'*

'Yes. I...'

At that moment, all of the mana in the area rushed towards their location, heating the air into a blinding white as it came.

Iris sprinted while leaning forward at a 45° angle, their mana leg muscles pushing hard into the dirt of the forest. The only thing keeping them on the ground was the increased gravitational pull. Zed saw the trees blur by as Iris dodged between them. Zed had felt heat from Drusso's improvised plasma ball, but hadn't been burned.

'Releasing control on three. One... two... three!'

Zed felt full control return to him. He stumbled briefly but quickly asserted control thanks to his enhanced mental abilities.

'Good job escaping the plasma, Iris.'

'It was a combination of running and putting up a magnetic field to keep it away from us.'

Zed sighed. He may have reacted as quickly and as well as Iris did if he used his time slow-down ability, but he wasn't sure. It bothered him that she was better at this than he was.

'We both have our strengths, Zed.'

'Do I have any strengths in combat compared to you?'

'Of course. Never mind your experience in hand-to-hand combat; your will is stronger, which translates to the mana reacting faster to your desires and obeying you at longer distances. When we learn how to create the remote minds, you won't have to create as many as I will because each one will be able to cover more area.'

'Well, I'm glad to know there's still a reason for keeping me around.'

'Don't worry, Zed. You'll always have a job with me as my boy-toy.'

Zed took the time to sense behind him. Drusso's mana had already been reformed as a sensor field and was quickly moving forward. Fortunately, it didn't advance as quickly as he was running.

Zed thought about ways to strike back. He could flank Drusso by crossing the road, as he doubted that Drusso could push the sensor field as hard as he was in all directions. He could also bury himself in the ground to evade the sensor field and then give him a surprise when he popped up. Both plans seemed risky, though.

'The remote minds are a huge advantage. I can maybe win now, but if I can retreat and learn how to create my own remote minds, I would have a much better chance.'

' "He will win who knows when to fight and when not to fight." '

'Sun Tzu?'

'Yes.'

'Well, let's hope he knew what he was talking about.'

**

Zed ran for a few hours. He thought about moving away from the road because it would make him very difficult to find, but he was afraid that Drusso would pass him and head to Formenos. He probably didn't know Zed was from there, but Zed didn't want to risk it. He needed to deal with Drusso before he returned to Dan and Laurel.

Zed decided to cross the road and go 100 meters into the treeline. That would be far enough that he should be outside Drusso's scanning range, but close enough for Zed to detect the scanning.

'Magic isn't the answer to everything, Zed.'

'What do you mean?'

'The easiest way for him to find you is to track you. When you ran at full-speed you were tearing up the ground.'

'Dang it. Good point. I slowed down towards the end, but you're probably right that he can find me.'

Zed did something he had read about but never thought he would need to do. He got up and very carefully went back the way he came, stepping in his previous footsteps. A good tracker would probably see what he had done since he couldn't do it while walking backward, but he was banking on Drusso being a noob like himself.

He followed his trail a little past where he had turned to cross the road, so he was headed back to Harlond. He then had Iris use telekinesis to lift him off the ground and up to the nearest sturdy branch. The forest was full of oaks, walnuts, and a tree he didn't recognize.

'They're American Chestnut trees, Zed. They're functionally extinct on Earth.'

'Huh. Too bad. They're nice looking trees.'

Zed started traveling through the forest on the trees, running and leaping on the branches. As dangerous as the situation was for him, he had a blast doing it. It reminded him of when Victoria healed his body and he played frisbee with Brutus. It was just pure joy in running and pushing himself in his balance and athleticism. After he figured he had run at least a couple of miles, he dropped back down to the ground and ran some more, trying to find a balance between good speed and minimizing his trail. After an hour of running he moved to 100 meters from the road again, but didn't bother crossing this time.

Zed found a comfortable place to sit cross-legged. Interestingly, his legs were far more flexible than before the tendon, ligament, and muscle replacement.

'Benefits of the Transcendent Body apparently.'

He pulled the Remote Minds crystal out to review its contents again. Normally he would have had Iris store its contents in her memory, but she was using that for the modeling and replacing of nerve cells, which he didn't want to interfere with.

283

'*Iris, please watch for Drusso while I'm studying.*'

'*Of course.*'

The Remote Mind technique was interesting. It was very similar to the technique used in mana contracts to monitor adherence to the contract, only the true Remote Mind could change in real-time through communication with its creator.

'*Iris, could you help me out here? This section uses some Álfar words that I don't know.*'

'*That phrase is "quantum entanglement".*'

'*What's that?*'

'*The simplest case of quantum entanglement is when a particle is split into two, like a photon. A single photon is split into two photons with the same properties. Do you remember when we talked about how the location of an electron is unknown, it just randomly bounces around in its "balloon"?*'

'*Yeah.*'

'*Well, all particles are like that. I don't mean they're all in a small balloon-like region like electrons. I mean that we never know exactly where they are or much of anything about them. Everything about them is random probabilities. Their position, their momentum, their polarity, their spin. Everything. Until we measure one of those things, we don't know what it is, just its probability.*'

'*Okay.*'

'*If you measure, say, the polarity of one of the photons, you "collapse" its probability into a hard number. It's no longer a probability because you know what it is. The cool thing about quantum entanglement is that, in a way, the two particles are one. So when you collapse the probability of one of them, you also collapse it for the other.*'

'*Okay, but what the heck does this have to do with remote minds?*'

'*It's how the mana user communicates with the remote minds. The mana user and the remote mind share a set of entangled particles. Instead of measuring the polarity, or spin, or whatever of one of the particles, the mind can impose the property that it wants. It can tell one of them to have vertical polarity and another horizontal. When it does, the entangled particles in the other mind become vertically and horizontally polarized, which transmits information. For instance, if vertical meant "0" and horizontal meant "1", then "01" would have been transmitted.*'

284

'*You would need a lot of particles to send much information.*'

'*Yes, you would. Fortunately, the particles are really small. Also, you can send more than one bit per particle by forcing more than one property to the value you want, but I think you get the gist of it.*'

'*Each side shares entangled particles. When one of them wants to say something, they force a bunch of particles to the values they want, and then it magically shows up on the other side.*'

'*Right! Nice job, Zed!*'

'*Why do I feel like a dog that you're patting on the head?*'

'*I have no idea, Zed, because you're not a dog, you're a baboon.*'

Zed rolled his eyes but decided to not respond. '*Can the entangled particles be reused? Like, if they set the polarity to vertical, can they set it later to horizontal?*'

'*No. Once the probability is collapsed, it's done. It's a one-time thing.*'

'*Doesn't that imply that the remote minds can only last so long, because once they have used all their entangled particles they can no longer communicate?*'

'*Yeah, it does. Good insight.*'

Zed and Iris continued in this vein, laying the foundation of his understanding of the technique and then moving on to learning the technique itself. It was mentally exhausting but also rewarding. He had come to enjoy learning how things worked.

'*Zed, Drusso is approaching.*'

Zed turned away from studying remote minds and focused on his surroundings. He felt a large sensor field "beam" sweeping the area.

'*Let's observe for a bit.*'

Zed stayed ahead of Drusso fairly easily, because the álfar couldn't move at full speed while sweeping his sensor field without missing large chunks of the forest. Zed had initially thought about approaching Drusso undetected by moving in a spiral toward him, always staying ahead of the beam. Apparently Drusso anticipated that tactic, though, since they saw the beam change directions occasionally.

'*He might also have a small omnidirectional sensor field,*' Iris said

'*Yeah.*' Zed paused and thought, '*Iris, what do you think his end-game is?*'

'*What do you mean? He wants to kill you.*'

'*Yeah, I know, and he had a pretty good shot at it when he surprised me with the armored carriage and then detected me with the sensor field. The thing is, now that he has lost the initiative, I don't see how he catches me. If he doesn't use a sensor, he doesn't find me. And if he does use a sensor, I detect him farther out than he detects me. It seems like a no-win situation for him.'*

'Hmm. When you put it like that, I see what you mean. The traditional approach in situations like this is to destroy the enemy's cover so they can't hide, or go after a target that will draw them out. That is why truly decentralized and mobile enemies are so difficult to deal with, because there is no target that will draw them out. The problem is that you do have such a target.'

'Dan and the others in Formenos.' Though he avoided thinking about her, he couldn't help but see Laurel's face. It brought both fond feelings and pain.

'Right.'

'How would he know about them?'

'He may not. We can't discount the possibility that he does, though.'

'So what do we do about him? Learning the Remote Minds technique will take weeks, if not more, so I can't wait for that before attacking him.'

'Do you have some other solution?'

'I could lead him away in another direction.'

'True. Assuming he doesn't already know about Formenos.'

'Yeah.' Zed sighed. People liked to say "violence never solves anything", but Drusso was a problem that was begging for some violence.

**

The next day was a frustrating one for Zed. He set up an ambush point with a clear line of sight down the road. He realized something was wrong when he detected Drusso's sensor beam. It wasn't coming from the road.

'Damn it! He's in the trees.'

He wasn't sure exactly how far out into the trees he was, but it was far enough that he couldn't see him before the sensor beam got close to his position, and near enough that the beam could cross to the other side of the road. Probably 50 meters from the road, give or take.

Zed retreated and thought about what to do. He tried ambushes a couple more times in the hopes that Drusso would move closer to the road, but the álfar was annoyingly disciplined. After a couple more ambushes failed, Zed smacked himself on the head.

'*Just get him when he goes to sleep.*'

The best solutions were simple.

Zed had to wait a few more hours before Drusso stopped. Once he had, Zed found a comfortable spot and asked Iris to set an alarm for four hours later. He studied the remote minds technique and let himself fall asleep when he grew tired.

'*It's time, Zed.*'

'*Any activity from Drusso?*'

'*He did a sensor sweep a couple of hours ago. Nothing since then.*'

Zed walked in a big circular arc to a position further into the trees than Drusso. He wanted to approach him by walking towards the road.

With camouflage and silence activated, Zed wasn't worried about his stealthiness. Still, he took his time. Things had been quiet and the sensor beam hadn't restarted, so Zed decided to move in. He stepped carefully. Even with his camouflage and silence field it was possible to be seen and heard if he stepped on a branch and caused it to move outside his fields.

He listened to the forest as he moved. There were the sounds of crickets, and the occasional hooting of an owl. No people though. With Iris' mapping help he was pretty sure he was headed in the right direction, but part of him worried that he was off course.

'*If I am, I guess I'll reach the road, in which case I can try again tomorr...*'

A flash erupted below him, and his ears that had been listening to the sounds of the forest were deafened as the pressure wave burst his eardrums and sent him flying.

Chapter 38

'*Zed, get up!*'

Zed was confused. Everything was blurry.

'*What ha...*' He lost his train of thought and then regained it. '*What's going on?*'

'*You need to reattach your leg, Zed, and start running. Pick up your leg.*'

'*Huh?*'

The blurriness was subsiding, and his thoughts became a little more coherent.

'*Pick up your leg, Zed!*'

Zed saw his leg from the foot to the top of his shin lying on the ground, bloody and ragged, a few feet away from him. He rolled over.

'*Son of a bitch, that hurts!*'

He did his best to ignore the pain and grabbed the leg.

'*Now reattach it to your leg, Zed!*'

'*How?*'

'*Just put it up next to your knee!*'

'*Can't you just take over, Iris?*'

'*No. This is Ring Iris. Brain Iris is still offline.*'

In his foggy state, Zed wasn't sure what that meant, but he put the torn part of his leg next to his knee and was amazed as it came together, as if they were the ends of two magnets.

'*That's cool...*'

'*No time, Zed! It won't be long before Drusso gets here!*'

Zed struggled to his feet and started jogging in what he hoped was the right direction.

'*Turn to your right! Your other right! Okay, good. Try to run faster if you can.*'

Zed's mind was slowly getting clearer. He felt like he was starting to get his bearings when he felt a strong sensor field appear around him.

'*Oh, crap...*'

The world turned red, then orange, then white. It wasn't an explosion this time, it was the air turning into plasma. He held his breath and kept running.

'*Zed, magnetic field!*'

'*Right.*'

Zed was in agony as his skin cooked, but he concentrated on two things: magnetic field and running. Blinded by the plasma, he tripped on some underbrush and fell to the ground, but the magnetic field formed around him and pushed the plasma away. He was still in pain, but it was greatly reduced, so he got up and kept running, faster than ever. Before long he saw the trees blurring by.

Zed slightly stumbled when something small bit him in the hip.

'*Iris, can you find out what that was?*' He didn't want to turn his head or activate his sensor field. Though his mind was in much better condition than it had been, he still didn't want to do too many things at once.

'*Okay. You're out of the plasma, Zed, so you can turn the magnetic field off.*'

Zed gratefully deactivated it and started dodging while running. Small somethings zipped by occasionally. One bit him in the shoulder.

'*Iris, what the hell are those things?*'

'*They're needles. Drusso is shooting them at us.*'

The needles were an annoyance, but not too dangerous as long as they didn't hit him in the heart, or some other critical location. What Zed was really afraid of was something like Silwan's plasma whip. Getting hit by that would likely mean his death.

'*What do you mean you're "Ring Iris"?*'

'*I'm the original Iris in the ring. When I moved into your brain I didn't "move", because I couldn't. I copied myself. The two of us have been working together since without you knowing because we were afraid that you would be weirded out by it.*'

'*I've got bigger fish to fry at the moment. Any ideas on what we should do?*'

The needles were wearing him down, and one had shot into his gut. Other than being painful it didn't seem to be causing any problems, but he'd heard of people dying from sepsis after gut shots caused digestive waste and bacteria to escape into the abdominal cavity. It didn't sound like a fun way to go.

'You don't have poop or bacteria in your guts, Zed! Concentrate on the fight!'

'Right.' The adrenaline and fear had his mind going 100 miles per hour, so he appreciated the refocus. 'So, any ideas?'

'I think it's time for you to learn how to fly.'

'I thought you said I didn't have the control for that yet.'

'Desperate times call for desperate measures. Also, that was when you had a lot less mana. You had to be really efficient with that mana to fly. With what you have now, it will be easier.'

'Okay. What do I do?'

'You've been learning how to do telekinesis, right?'

'Yeah.'

'Well, just push against the ground.'

'That's it?'

'To stay up in the air, yeah.'

'How do I move forward?'

'Push at an angle.'

'I'm not sure I'm strong enough to get above the trees.'

'You can use the telekinesis to pull yourself up the tree trunks, and then push against the trees instead of the ground.'

Zed thought about it as best he could while running for his life. Fortunately, though his body was a mess, his mind was running better all the time.

'Ring Iris, why hasn't Brain Iris come back yet?'

'I'm not sure. There's activity, so I don't think she's gone. She probably just needs more time.'

After a needle grazed his head, tearing some scalp off his skull, Zed knew that he couldn't stay here on the ground.

'Let's do this.'

Zed jumped into the air next to a tree and used telekinesis to "grab" the trunk and pull himself upwards, launching him through branches and up into the open night sky. For the briefest moment he was dazzled by the stars.

'Beautiful…'

'I'm glad that you have the ability to stop and smell the roses, Zed, but I don't think this is the time.'

Zed focused on maintaining his "flight", though as he pushed off from tree trunks it occurred to him that what he was doing was more like Spiderman swinging on his webs, except he was pushing instead of pulling.

He got better and smoother at it with practice. It wasn't particularly complicated. At least, it wasn't until a needle sliced in between two stainless steel ribs and lodged in his lungs.

'*Damn it!*' He coughed up a bit of blood.

'*Zed...?*'

'*Iris? Are you back with us?*'

'*Yes... What happened?*'

'*Drusso set an explosion trap for us, and it knocked us unconscious. Me for a second or two, you for about 10 minutes. Now I'm learning to fly in a flying needle obstacle course.*'

'*I... see.*'

'*When do you think you can take over some mana techniques?*'

'*Give me a minute.*'

Zed started throwing plasma balls behind himself. The main goal wasn't to hit Drusso, though that would be nice. It was to make him dodge, which would slow him down and put some distance between them.

'*Hell, even if it just made it harder for him to see me, that would be something.*'

Zed didn't know if it was the plasma balls, his dodging, or luck, but he wasn't hit by any needles over the next couple of minutes. He was concerned, though, that his arms were moving more slowly than what he was used to. Something was obviously going on, but he didn't have time to worry about it right now.

'*I think I can help now, Zed.*'

'*Great! Can you take over the telekinesis flying while using a sensor field to see the trees, so I can turn around and face Drusso?*'

'*Yes, I can do that.*'

'*Okay. Take over telekinesis on three. One... two... three!*' Zed released the telekinesis and started forming a laser. '*Turn us around, Iris!*'

Zed's body was jerked around so they were facing backwards while continuing to "fly" forwards. Zed continued to throw plasma balls at Drusso, which was visibly frustrating him. He tried to throw one at Zed, but after a short distance it slowed down too much to keep up with them, let alone reach Zed. Drusso ended up having to avoid his own plasma ball.

'*Any chance you could give me a targeting reticule for the laser, Iris?*'

'*Let me see… Yes, I can.*'

'*If it's too much, don't worry about it. Just keep flying.*'

'*No, I can do it.*'

Zed saw a targeting reticule in his vision that moved based on where he pointed his arm with the laser.

'*Now that is awesome,*' he grinned.

When he extended his arm out he saw that the skin was burnt black.

'*Holy crap!*' he thought in shock. The flesh looked like it was ready to flake off. No wonder he wasn't in as much pain. The nerves in his skin were dead.

'*Iris, how am I still alive?*' he asked, a little shook up.

'*Well, you're obviously not doing too well. It's not as bad as it seems though. While your skin does serve a purpose, that purpose is mostly aesthetic at this point. Your steel bones and mana-based tendons, ligaments, and muscles simply don't need blood, and cannot experience infection. So the flesh could be fried off of your legs and you would still be mostly okay. It's more of an issue in your upper body because those muscles haven't been completely replaced by mana yet. The long and short of it is, as long as your organs don't get too messed up, you're a difficult guy to kill now.*'

Zed nodded, pleased about his new resilience. The Zed that left Formenos would have died after the explosion and getting hit by the plasma.

Zed re-focused on Drusso. He was trying to catch up to Zed, only dodging when he had to. When he saw Zed raise his arm, though, he dropped below the tree line.

'*Damn it!*'

Zed lased the area that Drusso dropped down into, sweeping his arm back and forth at various heights. Given his weakened arms, the sweeps did not swing back and forth as quickly as he would have liked. That was not an all bad thing, though, as even his most powerful laser could not slice through the tree trunks instantly.

Zed stopped lasing and tried to use infrared vision to find Drusso, but there was too much residual heat from the fireballs and lased trees. He thought about dropping down to the ground to look for Drusso, but there were lots of partially downed trees thanks to his lasing.

'*Circle back to where he dropped down, Iris.*'

'Okay.'

Iris executed a series of sharp turns to bring them to a part of the forest that looked like a giant weed whacker had gone a little nuts. The largest trees were only partially cut through, while the others were decapitated at an angle, leaving the area denuded and messy. Zed tried to use his infrared vision to scan the area.

After a frustrating minute he found something. Under a fallen tree top was a pair of legs, cut just above the knees, lying next to the shorn hem of Drusso's sect robes.

'He left his legs behind. He was either incapacitated or in a hurry to leave.'

Zed looked for anything. A body. Tracks. Heat trail. He found nothing.

'I think we've lost him, Iris.'

'At least you won!'

'Yeah, but he won't make the same mistakes again.'

'Neither will we.'

Chapter 39

Zed sensed the mana in Drusso's legs before storing them in Iris' ring. He was surprised at how little they contained. He knew Drusso was a powerful cultivator, so there should have been more.

'Why do you think there was so little mana, Iris?'

'They leaked mana while we were looking for Drusso, of course, but I think the bigger issue is that he wasn't using his legs at the time, so he probably wasn't circulating mana through them.'

'Bummer. Oh well.'

Zed then thought about the more critical issue—the explosion that nearly got him killed.

'Iris, why didn't I sense that mana trap before I stepped on it?'

'Because it was dormant. It was passively sensing just like you were, so neither of you had an advantage in sensing the other. Returning to the analogy of the sensor field being like sonar, you can think of the mana trap as a mine. If a submarine uses its sonar, it will detect the mine, but the enemy submarine will hear it. If the submarine doesn't use its sonar, it and the mine will "detect" each other simultaneously when they touch. Unfortunately, that's too late for the submarine.'

'Huh. Makes sense. So how do I solve the mine problem?'

'Use your head. Use the sensor field judiciously. Avoid traps. There is no magic bullet.'

Zed didn't like that answer, but he couldn't find fault with it. There were no cookie-cutter answers to every situation. You still had to use your head.

Zed spent a little more time trying to find Drusso's trail. After he failed, he decided to head to Formenos.

Zed traveled slowly and stopped often to rest and heal. He could regenerate, but the mana needed materials to work with. It could and did use the carbonized flesh, but much of it fell off. Zed was glad that he couldn't see himself in a mirror.

He *could* see his arms, though, and they weren't pretty. All of the non-mana flesh was burned, with much of it carbonized. A large area on his right forearm was completely exposed, the flesh having fallen off.

Seeing the inside of his body was horrifying and fascinating at the same time. The muscles were white and glowed softly. The tendons were a light gray. The stainless steel bones were shiny and the expected shape, but otherwise did not look at all like what he expected. Instead of being smooth steel, they had numerous tiny holes, giving them a dimpled look.

'What's up with my bones, Iris?'

'I could say that a honeycomb structure is a good weight/strength tradeoff, but the real reason for the holes is that your marrow is still inside the bones and needs access to your blood.'

Zed nodded and held up his arm to look at the internals more closely. He had mixed feelings about his "transcendent body". On the one hand, he was awesome. On the other, he was basically the Arnold Schwarzenegger version of the Terminator.

'You're much more witty than he was, Zed.'

Zed chuckled. *'Thanks, but given how low that bar is I'll call that "damning by faint praise".'*

To replace the flesh that he lost, Zed ate and drank. He didn't want to waste the mana-rich food he bought at the auction on himself, so he pulled out some monster carcasses that he'd been carrying around for a while and cooked them. The carcasses had mana too, but not as much, so it wasn't as big a loss to his fellow Earthlings.

It was pleasant being in the forest. Zed could study and experiment to his heart's content and not be at anyone's beck and call. Gradually, his flesh started to heal. It was painful when the nerves regrew, but he dealt with it.

He sometimes worried about Drusso getting to Formenos before him. He knew logically that it was unlikely, but he couldn't help worrying. He took to talking himself down when he became anxious.

'I cut off his legs. It will take him a lot longer to heal than it will for me. Relax.'

It worked most of the time. The times that it didn't, he dealt with the fear and forced himself to stay the course. While waiting to heal, Zed worked on using telekinesis. He worked on his fine control, picking up small objects and manipulating them. He also worked on his flying.

'I wonder if I could make a telekinetic blade?'

'What do you mean?'

'What would happen if I pushed on a super small point? It would be like pushing a needle in, right? If I changed it to pushing on a really thin line, it would be like a blade.'

'Seems like it's worth trying.'

It worked... kind of. When he tried it on a tree he saw an effect, but it didn't work very well. With the telekinetic needle he could push through the bark and a bit into the wood. With the blade he wasn't even able to get through the bark. He was pretty sure that the biggest problem was that his fine control wasn't very good yet, so his "blades" were very dull. It would take time and practice.

Zed also worked on learning how to fight with the halberd. He practiced some katas to get a feel for the weapon and learn the basic strikes, blocks, and parries. Once he was ready, he asked to spar with Iris. He did have a few questions though.

'So, when we do this, will I be moving around in meat-space?'

'No. It will all be in your mind.'

'Will you be able to monitor what's going on in the real world while we fight?'

'Yes.'

'Okay then, let's do this.'

All was dark until he found himself in a white, featureless space. No walls, no anything. Iris was at his side. She was in her usual avatar, wearing a martial arts gi. Though the scene was boring except for Iris, Zed felt *great*.

'What's going on? Oh, right. No pain,' Zed thought with a sad smile. He'd gotten used to it and could mostly ignore it, but these days of healing had been full of pain. It was a relief to be here in Iris' virtual world.

Iris smiled at him. "I'm glad you can enjoy a little respite."

"So, what's with this?" Zed asked, gesturing at the nothingness around them.

Iris grinned. "I've been wanting to do this for a while." She paused and said, in her best Neo voice, "We're going to need weapons. Lots of weapons."

Many racks of weapons appeared in the distance and zoomed towards them. Zed would have been worried about getting crushed, but he knew Iris wouldn't do that. He felt a breeze as the nearest rack flew by him.

'The realism of the simulation is impressive,' he thought to himself. "Thank you."

The racks stopped, and there was a vast array of weapons in every direction. Swords and spears, clubs and mauls, bows and darts. Of course, right next to Zed was his halberd. Iris picked up a Greek hoplite spear. She also gestured at a Roman gladius and shield, Japanese katana, and European longsword. Those weapons lifted themselves off the rack and floated in the air.

"I don't think you have that many arms, Iris."

"This is to give you a chance to get experience against a variety of weapons."

After Zed picked up his halberd the racks faded away and were replaced by a traditional Japanese dojo. Iris gestured again, and the floating armaments placed themselves on the wall, ready for use. She still held the spear.

"Let's keep this simple," she said, "and not use any mana."

"Works for me."

She winked at him and said, "Come on, then."

What followed was a lot of embarrassment for Zed, but it was very instructive. He had thought that he was a good fighter, and he probably was. But when he went up against someone with the same physical advantages he had, almost instantaneous reactions, and thousands of subjective hours of experience with each weapon, there was just no contest.

Iris set the pain level to 15%. Enough to where it hurt, but not enough to be debilitating. That way she could stab him to her heart's content without feeling too bad about it. At first Zed was reluctant to cut Iris, but he got over it quickly when she showed no such hesitation.

Unfortunately, his opportunities to cut her were few and far between.

"Push your body harder, Zed. It can do more than what you're asking from it."

"I am pushing it," he growled.

"Not hard enough."

He was about to object and say that he was going as fast and hard as he could, but paused.

'Have I not been going 100%?'

297

Getting healed by Victoria had been liberating. Hell, it was life changing. But the subconscious fear that his body would go to crap again had remained.

'*I haven't gone 100%.*'

He was a little shocked at the realization. '*It's so stupid, because I know if something breaks I could regenerate it. Or heck, now that I have the mana fibers it looks like if something tears, it will just fix itself.*' But he was still reluctant to push too hard. His earlier injuries had been life changing too, and his body hadn't forgotten.

It was irrational. But, like a lot of subconscious, irrational fears, being aware of it helped. It took away some of its hold over him.

Once he saw it, Iris started working with him to find his real limits, and gradually face and release the fear. It would take time, but he would get there.

'*And when I do, I'll really be able to cut loose.*'

**

Over the next few weeks Iris and Zed continued to focus on fighting without mana. It was helping Zed to hone his technique and reactions, and overcome his fears. While Zed still mostly lost, the fights were far more even now.

He had learned to stop using the halberd like a spear that happened to have an ax and hook attached to it. He learned to use the weapon's entire repertoire. Much of what he'd learned with the spear, such as thrusts and parries, carried over. Now he could use the hook to pull a leg or catch a weapon. And then there was the ax. Zed liked the ax. He liked its simple effectiveness and the flexibility that it gave him in fights.

Zed also continued to work on the Remote Minds technique. He could create a single remote mind and use it to control mana. He was thrilled with the success, but he knew from seeing what Drusso could do with it that he still had a long way to go. He needed to be able to create more remote minds so he could extend out the bubble of mana around himself. To make progress after that, he had to connect remote minds to other remote minds instead of directly to himself. That would allow him to create chains extending out a long way, or meshes covering a great deal of area.

Learning the technique had taught him a great deal about its weaknesses. For one thing, an álfar or human couldn't give full attention to dozens of remote minds. When a remote mind wasn't being paid attention to, it simply continued with its latest commands. They could be given trigger events to alert the user, such as the detection of foreign mana.

Another weakness is that all of the mana that a remote mind controls is "outside" of itself, so it can be fought for and taken by another will that is either stronger or closer to the mana. If Drusso wasn't careful, Zed could steal a great deal of mana and weaken his sensor field at the same time.

Lastly, Zed found that the halberd could annihilate the remote minds. Zed thought it could probably disable them by disrupting the entangled particles they used to communicate, but the actual effect was much more drastic. They simply disappeared, sucked up by the weapon.

Though Zed didn't look forward to facing Drusso again, he was pleased at the surprise that would be in store for him.

Zed thought a lot about what to do about Drusso. He might not keep going. He might not know where Zed lived. But if he did... Zed didn't have any good answers. He considered waiting for Drusso by the side of the road, but what if he didn't come? How long would he stay?

'It would be better to set a trap for him, like he did for me.'

Zed was thinking about how to create a mana "mine" like Drusso's when it struck him that he was being an idiot. The mana contract technique was pretty much exactly what he needed, only instead of residing inside someone's skull, it would be wherever he wanted the trap.

The only real difference is that the trap wouldn't involve anyone else's mana or remote mind, but cutting that out shouldn't be too difficult. It was much easier to remove than to add. After playing around with it for a few hours, Zed decided to give it a try.

He picked a clear piece of ground and attached a small pool of mana to a static remote mind. The remote mind's instructions were simple—explode the pool of mana when it sensed ten units of mana that didn't belong to him.

299

Zed backed off and regretfully pulled out some of the mana food he had bought. It was a portion of roast beast. What kind of beast he couldn't have said, but it smelled good.

'Storage rings are awesome.'

He'd been experimenting all afternoon and hadn't realized how hungry he was. Despite his stomach's longings, Zed tossed the meat onto the mine.

"Kaboom!"

Zed smiled. It had only been a small explosion, but that was because he hadn't used much mana. The point was that it worked. Now he could watch for Drusso while still living his life.

**

At the end of those weeks, Zed was mostly healed. There was no reason to put off going back to Formenos.

'Why are you reluctant to go back, Zed?'

'I'm not sure. I think mostly because it's nice to have a little time with no one telling me what to do or expecting anything from me.'

'There aren't any other reasons?'

'Well, maybe.'

'You're good with people, Zed, but you're not very good at dealing with uncomfortable relationships.'

'Is anyone?'

'Touché. Though I suspect Laurel's mom is.'

Zed laughed. *'Yeah, you're probably right. The woman is steel in a velvet glove.'*

'Just remember that there are… options.'

'Yeah, I know.'

**

Zed felt nostalgia when he saw the walls of Formenos. He was coming from the south this time, but it still reminded him of arriving at the city with Brutus and Dan.

'I wonder how Brutus is doing.'

He hoped they could get back together to hunt and play. Zed wanted to see how Brutus had changed.

'*That reminds me. I need to set up the mines so that Brutus won't trigger them either.*'

Zed wanted to place the mines 100 meters from the city walls. He figured that Drusso would be less likely to use his sensor field near the city because it would tip Zed off to his presence. And if he did find the mines through his sensor field, that would be okay too because it would probably tip Zed off. It would be nice if the mines wounded Drusso, but the main thing was to be warned of his arrival.

Zed placed a line of the mines across the road, pausing for a few minutes to create each one. He had no idea what the guards thought of what he was doing, but it didn't matter as long as they didn't interfere.

Zed set the mines to trigger when they detected 500 units of mana that didn't belong to himself or Brutus. He figured that would be far more mana than anyone in Formenos, besides himself, would have.

'*Wait, what if Silwan comes through?*'

Grumbling to himself, Zed destroyed the mines, recovered the mana, and started creating new ones. The new ones triggered on 500 units of mana that didn't belong to himself, Brutus, Dan, Laurel, Silwan, or Annis.

'*If any other sect members show up, I probably don't want them around anyway.*'

Just to be extra careful, Zed extended the mines 10 meters beyond the road on both sides. When he finished he turned around and looked at the city's walls, and the columns of smoke rising above them.

It felt a little surreal to be home. Zed had longed to be here for so long, and now that he was he was nervous about walking in. He chuckled and shook his head. It was time to stop procrastinating and move forward.

It was time to see his friends again and help them prepare. They had less than six months to get ready for the coming of humanity and a worldwide war. It wasn't enough, but no amount of time would be. All he could do was move forward.

Notes on the Physics in the Story

String Theory

String theory postulates that everything in the universe, and I do mean everything, is composed of tiny strings of energy that vibrate in multiple dimensions. Under this theory, an electron is a string vibrating at a particular frequency, much like C♯ is a note in our musical scale. A photon is also a string, but a different note—perhaps a B♭. I borrowed from this idea when developing how mana works in the story.

While string theory is very appealing to physicists, it's had a bumpy history. In the 1990's, five competing versions of string theory posited that the strings exist in ten dimensions. The ten dimensions are the four we are used to (three dimensions of space and one of time), while I believe the other six are tiny, rolled-up dimensions similar to what I described in the story. I confess that I only understand this at the most superficial level.

A physicist named Edward Witten showed that the five competing theories were equivalent as long as you added an 11th dimension. That created great excitement in the theoretical physics world. Unfortunately, as far as this layman can tell, not much progress has been made since.

Lately, string theory has been plagued by two problems. First, little progress has been made in figuring out what the string theory equation is that harmonizes quantum mechanics and general relativity. Second, strings are so tiny that it is impossible for us to conduct experiments to determine whether string theory is correct or not. Many physicists have started to ask if it makes sense to work on a theory you can't test.

For the purposes of The Forerunner universe, string theory is correct, as long as you add a 12th dimension. Cause, you know, 12 dimensions would be way cooler than 11.

Wall Crawling

I thought about using the science behind how geckos stick to walls as the basis for Zed's wall crawling. I think geckos are cool, and the idea has a natural appeal. The main reason I didn't use the gecko approach was that the explanation for how they do it is really complicated. As you know, the magic system of the Forerunner universe is based on understanding, to as high a degree as possible, what it is you're doing, so it would be necessary for Zed to understand how geckos do it.

While Zed is no dummy, having him understand something that complex would probably tax most readers' suspension of disbelief. That, and I wasn't confident I could make it attainable and interesting to the average reader.

And if you think all of that is a cover for me not feeling like *I* completely understand it, well then you're just wrong. Completely and utterly wrong.

Ahem.

If you want the 100,000 foot view of how gecko wall crawling works, I'll give it my best shot. Geckos' feet have tiny branching hairs that are good at making contact with whatever surface they're on. Even though they're good at getting into cracks and such, that isn't the point of the hairs. They are just there to make really, really close contact. At that point, Van der Waal forces kick in and give them their "suction".

So how do Van der Waal forces work? Let's go back to how Zed's wall crawling worked. He intentionally moved electrons around to shove them to the side of the nucleus. He was making the atoms electric dipoles, meaning that one side of the atom was more positively charged (the side with the exposed nucleus) while the other was more negatively charged (the side with the bunched up electrons). The dipole was attracted to the electrons of the atoms of the surface he's trying to stick to, which creates the suction.

Van der Waal forces are similar. As was explained in the story, the electrons are constantly moving around. Sometimes they will be, through pure randomness, mostly to one side of their "balloon" regions, and sometimes they will be on the other side. This creates electric dipoles, only they are very short-lived, because as the electrons continue shifting around, the dipole changes. Still, these short-lived electric dipoles are enough to create attraction to the atoms on the surface that the gecko is trying to stick to.

The atoms on the surface, by the way, are also creating those short-lived electric dipoles for the exact same reason. The attraction between the atoms is not very strong, but it's enough for the geckos. It probably wouldn't be strong enough to hold up a 200 lbs man, though, so I suppose that was another reason to not use the gecko method.

Anyway, if you are interested in the topic, I recommend looking up more information online.

Made in United States
Orlando, FL
26 October 2023

38241960R00188